The End of Atlantis

Chronicles of Atlantis
Book 3

FANTASTICAL REALM
PUBLISHING

This book is dedicated to Paul, my loving husband, critique partner, and scene enhancer. And to my father—without him, consistently placing fantasy books in my hands, my love for fantasy and sci-fi would never have grown.

Fantastical Realm Publishing
Book List
Author Sarah M. Wasson

Chronicles of Atlantis
The Beginning of the End – Book 1
The Journey Continues – Book 2
The End of Atlantis – Book 3
Royal Line – The Search –
A Chronicles of Atlantis Short Story

A Prophecy Foretold Novel
Twins of Fate – Book 1
Wizard's Hat – Book 2
Infinite Medallion – Book 3 - forthcoming

Short Stories
To Train a Falcon

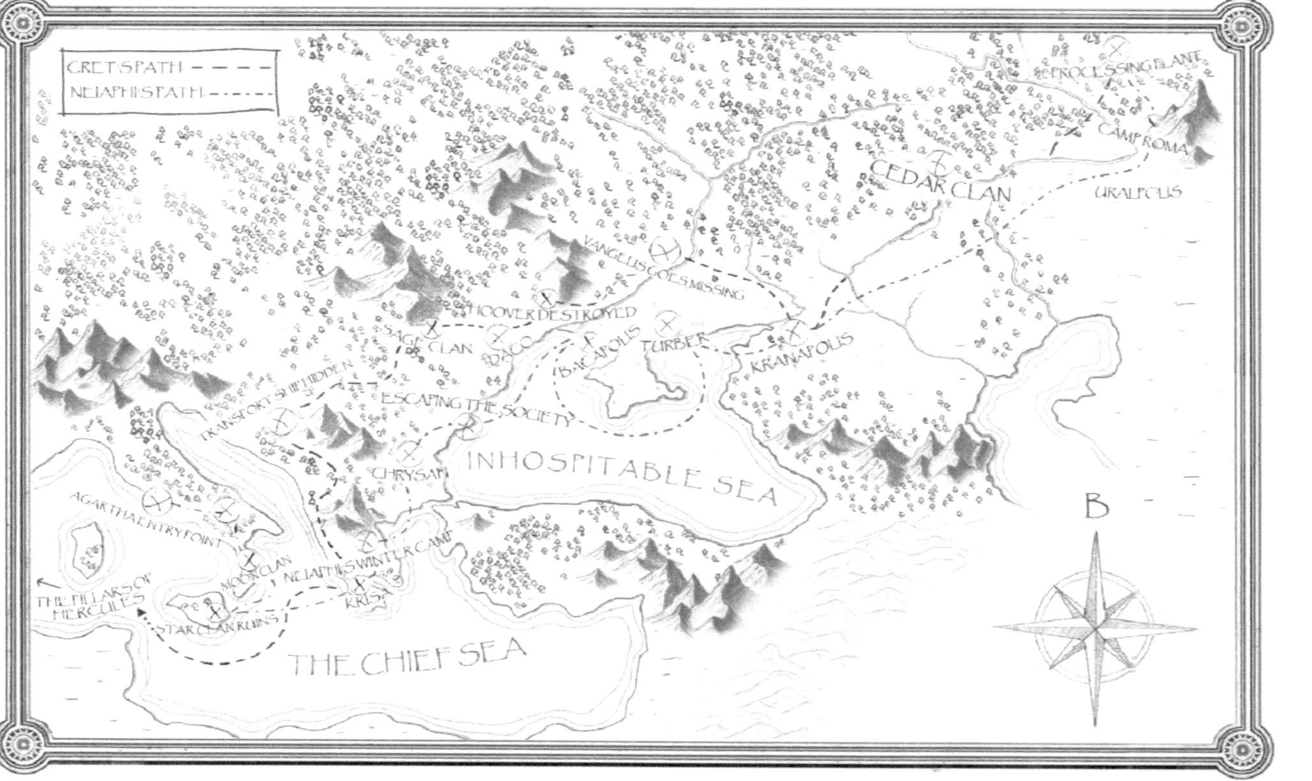

GRETS PATH
NEIAPHIS PATH
THE CHIEF SEA
INHOSPITABLE SEA
THE PILLARS OF HERCULES
AGARTHA ENTRY POINT
MOON CLAN
STAR CLAN RUINS
NEIAPHIS WINTER CAMP
KRISA
CHRYSAN
TRANSPORT SHIP HIDDEN
ESCAPING THE SOCIETY
SAGE CLAN
DACO
HOOVER DESTROYED
VANGELIS GOES MISSING
BACAPOLIS
TURBER
KRANAPOLIS
CEDAR CLAN
RE-PROCESSING PLANT
CAMP ROMA
URALPOLIS
B

∞ PRELUDE ∞

Neiaphi stood at the ship's stern, waving goodbye to her family as they sailed into the bay. Andonis stood beside her, one arm wrapped around her shoulders, while Cypress sat attentively on the other side. Was this the right decision? A new chapter of her life was beginning, but was she truly ready for it?

"Are you okay?" Andonis asked, giving her shoulder a reassuring squeeze.

"I will be," she replied, forcing a smile. "How about you?

His body went rigid at her question, and for a moment, he seemed lost in thought.

"Yeah, why wouldn't I be? I'm going on an adventure with my girl, helping creatures I didn't even know existed until recently, save their species from some strange, angry wolves that aren't wolves. Who wouldn't be okay?" He cleared his throat and chuckled, trying to lighten the mood.

Neiaphi turned to face him, her expression serious. "You didn't have to choose this path."

You had other options, right?"

"I had others," he admitted with a nod. "But this is the only one that felt right. I can't explain it. When I met Lyric, it just... clicked. I knew I had to help her. It feels right somehow."

"Then this is what we need to do," she said with certainty, her voice steady.

On the second day, the ship finally approached the shore. "Is this it?" Lyric asked the captain, her heart racing.

He eyed her nervously. "That's the island Pythia told me to take you to." After a pause, he added with a nod, "No one lives there, you know?"

"Not anymore," she whispered, a chill running down her spine as she stepped away from him. Turning to her group, she said, "As soon as we land, we'll split into two groups. Justic, Andonis, and Neiaphi will be with me." Everyone nodded, gathering their belongings in preparation.

The captain's voice called out, "This is as close as I can get; I'll lower the cargo raft.

"Everyone aboard!"

Several crewmates rowed them to shore, the tension palpable as everyone braced for the unknown.

"Let's establish a base camp here," Ambrite suggested as the cargo raft drifted back out to sea. "We'll reconvene in three days, or sooner if you discover anything or run into trouble. Return here immediately. For now, let's spend the night and set out fresh with the sunrise."

Nods of agreement rippled through the group, a shared determination settling over them.

"He left the ship with the creatures, sir," the crew member reported. Brutus snarled, "We are called centaurs, two-legs."

"Does it matter what everyone is called?" Hepluosis asked, raising his hands in a placating gesture. "The important question is, what are they doing on this island?"

"We'll swing around to the other side of the island and spread out," Captain Rirmell ordered. "If you see anything of interest, report back. If you spot members of their group, stay hidden. Observe and follow, but do not engage, unless that pilot is completely alone and won't be missed for several minutes."

"Yes, sir!" the soldiers barked in unison. Hepluosis, Six, and the centaurs gave quick nods of agreement. Captain Rirmell noticed the subtle exchange but kept his thoughts to himself.

"There it is, boys! Welcome to the Pillars. Now let's get you conscripted into the Royal Atlantean Navy," Captain Matteas announced.

"Will it be difficult for us to get enlisted?" Tivadarios inquired.

"Well, I don't doubt two of you will be welcomed," he said, casting a pointed glance at the centaurs.

"What's that supposed to mean?" Myreia huffed, crossing her arms.

"No insult intended, ma'am. I just don't see how a naval ship would make use of you and your mate," he replied.

"We'll show them just how valuable we can be," Cret said flatly. His eyes lifted to the massive stone statue towering over the bay, a man straddling the harbor, sword raised high and shield at the ready. The colossus loomed as a defiant sentinel, marking the entrance to the Great City of Atlantis.

"Do you think she's okay?" Altesse asked, glancing down at Annas, who slept peacefully in her arms.

"I'm sure she's fine, dear. She has Andonis by her side, and Pythia assured me we would see her again," Neiluios replied, trying to sound reassuring.

Altesse looked up at him, her brow furrowed. "Can she truly be trusted?"

He shrugged. "So far, I see no reason not to. Don't worry; we'll see her again." Altesse rested her head against his side, letting out a soft sigh.

"The horses have escaped again," Lars growled, pacing back and forth along the shoreline.

"Calm down, Lars. We'll catch them soon enough," Staps replied, baring his massive jaws. "My sire was part of the raiding party that destroyed the settlement on that island. There's nothing there for them. They'll be back, searching for the second machine, before long."

"If everything was destroyed, how would they know where to look for it?" Lars retorted, his shoulders hunched, head low.

"Don't worry about that. We left clues for any stragglers to follow. They'll lead the prey straight to us. Now, pack up. We have an ambush to prepare." With that, the pack erupted into howls, shadows trailing after their leader, hungry for action.

"They are coming!" Dyna exclaimed, gazing out the window of her sitting room in the Center Palace.

"Who is my lady?" asked her attendant, glancing up from her tasks.

Dyna looked down at the young woman kneeling before her, adjusting the final touches on the elegant gown she would wear to the banquet that evening. She hadn't realized she'd spoken aloud.

"That's not important," she murmured, then smiled. *They're almost here. The final pieces are falling into place. Salvation is almost upon us,* she thought.

∞ **1** ∞

ᘓTLANTEAN ᘓAVY

Cret and Tivadarios strolled up the gangplank of the largest sailing vessel they had ever seen. Captain Matteas had assured them the man in charge of enlistment was aboard, Cret only hoped he was right. The ship rocked gently against the dock, its mainsheet spread across the deck while sailors worked on repairs.

Cret glanced around the bustling port, struck by how drastically his life had changed in so little time. Back on Romota, his path had been simple—charted from birth, predictable, secure. Earth had offered no such certainties. Here, his life had been hijacked, exploited, and nearly extinguished. If not for the Loyals—and the unexpected aid of the centaurs— he would not be standing here now, let alone considering enlistment aboard an Atlantean warship.

They stepped onto the deck, where the scent of salt and pitch clung to the air. Sailors hurried past, ropes slung over shoulders, orders shouted, rigging tightened—too busy, or too indifferent, to notice the two newcomers. Not a single glance turned their way.

"Excuse me, I'm looking—" Cret called after a sailor striding past. The man didn't slow, muttering a grunt before vanishing below deck.

"Hello, I was sent—" he tried again with another, only to be brushed off with the same indifference.

Cret exchanged a weary look with Tivadarios. This wasn't going to be easy. "Well, this is getting us nowhere fast,"

Tivadarios muttered.

"Let's try the quarterdeck. Maybe the captain's up there," Cret replied.

They had barely taken a few steps when a sharp voice rang out. "Halt! Who goes there? I don't tolerate stowaways on my ship."

The two men froze as a burly crewman stepped into their path, glaring at them.

"We were sent here," Cret said quickly. "We're looking for Lieutenant Pav. Can you direct us to him?"

"Her," came a firm voice from the cabin.

A woman stepped into view, her uniform immaculate, her posture rigid, and her gaze sharp enough to cut through steel. "I'm Lieutenant Pavlina," she said. "Now tell me, who sent you?"

"Captain Matteas sent us," Tivadarios said.

"So, you're here to enlist?" Pavlina's eyes swept over them in a swift, appraising glance. Her lips pressed into a thin line, giving nothing away—but the faint lift of her brow suggested she wasn't impressed.

"Yes," they answered in unison.

"We have two others with us as well," Cret added quickly. She frowned. "You don't look like sailors."

"We're not, ma'am."

"You'll address me by my command title," she snapped.

"Yes, Lieutenant. My apologies," Cret replied. "No, we're not sailors."

"Not warriors either, I'm guessing." She crossed her arms. Both men shook their heads. "Then why are you here?"

Cret straightened. "Pythia told me Atlantis needed my help. Tivadarios and I, along with two others, came at her request."

"Well," Pavlina said coolly, "unless you're a mysterious traveler from a distant planet, I have no use for you."

Cret and Tivadarios exchanged a glance. Cret hesitated,

then dipped his head in a small, deliberate bow—wordless, but clear.

Pavlina's eyes widened. For a beat, she just stared. Then her gaze sharpened. "I see," she said, her voice suddenly tight with control. "Come with me."

She spun on her heel and strode toward the cabin. Cret and Tivadarios followed, ducking into the cramped room behind her. The door slammed shut, the sound reverberating through the narrow space. "Explain yourself," she said quietly, but carrying the full weight of command.

Cret hesitated. "I've been warned not to speak too freely. I hope I don't offend, but… do you know the name of the distant planet, or the mysterious traveler?"

Pavlina studied him, then gave a single nod. "I'm Cret. From Romota."

Her breath caught, and her eyes widened. She stared at him in stunned silence before whispering, "By Zeus… the witch spoke the truth."

She sank into the chair behind her desk, as if the revelation carried physical weight. With a silent wave, she motioned for them to sit. For a long moment, she said nothing, her brow furrowed in thought.

"And the other two," she asked finally, "do they truly have the body of a horse—and can speak?"

"Yes," Tivadarios replied, his tone steady. "They're called centaurs. They're waiting for us aboard Captain Matteas's ship."

Cret leaned forward slightly. "Do you have any idea what kind of help I might offer Atlantis?"

Pavlina shook her head. "No. I've been wondering that myself. I don't know what the witch meant. Our Navy controls the waterways here—and around Atlantis. The Society poses no real threat. I just don't see how you two, as outsiders, especially with two creatures who have horse bodies, could be of use on a naval vessel."

Cret nodded slowly. "Neither do I. Pythia only said Atlantis needed my help. I'll do whatever I can. My companions feel the same."

"Well then," Pavlina said, "I need to find a way to keep you aboard and explain your friends to the crew. I doubt they'd be willing to stay hidden below decks."

"They'd take offense to that," Tivadarios replied.

"I thought as much, but it was worth asking. Let me consider the matter. Come back tomorrow, I'll have our answer."

"Thank you, Lieutenant Pavlina. Until tomorrow."

Lieutenant Pavlina stepped into the clearing where Cret's small party had camped the night before.

"Lieutenant! How did you find us?" Cret exclaimed.

She smirked, tossing two bundled parcels toward him. "I have my ways. Here—put these on."

Her eyes then widened as she spotted the centaurs nearby. "Oh my… are these the centaurs?"

"This is Myreia, and that's Bal-air," Cret said. "Have you found a job for us?"

Pavlina's smile widened. "In a way." She turned to Myreia and Bal-air, then bowed with surprising formality. "Cret and Tivadarios are ambassadors, escorting the King and Queen of the Centaurs to Atlantis."

The centaurs gawked at her. Bal-air folded his arms, scowling. "No chance. I don't think so."

"It's the only way I can get the four of you into Atlantis," Pavlina shot back. "Cret and Tivadarios can pass as sailors. But for centaurs?" She shook her head. "There are no positions—official or otherwise. This is the only path."

"Thank you for your help," Cret said quickly, stepping in before Bal-air could retort. "When do we leave?"

"I've commissioned the Royal Transport," Pavlina replied. "It sails in the morning."

Tivadarios raised an eyebrow. "Won't we get in trouble when they realize we're not who you say we are?"

Pavlina's expression hardened, though a hint of mischief lingered in her eyes. "I'll be with you. Let me worry about that. Be ready at dawn."

She turned and disappeared into the trees.

"I don't like this idea," Myreia muttered once the lieutenant had gone. "I am not royalty material." She huffed and flicked her tail.

"How would they know?" Cret asked. "I doubt anyone in Atlantis has ever even seen a centaur—let alone knows how a king or queen should act."

"We do not have royalty," Bal-air said flatly.

"Exactly." Cret grinned. "Which means Centaur Royalty on Earth speaks and behaves just like you two. Your majesties." He gave them a playful bow.

Myreia sniffed and lifted her chin, but a smile tugged at her lips. "Very well. First royal decree: no bowing."

The Royal Transport was smaller than the ship where they had first met Pavlina, yet it remained an impressive vessel. Its hull gleamed with the darkest mahogany Cret had ever seen, rich, polished, and glossy as glass. Ornate, gold-laced scrollwork adorned the masts and railings, curling like vines in the sunlight. The deck itself was a marvel, its vivid mosaics inlaid directly into the planks. Even the cream-colored sails were trimmed in gold, and the mainsail bore what Cret assumed to be the Royal Crest: a silver griffin locked in battle with a golden pegasus.

Cret and Tivadarios walked up the gangplank side by side. Cret kept his chin high, trying to project an air of importance, though he wasn't sure he managed it. Beside him, Tivadarios fussed endlessly with the sash on his robes, tugging it this way and that.

"Stop it," Cret hissed under his breath.

Bal-air followed, with Myreia close behind. She had repurposed his heavy winter cloak into a short drape that hung across his shoulders and halfway down his back. His club was strapped securely there as well, with a carved bone knife resting at his waist. Myreia had altered her cloak too—draping it across her shoulders and chest before letting it flow down her back like a saddle blanket. To finish her look, she had woven a crown of flowers and tucked more blossoms into her thick curls. Her bow and quiver rested across her back.

Together, they were an impressive sight.

"Welcome, ambassadors—and Your Majesties—to *The Gilded Pegasus*," Pavlina announced. She now wore a formal uniform of gold and green and bowed deeply. "Allow me to show you to your cabins. If you need anything while aboard, this is Stavos, your attendant."

Stavos, a short, slender man with graying hair and kind eyes, bowed low at the waist. "May I take your bags, sir?" he asked. Cret handed him the single bag they had brought.

Pavlina led them toward the stern. "Your Majesties will be staying in the captain's quarters," she explained. "I hope you're not offended—it's only that the stairway to the Royal Quarters cannot accommodate your size." She bowed again, her expression tinged with apology. Around them, several crew members stared openly at the centaurs, mouths slightly agape, eyes wide with awe and disbelief.

"I'm sure the accommodations will be adequate," Bal-air replied, lifting his chin and infusing his voice with exaggerated dignity.

Pavlina gave a small, amused smile, then swept open the double doors with a flourish and another deep bow. Both centaurs ducked their heads to step inside, their movements only slightly awkward.

The cabin had been carefully prepared: two thick mattresses lay neatly on the polished floor, and a nearby table displayed an elegant spread of fresh fruit, assorted nuts, thinly sliced meats, and a pitcher of deep red wine.

"I took the liberty of arranging breakfast for your arrival," Pavlina said. "If something isn't to your liking, please let Stavos know."

"This will do nicely, thank you," Myreia replied, popping a grape into her mouth with practiced regal ease.

"This way, ambassadors." Pavlina gestured for Cret

and Tivadarios to follow, leading them down to the next deck, where the guest quarters awaited. Though smaller than the captain's cabin, the rooms were still finer than anything they had experienced aboard a ship before—and, for once, each had a private space of their own.

"You're going all out," Cret remarked once the door closed behind them. "I have to say, I'm impressed."

Pavlina gave a slight shrug. "I need the crew to believe the story. If I can't convince sailors accustomed to serving royalty, I'll never get you past the gates of Atlantis. Appearances matter."

"You've done more than enough. Thank you."

"You have free rein of the ship," she added curtly. "Just stay out of the crew's way."

Cret nodded.

"We'll set sail shortly. If the weather holds and there are no… complications, we should reach Atlantis in a few days."

"What kind of complications? The Society?"

Pavlina's face tightened. "I wish they were our only problem," she said flatly.

∞ **2** ∞
ᎢHE ᏟLANS

Lyric felt herself drawn toward the heart of the island, as if every winding path conspired to lead her there. The forest pressed close around them, trees thickening, underbrush snagging at their hooves. Overhead, birds trilled and chirped, their calls weaving through the canopy in a chorus that seemed both welcoming and watchful.

She glanced back at her companions—her brother, Justic, and the two two-legs she had only just met, Andonis and Neiaphi. Traveling with humans still felt strange, unnatural even. She gave her head a small shake, as though she could toss away the thought, and fixed her gaze once more on the forest ahead.

If anyone had told her a year ago that she would be helping humans—and accepting their help, she would have laughed in their face or called them mad. Centaurs and humans didn't get along. That was what she had been taught her entire life.

At last, the trees gave way, and they emerged into a clearing scattered with the husks of old brick buildings. Roofs had collapsed long ago, and jagged walls jutted upward like broken teeth. Weeds choked the stone foundations, while thick vines climbed pillars and twisted through shattered windows, as if the forest itself were dragging the ruins back into its embrace.

Justic and Andonis moved ahead into the overgrown settlement, curiosity in their steps.

Neiaphi lingered at the edge, slowly turning in a circle as her eyes drank in the sight.

"Do centaurs normally live in buildings like these?" she asked, her voice quiet with wonder.

Lyric shook her head. "I've never seen anyone live like this." "Lyric, over here!" Justic's voice echoed from one of the ruins.

Without hesitation, Lyric broke into a trot, leaving Neiaphi standing alone at the clearing's edge.

Neiaphi's eyes swept across the silent ruins, unease tightening her posture. After a few heartbeats of hesitation, she broke into a jog, calling out, "Cypress!" Her companion bounded to her side, falling into step as she hurried into the settlement.

Lyric trotted past cracked foundations and tangled brush, stepping into the structure where Justic had vanished. "What did you find?" she asked, her voice low with curiosity.

"You need to see this," Justic said, pointing to a symbol etched into the crumbling wall.

Lyric stepped closer. Her breath caught in her throat. Etched into the crumbling stone was a symbol she knew too well—the same mark that hung around her neck.

This was the place.

But why had it been abandoned? And how long ago?

Andonis crouched beneath the symbol, brushing away layers of dirt and moss that had collected over the years. Beneath it, he found a few jagged shards of metal. He examined them briefly, then let them fall with a clatter.

"Whatever machine was here," he muttered, "it's long gone. There's barely enough left to guess what it even was."

He stood, shaking his head, then his gaze caught on something behind them. His face went pale.

"What's wrong?" he asked, his voice sharp with alarm.

Lyric and Justic turned quickly, following his gaze to Neiaphi.

Neiaphi's terrified expression softened into sorrow. "Nothing. I'm fine," she murmured. "Just startled, being alone for a moment. It's nothing."

Andonis stepped forward and pulled her into a gentle embrace, leaning close to whisper something in her ear. She nodded slowly, the tension in her shoulders easing.

Lyric turned back to the wall, her gaze lingering on the faded symbol above the twisted remains of the machine. She brushed aside a vine creeping across the stone, uncovering more of the engraving, of the same mark etched on her necklace.

Her fingers traced the shallow, recessed lines, as though something had once been set there. Her brow furrowed.

Curiosity growing, she slipped the necklace from her neck and held it over the carving.

Slowly, she aligned the pendant with the ancient symbol.

A soft chime resonated from somewhere deep within the stone—then, suddenly, a blinding light burst forth, engulfing her in brilliance.

Lyric gasped, stumbling back. "Ah!" she cried out. The others spun toward her, eyes wide in alarm.

"What just happened?" Andonis asked, eyes darting between Lyric and the wall. "I… I don't know," she said, still blinking spots from her vision.

"Are you okay?" Justic asked, stepping closer.

Lyric nodded, then exhaled slowly, trying to steady her breathing. "I saw the symbol from my necklace here, so I lined up the pendant. The moment I did, there was a sound, and then… that light."

Neiaphi stepped forward, thoughtful. "It must be a key. Your necklace, it, activated whatever's left of the machine."

Lyric glanced back at the wall. The symbol still faintly glowed, pulsing softly before dimming again. She tucked the necklace away.

"So… what now?" Justic asked, scanning the ruins.

Lyric didn't answer right away. She turned and moved

toward the next building, her steps cautious but purposeful.

"We keep looking," she finally said. "Whatever this place was… I think it still remembers something."

"Pelagios, look what I found!" Simandro called as he stepped into the clearing. The centaur and the human advanced cautiously, scanning the ruins.

Justic spotted them and trotted over. "Where are Ambrite and Peleros?"

"Our path forked," Simandro replied with a shrug. "We decided to cover more ground." Pelagios eyed the crumbling buildings. "So, what did you find here?"

"The technology we were sent to locate—what's left of it, anyway," Justic said. "It's been destroyed."

Pelagios frowned. "Recently?"

Justic shook his head slowly. "No, it doesn't look like it. The damage is old."

Lyric's voice rang out from deeper within the settlement. "Justic, we found something." The centaur turned. "Come on," he said, motioning for the others to follow.

As they hurried through the ruins, two more centaurs emerged from the treeline. Simandro gave them a quick wave without slowing, and he and Pelagios pressed on toward the half-collapsed structure where Lyric had called. Their pace quickened with anticipation.

"What did you find?" Pelagios asked as he stepped into the crumbling structure.

"It's a journal," Andonis said, brushing dirt from the cracked leather cover. "I'm not sure how it survived this long."

"Can you read it?" Ambrite asked, joining them.

Andonis shook his head. "I don't understand this language. It's familiar yet not."

Neiaphi took the book from him and carefully leafed through the brittle pages. "I understand some of it," she said softly. "It's an old dialect. The last entries describe a siege—

weeks, maybe even moons, of being under attack. They were cut off from the mainland. The transponder had to be protected at all costs, but they weren't sure they could escape with it intact. They had a single chance, one plan: head inland and seek refuge with the Moon Clan, if they could reach them."

She looked up at the group; her expression was solemn. "The author left this journal as both a record and a warning. They didn't want it falling into the wrong hands. It's signed… Tempis, Supreme Elder of the Star Clan."

Silence fell.

"Does anyone know where to find the Moon Clan?" Andonis asked. The centaurs exchanged uncertain looks and shook their heads. "Well, now what?" Peleros asked. "Where do we go from here?"

Lyric's brows furrowed. They had come so far—why would Pythia send them here if the transponder wasn't in the ruins? Shouldn't she have known it had been moved? Or were they overlooking something crucial?

After a long pause, she said quietly, "Let's make camp here for the night. We'll decide our next step in the morning."

Everyone nodded, their faces heavy with both weariness and questions.

Andonis and Neiaphi sat back-to-back on a fallen log, their eyes sweeping the darkness in opposite directions. The forest had fallen silent—a stillness so complete that even the wind seemed to hold its breath.

Neiaphi shivered. She told herself it was the chill, but it wasn't. The dark still unsettled her, ever since Kayson. During her captivity, she would sometimes wake to find him staring at her in the shadows; other times, she would wake to emptiness—his absence as unnerving as his presence. Even now, she wasn't sure which was worse.

"Are you okay?" Andonis asked gently, his voice low enough not to disturb the others. She hesitated before answering. "Yeah… just the dark. It still gets to me sometimes."

He shifted slightly to glance over his shoulder. "Why don't you get some rest? I've got the watch."

She shook her head. "No. Four eyes are better than two," she said, trying to sound steady. He didn't argue, just nodded and returned to scanning the trees.

Time passed slowly.

Eventually, Andonis rose and went to wake Ambrite and Justic for the second watch. Neiaphi stayed where she was, knees drawn to her chest, until he came back and gently guided her toward the blankets.

She didn't resist. Curling up beside him, she let her body finally relax, comforted by the steady rhythm of his breathing nearby.

Lyric walked through the settlement in awe. The crumbling ruins were gone. In their place stood a vibrant village alive with color and sound. The buildings were sturdy— not new, but well-maintained—their red bricks glowing warmly in the morning sun. Birds chirped from the trees, hopping between rooftops, while flowers bloomed along the footpaths. It felt as though time itself had reversed.

Several centaur foals peeked nervously from behind a doorway, their wide eyes filled with fear. Adult males patrolled the village's edges, gripping sleek metallic weapons unlike anything Lyric had ever seen—so different from the handmade bows of her people. Other centaurs moved with quiet urgency, bundling supplies and tying them with practiced hands.

No one looked at her. No one saw her.

She moved among them unnoticed, ghost-like.

A chill ran down her spine, but she pressed on toward the building where she and the others had once found the transponder's remains. Now it stood whole, glowing softly, humming with life, its core pulsing with a warm amber light.

An old centaur woman lay before it, her fingers moving expertly across the panel. Lyric froze, her breath caught in her throat. The woman looked exactly like her mother—only older. Wiser. Stronger.

Her heart pounded.

Could this be... my great-grandmother? "Grandmother!" A child's voice called.

A young centaur filly burst through the doorway—and passed straight through Lyric's body like a whisper of air.

Lyric gasped and stumbled back, her hands trembling. The child hadn't seen her. Hadn't even sensed her. I'm not here, she realized.

"Yes, dear one," the old woman answered gently.

Lyric's eyes widened. The child was the very image of the old centaur herself—only younger. The resemblance was uncanny.

"I'm scared," the filly said, her small voice trembling. "Father's been gone so long.

When will he come back? Everyone's packing. Are we leaving? All of us?" The old woman placed her hands on the little girl's shoulders.

"There's nothing to fear, Aleena," she said softly. "All will be well soon." "Aleena," Lyric whispered, her breath catching in her throat. "That's my mother!"

The little girl sniffled, wiping her eyes with the back of her hand. "Are you sure?" she asked timidly.

"Have I ever lied to you?"

Aleena shook her head. The old woman smiled, unclasping the necklace from around her.

She leaned forward and fastened it gently around the girl's neck. "I want you to have this."

Aleena's eyes widened. She lifted the pendant with reverence, tracing its smooth edges with her small fingers.

Lyric touched her necklace. It's the same one; this is the moment she received it.

But then the thought struck her: Why hadn't my mother remembered any of this? Aleena had been old enough to carry such memories. What had happened to her after they left this place?

"Come, child," the old woman said, rising slowly. "I have one more thing to do before we leave."

Lyric followed as they stepped out of the building and into the bustling village. Centaurs bowed their heads in reverence as she passed. Most kept silent, though a few murmured respectful greetings.

"May the Gods protect us today, Elder Tempis," a male centaur said as he walked by. The elder only nodded and continued toward the quiet forest beyond. There, nestled among the trees, stood a small, crooked hut.

"Why do you live out here, away from everyone, Grandmother?" Aleena asked. "I prefer my solitude," the old woman replied. "Now, come inside, please."

The interior was dim, lit only by thin rays of sunlight filtering through cracks in the walls. The old woman struck a match and lit a stubby candle, its glow casting flickering shadows across the room. At the center lay a bundle wrapped in cloth. Shelves lined the walls, mostly bare, holding only a few knick-knacks and a couple of worn books. Dust outlined the spaces where other belongings had once stood, lost, stolen, or forgotten.

She crossed to the farthest shelf and carefully brought down three small, ornate boxes, each painted in a different hue. She placed them on a table.

"Come here, dear."

Aleena stepped forward, her eyes fixed on the boxes. "What are these?" she asked.

"Just boxes," the woman replied. "But I want you to choose one to hold something very special. Can you do that for me?"

Aleena nodded slowly, her small hands fidgeting at her sides.

The green one, Lyric thought instinctively. She always picks green.

Aleena's fingers hovered over the boxes before settling

on the one in the middle—a deep forest green.

"Is this one okay?" she asked.

"Perfect, dear. Now go help your mother." Aleena nodded and scampered out the door.

The old woman waited until she was alone. She turned to a nearby shelf and drew out a thick book, its cracked leather binding worn but familiar. She placed it inside the green box. Then, with practiced ease, she flipped the box over and revealed a hidden compartment in the base.

From a pouch at her waist, she withdrew a folded parchment. Lyric edged closer, straining for a clearer view..

The woman unfolded it slowly. It was a map. Lyric's heart lurched. A map, but leading where?

The woman studied it in silence, then folded it with deliberate care and slipped it into the secret compartment. She closed the box with a soft click, her fingers lingering on the lid.

Lyric bolted upright, chest heaving. Her eyes darted across the darkened clearing. The fire crackled softly, casting restless shadows on the ruined walls. Crickets sang in the trees. Everything seemed ordinary.

But her heart still pounded.

Sweat beaded her forehead. Her hands trembled as she pushed her hair back. The necklace against her skin shifted and brushed her collarbone. She flinched; it was hot, pulsing with a faint glow, before fading back into darkness.

"Just in time, it's your watch," Justic said, stepping into view.

She blinked at him, disoriented. "O-oh. Okay. I'm ready," she said, her voice unsteady.

Justic studied her for a moment, concern flickering across his face, but he said nothing.

He gave a small nod and retreated toward his bedroll.

Lyric had the final watch of the night. A small mercy, though she doubted she could've fallen back asleep even if she tried. Her heart thudded against her ribs as she stared toward the horizon, willing the sun to rise. Somewhere out there was the box, the key they needed. A map to the Moon Clan.

She shut her eyes for a moment, breathing slowly and deeply, trying to steady the tremor in her chest.

When the sun finally began to crest above the trees, Lyric stoked the fire and set a kettle of water on the hot stones. She added a handful of herbs and let them steep, the soothing scent rising with the morning mist.

From their supplies, she took the last of the leftover rabbit from the night before and skewered it over the flame. As the meat began to roast, its savory aroma drifted through the crisp morning air, stirring the others in their makeshift camp. But Lyric didn't wait for them to wake. She slipped away, heading straight back into the crumbling building where they'd found the journal.

Andonis and Justic spotted her sudden departure. "Lyric, where are you going?" Justic called.

She didn't slow.

They exchanged a glance and bolted after her.

Lyric threw the door open and rushed inside, dropping to her knees. She scoured the ground, yanking up weeds and pushing aside loose stones, her hands moving frantically.

"Where did you find that journal?" she demanded as Andonis entered. Her eyes were wide, almost feverish, as she kept digging.

"Over here," he said, crossing the room to what remained of a crumbled shelf. He knelt beside it and pointed. "It was in this little box, just down here."

"Box? Where?" Lyric barked, rushing over to him. "Here." Andonis handed it to her. "It's empty now."

She snatched the faded green box from his hands and fell silent, eyes scanning every inch. Her fingers traced along the edges until they found a latch — barely noticeable.

Click.

The bottom popped open.

Lyric froze, breath caught in her throat. With a trembling hand, she reached inside and pulled out a folded piece of parchment.

"What is that?" Andonis asked, stepping closer.

Justic moved in beside him. "How did you know it was there? What is it?"

Lyric stared down at the parchment, her voice barely above a whisper. "The map to the Moon Clan."

"What are they even looking for?" Six muttered, more to himself than anyone else. "How should I know?" Hepluosis snapped.

He'd been wearing his temper like a cloak lately, and his patience was thinning—like the first ice of winter, fragile and ready to crack.

Six hadn't known him long, just long enough to know when to tread carefully.

He glanced around at their small group, crouched in the shadows, as they watched a handful of centaurs and three humans sift through the ruins of an abandoned village.

His master, Hepluosis, had learned that members of the Society were searching for a pilot, someone who had been traveling with the centaurs. Cret had been with them until he vanished. That disappearance had sent Hepluosis into a fury, and now he was hell-bent on finding Cret… and doing what, exactly?

Six wasn't sure. Kill him, maybe?

Hepluosis's gaze lingered on a girl with the centaurs. Six thought her name was Neiaphi. His master had mentioned her a few times, though never in detail. For reasons Six didn't understand, Hepluosis watched her with an obsession that made him uneasy.

By the fire, Neiaphi carefully turned a rabbit roasting on a spit. Two centaurs and the pilot sat close by, while the rest of the group continued combing the ruins.

"We're wasting time," rumbled Brutus, a massive centaur with a blood bay hide. His voice was a low growl. "They're lightly armed, and they've split up again. We should rush them and end this now. I still need to find those two-legs and bring them to justice."

Brutus and his followers had been tracking Cret, Tivadarios, and the centaurs when Hepluosis and Six had crossed paths with them.

"Patience," Captain Rirmell said coolly. "I want to see what they're after."

"It doesn't matter to us," Brutus snapped. "I want those centaurs. They must pay for their betrayal."

"Not even a little curious about what they're doing?" Rirmell pressed. "A solid black-coated female is leading them. Your leader might want to know what she uncovers."

Brutus crossed his arms over his chest, but said nothing.

"We'll keep following them," Rirmell said. "Whatever they find might be valuable to my people as well."

Justic dragged a small table out of one of the abandoned buildings, with Andonis steadying the other end as they carried it over to their makeshift camp.

Lyric unfolded the map with care and spread it across the tabletop. The others gathered around, drawn in by the quiet gravity of the moment.

"We're here," Andonis said, pointing to an island marked with a small star.

"And the Moon Clan..." Justic trailed his finger inland, stopping at a crescent-shaped symbol. "Looks like they're here."

"So, what does this symbol mean?" Ambrite asked. "The Lightning Clan?"

"I guess so. Makes sense," Lyric replied. "Have you ever heard of these clans?" All but Simandro shook their heads.

He spoke after a long pause, his voice low and thoughtful. "My grandmother used to tell me stories about where we came from. She said that when we first arrived on this planet—from the stars—we lived in three great clans: the Sun, the Moon, and the Star. Those were our seats of power."

He paused, as if searching for the right words.

"But power breeds ambition. Some within those clans wanted more, and new clans began to splinter off. Most lived peacefully with the humans. Trade was common—goods, technology, and knowledge."

His tone darkened. "But the Lightning and Thunder Clans… they believed centaurs should rule. They turned against the two-legs and waged war. It didn't last long. The humans crushed them."

A silence settled over the group.

"After that, the humans turned on the rest of us, the other clans. That's when we vanished into the forests, into hiding."

"Why have I never heard this story?" Ambrite asked. Simandro shook his head, the sadness plain on his face.

"One night, around a hunting fire, I asked our chief if he knew where the original clans had once lived. The look he gave me… it withered me on the spot. I didn't understand why."

He paused, his voice tightening.

"The next day, I went looking for my grandmother. She was gone—banished, my father told me. Banished for speaking what should never have been spoken… for telling me that story. If I hadn't said anything, she would still be with us."

He looked down. "It was my fault. But she never warned me not to speak of it." Lyric gently placed a hand on his shoulder.

"We've all been cast into darkness," she said softly. "And it's only brought us harm. We don't belong on this planet. We need to leave."

"Just find me a ship," Pelagios said with a nod, "and I'll get you home." "Thank you." Lyric smiled at him, warm and grateful.

Neiaphi noticed the flicker of a scowl shadowing Andonis's expression as he watched Lyric and Pelagios. She cleared her throat pointedly.

"So… where to next?"

Andonis jumped, as if startled out of a thought. Lyric blushed, quickly folding up the map.

"Back to the beach where we landed," Ambrite said. "Our ship should return by sunset tomorrow. Then it's on to the Moon Clan."

The trip back to the beach was quick and uneventful. By dusk, they had set up another makeshift camp to wait for the ship's return.

Neiaphi sat on a large driftwood stump, the setting sun casting long golden shadows across the sand. Cypress lay at her feet, tail thumping gently as she scratched behind his ears.

At the sound of approaching footsteps, Neiaphi tensed—until she counted four hooves instead of two feet. She exhaled and relaxed.

"What's troubling you?" Peleros asked, easing down beside her. "Nothing," she replied softly.

He chuckled, a warm, low sound. "I don't know much about females… two-legs… or female two-legs," he added with a half-smile, "but I can still tell when something's wrong."

She gave a quiet sigh, but said nothing.

Peleros continued gently, "I can't imagine what it's been like for you, coming here. None of this can be easy. Especially not for someone so young."

He paused, studying her face. "Is it trouble with your mate?"

Neiaphi shook her head. "We're not married," she murmured. "So… he's not my mate."

"I can smell your attraction to Andonis," Peleros said. "And his attraction to you. In our world, sometimes that's all that's needed."

Neiaphi turned to him, eyes wide in astonishment.

He laughed softly. "Yes, I can smell attraction. I suppose that makes us more animal than human in some ways. But it certainly simplifies things; there's no guessing how someone feels."

"That would be… handy," she said, glancing away.

He nodded thoughtfully. "I think I can help you just a little." "How?"

"Because I can also smell Andonis's attraction to Lyric. And I think you've already begun to sense it, too."

Neiaphi hesitated, then nodded slowly. "Does she… return his feelings?" "No," Peleros said simply.

"But she knows, doesn't she?" He gave a short nod.

"Will she say anything?"

"Not unless he does something more… physical about it."

Neiaphi stayed quiet for a long moment before speaking. "It's probably nothing more than curiosity," she said at last. "If I focus only on her human features, I can see what he might find appealing. But as a whole…" She shook her head. "No offense intended."

"None taken." Peleros smiled. "Add a couple of extra legs and a flowing tail, and you'd be considered highly desirable."

Neiaphi giggled at the mental image of herself as a centaur. "Thank you." "For what?"

"Putting my mind at ease, I guess."

Peleros gave a small nod, then rose and left her alone with her thoughts.

Not long after, she heard more footsteps—lighter this time. Just two legs. "Would you like some company?"

Andonis's voice was quiet, almost hesitant.

She didn't answer immediately. Instead, she shifted to the side and patted the space beside her on the driftwood stump.

He sat down, stiff at first, unsure of what to do with his hands. She glanced sideways at him—the discomfort etched across his face was unmistakable.

With a small sigh, she rested her head gently against his shoulder.

He relaxed almost at once. Without a word, he reached for her hand and held it.

They sat in silence, watching the last sliver of sun slip beneath the horizon. After a long while, Andonis said softly, "Come on. Let's get something to eat." "I'm not hungry," she murmured.

He turned slightly toward her, concern threading through his voice.

"What's wrong?"

Neiaphi shrugged again.

"That's not an answer," Andonis said gently.

He reached out, tilting her chin up so she had no choice but to meet his eyes. Her voice cracked when she finally spoke. "Do you still love me?"

Andonis's expression shifted—first to pain, then to regret. "Of course I do. Why would you even ask that?"

She lowered her gaze. "I've seen the way you look at Lyric. You like her… don't you?"

Andonis didn't respond right away. Then he wrapped his arms around her and pulled her into a tight embrace.

"I'm so sorry," he whispered. "Yes, I've been… drawn to her, fascinated maybe. But I never meant to hurt you. I wasn't thinking. I love you. You're the one I'm meant to be with—no one else."

Neiaphi gave a small, sad smile. "It's okay. She is pretty, you know." "Possibly. But she's not you."

He leaned down and kissed her gently.

After a beat, he murmured, "Come on. Let's get closer to the fire."

She nodded, took his hand, and followed him back toward the glow of the flames.

"About time the lovebirds joined us," Pelagios teased as Neiaphi and Andonis approached. "Lyric said no one could eat until everyone was here."

Neiaphi froze, shock crossing her face. "Oh no. I didn't mean to hold everyone up!" "I never said that," Lyric muttered under her breath, shooting Pelagios a glare.

A stick sailed past Pelagios's head, and he ducked with a laugh. "Hey, careful! That nearly took my ear off." His eyes twinkled as he raised his hands in mock surrender. "All right, all right, my mistake. Must've imagined that part." He gave Neiaphi an exaggerated bow and a sheepish grin. "Forgive me. Just joking."

Neiaphi relaxed slightly, though a blush lingered on her cheeks.

"Come on," Andonis said, his tone cooler. "Let's eat."

The group settled into a quiet meal, each person lost in their thoughts as the fire crackled softly, and the sky darkened overhead.

By midday the next day, everyone was back aboard the ship. The captain, visibly irritated, waited only long enough for the last centaur's hoof to strike the deck before shouting for departure.

Lyric approached him with the map in hand and pointed to their destination. "Why there?" he grumbled, eyes narrowing.

"That's our concern," she replied calmly. "Just take us."

The captain muttered something under his breath—too low to make out, but not friendly.

Andonis stepped forward, his tone sharp. "Is there a problem?"

The captain turned and gave him a withering look.

"Only if you're planning to stroll into the heart of the Society, traveling with creatures they've never laid eyes on. Creatures they'll kill before asking questions. But hey, if that's your plan, then sure. No problem."

With that, he shoved past Andonis and barked orders to his crew.

Neiaphi moved closer, grabbing Andonis's hand with both of hers. He gave her a reassuring squeeze.

"Don't worry," he said lightly. "If we were sailing into danger, I'm sure Pythia would've warned us."

Lyric arched an eyebrow, saying nothing, but her silence spoke volumes.

∞ 3 ∞
THE PILLARS

The Pillars loomed on the horizon—far more imposing than Cret had imagined. He hadn't known what to expect, but certainly not this—a colossal stone figure of a man, legs braced across two rocky cliffs, one foot on each side. In one hand, he raised a great sword toward the sky; in the other, a massive shield angled toward the sea, as though holding back the ocean itself.

His back was to the endless blue, an eternal sentinel watching the continent.

The land narrowed into a natural bottleneck of stone, forcing all movement—by land or by sea—to pass beneath the statue's legs. It was a gate, a warning, and a challenge.

Fishing vessels bobbed in the waters at its flanks, their sails snapping in the salt wind. But beyond them waited the true danger: warships. Sleek and dark, they drifted like predators among prey, bristling with weapons and taut rigging. Soldiers paced the decks with practiced vigilance, their eyes sweeping across the fishing boats and merchant ships with thinly veiled suspicion.

Cret swallowed hard. They were almost there.

Beside the statue's right leg, a broad patrol vessel hovered, stopping each merchant ship for inspection. It blocked the only passage forward, a narrow channel threading through a chain of jagged islands.

Tivadarios glanced nervously at the ship. "Do you think they'll let us pass?" "I hope so," Cret replied, eyes fixed on the vessel.

Tivadarios swallowed and asked, "What will we do if they don't?"

Cret shifted uneasily, shrugging. "I don't know. Pythia never said. I just hope she's been in contact with someone inside."

Tivadarios shook his head, frown deepening. "We come from a highly advanced civilization, but Pythia... she unsettles me."

Cret nodded in agreement. "She uses technology forbidden on Romota. I'd love to see it in action."

Myreia approached them, wide-eyed. "How is that even possible?" She asked in a breathy voice.

"What?" Cret asked, confused.

"That statue. How can anyone build something that size?"

Cret glanced up at the towering figure. "Back on Romota, the king's statue is about that size. I guess this one was made before they banned technology here."

Pavlina appeared beside them, impeccably dressed in her finest uniform. Her brass buttons gleamed, and her shoulder bars were trimmed with gold braid and tassels that swayed with every step.

"Ready for the show?" she asked with a sharp smile.

"Are you sure about this? What if they find out we're not who we claim to be?" Tivadarios's voice dropped to a whisper.

Pavlina's eyes hardened. "If you're caught, you'll be executed. And I'll be tortured as a traitor." Her words cut through him like a cold wind.

The color drained from Tivadarios's face. Pavlina smirked, then gave his shoulder a quick punch. "So, let's not fail, alright? It'll be fine."

He winced, rubbing the spot. "Stars, I didn't know you could hit that hard."

She smirked. "Aw, you're just saying that. Now come on, 'Ambassadors,' we've got work to do."

Their ship eased into line behind seven other vessels.

Bal-air frowned, watching the slow procession. "How long will this take?"

"It depends on the cargo and passengers," Pavlina said. "If it drags on, we'll have to wait until morning."

Cret scanned the horizon, eyes straining. "I don't see the city. How far is it?" Pavlina's smile turned mysterious. "That," she said, "is a surprise."

Time dragged as each ship ahead of them was inspected one by one. The sun sank lower, already halfway below the horizon, when it was finally their turn—only to be stopped.

"I'm afraid we'll have to wait until morning. The port's closing," Pavlina said with a sly grin. "But I know a great place nearby—good food, strong ale, and plenty of pretty girls to keep you boys entertained." She winked.

Tivadarios's cheeks flushed. After a moment, he asked, "So, tomorrow, we'll be first in line?"

"Only if we get there first. Some merchants plan to spend the night drifting around, and at first light, they'll all race to be first. We'll do our best to beat them."

Bal-air let out a frustrated huff. "Doesn't being on the Royal Transport give us any priority?"

Pavlina pointed up to the mainmast, where a plain white flag snapped sharply in the wind. "Only if we were flying the Royal Seal, and that's only allowed if a member of the Royal Family is aboard. Then we could sail straight through without a second glance."

"Can't we just pretend?" Tivadarios asked, eyes fixed on the white flag curling and unfurling in the breeze.

"That, my friend, would lead us to a fate worse than death." Pavlina's tone was sharp but laced with dark humor.

"I think we should maintain a low profile tonight, Just a clean bed and a hearty meal," Cret said without removing his eyes from the statue.

Pavlina's lips thinned into a thin line. She looked like she was going to argue but changed her mind. "We'll be staying at the Royal Stag Inn tonight. I'll secure rooms for all of us."

The Royal Stag Inn was a narrow, tall building perched near the coastline. Inside, the main room glowed warmly around a large open fire pit, its flames casting flickering shadows across the rough-hewn beams.

A short, plump woman greeted them with a broad, toothy smile that didn't quite reach her eyes. "Lieutenant! What a surprise! I wasn't expecting guests this evening. How many will there be?"

"Ambassador Cret and Ambassador Tivadarios, plus two others joining us shortly," Pavlina replied smoothly.

"Ambassadors, you say? My, my… Not many return to Atlantis these days. And where might you hail from?" The innkeeper's eyes narrowed slightly.

"We've traveled far from the east," Cret answered, his voice steady but cautious. The woman's gaze lingered a moment longer. "That's… an unusual answer."

"It'll make sense soon, Nataly," Pavlina said quietly. "Our guests are unlike anything you've ever seen. We need to keep a low profile—they're royalty and want to remain hidden. They're out back. Please don't be alarmed when you see them."

Nataly nodded briskly, her eyes wide with curiosity.

Pavlina led them through the bar to the kitchen. A couple of patrons glanced their way with mild interest, but Pavlina ignored them. Once behind the bar, she swung open the back door. Myreia and Bal-air stepped inside, ducking low.

Nataly's eyes widened even more.

"May I introduce King Bal-air and Queen Myreia of the Centaurs?" Pavlina announced.

Nataly sank into a deep curtsy. "It's an honor to meet you, Your Majesties," she said, her voice hitched slightly.

She straightened and cleared her throat, hesitating before asking, "If I may be so bold… when did the centaurs get a king and queen?"

The room fell silent. Everyone stared at her, stunned. Cret was the first to break the quiet. "You know about centaurs?"

Nataly smiled wistfully. "Oh yes. I haven't seen one since I was a child. Our village was close to a centaur settlement, until the falling out. But royalty? That's new to me."

"Falling out?" Myreia's brow furrowed. "What happened?"

Nataly brushed off her apron. "Why don't we get you settled in? I'll close up the inn, and then we can talk in peace."

"That sounds like an excellent idea," Pavlina agreed with a nod.

A few fingers of time later, everyone gathered near the crackling fire, the warm glow casting dancing shadows across their faces. They sipped mugs of steaming cider, the rich scent mingling with the wood smoke.

"So, my wonderful four-legged friends," Nataly began with a teasing smile, "which clan do you hail from?"

"My clan is Sage," Myreia said softly.

"And mine, Birch," Bal-air added.

Nataly's eyes sparkled with recognition. "Interesting— you're not from the same clan. That's quite unusual. I might know someone from your clan, Bal-air. When I was young, my village was near the Birch lands."

"Perhaps you know our elder, Osaga," Bal-air offered.

Her fingers drummed thoughtfully against her chin. "Osaga… That name does ring a bell, but it's been many years."

She paused, then tilted her head. "So, what brings you all to Atlantis?"

The centaurs exchanged glances, but before anyone could answer, Pavlina spoke for them. "They spoke with

Pythia," Pavlina explained. "She told them to go to the city."

"Oh, I see." Nataly chuckled softly. "Which means you have no idea why you're going

Cret leaned forward. "Can you tell us about the falling out? Just the basics, maybe?"

Nataly nodded. "I don't know all the details; I was only nine or ten when it happened. But from what I remember, my village and the Birch Clan lived peacefully. Our homes were only about half a day's leisurely walk apart. The centaurs would come to trade with us, and we'd visit them. We shared feasts and celebrated festivals."

Her voice faltered. "Then, one night, everything changed."

She glanced down at her mug before continuing. "The centaurs came into our village under the cover of darkness, armed. They rounded up our leaders and interrogated them until dawn."

Bal-air's voice was steady. "What were they asking?"

"Why would we burn their village?" Nataly said bitterly. "We hadn't done it, of course. Our leaders tried to explain, but the centaurs wouldn't believe us. Their elder was trapped in the flames and died. In retaliation, they killed our town's leader, declared the debt paid, and then vanished." She lowered her gaze, the pain clear.

"Did your village ever find out who was responsible?" Tivadarios asked gently.

Nataly shook her head. "No. My father and others searched for answers. They found footprints of men entering the village, but none leaving. It was as if the attackers had simply ceased to exist. After that, our village relocated, afraid we'd be next. I never saw another centaur again, and as the years passed, fewer people even remembered they existed."

Bal-air remained silent for a long moment. "My grandmother told me stories of monsters attacking by night. She warned me never to trust the two-legs. I thought they were just tall tales—like the wooden cities that floated on water or the star-traveling ships."

"Wooden cities?" Tivadarios frowned.

Bal-air shrugged. "I now know they were ships. Sailing vessels."

They were back aboard *The Gilded Pegasus* well before first light, but even with the sun still below the horizon, they weren't first in line.

"Sixth in line isn't too bad," Pavlina remarked, glancing over the waiting ships. "Really?" Cret asked, skeptical.

"All those merchants have likely been sleeping aboard their vessels. We'll be underway well before midday, fear not."

As the pale light of dawn stretched across the sky, their ship edged closer to the inspectors' platform. Two men stepped aboard, flanked by three fully armored guards.

"Greetings, Inspector Marlek. I trust the Gods have been smiling upon you," Pavlina said with practiced formality.

"Lieutenant, wasn't expecting to see you so early," the inspector replied, surprised. "Unexpected visitors to the Royal Palace," she explained with a subtle bow, then extended her arm toward her passengers. "It is my honor to introduce Ambassadors Cret and Tivadarios and their Majesties, King Bal-air and Queen Myreia of the Centaurs."

The inspector's eyes nearly bulged from his head as the royal couple stepped out of the captain's quarters and onto the deck. Two guards immediately drew their swords, while the third raised his shield and stepped back.

"Stay calm, gentlemen," Pavlina said firmly. "No one here means harm. They come on a mission of peace."

The inspector masked his surprise with a practiced cough, clearing his throat as he glanced at the scroll in his hand and made a quick notation.

"Your ship will need to be searched. Do you have any other passengers or items to declare before we board?"

"No, Sir. Welcome aboard." Pavlina bowed once more.

The two inspectors and three guards stepped onto the deck. From the small building on the man-made island, four additional guards appeared, each carrying a bow.

The inspection was swift and thorough.

"Everything appears to be in order," Marlek said with a brisk nod. "You may proceed.

Stay the course and do not deviate from the path."

"Thank you, Marlek. I know the way."

The Pegasus's sails unfurled as the ship slowly lurched forward, guided by a pair of oxen trudging along the dock.

Several small fishing vessels clustered near the towering statue's massive legs. One merchant ship that had entered ahead of them was still visible in the distance, but no others remained in sight.

"Huh," Cret huffed, crossing his arms. "What is it?" Pavlina asked, glancing at him. "I expected warships guarding these waters."

She smiled knowingly. "They patrol closer to Atlantis itself. Nothing gets through the Pillars without permission." She paused, her eyes gleaming. "But the shoreline beyond is wild. That's where the Predators roam. They're quite the sight, if you're lucky enough to see them and live to tell about it."

With a hearty laugh, she clapped Cret on the back. "Stay the course, men! Keep the colors flying! We'll see home with the rising sun!" she shouted, her voice carrying across the deck.

The crew sprang into action, adjusting sails as the first pale light of dawn edged over the horizon.

∞ **4** ∞
MONSTERS

The shoreline looked much like every other Neiaphi had seen since arriving on this planet: jagged rocks, long stretches of sand, and dense forests pressing inland. The captain guided his vessel to a desolate beach, unloaded his passengers swiftly, and turned the ship back toward the horizon.

Three humans, five centaurs, three horses, and a dog stood in silence on the sand. Hundreds of tiny shells shimmered in the rising sun like scattered diamond dust. They watched as the ship slipped beyond the water's edge, leaving only the whisper of waves and the distant cry of seabirds behind.

"So, where to next?" Pelagios looked expectantly at Lyric.

"The Moon Clan is about a four-day ride north, if this map is right. We don't know how many settlements are in the area, though. Any suggestions?" Lyric replied.

"Neiaphi, Pelagios, and I will ride ahead in the open," Andonis said, tightening the cinches on both his and Neiaphi's horses. "The rest of you should spread out and stay hidden as much as possible. We'll take it slow to avoid separation. Once we find the first town, we'll gather supplies and hopefully get a better map."

They rode steadily beneath the sinking sun, which washed the sky in molten hues of crimson and gold. Ahead, a small village came into view, its mud-and-grass houses clustered together. The group agreed Andonis should approach alone.

He urged his horse forward, the muted thud of hooves soft against the dry earth. As he entered the village, three men stepped out to meet him, one with a hand on his sword hilt, the other two leveling bows squarely in his direction.

"Hello," Andonis called out, raising his hands in a peaceful gesture.

"Stop right there. What business do you have here?" The man in the middle growled. "Just passing through. Looking for supplies," Andonis replied with a broad smile. "We have nothing for you," the man said sharply. "Move along."

"We don't want to be a burden. Do you know how far it is to the next settlement?"

"Two days' ride further north. You'll find a sizable town, but they're not friendly to outsiders."

"Thank you." Andonis bowed his head slightly, a wiry smile tugging at his lips. He backed his horse several steps before turning to leave.

When he returned to the group, a dark shadow crossed his face. "We'll have to press on," he said quietly. "Let's move deeper into the trees and find our friends."

"That must be the 'sizable town'," Pelagios said, his gaze fixed on the cluster of buildings nestled in a valley where two sluggish streams split apart.

"Wait here. I'll see how friendly they are," Andonis said, urging his horse into a brisk trot.

As he rode deeper into town, the narrow streets grew crowded. People filled the lanes, their hands empty but their eyes cold. Many paused to stare, their expressions hardening with every step of his mount. Andonis offered a polite nod, but the scowls only deepened.

He guided his horse straight to the fountain in the town

square, scanning his surroundings. A weathered tavern stood to one side. Dismounting, he tied his horse to the hitching post and approached the door.

Loud music and drunken shouts spilled into the street. Andonis pushed the heavy door open and stepped into a haze of stale ale, sweat, and ash, undercut by a sharp, acrid stench that turned his stomach.

No one spared him a glance as he made his way to the bar.

"What'll it be?" barked a burly man behind the counter, dragging a filthy rag across his brow.

Andonis forced down a grimace. "I'm looking for a place to buy supplies."

The bartender coughed harshly, then wiped his nose with the back of his hand, then leaned closer. "Market's closed. Inn's full. Try again tomorrow." His eyes narrowed. "Now, what are you drinking?"

Andonis hesitated. He didn't want to linger, but information often came with a price. "The house specialty," he said evenly.

The man grunted, slid a mug of sour ale across the counter, and scooped up the coins with snake-like speed. Without another glance, he turned to shout at two men already on the verge of blows.

Andonis scanned the room. Two weary servers wove through the crowd, trays balanced in their hands as they endured the groping of rough men who hadn't bathed in weeks. A dice game in the corner collapsed into a brawl, tables overturning as fists and mugs flew. The barkeep tried to intervene, shouting hoarsely, but the chaos swallowed him whole. The brawl quickly devolved into a full melee, with patrons either joining in or cheering wildly.

Andonis stayed a few minutes longer, then headed for the door, setting down his still-full mug on the nearest table.

Outside, he drew a deep breath of clean, crisp air.

"Are we welcome there?" Pelagios asked as he returned to camp, a short distance from the town.

"Welcome enough for what we need," Andonis replied. "You and I will go back tomorrow. Neiaphi stays here. That place isn't for a lady." His scowl deepened.

"Can't be that bad," Neiaphi said, though her voice faltered under his glare. "That bad. And worse. You stay here, with the centaurs."

"We should strike tomorrow, when they split up!" Hepluosis whispered urgently, eyes fixed on his prey just a hundred yards ahead.

Rirmell's reply was low and rough. "No. Not yet. I need to know what they're after first.

We follow, nothing more, for now."

Slowly, they retreated into the shadows to wait for morning.

The rising sun chased the centaurs and Neiaphi into the safety of the trees, while Andonis and Pelagios rode into the town.

Neiaphi sat on a log, calling Cypress to her side. She scowled toward the village and the two men heading in.

Peleros approached quietly and settled beside her. "He's only looking out for you, you know?"

She blinked, shaking her head as if to clear the fog. "Who?"

"Andonis. Don't be angry with him."

"I'm not angry," she said softly, though the tightness in her voice suggested otherwise. "Then why are you scowling and boring a hole into the back of his head with your eyes?"

Peleros asked, a teasing note in his voice.

Neiaphi sighed. "I was just thinking about everything I've been through since coming to this planet."

"Reflection is good, but you need to focus on the now

and what's coming next. Always looking back will leave you stumbling—and lost in your journey through life."

She nodded slowly. "Wise words. I've been thinking about the future a lot, too. It's just easier to critique the past than to predict tomorrow."

The sun was nearing midday when Andonis and Pelagios returned, each with full bags tied to either side of their horses.

"I see you were successful," Lyric remarked.

"It cost more than it should have, but we have enough supplies for several days. I even managed to get a map of the area," Andonis said, unrolling the worn parchment and weighing its corners down with stones.

Everyone gathered close. "We're right here," he said, pointing.

"There's another settlement further along this stream, but from what the traveler said, most of the others are closer to the shoreline."

"What are these marks?" Justic asked, pointing to the strange symbols on the map. "Those are the places I want us to check first," Andonis said. "The traveler told me they're the ruins of dwellings once home to fearsome monsters—said to be the cursed children of a four-legged demon and a village maiden he had captured. These cursed children were mighty warriors who slaughtered anyone who came near."

Lyric leaned in, whispering, "What happened to them?"

"No one really knows. The legend says two other monsters appeared, and a great war broke out between the three. Afterward, they all vanished into the shadows."

"Does the legend describe the three different monsters?" Neiaphi asked, her voice barely above a whisper.

Pelagios looked up, meeting her gaze. "The cursed children—the mighty warriors—are described as having the body of a horse twisted unnaturally with that of a man. Their words, not mine," he added with a grim smile toward the centaurs.

"The second is said to have the body of a man but the head of a monstrous bull. And the third… well, it could change shape. It was the most terrifying of all, able to appear as a normal man or transform into a huge, intelligent wolf."

Neiaphi's eyes widened. "A large, intelligent wolf?"

"That's what they say." Andonis placed a steady arm around her shoulders. "We'll stay here tonight and set out at first light."

"So, the people here have legends about our kind," Staps growled, his eyes sweeping over the pack as they melted into the shadows beneath the trees.

"What does that mean for us?" one low voice asked nervously.

Staps snapped at him sharply, forcing the wolf to lower his head and tuck his tail between his legs.

"Being feared as monsters…" Staps paused, then added with a sly grin, "We can use that to our advantage."

Several wolves nodded in agreement.

"Lars, you're with me. We'll probe the depths of their fear. The rest of you, follow the horses and humans; we'll catch up soon."

His pack let out a chilling howl before disappearing into the darkness, leaving only Staps and Lars behind.

Staps nodded to Lars, closed his eyes, and shifted his form. Lars stepped forward, allowing Staps to remove a pack from his back before he, too, shifted.

Quickly dressed, Staps stretched his limbs and neck.

"How long has it been for you?" Lars asked once Staps was fully dressed.

"Almost a year," Staps muttered with disgust. "I hate this form—too weak. It needs clothes."

Lars nodded in understanding.

"Let's move. We need to get back to the others," Staps said.

Slipping the pack over his shoulder, Staps walked upright like a man—because that was what he was—now.

The first mark on the map led them to a clearing that might have made a perfect campsite, but there was no trace of any settlement. They pressed on.

By the time the sun dipped low, draping the land in long, jagged shadows, they had reached the fifth mark. The valley was strewn with piles of stone—remnants of collapsed walls—and a few buildings still stood, their frames stubbornly defying time.

"Finally!" Lyric breathed, relief evident in her voice. They split into pairs, spreading out to search the ruins.

"Look at this!" Justic called, crouching near the village's central well. Weathered drawings clung faintly to the surrounding stones—ancient records left behind.

The crude etchings depicted fierce battles: centaurs locked in combat with bull-headed men, wolves, and humans.

"Minotaur," someone murmured reverently.

"What's a Minotaur?" Pelagios asked, stepping closer to study the drawings.

"The bull-headed men," Simandro growled. "I thought the descriptions sounded like them, but now I'm certain. They're vile creatures, more beast than man. Pure savages, bloodthirsty and merciless."

They walked slowly around the well, tracing the story etched into the stones. The Minotaur and wolves had attacked under the cover of night, setting fire to everything that would burn. Centaur foals fled into the woods with the elderly, while the men and women grabbed whatever weapons they could to fight back.

Neiaphi ran her hand gently over the worn edge of the well. "As the sun rose, and the fires raged, the centaurs pushed the attackers back into the trees. The elderly and children returned afterward to bury the dead. According to this, only three adults survived if they were drawing everyone."

Lyric crouched down, pointing to one of the figures. "Look at this filly—she looks just like Mother. She made it here… only to be driven away again. Why doesn't she remember any of this?"

Justic shook his head, troubled. "Where did they go after this?"

"East," Andonis said, gesturing toward the final image.

A crude map was sketched on the crumbling wall, depicting the shoreline with a dark cloud hovering over a small village and several large boats anchored offshore.

"Thunder Clan?" Lyric asked, glancing toward Simandro. He nodded solemnly. "Then that's where we go next."

"It will take many days," Andonis reminded them.

Lyric stood, determination flickering in her eyes. "Then let's not waste any time."

∞ **5** ∞
ᴛHUNDER ᴄLAN

Staps stalked through the village streets, his sharp gaze daring anyone to meet his eyes. He despised humans— their cramped villages, their tiny houses, and the sour stench that clung to everything. Wrinkling his nose, he stepped around a heap of rotting refuse piled in front of the inn.

He had tasked Lars with sniffing out whatever the villagers might know about his kind—or any other nonhumans. Staps avoided speaking to humans whenever possible; their words felt like poison on his tongue.

"Watch out!" he bellowed as a staggering man lurched out of the inn and slammed into him.

With a single rough shove, Staps sent the man sprawling in the dirt. "Watch yourself," the man snarled drunkenly.

"Humans," Staps spat, his voice thick with contempt.

Up ahead, Lars emerged from the butcher shop, lugging a large package. "Time to go," he called, already heading toward the edge of the village.

Staps quickened his stride to catch up, eager to leave behind the suffocating filth of the human settlement.

"What did you learn? And what's that you're carrying?" he asked, eyeing the bulky parcel balanced on Lars's shoulder.

"Mutton," Lars replied with a wide, toothy grin. "How did you get it? We have no currency here."

Lars smirked and started jogging. "I convinced them the legends were real," Staps growled. "What did you do?"

"They treat those stories like bedtime tales for children,

meant to keep them away from the ruins. Still, they believe the Gods guard the place—and that anyone who desecrates it will fall under a curse."

"And the mutton?"

Lars laughed. "Let's just say I gave them a little… incentive to part with it." Staps snatched the package and gave Lars a sharp slap on the back of the head. "Ouch!"

"Come on. We need to get back before they realize what's missing."

They slipped into the shadows of the trees, shedding their human clothes as they shifted back into their true forms. Staps devoured the mutton with ravenous bites, while Lars gathered their discarded garments and stuffed them into a backpack.

"Leave some for me," Lars snarled, eyeing the meat. Staps growled, bearing his teeth.

"Please," Lars said in a mock-whimper before shifting fully into a wolf.

"Move it. Night's coming." Staps let out a long, piercing howl and lunged forward into a sprint. Lars swallowed the last bites of mutton, clamped the pack between his jaws, and bounded after him.

After several days of hard travel along the coastline, Lyric's band finally arrived at the location marked on the map.

"I don't understand," Lyric said, circling the lone stone monolith. The clearing held nothing else—no ruins, no worn paths, just one trail from the coast and another leading north. "There should be ruins here… something."

"Well, maybe people came and repurposed all the stones," Justic said passively.

"Every last one? Not even a trace left behind? Look at this place—it's untouched, like freshly fallen snow. No rabbit tracks, nothing." She pointed at the pristine ground, then tilted her head skyward, slowly turning in place. "Even the birds avoid it. See?"

Two finches abruptly veered away from the clearing, changing direction midflight as though striking an invisible wall.

"There must be something here. Is there any writing or drawings on the monolith?" Simandro asked.

Neiaphi and Andonis circled the monolith slowly, scanning it from top to bottom. At last, they shook their heads. With a sigh, Neiaphi knelt and brushed aside the flowers and grass growing at its base.

She gasped, "Over here, I think I found something." Tugging the grass out by the roots, she dug into the dark red soil. Her fingers grazed something cold and smooth beneath the earth. Carefully, she swept the remaining growth aside, revealing ancient carvings etched deep into the stone— intricate symbols unlike any script they had ever seen. Faint light pulsed along the grooves, an eerie, rhythmic glow, as though the monolith itself were alive and guarding a hidden secret.

She traced the lines with reverence. "This place… It's protected. Not by walls or guards, but by something else. This has to be it! Ancient technology."

Andonis knelt beside her, frowning, picking up a handful of the red soil.

"What is it?" Lyric asked him.

"The soil, see?" He held the dirt up for her to see.

"It's red dirt. I don't see your point."

"Look around outside the clearing; what color is all the surrounding soil?"

"Black!" She exclaimed with wide eyes. "Why is all the dirt in the clearing different from the surrounding land?"

"Look at this; it looks like your necklace, Lyric." Neiaphi looked up at the filly. She pointed to a small circular indentation at the base of the monolith.

Lyric bent down to get a closer look while she ran her fingers across the pendant of her necklace. "What does this mean? Were they here and then left again? Where did they go from here?" She stepped even closer, eyes narrowed. "No tracks, no birds… It's as if the very air around this place refuses to let anything near."

Simandro tightened his grip on his sword, glancing warily into the shadows beyond the clearing.

"If you don't mind, can I?" Pelagios pointed to Lyric and then turned his palm over, asking for the necklace.

She hesitated momentarily before sliding the leather thong over her head; she held it close. "Do you think it's like back at the Moon clan? A key?" He nodded. "Be careful with it."

Pelagios bowed his head, one hand pressed to his heart. "With my life," he said, the corner of his mouth lifting into a shy grin.

Lyric carefully handed him the necklace. Their fingers brushed for the briefest moment before Pelagios took it and examined the pendant, turning it over in his palm. At last, he matched it to the indentation on the monolith.

"Here goes nothing," he muttered, pressing the necklace into place.

At first, nothing happened. Then the stone began to hum a low vibration that made the air tingle. The carved symbols flared to life, glowing brighter until the entire clearing shimmered with eerie light. Suddenly, the ground shook violently, followed by a sharp crack and a roar like grinding thunder. Gasps escaped from the onlookers as the tremors drove them scrambling for shelter among the trees. A billowing cloud of dust and debris shot skyward with another explosive burst. From deep below came a rolling rumble, and the soil in the clearing slowly parted like a curtain drawn aside, to reveal a hidden staircase descending into the earth.

Neiaphi walked back into the clearing first, eyes wide. "This… this is a doorway."

"And it's been waiting for you," Pelagios said quietly, looking at Lyric with a mix of awe and concern.

Lyric swallowed hard, her fingers brushing against her neck where the pendant used to rest. "Then we need to find out what's down there."

Sword in hand, Andonis strode forward, raising his free hand to signal the others to stay back. He crept toward the staircase, coughing as thick, stagnant dust settled and coated the clearing. After a few moments, the haze began to lift, though a mix of hope and unease hung heavy in the air. At the center, the stairway yawned open, leading down into darkness. Andonis stepped closer, pausing at the edge before placing his foot on the first step. The stone staircase was not built for human legs; the steps stretched three paces wide and two paces deep. "We're going to need torches," he called back.

Lyric stepped forward, her eyes darting nervously between the dark stairway and the wary faces behind her.

"Torches," she echoed. "I'll get some from the horses."

Justic and Simandro nodded, already moving to gather kindling and dry branches from the nearby woods. Neiaphi moved among the horses, soothing them with gentle words.

Pelagios lingered near the monolith, his gaze fixed on the abyss below. "This place… it feels more magical than tech-based," he muttered, almost to himself.

"And dangerous," Andonis added, gripping his sword tightly.

The group prepared quickly, their torches soon flickering to life, casting wavering light over the jagged stone steps. One by one, they descended cautiously, the air growing colder and heavier with each step.

They moved cautiously, testing each step as they descended. By the fourth turn of the stairs, their torches were the only source of light. At the fifth, a stone sconce jutted from the wall, its surface etched with tiny, star-shaped carvings. Lyric halted, curiosity sparking, and reached into the empty holder where a torch once might have rested. She flinched, pulling her hand back, her fingers slick with a strange, oily film. Rubbing it between her fingertips, she raised them to her nose.

"What do you think this is?" she asked Andonis. He touched the residue and smiled. Taking her torch, he pressed the flame to the sconce. Instantly, the oil caught, blossoming into a bright, steady fire. In its glow, a spiraling channel carved into the wall came into view, carrying the light downward along the stairwell. Within moments, the entire passage glowed with warm illumination.

"Oh, my!" Neiaphi breathed, her eyes roaming the stairwell walls. Every surface was alive with intricate carvings: stars, suns, and moons adorned the upper sections, while trees, mountains, and animals sprawled across the lower. Even the steps bore scenes—humans and centaurs, villages and boats etched into the stone. Cypress yipped softly and nudged her hand. "It's okay, boy," she murmured absently, scratching behind his ears.

They descended further, each footfall echoing into the unseen depths. Time stretched, the stairway seeming endless, until at last they reached the bottom. There, where the channel of torchlight ended, the passage widened into a vast chamber. Along its walls glimmered faint, ancient markings, symbols identical to those carved into the monolith above, casting a subtle, otherworldly glow.

They lifted their torches high, casting flickering light into the vast chamber. Ambrite slipped to the left, running his gaze along the walls until he discovered another torch channel. With a swift strike of flint, he set it alight. Fire leapt into the groove, racing along its carved path. One by one, the hidden channels flared to life, flooding the chamber with radiance and spiraling back toward the stairwell, until the entire space glowed with living fire.

Then they saw what they had been searching for on the far side of the chamber. "The Communication Machine," Lyric whispered.

"Do you think it still works?" Justic asked.

"Only one way to find out." Pelagios walked quickly to the machine, looking at the control board. "This is old technology, but I recognize it. If it's still functioning, I can get it on."

Lyric hurried to his side. "Are you sure?" He placed a

hand on her arm and nodded.

Lyric's voice barely rose above a whisper, "This is only the beginning."

Pelagios crouched before the Communication Machine, brushing years of dust and grime from its intricate dials and levers. The faint hum of residual power sparked hope in the group.

Lyric stayed close, watching his every move. "Do you need anything?" she asked quietly. "Just a moment to reconnect the circuits," Pelagios murmured, his fingers deftly twisting wires beneath the panel. "This technology is ancient, but it's still based on principles I understand."

Andonis and Neiaphi began examining the chamber's walls. Suddenly, the machine sputtered to life with a low buzz. Pelagios adjusted a dial, and a faint blue light flickered on the display. "It's working."

Lyric exhaled, relief flooding her face. "Can you send a message?"

"I think so," Pelagios said, eyes narrowing in concentration. "We need to establish a clear signal first."

The ancient machine began humming steadily, a lifeline to a home—a planet most centaurs didn't know existed.

Lyric stepped forward, her voice steady but thoughtful. "We need to let them know who we are, where we are, and what we seek. Something clear, but not too detailed—just enough to prompt a response."

Pelagios nodded, fingers poised over the ancient controls. "Agreed. Too much info could alert the wrong ears."

Andonis rubbed his chin, considering. "What about this: 'This is Lyric of the Moon Clan, seeking allies. We stand at the ancient monolith, in need of guidance and aid."

Lyric smiled slightly. "Simple, direct, and respectful."

Pelagios began feeding the message into the machine, its low hum rising with each movement.

"Ready to send on your mark," he said, glancing up at Lyric. Their eyes met, holding for a heartbeat.

"While you work, Simandro and I will head back

up—just to be sure no one stumbles onto us," Peleros added.

"I'll join you and see if I can find something for us to eat," Ambrite replied. "I'll help." Volunteered Neiaphi. "Would you like to help Andonis?" Andonis was staring at Lyric and Pelagios. "Andonis?" she asked again.

"Oh, um, yeah, I'll help too," he said after clearing his throat.

∞ **6** ∞
ᴀBOVE THE ᴄLOUDS

Sephi lingered by the door, gazing at the dense canopy above, where sunlight filtered through like scattered jewels. The scent of pine and damp earth filled the air, a fragile reminder of the peace they had found here.

She turned back to the small, tidy hut, her fingers brushing the rough wooden table where memories lingered—laughter shared, plans made, and worries whispered into the night.

"I hope wherever they are, Cret and Tivadarios are safe," she murmured.

Outside, the wind shifted, carrying a faint chill. The journey ahead would be long and uncertain, but the hope of reunion—of family—was the light they all clung to.

Sephi stepped outside, inhaling deeply. Beyond the clouds, the sun still shone, waiting for them to reach its warmth again.

"Do you think Cret's okay? Will we see him again?" she asked as Crelian approached.

She had asked him the same questions almost every day.

"Yes… I have faith," he said, as he always did. But in truth, doubt gnawed at him. With every passing day, week, and moon, his hope of seeing his son again grew fainter.

Word had once reached them from a centaur: Cret and Tivadarios were being held captive. With Lyric's help and the aid of others, they had broken free, swearing they would return as soon as possible. But since that message, no further sign had come. Crelian bowed his head, silently praying they had found safe shelter for the winter and that fate would guide them home again.

"We'll be pressing on again the day after tomorrow," he said. Sephi nodded and continued to pack.

"In a small way, I will miss this place," she said quietly. Crelian patted her hand and departed from their hut.

Simos pushed his small group hard each day, only allowing them to rest one day after five days of travel. But in truth, he didn't have to ask them too hard; they were eager to get to Atlantis.

They were hit by heavy rainfall the second week, which halted their progress entirely for three days.

As each day passed, Simos's mood grew sullen. Without the Hovers to enhance their speed over the harsh land, he worried they would not reach their destination before winter caressed them again with its icy fingers.

The Planting Moon ebbed, and the Growing Moon was creeping up on the weary travelers when they finally neared Chrysafi. Simos halted his group in the cover of the forest and approached the trading town alone. He moved slowly toward the nearest guard post. The village buzzed with life— merchants haggling, traders unloading, travelers weaving in and out in a steady flow. Only one guard bothered to stop wagons and question newcomers; the others kept their eyes fixed on the surrounding forest.

Without a word of greeting, Simos was waved through the gate. The instructions had said he would need to speak to the guards for access, but clearly, circumstances had changed. He pressed on, scanning the shop signs as he walked. According to the directions, he was to look for a butcher. Simos paused outside the shop. The sign of the green hog with purple spots swung idly in the evening breeze. The small storefront was nestled between an apothecary and a seamstress's shop. Lanternlight flickered across the cobblestones, stretching long shadows that gave the street a watchful, uneasy air.

He shuddered but the uneasiness lingered as he scanned the surroundings. The lighting seemed excessive, as though someone wanted every corner of the night visible and observed. The guards' attention was still fixed outward, toward the trees, not inward at the people. Something was off.

Pushing open the heavy wooden door, Simos stepped inside. His boots echoed softly across the dim shop. The scent of cured meat hung in the air, laced with something metallic—like blood, though not fresh. An older woman stood behind the counter, a long white apron covering her from neck to ankle, a broom resting in one hand. Her sharp eyes fixed on him, silent, waiting for him to speak.

"What's going on here?" Simos asked quietly, keeping his voice steady despite the unease curling in his gut. "Why so many guards watching the forest, and all this light at night?"

She paused her sweeping, her lips twitching into a faint, grim smile. "You're asking questions, traveler. That's dangerous around here. What can I do for you?"

"I was told you had the best purple pickled pigs' feet in town," he replied, repeating the phrase announcing his loyalist ties.

The words hung in the air for a beat; a deliberate code passed like a coin. Her eyes narrowed, and for a moment, neither of them moved.

The woman grinned and seemed to relax. "One moment, sir. Seraph? "Yes, Mother?" A little girl poked her head out from the back room. "Purple pickled pigs' feet, please."

The little girl's eyes went wide. "Please follow my daughter."

"Thank you, ma'am." Simos nodded to the woman and followed the girl into the back room.

The back room was dimly lit by a single lantern

hanging from a low beam. The air carried the tang of vinegar and spices, layered over the earthy scent of preserved meats. Seraph moved ahead, guiding Simos past shelves lined with jars and cured cuts. Her small footsteps were nearly silent against the worn wooden floor.

"Pa?" she said meekly to the large man in the bloody apron. He looked up just as his cleaver slammed through the leg joint of a sheep. "Purple pigs… Um, pickled… purple…" she stammered.

"That's okay, Seraph; go help your mother," he grumbled.

"Yes, Pa, sorry," she squeaked and fled the room.

The butcher shook his head and smirked. "Best purple pickled pigs' feet in town."

"Nothing but the best for me," he answered with the required reply.

"Welcome to Chrysafi, friend; what can I do for you?"

"Our friends from Romota haven't passed this way yet, have they?" He nodded. "Just before the snow fell. How do you know of them?"

"My group rescued the ones they left behind."

The butcher's face broke into a huge smile. "Thank the gods; everyone thought them lost for good. Might you be needing some transportation then?"

"Any that you have will be greatly appreciated."

"Then I have a surprise for you. In the morning, return here with several of your people. I will have supplies ready for you. Camp one more night, then continue to the shoreline of the Chief Sea; ships will meet you there. Once across, swift transports will be waiting to speed you to Krisa."

"Krisa? I've heard of that place, thought it mere legend, though."

"Oh, it is real. The Oracle of Delphi will help you from there."

"Many thanks. I will see you in the morning. Oh, one more thing, why all the lanterns?"

"Wolves—the largest anyone has ever seen. Watch

your backs, and keep the fires burning bright all night, my friend. See you in the morning."

The weight of hope pressed heavily on Simos's shoulders as he stepped into the cool night air. Lanterns cast long, wavering shadows across the deserted streets of Chrysafi. His breath drifted in pale clouds, each one quickly swallowed by the darkness. From somewhere beyond the village, a wolf's howl split the silence—deep, resonant, and too close. Another answered, then another, until the night itself seemed to tremble with their voices.

Simos drew his cloak tighter and began the quiet walk back to camp, already planning how to ready the others for what lay ahead.

Tomorrow, they would return to the butcher, gather supplies, and take one more step toward the fabled lands of Atlantis.

But tonight, the wolves watched from the woods. And the fires would have to burn bright.

Simos stood before his traveling party, raising both hands to quiet the flood of questions hurled at him. A broad smile spread across his face. "Please, my friends, one question at a time," he said warmly. "Yes, as some of you have already heard, I met with our contact in Chrysafi. They'll resupply us tomorrow. The following morning, we march to the shore of the Chief Sea. There, ships will be waiting to carry us across."

"What mode of transport will be awaiting us?" Someone yelled out.

He shook his head. "I do not know, but I was told that we will be very grateful to have it. Let's get some rest tonight and tomorrow. I need four volunteers to come with me to get the supplies in the morning." He glanced into the crowd, seeing at least ten hands in the air.

He pointed at Crelian.

Crelian stepped forward without hesitation, his jaw set

with determination. "You can count on me, Simos."

The other three volunteers, strong and steady, fell in line beside him, their faces a mix of anticipation and resolve.

Simos nodded approvingly. "Good. We move at first light. Until then, double the watches, keep the fires burning bright, and stay alert. These woods have teeth, and they won't hesitate to bite."

A ripple of murmurs passed through the crowd, but the steady glow of the fire—and Simos's calm authority—anchored their nerves. As the night deepened, the camp settled into uneasy quiet. Flames crackled and hissed, holding back the shadows, while watchful eyes scanned the darkness beyond, waiting for whatever might emerge.

The Chief Sea lived up to its name—vast, shimmering, endless. By midday, they reached its shores. The air was still, heavy with salt, and gentle waves lapped lazily at the white sand. Several children broke from their parents, racing to the water's edge with laughter and squeals as they splashed in the shallows.

Three days passed before ships appeared on the horizon—tiny, bobbing specks at first.

Another full day crawled by before they drew close enough to lower rowboats into the surf.

The creak of ropes and the steady splash of oars soon filled the air as the last passengers and supplies were ferried aboard. A salty breeze rose and swelled, billowing the sails, whispering of a swift, hopeful passage ahead.

Children clung to their parents, eyes wide with excitement and a touch of apprehension, while the adults exchanged hopeful glances.

Simos stood on deck, gazing across the shimmering expanse of the Chief Sea. The sun was sinking low, its golden light dancing across the waves.

"I hope the gods will be smiling on us," Simos said,

approaching the captain.

The captain was a short, burly man with more hair on his face than on the top of his head. "I believe they already are. The winds are quite favorable for a swift crossing."

Simos nodded his head briskly. "Good."

The captain gave a curt nod. "We set sail at first light. Rest well."

The captain was right. In less than two days, the opposite shore came into view, and soon enough, the entire party stood once more on solid ground. Simos scanned the beach for their contacts. "Where are they?" Crelian inquired.

Simos shrugged, "Let's head inland a bit and make camp for the night."

They gathered their belongings, moving cautiously away from the shoreline. Sand gave way to grass and scattered stones, while the dense forest loomed ahead, its shadows stretching long under the fading light.

Simos scanned the tree line, his senses alert for any sign of their allies. The silence felt heavy, broken only by the distant call of birds settling for the night.

As the first stars pierced the darkening sky, the group built a modest camp. Fires flared to life, their flickering glow casting a shadow across tense faces. Yet beneath the warmth of the flames, unease lingered. Tomorrow, they hoped, would bring their allies.

Darkness soon cloaked the land, and the glow of their fires grew ever brighter against the night. In the distance, a low rumble echoed, distant at first but steadily growing. The ground began to tremble beneath their feet as the sound swelled to a deafening crescendo. Simos and the other Loyals looked around nervously; Crelian and his followers smiled with delight.

A blinding light cut through the darkness as a massive

transport ship descended from the sky. Heat, smoke, and wind blasted outward, scattering dust and leaves in a swirling cloud. The craft touched down with surprising grace, releasing a hiss of air that echoed across the clearing. Crelian smiled as he approached the ship.

Ding, Ding, an alarm bell chimed, and a ramp door opened, blinding Crelian momentarily with its interior light. Holding a hand up to shield his eyes, he waited impatiently for whoever was on the ship to emerge.

A man dressed all in black ambled down the ramp. His purple-trimmed cloak stirred with a gust of wind.

"Simos?" He asked. Crelian shook his head and gestured behind him, yet for the first time in many moons, a flicker of certainty burned within his chest. Simos hesitated for a moment before approaching.

"I am Crelian," Crelian told him, holding his arm out.

The man's sharp eyes flicked over Crelian before taking the offered arm with a firm grip. "It is an honor to meet you, Crelian. I am General Axum. Simos, I presume?" he asked, voice calm but edged with authority.

"Yes, it is an honor, General." Simos bowed at the waist.

The General smiled, "I've been sent to guide you onward to Krisa. Let's get everyone on board. We will be in Delphi by morning."

Everyone close enough to hear gasped, and then excited murmurs broke out.

"You heard the general; let's get packed up," Crelian shouted.

Behind him, the ship's glow dimmed slightly, revealing sleek, humming engines that seemed almost alive in the night air. The group exchanged looks, the tension between old doubts and new hope palpable.

The group moved quickly but carefully, their previous weariness replaced by a renewed surge of energy. The glow from the ship cast long shadows on the sand as the ramp lowered once more, beckoning them aboard.

Simos helped the weary and the young up the ramp, his eyes meeting those of Crelian, who nodded with quiet determination. The night air buzzed with anticipation, and even the wolves' howls seemed to soften in the distance.

As the ramp closed behind them, the cool night air was replaced by the hum of machinery and the faint scent of ozone—signs of a journey unlike any the Loyals had taken before.

Once inside, General Axum led Crelian and Simos to the flight deck. He gestured toward comfortable-looking seating arranged around glowing panels and maps. "Rest now. We will chart the course to Delphi. The Oracle awaits."

Simos settled in, the weight of the journey momentarily lifting. Outside, the stars shimmered brighter than ever—as if the gods themselves were watching over their voyage.

The soft hum of the engines filled the cabin as the ship carved through the sky, leaving the world below swallowed by clouds. Crelian's eyes traced the shimmering moonlight reflecting off the clouds, giving them an ethereal silver glow.

Simos slowly opened his eyes, still feeling the strange rush of movement, his heartbeat steadying. "It's… beautiful," he whispered, his voice tinged with awe.

Crelian gave a slow nod, his gaze never leaving the window and the endless expanse of clouds beneath them. "We're not just heading to a new land, Simos. We're crossing into something greater—something far beyond anything you've ever known."

The ship's gentle vibrations steadied, and ahead, the faint outline of jagged mountain peaks pierced the cloud blanket. Delphi was drawing near.

Simos gripped the arm of his chair tightly; his vision started to swim; he clamped his eyes shut. Crelian patted him on the back. "Never gone this fast?" he asked with a chuckle.

"Never thought this kind of speed was possible." He gulped.

Crelian laughed again. He strode closer to the view screen, watching the clouds zip by. The moon hung high above, casting a silver sheen across the billowing clouds. They glowed softly in the night, like waves lit from within. He leaned forward, squinting through a narrow break in the cloud cover, but the land below remained hidden, shrouded in shadow, as if the earth itself was holding its breath.

"If you don't need us, I'm going to get Simos here somewhere that appears stationary." The general grinned and nodded his head. Crelian grabbed Simos by the shoulders, turning him away from the screen, and led him down the dimly lit corridor, the gentle hum of the engines accompanying his thoughts. The soft carpeting underfoot, the electric glow of the lights, and the faint hum of the engines were oddly comforting, a steady rhythm amidst the unknown.

After leading Simos to his cabin, Crelian found himself wandering the ship. He knew his wife and daughter would be sleeping and didn't want to disturb them. He found the mess hall; there was someone still in the galley.

"Can I offer you anything before I leave?" he asked.

"Not hungry, but thank you." He walked around the room. He appeared to be at the front of the ship; a large window showed the darkness outside, with an occasional cloud illuminated by the moon.

The galley crewman paused at his table, placing a steaming mug down, and then walked away without a word.

Crelian's mind wandered back to the last time he'd seen Cret—the boy's bright eyes full of hope despite the dangers they faced. Would this new journey bring them back together? Or was the sky now a barrier between them?

With a deep breath, Crelian stood, leaving the mug untouched, and headed toward his quarters, the weight of uncertainty settling over him like the clouds outside the ship's windows. Yet beneath it all was a spark of determination—no matter what, they would find their way.

True to the general's word, they started their descent in the graying light of dawn. Crelian gathered everyone in the mess hall to watch their approach.

He glanced around the room, a sudden wave of remorse

washing over him, yet beneath it, a flicker of hope stirred. The last time he stood in a gathering hall aboard a ship, preparing to disembark in an unknown land, there had been many more by his side. His son among them. He shook his head. They would be together again soon. At least, most of them. Some had been left behind, stationed at various points, just as planned. But his son's whereabouts remained a mystery.

Outside, the crew moved with practiced efficiency, unloading the wagons and gear. Crelian stepped out, scanning the dense forest surrounding the landing site. Towering trees swayed gently in the morning breeze, their thick canopies whispering in a language not yet familiar. The ground beneath his boots was solid, earthy, and reassuring after the otherworldly drift of the skies.

"Where do you all hail from?" Crelian asked the General.

"Atlantis, we don't usually fly this way inland," he replied. "Where do you normally patrol?"

"We usually go to the lands to the west, but The Oracle contacted me directly. I hope you are worth the reprimand I might receive," he said grimly.

"I apologize if we get you into any trouble."

The general waved his hand dismissively. "I'm sure I've been in worse trouble before. God's speed. I wish I could take you to Atlantis."

Crelian's mouth dropped. "You could have?"

The General shook his head. "I asked the Oracle, but she said a quick journey was not for you. You must meet with her at Delphi; she has important information for you."

"Where do I find this Oracle?"

"I'm sure the others you're meeting there will know. She's most likely already met them."

"Then we move quickly. We're not just here to find safety, we're here to find answers. And maybe… to find those we've lost." The familiar weight of leadership settling across his shoulders.

Around them, their companions exchanged glances.

Hope and uncertainty danced in equal measure across their faces. Yet in that moment, something unspoken passed between them, a shared resolve. This was only the beginning.

Their horses moved at a steady pace, hoofbeats muffled by the thick carpet of fallen leaves. Shafts of sunlight pierced the forest canopy, scattering dappled light across the winding path ahead.

Crelian rode beside Simos, his voice low. "So, Delphi is our next stop. What do you know of this Oracle?"

Simos gave a slight shrug. "Only that she's said to be wise beyond measure, able to see what others cannot. Kings, warriors—even skeptics—go to her. Most leave changed."

Crelian nodded slowly, hope flickering in his chest. "And you believe she holds the key to finding Cret?"

Simos's gaze hardened, eyes narrowing. "She holds many keys. Whether yours is among them… only time will tell."

Behind them, the rest of the group moved in a steady procession, the future ahead uncertain but charged with possibility. The road to Delphi had begun.

Crelian nodded, his heart lifting with renewed hope. A short distance away, across a large open meadow, was a village nestled at the base of a hill. On top of the small mountain was a gleaming white temple. The scent of wood smoke on the wind greeted them.

When they were halfway across the meadow, a group from the village started their way.

Once close enough to distinguish features, Crelian spurred his horse forward.

A rider broke from the other group as well. As they neared each other, Crelian saw they wore the same smile, full of relief and happiness.

"Crelian, so happy to see you," Neiluios said. "Likewise, how's the family?"

"Doing good and going to be so relieved to see everyone. Come, there is someone eager to meet you, the Oracle of Delphi."

Neiluios led the way up the gentle slope toward the temple, its white marble gleaming softly in the morning light. The path was lined with ancient olive trees, their silver leaves whispering in the breeze.

At the temple entrance, a tall woman awaited them. Her eyes sparkled with a knowing calm, and her presence seemed to command both respect and warmth.

∞ 7 ∞
MERCHANTS

"All hands on deck!" Captain Vaso bellowed. "Man your stations!"

The Gilded Pegasus bucked violently beneath the storm's fury. The tempest had come from nowhere. Lightning split the sky, illuminating towering waves that crashed against the hull, each one a monstrous hand trying to drag the ship into the roiling deep.

Myreia and Bal-air clung to the mainmast, hooves slipping on rain-slick wood as they fought to keep upright. Nearby, Cret and Tivadarios wrestled with the rigging alongside a knot of sailors, struggling to haul down the thrashing sail before it tore loose. Officers barked orders over the howling wind, their voices ragged but unyielding, as the crew scrambled to obey.

The ship lurched forward, her bow plunging deep into the throat of a massive wave. Before she could rise, another slammed her broadside. The sea battered the Pegasus mercilessly, each swell threatening to rip her apart.

"Look out!" someone shouted.

A thunderous crack split the night as the forward mast snapped halfway up. The upper section crashed down, caught mid-fall by rigging that swung it sideways in a wild, deadly arc. Sailors dove for cover, boots sliding across the drenched deck.

Pavlina froze in horror as one man stumbled too late. The splintered mast smashed into his chest with a sickening crunch, hurling him overboard like a rag doll.

"Man overboard!" she screamed.

Another sailor sprinted to the railing, rope in hand, and hurled it into the boiling sea. His eyes darted frantically across the foam. For a fleeting second, Pavlina saw the crewman's form, arms flailing, eyes wide with terror, before the churning waves swallowed him whole.

Then, as suddenly as it had come, the storm ceased.

"What in the name of Poseidon and all his sons was that?" the captain growled.

In the distance, a smaller vessel limped across the water, both masts shattered and its hull listing badly.

"Helmsman, make for that craft!" the captain barked. "Aye, aye, Captain! Raise the sails, make ready!"

"Lower the foal! You four—get over there. See if anyone's left alive."

Four sailors scrambled into action, unfastening the rowboat and clambering aboard. Two others took their places at the winches, lowering the boat into the now-calm sea.

At the railing, Cret watched intently as the small vessel rocked over the swells. On the deck of the crippled merchant ship, four figures waved desperately.

The rowboat drew closer, its progress slow but steady. When it finally reached the listing vessel, one of the stranded crew tossed down a rope, guiding the rowboat alongside. A pair of heavy sacks was hurled down, landing with dull thuds, before the survivors began descending the rope ladder one by one.

BOOM.

A cannon roared from somewhere behind the merchant ship. The shot punched through its side with a thunderous crack. Two figures were flung from the ladder, crashing into the water below. A third still clung to the rungs near the top, trembling but holding on.

Everyone in the rowboat shouted and waved. "Jump!"

Another cannonball struck. The vessel buckled, and the last person was flung into the sea. As the merchant ship slipped beneath the waves, the last survivor was hauled from the water. The sailors aboard *The Gilded Pegasus* rowed hard, racing back to their ship.

"Ready the cannon—do not fire until I give the order!" the captain barked.

The attacking ship bore down on them, cutting through the foam like a predator chasing wounded prey. Its black hull loomed larger with every heartbeat, sails straining with the wind as it closed the distance.

Cret moved beside Pavlina. "Who are they? The Society?" Her expression darkened. "I wish they were," she muttered. He frowned. "Then who?"

"The Lemurians," she spat the name like venom. Cret blinked.

"Who are the Lemurians?"

Before she could answer, Pavlina turned and shouted, "Captain! Lemurians!"

The captain slammed his fist onto the map table. "Curse them to Hades," he growled. "Weapons at the ready!"

Tivadarios ran over, panting. "What's going on?"

"I'm not sure," Cret said, eyes locked on the approaching ship. "But whoever the Lemurians are, I'm guessing they didn't come to parley."

"As if the Society wasn't bad enough corrupting and enslaving the population now the once-peaceful Lemurians want to wipe us off the map," Pavlina said with a sneer.

"Wipe who off the planet? Atlantis?" Tivadarios asked, eyes wide.

"Yes. Atlantis and anyone loyal to her." Pavlina's voice sharpened. "They've convinced themselves we're poisoning the world, stripping its resources, and enslaving the people."

Tivadarios leaned toward Cret. "Isn't that what the Society says, too?" Cret nodded, silent.

The Lemurian vessel cut through the sea like a blade—sleek, black, and gilded with gold. Its sails hung limp, flapping uselessly, no oars to help its passage, yet the ship moved with uncanny speed, skimming the waves without wind. A blue flag with a golden seven-petaled flower flapped in the wind atop their mainmast.

"Power propulsion?" Tivadarios whispered to Cret.

He nodded. "Not opposed to technology, like the Society."

The four merchant sailors scrambled aboard the Pegasus—three of them were women.

"You four, stay with Ambassadors Cret and Tivadarios. Keep out of the way," the captain ordered sharply.

The merchants nodded quickly, eyes wide with fear. Myreia and Bal-air stepped forward to join them.

The eldest woman gasped softly, clutching her hand to her mouth to stifle a scream.

"Be calm," Cret said gently. "They won't harm you. They're Centaurs—and this is a mission of peace."

She nodded, but her eyes never left the centaurs.

The Lemurian vessel swung its stern to broadside the ship.

"Steady, no one fires until I give the word," the captain commanded.

After tense moments with both ships locked side by side, a sailor called out, "Their cannons are quiet, sir."

"Don't let your guard down. Stand ready!" the captain snapped.

The Lemurian deck was empty. Then, without warning, the rigging groaned, and the sails snapped taut in the wind, though not a single crewman was in sight.

The sleek black ship caught the breeze and slipped away silently, as mysteriously as it had appeared.

The captain and Pavlina strode toward the new passengers. "Explain that!" the captain barked, pointing at the retreating vessel.

The male merchant cleared his throat and stepped forward. "Explain what, Captain?"

The captain's eyes narrowed as he appraised the man. "Why did they attack your ship and sink it and leave us untouched?"

The merchant bowed his head. "They fear the might of Atlantis." "Don't blow smoke up my sail. What were you carrying?"

The merchant forced a smile and shrugged. "Fruit and cloth from the Far East. Nothing they'd want." He gestured vaguely toward the retreating Lemurians and bowed slightly.

"Save the act," Captain Vaso snapped. "The Lemurians wouldn't destroy a vessel with no Atlantean insignia over fruit and cloth." He stepped closer, voice low and commanding. "I am Captain Vaso of the Atlantean Royal Navy. Enough games. Tell me who you are."

"I am Aten." He bowed deeply.

Cret studied the newcomers at last. Aten was tall and slender, his skin a deep olive, his black hair falling loose about his shoulders. Two of the women shared his complexion, while the eldest's skin was a rich, warm mocha.

"This is my wife, Amunta, our daughter Samira, and Mesta, my daughter's attendant. We must meet the King of Atlantis. It's of utmost importance."

"How did you survive when the rest of your crew didn't? Where are the others?"

Aten lowered his head, grief weighing his words. "There were two more. One was swept overboard when the sudden storm struck. The other… gave his life, pushing my daughter out of the path of a falling mast during the storm."

The captain nodded grimly, lips pressed tight. "Aye. We lost one to that storm, too. Terrible business."

"What business do you have with the King?" Pavlina asked. "That's private—between me and his Highness."

Pavlina raised an eyebrow. "How'd you make it through the Pillars with a comment like that?"

Aten stiffened, his jaw tightening before he wisely snapped his mouth shut.

Amunta placed a calming hand on his arm. "We didn't share that part with the inspectors," she admitted softly. "We carried fruit and clothing, intending to sell them first—before seeking an audience."

The captain leaned close to Pavlina, whispering sharply. She shook her head and murmured a quiet reply. His scowl deepened, storm clouds gathering across his face.

"We'll take you to Atlantis and see you through the entry port," Pavlina said firmly, her eyes narrowing at the captain in warning. "What you do afterward is your choice."

Aten bowed with measured grace. "Thank you, Lieutenant Pavlina. If I may ask—what was the alternative?"

The captain's voice came out rough, edged with irritation. "Leave you in the Foal with enough food and water until a Predator could pluck you from the sea and drag you back to the Pillars." He spun on his heel before Aten could respond, barking fresh orders to the crew.

Mesta's eyes brimmed with tears. Pavlina laid a gentle hand on her shoulder. "Don't worry," she said warmly. "I'd never let that happen. Vaso's bark is far worse than his bite." A small smile tugged at her lips. "Come on, let's find you a place to rest."

We'll be in Atlantis soon."

The evening was calm and clear. Stars twinkled overhead beneath a full moon. The ship gently rocked with the waves; the sails hung limp in the still air.

Tivadarios walked slowly across the deck. On the other side, someone else was awake, cloaked, and gripping the railing tightly. A stray breeze tugged at their hood, pulling it back to reveal long black hair.

He stopped, mesmerized. Bathed in moonlight, Samira's hair shimmered as if flecked with gold.

Drawn forward, he changed course and approached her quietly. Clearing his throat softly, he broke the silence.

Samira jumped and spun around. Tivadarios raised his hands in peace. "Sorry, I didn't mean to startle you. Mind if I join you?"

She shrugged, wordless.

After a pause, he found his courage. "My name's Tivadarios. But you can call me Darios."

Samira turned to face him. "I'm Samira."

"Um, yeah—I know." He rubbed the back of his neck, feeling a bit awkward. "So… Where are you from?"

She pursed her lips thoughtfully. "I'm not sure how it translates exactly, but it means something like 'The Black Land.'"

"That doesn't sound very inviting."

Her face brightened. "Oh, but it is. The 'black' refers to the rich, fertile soil of the mighty Kemi River. The river appears dark due to the soil it deposits during its annual floods. It's a beautiful place—lush fields surrounded by golden sands."

"Sounds like a place I'd love to visit. Do you get to swim in the river often?"

Her expression shifted to mild horror. "Not unless you want to be eaten by crocodiles." "I've never met a crocodile," he replied with a crooked grin, "but judging by your face, I'm certain I don't want to."

"Where are you from?" she asked.

His smile faded slightly. "Um, far to the east. A place called Laos."

"Never heard of it. It must be far. I've traveled a lot with my father, and that's not a name I know." She pouted lightly.

"What?"

"Oh, nothing."

"No, it's something. What is it?" he pressed.

She hesitated. "It's just… You don't look like you're from the east. The people there usually look different."

Tivadarios paused, then smiled. "Well, like you said, you've never been that far east." Samira studied him for a moment, then smiled back.

"You have a pretty smile."

Her face turned away, cheeks flushing. A sudden gust of wind blew her hair across her face. Tivadarios reached out, gently brushing a strand behind her ear. She froze, stiffening at his touch, but he seemed unaware.

"I… uh, better get back to my father," she murmured.

"I'll walk with you," he offered.

"No, thank you. I can find my way."

"Oh, okay. I'll see you in the morning then. Sleep well, Samira."

She turned quickly and hurried across the deck. Her cloak and long robes swished with each step, the steady breeze tugging her hood back and sending her black hair streaming behind her in a graceful dance.

Tivadarios watched her go, his eyes lingering on the hatch to the lower decks for several long moments. Then he turned toward the sea. The bright moon made the waves sparkle like scattered jewels.

∞ **8** ∞
ᏉISION

"Welcome, Crelian. I am pleased to finally meet you." Pythia bowed her head gracefully, her voice carrying both warmth and weight, before gesturing for him to follow.

Neiluios had told him the priestess wished to speak with him alone, and now, curiosity and unease warred within him as he trailed behind her. She moved with serene confidence, her white gown flowing like liquid light with every step. They descended a narrow flight of stone stairs, the air growing cooler and stiller with each turn. At the bottom, she guided him into a small, dimly lit chamber where the flicker of oil lamps painted restless shadows across the walls. Pythia settled into one of the two chairs set at the center of the room and, with a calm gesture, motioned for him to take the other.

"Where is my son?" he asked.

Pythia smiled gently. "What have the others told you?"

"Not much. Only that he arrived here with some new friends and has already left."

"Yes," she nodded softly. "He came with a group of centaurs and a stranded pilot from your world."

Crelian's mouth fell open. "Where are they now? Why did they leave? I noticed Neiaphi isn't here either—is she with them?"

Pythia lifted her hands gently to still the flood of questions, her serene smile both calming and unsettling. "Be at ease. I sent Cret, Tivadarios, and two centaurs to Atlantis—they are needed there. He departed before Neiaphi arrived with the others. Neiaphi, her promised, the pilot, and the remaining centaurs are searching for a way to save their kin."

"Will I see my son again?"

She frowned. "I haven't seen that future yet. The future is not always clear. Many forces are at play, their outcomes intertwined. If one fails, it doesn't mean all are doomed. There is always hope."

"You speak in riddles," he said, shaking his head. "What do you want from me?"

"You and the others will make it to Atlantis." Crelian released a shuddering sigh. "But most will not remain there long. Atlantis is not destined to hold power for much longer."

"The Society?" Crelian asked, voice barely a whisper.

"The city will not be standing much longer," Pythia replied flatly.

Crelian was struck silent. The mighty city of Atlantis was doomed. After a pause, he finally asked. "What role am I to play, then?"

Pythia cupped her hand to her right ear, closing her eyes briefly before smiling warmly. "You will bring your family to Atlantis. When the time comes, you will flee with the others. They will be divided into two groups—neither path is good or bad. You must decide which way to go."

"I will choose where my son goes."

"Do not choose now. Much will happen before then. I do not know which path your son will take, or if your paths will cross again. There is still much left for him to do."

Crelian frowned. "You said a moment ago that you hadn't foreseen the future, but now you speak as if you have."

"That's how prophecies work," Pythia replied softly. "They come when they will, not when I want—or need—them. We've been lucky this evening."

"Funny," Crelian said, shaking his head. "I don't feel fortunate. I think I have more questions now than when I first arrived."

Pythia leaned forward and placed a gentle hand on his knee. "Don't fret. I see happiness in all your futures. I see you and your wife at your daughter's wedding, many children in her life… and your son—married as well…"

"To whom?" he interrupted.

Pythia closed her eyes briefly, then frowned. "I cannot see her face. All I know is she has brown hair—and Cret's smiling face as he looks at her."

"As long as he's happy, his mother and I will be, whoever she is." He nodded thoughtfully. "Thank you for easing my heart. Though I still don't know what the future holds, I do know we'll all be happy." He sighed, sinking back in his chair. "That's all I've wanted since arriving on this planet. Our lives were planned on Romota, but everything spun out of control when we came here. Thank you for your insight."

Pythia bowed her head. "It's always a pleasure to bring good news, even if my job isn't always easy."

I can imagine. Again, thank you." Crelian stood, ready to leave.

Suddenly, Pythia thrust her hands toward him, a strangled cry tearing from her lips. Her eyes rolled back, eyelids fluttering shut, and her voice dropped into a deep, garbled tone:

"Beware false friends of purple and gold, and seek the unlikely, illuminated in light. Centaurs will choose flight or burrow. A ship of fire will return the lost to their home—but not all will be welcomed. Those who burrow, those who stay—some will be saved, some lost."

Her head snapped back, then slumped forward onto her chest. An eerie orange glow pulsed from her right ear.

From the shadows, a figure rushed to her side.

Crelian stood frozen. "What just happened?" he finally whispered.

An acolyte held a small vial beneath Pythia's nose. "Sometimes her visions come this way. She'll be fine."

Another acolyte appeared from the gloom and approached Crelian, pressing a parchment into his hand.

"What is this?"

"This is the Oracle's vision. I transcribed it as she spoke. Please take it with you." Crelian studied the paper. "But what does it mean?"

The acolyte shook his head. "I don't know. You may return in the morning and speak to the Oracle again. She might be able to help."

With a slight bow, the acolyte gestured for him to leave.

As Crelian walked out of the temple, he read the vision once more. The words offered no more clarity than the voice he had heard. "I should share this with Addident and Neiluios," he muttered to himself. "Maybe something they've been told will help me understand it."

The following morning, Crelian spotted Addident pacing along the camp's perimeter. "That's a strange message," Addident said, handing back the parchment. "I'm not sure what to make of it."

"I'll return to the temple and see if I can get any answers."

"We leave tomorrow," Addident said. "Let me know if she gleans anything."

Crelian nodded and set off toward the temple atop the hill. The morning air was crisp but pleasant, a light breeze fluttering through the trees and rustling the fresh leaves bursting from their buds.

At the massive temple doors, firmly shut, Crelian found a thick rope hanging to the right.

He tugged it once, and a deep bell rang out.

After a few moments, an acolyte appeared and swung the doors open.

"The Oracle is not seeing anyone today. Please return at another time." The acolyte slipped back inside.

"Wait, I was told to return this morning."

"Sorry, no one today."

He placed his hands on the door, stopping it from

shutting. "I demand to be seen."

The acolyte glared at him. "The Oracle is not well; return later." And then slammed the door shut.

Crelian pounded on the door. "Hey, open up!" he shouted. Silence answered him. Reluctantly, he trudged back down the hill to start packing once again.

"Why can't the pilots just fly us in their ship?" Sareen asked.

Sephi smiled at her daughter. "Your father already told you, sweetheart. They aren't allowed to fly their ship into Atlantis. The only way to enter is through The Pillars by sailing ship."

Sareen pouted. "It's not fair. If they could, we'd probably be there in two days."

"Come on, little one. Let's finish loading up."

Sephi and Sareen walked over to their wagon, placing the last few items aboard. Just then, Crelian approached.

"Are we leaving soon?" Sareen asked him eagerly. "Momentarily, my dear," he replied, his voice heavy.

Sephi placed her hands gently on his cheeks, coaxing him to meet her eyes. "What's the matter?"

He shook his head, trying to pull away, but she held him firmly. "That's not an answer I'll accept. We've been through too much together for that. Please, tell me."

He sighed deeply and slowly nodded, taking her hands in his. "It's the Oracle's vision. It doesn't make sense. She won't see me again to explain, and now we're leaving."

"I've spoken to several people here," Sephi said softly, "and from what I've heard, that's how her visions usually are. When she offers her own opinion, the meaning is clear. But when the visions take over her, the message is shrouded—only to be revealed later. We just have to hold onto the words until they make sense. She's using technology that has been banned on Romota for decades. Nobody here understands how it works."

Crelian leaned forward and kissed his wife's forehead. "Thank you. I always knew I married you for your level-headedness," he teased.

"Oh, you," she said, playfully slapping his shoulder. "Now, let's go find our son."

Their two ships sliced effortlessly through the rolling waves, the sails snapping taut in the stiff wind. Neiluios stood at the bow of the lead vessel, fingers tight around the railing as the ship dipped and bucked beneath him. Over a year had passed since they'd boarded the transport to this strange planet. It felt like only yesterday that he, his wife, and daughter had set out, just the three of them.

Now, he found himself traversing unknown lands by countless means, journeying toward a distant city while hunted by enemies he barely understood. His daughter was off on her perilous adventure, and his wife had recently given birth to their twin sons. The carefully mapped life his parents had envisioned for him was unraveling fast, teetering on the edge of chaos.

Neiluios drew a deep breath, holding it for several heartbeats before releasing it slowly, the tension slipping from his clenched jaw with a soft hiss.

A few swells later, Crelian approached and stood silently at Neiluios's side. "Glad you finally caught up with us," Neiluios said after a moment.

"Me too. Sounds like I missed all the fun, though."

"If by fun you mean people chasing us left and right, those abnormally large wolves trailing us, and them snatching my boys only to return them weeks later… Yeah, you missed all the fun." Neiluios chuckled softly.

Crelian slapped him on the back. "Oh, I'm sure there's still plenty of fun left to be had." He smiled wryly.

Neiluios shook his head, smiling. "The fun never stops

on this planet." "Is there any way to get word to Neiaphi or Cret?" Crelian asked.

"Not that I know of. I wish I knew if they were alright. That woman, Pythia, said she didn't know if they'd succeed in their quests, but that the odds were in their favor."

Crelian frowned. "I don't like that woman."

"Me neither." Neiluios shrugged and rolled his neck. "Let's just hope we get through The Pillars and safely to Atlantis. I want the next phase of our lives to begin—settling down, discovering how I can best serve the crown, seeing Neiaphi married, and raising my boys."

Crelian turned, leaning on the rail. "I've heard Neiaphi has been spoken for. Good man, I assume?"

Neiluios cleared his throat before replying, "Andonis." He nodded. "He's a good man. I've been meaning to talk to you. I'm sorry to back out of our agreement. Even though I like Andonis, I wish it had been Cret instead."

Crelian placed a hand on Neiluios's shoulder. "I know, my friend." He shook his head. "You had no way of knowing we'd meet again. You did what you had to for her sake."

"Just so you know, she struggled with the choice. She truly believed she'd see Cret again, but everyone told her she was wrong." Neiluios hung his head. "We should've listened to her."

"It'll be fine. Young hearts mend quickly. Did Cret find out when he came through Delphi?"

Neiluios nodded.

"How did he take it?"

"I'm not sure. He spoke with Pythia, left a letter for Neiaphi, and departed. His letter says he's fine and wishes her the best. Did he get close to anyone since leaving Camp Roma?"

Crelian shook his head. "Not that I saw."

"That's too bad. It would've made things easier, I think." "He will find his path, just as she found hers."

∞ **9** ∞
THE PILLARS OF HERCULES

The Pillars of Hercules loomed on the distant horizon all day. The ships sliced through the restless waves, pitching with each swell. Everyone crowded the main decks, their eyes locked on the towering silhouette ahead. The colossal statue of a battle-clad man grew larger—agonizingly slowly.

"Greish!" Crelian called out, spotting him across the deck. "Lieutenant now, I hear." "Yes, sir, Crelian, sir," Greish snapped to attention.

"Relax. I haven't seen you around lately."

"I'm stationed on the other ship. Came over this morning. I'm glad your party linked up with us. I haven't seen Addident this relaxed in ages." He chuckled softly.

Crelian laughed. "You call that relaxed?" He gestured toward Addident and Neiluios, who were loudly arguing nearby.

"Well, you haven't been around much, sir. What are they yelling about?" Greish asked. "Something about making sure we're ready for inspection when we reach The Pillars. So, how have you been?"

"Keeping busy. I've been tasked with training the dogs and the young recruits."

Crelian smiled and clapped him on the shoulder. "I knew you'd go far once you got away from Hepluosis."

Greish's expression darkened, and he sighed. "He's a troublemaker, that one. Whatever happened to him?"

"One night, he and his servant vanished. No one's seen them since," Crelian replied. "That's strange, indeed."

Crelian nodded somberly but quickly changed the subject. "Any young ladies in your life now? I've seen a lot of new faces around here."

Greish grinned widely. "Yes, sir. Her name's Alexa."

"When will you be married?"

He shrugged. "She wants to wait until we reach Atlantis. No point rushing without a stable roof over our heads."

"When we land, I'd love to meet her."

"Yes, of course. She's become Neiaphi's best friend and has heard all about your family.

I'm sure she'll be excited to meet you."

Greish glanced toward the captain's quarters. "If you'll excuse me, it looks like I'm needed."

"Good to see you again, Greish."

A small portside village was bathed in the soft glow of the rising sun. Waves lapped rhythmically against the rocky shore, drawing their ship ever closer. Neiluios, Aner, Paragon, Simos, and Addident stood at the bow, eyes fixed across the brightening waters toward the immense statue towering over the strait. The colossal figure of Hercules stood with one foot planted firmly on each rocky outcropping, a sword gripped in one hand and a shield in the other.

"So, that's the mighty Hercules," Simos said softly, his voice filled with reverence.

Addident glanced toward the docks. "How do we proceed from here?"

"I was told to find the transit officer near the harbor," Aner replied. "Hopefully, we'll be cleared to move on before midday."

"Take Neiluios and Greish with you," Addident said firmly. "May the Gods smile upon us today."

"I'll send word to Greish and have him meet us on shore," Aner responded.

The sign for the transit office swung gently on its hinges, stirred by a soft morning breeze. Though it was still early, a lone candle flickered in the window, casting a warm glow into the dim street. Simos stepped inside first.

At the center of the room sat a young man behind a cluttered desk, his head bowed low as he shuffled through a stack of papers. The silence stretched for a few moments before Simos cleared his throat. The young man startled, lifting his gaze sharply, eyes wide with surprise. "I'm sorry, I didn't see you come in. How may I assist?" he asked, his voice tentative but polite.

"We have two ships that require entry into Atlantean waters," Simos said firmly.

"Do you now?" The man furrowed his brow, his fingers pausing on the papers. "Have you and your crew been through before?"

"Our captain and his crew have, but not the passengers," Paragon answered steadily. The man's expression tightened. "Well, I'm afraid that may be a problem."

"How so?" Neiluios stepped forward, his tone cautious but insistent.

"The Transit Officer is out ill at the moment," the young man explained, his shoulders slumping slightly. "I don't have the authority to approve newcomers. You'll have to wait."

"For how long?" Aner asked, trying to keep frustration out of his voice.

"I don't know," the clerk admitted, shaking his head. "Check back tomorrow. But not too early; he never comes in that soon."

The five men exchanged uneasy looks, then silently left the transit office and made their way back to the waiting longboats, which bobbed gently at the dock.

"Do we wait on the ships, or should we set up camp? We might be here for a few days," Neiluios said thoughtfully, scanning the quiet village nearby.

"We'll let the captain decide," Paragon replied, casting a glance toward the harbor where the ships lay anchored.

They decided to sail a short distance from the village and make camp along the shore. A small delegation stayed behind in town near the transit office, tasked with checking in daily. On the fifth day, the transit officer finally returned to his post, still looking somewhat under the weather.

After some negotiation, they persuaded the officer to come to their makeshift camp to meet the entire group, sparing them the journey back and forth to town.

On the sixth day, just after midday, Officer Stelios arrived with his assistant. He was greeted first by Addident and the other leaders.

"Good day, gentlemen," Stelios said, his smile polite but his eyes cold and calculating. "That's quite a sizable force you've brought here."

"Please sit; we have quite a story to tell you." Addident beckoned him to sit next to the fire. Then he cleared his throat and glanced at Aner and Paragon, who nodded. "As an officer for Atlantis and the one in charge of admittance to the Great City, I hope what I'm about to reveal to you doesn't come as a surprise," Addident told him of their mission and why they were sent to Atlantis. When he got to the part about Camp Roma, Officer Stelios interrupted.

Officer Stelios leaned forward, his brow furrowed. "I'm confused. I was told that a large group would be coming here from Home Base, which is what we call Romota. Those who don't know about Romota often assume we're referring to Atlantis. You were expected last year and never arrived."

"Yes, the Society intercepted your message and then

sent new coordinates for our landing," Addident replied.

"It's only by the graciousness of the Gods that we found out about what happened and were able to rescue them from the Society," Simos agreed.

Addident and Crelian continued the tale of the journey thus far without any further interruptions.

After they were finished, Officer Stelios sat quietly. "I'm relieved you have arrived here safely. I wish all of you had made it this far, but I'm glad that you were able to reinforce a few posts along the way. I'll ensure you have a safe and timely passage the rest of the way from here. "As for your daughter Neiaphi and those traveling with her, we'll watch for them and make sure they get through as well." Neiluios bowed his head in thanks. "Get some rest this evening and board your boats at first light. The inspectors will be expecting you. Your ships will still be subject to search, so ensure everyone is on the main deck during the inspection. I wish you much speed and all the safety the gods can lend." Officer Stelios stood, signaling the end of their meeting.

Addident rose as well, offering a firm handshake. "Thank you, Officer. Your help means more than you know."

Stelios nodded, a rare flicker of warmth in his eyes. "May the Gods watch over your journey from here. Atlantis is not a city to be taken lightly."

As Stelios and his assistant departed, the group settled into their camp, the weight of the coming inspection pressing on their minds. Yet beneath it all was a cautious hope, the hope that after so much struggle, they might finally set foot in Atlantis and face whatever awaited them there.

The ships glided steadily forward, the rhythm of the waves calming the nerves that had tightened during the long inspection. From the decks, the passengers watched as the colossal statue of Hercules loomed ever larger, its stern gaze seeming to welcome—or perhaps warn—them.

Crelian stood near the bow, eyes fixed on the towering pillars. Beside him, Addident adjusted his cloak against the brisk sea air.

"It's been a long wait," Addident said softly. "But soon, we'll be inside the city's walls."

Crelian nodded, his thoughts heavy. "I wonder what awaits us there. The Oracle's words echo in my mind."

A gentle breeze swept across the deck, carrying with it a sense of both promise and uncertainty as the ships pressed onward toward Atlantis.

It took the inspectors most of the morning to inspect both vessels, and the sun was nearing its zenith when their sails unfurled to catch the stiff wind and finally be on their way to Atlantis.

∞ **10** ∞
ℒEMURIANS

"All hands on deck! All hands on deck!!" The sailor in the crow's nest cried out.

The ship's warning bell chimed loudly, and everyone scrambled out of the lower berths to man their stations. Cret and Tivadarios joined them.

"Lemurians off the port bow, Captain!" Chaos erupted as sailors shouted orders.

The larger ship was cutting through the choppy waters with frightening speed. A flash from the other vessel was the only warning they received before a cannonball smashed through the side of their ship just above the waterline. They had no time to react as more and more shots thundered through the night.

"This is it, boys. We'll be meeting Hades tonight. Say your peace, and maybe you'll be taken to Mount Olympus instead. It has been an honor serving with you all," the captain said, holding his sword with one hand and gripping the wheel tightly with the other.

As quickly as the violent barrage started, it stopped.

"What do they want?" Tivadarios asked. All Cret could do was shrug.

The first longboat thumped against their vessel; everyone onboard held their collective breath as the first sailor boarded.

The man in the lead was an officer; he wore a bright blue and silver jacket, silver leggings, knee-high black boots, and a black hat with a large blue plume on top.

The rest of the men in the first longboat climbed up the ladder rapidly and took up positions on either side of their commander, swords drawn.

Lieutenant Pavlina and Captain Vaso approached the invaders, swords sheathed and scowls on their faces. "How dare you attack *The Gilded Pegasus*!" Vaso barked.

"We are looking for saboteurs and stowaways," the commander stated flatly with a thick accent.

"We have no stowaways onboard, and even if we have a stowaway on our ship, I don't see how it is any of your business," Pavlina spat.

"I see you don't deny the saboteurs?" He smirked.

Pavlina glanced at Captain Vaso before answering. "We picked up some driftwood from a wreck. I don't know their story."

"They are from the lands of the Pyramids; you will hand them over to us now." "They have committed no crimes that I know of."

"They have committed crimes against the Lemurians."

"I will have to take them to Atlantis; if the king agrees with your claim, they will be released to you."

"Unacceptable," he growled.

"Then you will be responsible for escalating this war," Captain Vaso said.

"I have my orders. You'll hand over the saboteurs and the stowaways." The Lemurian commander elevated his voice.

Pavlina held up her hands. "What stowaways? I already told you we harbor no stowaways."

"You have four individuals onboard who do not belong on this planet. I'm to take them to my king for questioning."

"Our guests have business of grave importance with our king," Pavlina said.

"They. Will. Be. Delayed." He paused deliberately between each word, his tone cold.

"Over my dead body," Pavlina snapped.

"That can be arranged." The commander drew his sword with a steely hiss.

Before the situation could escalate, Cret stepped between them, hands raised. "There will be no bloodshed on my account. Please—let's resolve this civilly."

Pavlina and the commander locked eyes, tension thick in the air.

"My name is Cret. This is Tivadarios, and with us are Bal-air and Myreia." He gestured calmly as he spoke. "Let's take this to the captain's quarters."

After a moment's hesitation, the Lemurian commander gave a curt nod.

Once inside the captain's quarters, Cret finally got a clear look at the Lemurian commander. His complexion was a deep, copper-tinged brown, nearly as dark as Bal-air's. His black hair shimmered faintly with green, and his eyes shifted subtly between slate, copper, and green as he moved. But it was his height that stood out most; he'd ducked to enter the room, and Cret guessed he and Bal-air would stand eye to eye.

When Bal-air and Myreia rose and stepped forward, a flicker of surprise crossed the commander's face—but it vanished almost immediately.

"This is Bal-air, and this is Myreia," Cret said, his hands resting lightly behind his back. "What seems to be the issue?"

"The saboteurs will come with me, as will the stowaways. I don't see the confusion," the commander growled.

"May I at least have your name?" Cret asked calmly.

"I am High Commander Zelphar of the Immaculate Lemurian Navy, on the Western Ocean."

"Then, High Commander," Tivadarios cut in, "why do you keep calling us stowaways?" Zelphar's eyes narrowed. "You're new to this planet. And you are unwelcome."

"I wasn't aware that was a crime," Cret said evenly.

"That alone is not a crime," Zelphar replied with a curt nod.

"Then what have we done?"

"It's not what you've done—but what you will do." He crossed his arms and drew himself taller.

"What we will do?" Cret asked, incredulous. "I don't even know what I'll do tomorrow.

"How can you punish us for something that hasn't happened—and may never happen?"

"The Mystic Rania has foreseen it," Zelphar said. "All those from Romota, will come with me."

"Rania is no seer of futures!" Pavlina snapped. "The Oracle has already met with Cret and the others. They are following her instructions."

"Pythia? Bah." Zelphar spat to the side. "The Mystic Rania sees truth, not riddles."

Cret raised his hands again, calming the storm in the room. "Please. Whatever Pythia or Rania believes they've seen, it changes nothing for me. I'll go. I'll speak with your Mystic and your King. My future isn't fixed. I want only to return to my family and live a peaceful life."

Zelphar gave a slow, approving nod. "Well spoken, Cret. We depart immediately. You four—and the other three—will come."

"Only those who choose to leave this vessel will do so," Pavlina said flatly. "No one will be taken by force."

"My dear Pavlina," Zelphar replied, shaking his head in mock pity, "you are in no position to make that decision."

Pavlina's hand went to her sword, but before she could draw, the doors burst open. Aten entered, robes swirling around him, his wife and daughter close behind.

"That won't be necessary, Lieutenant Pavlina," he said calmly. "We will go willingly, but only under Cret's protection."

Pavlina turned to Cret. He shrugged, then nodded.

"Fine," she muttered, her voice low and edged. "But I'm coming with you."

Zelphar's eyes narrowed, but after a moment's glare, he gave a curt nod and turned sharply on his heel. Without another word, he strode out and began barking orders to his soldiers in a sharp, unfamiliar tongue.

A short time later, Pavlina and the rest of the group stood on deck with their belongings in hand, awaiting departure. While they had been inside, three more longboats had moored alongside *The Gilded Pegasus*.

"Are you sure about this, Pav?" Vaso asked quietly.

"It'll be fine." Pavlina grinned. "I've always wanted to meet the Eclectic Utopian King of Lemuria." She flung her hands dramatically into the air, then dipped into an exaggerated curtsy—so deep she nearly landed on the deck.

Several Lemurian sailors scowled at her mockery. One even reached for his sword.

Cret looked at the Lemurian sailors with unease. The tension was thick—hanging in the air like a blanket of fog. Cret couldn't help but reflect on the uniqueness of the Lemurians. Each was tall and slender. Some appeared to be over ten feet in height, while most were only two or three feet taller than him. All had the same greenish sheen to their hair, regardless of whether it was golden blonde or deep black. Their skin tones were the most striking. Ranging from pale white to deep black and all shades in between.

"If I were you," Zelphar said, voice low and tense. His shifting eyes settled on green that almost glowed. "I would not do that in his presence. The Illustrious King Luthais— Patriarch of Earth and Warden of All Who Reside Upon It— does not possess a sense of humor."

Pavlina raised her hands in surrender. "Wow. That's some title." Then, more sincerely, "I'll remember my place. In all seriousness, I have always wanted to see your court. How long until we arrive in Lemuria?"

Zelphar gave her a tight smile that never touched his green-shifting eyes. "Sorry to disappoint you. His Illustrious is but a day's sail away. You will not be seeing the court this time."

Cret and the others were blindfolded as soon as they were seated in the longboats. "Is this necessary?" Pavlina asked, her voice sharp with irritation.

"Yes," came the curt reply.

"Well then, how exactly are we supposed to board your ship?"

"We'll raise the boats. Now be silent," snapped the officer in charge, his tone making it clear the discussion was over.

They rode in silence. Deprived of sight, the journey felt endless. Every splash of water, every creak of wood stretched time out thin and taut.

Finally, their boat thudded against a larger hull.

Above them, bells chimed and sailors shouted to each other in their strange, harsh tongue. Cret strained to make sense of it, but nothing was familiar—no root, no pattern, no hint of shared language.

Moments later, the boat rocked and tilted as it was hoisted upward. Ropes groaned. Then the swaying ceased.

"Now, will you take off the blindfolds?" Pavlina asked, more demand than a question.

No answer. Instead, rough hands gripped their shoulders, guiding—or shoving—them forward. After several uncertain steps, they were forced down.

"Sit down!" barked a voice.

"What's going on here? I thought we were guests, not prisoners!" Pavlina shouted as a rope tightened around her wrists. "Zelphar, where are you?"

"I'm here." His voice drifted in cool and composed. "Don't fret, Pavlina. You are a guest aboard my ship. If you were a prisoner, you'd be gagged and thrown in the cargo hold." He paused for emphasis. "But you are not an invited, honored guest. You will remain here until summoned."

To her credit, Pavlina held her tongue.

Time had lost all meaning. At some point, something warm was shoved into Cret's hands. A bowl.

He sniffed cautiously.

"It's not poison. Just drink it, Atlantis t'skum," a sailor sneered before moving down the line.

"T'skum?" Cret echoed, puzzled.

"I don't know much Lemurian," Pavlina said, "but I've heard that word before. Pretty sure it's not a compliment."

"I didn't think so." Cret sipped the soup. It was spicy, warming—and surprisingly good.

"My mouth's on fire," Tivadarios whimpered. "I'm going to need water after this."

"Mild, really," Samira said quietly. "Pleasant, even."

"Mild?" Tivadarios groaned. "If I weren't starving, I'd stop eating. I expect actual flames to shoot from my mouth any second."

That earned a round of quiet laughter. A moment passed.

"Are they going to make us sleep like this?" Cret asked, glancing at his bound wrists.

"I think so," Pavlina replied. "Let's hope their king gets here early."

The sun's warmth on Cret's face was the only sign that morning had finally come. All through the night, the ship's noises had never ceased—creaks, murmurs, footsteps—so when a sharp whistle pierced the air above them, they all jumped.

From near the bow, someone began shouting orders in their strange, guttural language. Immediately, the deck vibrated as sailors hurried back and forth. Heavy footsteps pounded up the stairs from the lower berths.

"Sounds like the king might be here," Pavlina whispered, leaning close to Cret. "I'm not sure what the protocol is when meeting a king," he whispered back.

"Follow my lead. I don't know their protocol either; I'll use Atlantean customs.

Hopefully, he doesn't chop off our heads." Cret

swallowed hard.

"Chop our heads off!" Tivadarios whispered, his voice trembling.

"Let me do the speaking. Do not speak unless spoken to. Do I make myself clear?"

"Yes, ma'am," they replied in unison.

A few moments later, a sharp kick struck Cret's feet. "On your feet, all of you. You have been summoned," a sailor barked.

They scrambled up, their wrist bindings were cut, and they were prodded forward. "Kneel," a harsh voice commanded, just before Cret felt a heavy shove to the backs of his knees, forcing him down. The sounds told him the others were treated the same.

His blindfold was yanked away. He blinked against the sudden brightness of the sun, raising his hands to shield his eyes.

When his vision cleared, he saw the figure seated before them, the sun casting a golden halo around him. This was undoubtedly the king.

He wore a deep royal blue cloak trimmed with silver. A massive crown of gold, silver, and sapphire rested heavily on his head, nearly concealing his hair, which peeked out, grey with a faint green sheen. His skin was pale, nearly albino, lined with the wrinkles of age. Each finger on both hands was adorned with a jeweled ring.

Pavlina brought her hands first to her mouth, then to her forehead, back to her mouth, and finally clasped them over her chest. She bowed so low that her forehead touched the ground before her knees, and remained there until the king gave her leave to rise.

"Greetings, Lieutenant Pavlina."

She sat up slowly, repeating the hand gestures before speaking.

"Greetings, Illustrious King Luthais, Patriarch of Earth and Warden of all that reside on it."

King Luthais raised a hand, interrupting gently.

"Please, there's no need for formal titles; we know you do not truly believe we are king of all who live on this planet. Still, we are curious why you have come."

"My vessel was hostilely boarded, and my passengers were forced off. I have come to ensure their safety," Pavlina replied firmly.

The king chuckled softly. "Our High Commander takes his orders seriously. But we make no apologies for him. It seems he found your saboteur—and those from Romota. We are more intrigued by the centaurs, however. We had no idea there were any remaining in this part of the world."

"What are these three accused of, Your Majesty?" Pavlina asked. King Luthais's eyes gleamed with satisfaction.

"Your king will be pleased to hear we've apprehended three from the land of the Pyramids. They've been attacking both our ships and convoys…"

"We have not," Aten interrupted, his voice sharp and defiant. "We've been trying to prevent the war between you and Atlantis."

Before he could say more, a sailor's backhand struck him across the face, splitting his lip.

The sailor reared back, ready to strike again—until King Luthais clicked his tongue sharply. "That is not how it appears," the king said smoothly. "But do not worry. You will receive a fair trial."

Pavlina pressed on, voice calm but firm.

"What exactly have they done?"

"One of our vessels was set ablaze," the king replied, "and an Atlantean ship nearby had its rigging cut and sails slashed."

"And where did this take place, may I ask?" Pavlina inquired.

King Luthais waved a hand dismissively. "Not far from where we are now."

"So, let me get this straight," Pavlina said, narrowing her eyes. "One of my ships had its mobility disabled, and one of yours, which just happened to be in Atlantean waters, was set ablaze. The real question is, what was that ship, or this one, doing in my waters?"

The king slouched slightly, his frown deepening. He remained silent. After a long pause, his gaze shifted to Cret.

"Why are you here?" His voice was cold and sharp. Cret frowned in return.

"I was forced onto this ship by your men."

"That's not what we meant," Luthais said, voice dropping to a near whisper. "Why are you on this planet?"

"We are here by the will of the King of Romota."

"But why were you sent here? The official story, if you will." King Luthais rolled his hand with a flourish, a hint of amusement in his eyes.

Cret cleared his throat. "I don't know the official story, Your Highness; none of us do. Before we left Romota, my father was told that Atlantis and the Krill Colonies needed officials and guards to prevent a potential uprising. We were assigned a five-year term." He paused briefly before continuing. "While in transit, we learned that once we entered this planetary system, we could never return. After we landed, we discovered our ship had been redirected, not to Atlantis, but to a Society camp. They claimed it was for assessment. But once they decided we were a threat, they split us up… and tried to eliminate us." He met the king's gaze. "A group called the Loyals rescued both of our groups. They've been helping us reach Atlantis ever since."

Everyone sat in silence as the king considered Cret's words. "Explain the centaurs," Luthais finally said, breaking the quiet.

"Before I left Romota, the Centaur King entrusted me with a mission: to find proof that centaurs still live on this planet and to send word back to him. I did find one, and I helped her reach the Oracle. She continues her journey now. These two chose to accompany me."

"Where are you headed?"

"The Oracle told me I'm needed in Atlantis."

Luthais rubbed his chin thoughtfully.

"And how are you supposed to send word back to this Centaur King?"

"He gave me a transmitter. I showed it to an elderly female centaur, but she never returned it. I don't know where it is now."

"That's a pity; we would have liked to see this interplanetary device. Why does Atlantis need you?"

Cret spread his hands slightly, a hint of frustration in his voice.

"That's what I asked the Oracle. She wouldn't tell me. Said I'd know when the time was right."

"Pythia always speaks with a forked tongue," Luthais said, clicking his tongue. "You will all remain our honored guests this evening and join us at our table. You may rise." Everyone started to rise. "Not you," he snapped. "You will be taken below."

He flicked his fingers, and six sailors stepped forward, swords drawn.

"Wait—surely Samira cannot be held for her father's crimes!" Tivadarios's voice rose in panic.

A slow, cruel smile tugged at the corners of Luthais's mouth. "My dear boy… she is the saboteur, not her father."

With a flick of his wrist, Samira, her attendant, and her parents were shoved toward the lower decks.

Zelphar stepped forward. "This way, please. You'll remain in the captain's quarters until summoned. If I were you, I'd stay inside."

∞ 11 ∞
Visitors

A sharp sound shattered the calm night—three short beeps, followed by two long ones, then the pattern repeated.

"What is that?" Ambrite was on his feet first, bow in hand.

Lyric jolted awake, blinking at the dying fire where she had been dozing. Pelagios sprang up and hurried down the spiral staircase.

"The machine!" Lyric called, following him swiftly.

A few moments later, everyone gathered around the communication machine. "What is it? Is it a message from King Rees?" Justic asked eagerly.

Pelagios read aloud, "Greetings, Krill Colony Centaurs. We are beyond pleased to hear from you at last. Our envoy has found you, and we are sending a transport to bring you home. It will take some time to arrange. We'll use these coordinates as the arrival point. Please have all Centaurs at these coordinates in eight Plexur lunar cycles. Confirm receipt of this message."

"How long is a Plexur lunar cycle?" Justic asked.

Pelagios hesitated. "Um, let me think... The Plexur moon's cycle is a bit longer than the lunar cycle here."

"Why do you call it the Plexur moon and not just the moon?" Ambrite asked.

"Romota has two moons. Well, three, but the last one only circles every other year." He waved off the question like it didn't matter. "They'll arrive in about ten Earth moons, so we should plan for everyone heading to Romota to be here in nine.”

“How can they get here so quickly?” Neiaphi asked. “It took my people five years.”

Pelagios shrugged. “They must have access to a cruiser. Those travel much faster than transports.”

Lyric sighed heavily.

“What’s wrong?” Justic asked.

“I’m just wondering what I’ll tell everyone. How do I convince them to go? Should we go? Do I even want to go?” Lyric’s voice was heavy with doubt.

A calm, gentle voice interrupted. “I believe I can help answer those questions, child.”

Everyone spun around to see a tall woman standing before them. Her alabaster skin almost glowed, framed by platinum blonde hair. She wore a shimmering silver gown that flowed to the floor, with a matching cloak draped over her shoulders.

Andonis drew his sword, holding it ready. “Who are you?” he demanded.

The mysterious woman raised her hands peacefully. “Be at ease, my child. I mean you no harm. Please, come back to the fire—we have much to discuss.” Without waiting for a reply, she glided smoothly up the stairs.

“Should we follow her?” Neiaphi asked.

Cypress glanced up, yipped once, and trotted after the woman.

Andonis shrugged. “Cypress doesn’t seem to mind her. I’ll lead.” Ambrite fell in step beside him, and together they ascended the stairs, shoulder to shoulder.

“What do you want with us?” Andonis demanded loudly as he reached the top step. He held out a hand, signaling for the others to stay back deeper in the subterranean staircase.

“Please, come forward and break fast with us,” the

woman said calmly. "We mean you no harm, as I said before. We are here to help—and to offer the centaurs another option. Now, please, allow everyone to join us."

"I think it'll be alright, Andonis. Let's hear what they have to say," Ambrite urged.

Neiaphi and the others cautiously stepped forward, emerging into the clearing where five more strangers sat around the now fully alive fire. They were preparing something that filled the air with a wonderful, inviting aroma.

"Who are you? Where are you from?" Lyric asked, her voice steady but curious. The woman in silver smiled warmly and motioned for them to join around the fire.

A steaming bowl was passed to each of them. Neiaphi examined hers, stirring the soupy mixture to reveal an assortment of roots and vegetables.

The newcomers began eating without answering, exchanging quiet glances among themselves before tentatively tasting the meal.

"Oh, this is surprisingly good. I've never tasted anything like this," Pelagios remarked.

The strangers smiled but said nothing, returning their attention to their food.

When everyone finished, one of the women rose and quietly gathered the bowls, disappearing into the shadows beyond the clearing.

"Now, we may talk. We do not speak while eating. When nurturing our bodies, we center ourselves and focus our core."

Lyric frowned, impatience clear in her voice. "Will you answer our questions now?" "But of course, my child. We are Agarthans—from Agartha."

Andonis raised an eyebrow. "Okay, but that just opens up more questions than it answers."

The woman smiled serenely. "Agartha lies far beneath us."

Pelagios looked down at his feet, baffled. "Beneath us?"

Nervously, Neiaphi asked, "What's your name, please?"

"Ah, Neiaphi—it's a pleasure to finally meet you."

Neiaphi's mouth dropped. "H-how do you know my name?" she stammered.

"We've been sent to help you—all of you."

Pelagios's frustration surfaced as he raised his voice slightly. "Okay, wait one minute. You're raising more questions than you're answering."

"I am Shalendra," the woman in silver said, nodding gracefully.

"How exactly are you going to help us? You mentioned another option," Lyric pressed, eager to steer the conversation.

"Yes, we are here to help. As you know, the Society and Atlantis are locked in a battle for power across this continent. But what you don't realize is that Atlantis is fighting a two-front war."

"And who's the other side?" Andonis asked, eyes sharp. "The Lemurians."

"The who?" several voices asked in unison.

Shalendra smiled gently. "The Lemurians. They came to this planet long before the Atlanteans. They settled on the opposite side of the world and lived as peaceful stewards, helping all lifeforms flourish and become their best selves. They took only what was necessary and avoided interfering with the natural development of other species. When we first encountered them, we respected their choices and left them to their ways."

"It was many, many years later when we reemerged and saw that a new race had appeared—the Atlanteans. Unlike the Lemurians, they were not peaceful. Their leader filled the land with the unwanted and enforced control through ruthless wardens. They ripped resources from the earth, taking more than was needed, and sold these treasures to off-world races. Resources that once replenished slowly but surely were now depleted rapidly.

"We approached them, pleading for restraint and

respect for the planet. As you might expect, they refused. The Lemurians, committed to balance and harmony, have made it their mission to stop this exploitation. We, too, have tried to restore peace, but so far, our efforts have been in vain. A war is coming—a devastating war that threatens the very future of this world."

"Can't you stop it?" Ambrite implored, eyes wide with hope.

Shalendra shook her head gently. "We possess great technology, but it is not meant for war. We are a peaceful people. Rather than trying to broker peace between these two warring factions, we've chosen a different path."

She paused, her gaze sweeping across the group. "We seek out those who are deserving—those who want to escape the coming storm. We offer them sanctuary and a chance to live in peace with us. We're also searching for those not native to this planet, like the centaurs and the griffins. Atlantis introduced many species here, and the Lemurians have vowed to purge all from Romota's bloodline. We don't believe they all deserve death."

She let her words hang in the cool night air. "In nine moons, we will gather everyone we find here at this location. They will be given three choices: return to Romota, come with us to Agartha, or remain on the surface with an uncertain future."

"Griffins cannot speak like us; they are animals, like horses," Lyric said, frowning. "How will you communicate this to them?"

Shalendra smiled gently. "There are those among us who can speak with lesser beings. All creatures communicate in their way—you just have to know how to listen and speak their language."

"What did you mean by 'top side'?" Justic asked, puzzled.

"Just that," Shalendra replied simply. "Up here, on the surface of this land, is the top side."

He frowned, considering her words. "But then, what is

the bottom side?"

"Agartha lies at the center of this planet."

The revelation left everyone speechless, the weight of the idea settling heavily.

Pelagios was the first to break the silence. "There's nothing at the center of a planet but molten rock."

Shalendra shook her head softly, while a few of her companions snickered quietly. "There is molten rock, yes, but much, much more than you can imagine."

Lyric stood, flicking her tail thoughtfully. "So… how do we begin?"

The woman in silver smiled serenely, ready to answer, but far beyond the clearing, two figures slipped away silently.

Hepluosis and Captain Rirmell moved cautiously on their bellies, then rose to their feet once safely distant, quickening to a jog. Neither spoke, their minds buzzing with everything they had just heard.

When they reached their camp, they gathered the others and shared every detail of the encounter, the weight of the message sinking deep.

"A whole land beneath our feet? How's that even possible?" Brackus, a tan centaur, asked skeptically.

Rirmell shot him a sharp look. "Don't waste time questioning what doesn't matter. What matters is there'll soon be fewer unwanted beings on this planet—at least above ground. Frankly, I don't care how they leave, as long as I don't have to see them anymore."

Talite's deep voice cut through the murmurs. "Who says all of them will leave?" Rirmell's scowl deepened. "Then we'll deal with the ones who refuse. I want eyes on that clearing, day and night. The moment they move, I want to know. We will not lose track of them."

All the centaurs exchanged looks—first surprise, then a slow burn of anger kindling behind their eyes.

Shalendra moved gracefully to assist Lyric and Pelagios in crafting the reply message to Romota. Around the fire, others scoured over intricate maps the Agarthans had provided, tracing routes and landmarks with keen attention.

Neiaphi sat off to one side, throwing a stick for Cypress to fetch. A tall, solemn figure approached her.

"Neiaphi? I am Asan," the man said with a deep, respectful bow. "I will be accompanying you on your journey to Atlantis."

Neiaphi shook her head firmly. "I'm not going to Atlantis. We're helping the centaurs. Isn't that right, Andonis?" she asked as Andonis came near.

Andonis hesitated, his brow furrowing. He glanced up at the early morning sun just beginning to peak over the trees. "I… I'm not sure. Maybe you should go to Atlantis first, and then I'll meet back up with you there," he said, voice uneven. "I still want to help, but it might be safer if you're with your parents. It's just... safer."

"How can you say that?" Neiaphi's voice cracked with frustration and hurt. "After everything we've been through, you want to just... part ways?" She stood abruptly, eyes flashing with pain. Without waiting for a reply, she stormed off, her footsteps heavy against the earth.

Andonis hurried after her, grabbed her shoulder and spun her to face him, his expression anguished. "I do. I do want that. I just… I thought sending you away would keep you safe. Everything feels like it's falling apart, and I don't know how to fix it. But the one thing I thought I could do was protect you."

Neiaphi's eyes shimmered. "You don't protect someone by pushing them away. You protect them by standing with them." Her voice softened, but the hurt still laced every word. "If you're too afraid to do that, maybe you don't want what I thought you did."

Andonis stepped closer, lowering his voice. "I'm not afraid of standing with you. I'm afraid of losing you."

"Then don't walk away from me," she said quietly.

"Don't ask me to go where you won't follow."

There was a long silence between them, filled only by the distant sounds of the camp.

Then, finally, Andonis nodded slowly.

"I'm sorry," he whispered. "You're right. Wherever you go, I go."

Neiaphi searched his face for a long moment, then gave a small, sad smile. "We are supposed to figure it out together."

"I do—"

She held up a hand to stop him, eyes downcast. "Life partners stick together. They face everything side by side. If you were truly committed to us, you would never have asked me to leave."

Her voice trembled, she lifted her gaze to his, eyes shimmering with unshed tears. "No matter what happens on this trip, I want to be with you."

Andonis took her hands and pressed them to his chest. "I want that too. But I can't stand the thought of you being in danger."

She shook her head. "I've been in danger since I arrived on this planet. Whether I'm here with you or back with my parents, that doesn't change. You risked everything to save me from Kayson. You promised to stay by my side. And now you want to send me away—with someone we barely know."

She pulled her hands free. "Do you still love me?"

"Of course I do. That's why I want to keep you safe."

"Atlantis is in the middle of a war. You think I'll be safer there—without you?" Her voice rose, disbelief written across her face.

Andonis opened his mouth to respond, then closed it again. His brow furrowed as her words sank in.

"I'm continuing to Atlantis," she said at last. "I release you from our arrangement."

Andonis grabbed her hand and dropped to his knees. "Please, don't say that. I don't want this. I'm sorry. I'll go to Atlantis with you, or we can keep traveling with the centaurs. Whatever you want. Just... don't leave me."

She shook her head gently and pulled her hand from his. "I never left you, Andonis. You left me—some time ago." Her voice was soft but steady. "I want you to be happy," she added, a catch in her throat. "I… I hope you find it."

She leaned down and pressed a kiss to his forehead, then turned and walked away, leaving him kneeling in the dust.

"Asan," she called out, her voice firmer now, "I'm ready to leave when you are."

"As you wish, my lady. We'll depart before midday," Asan said, bowing low.

Neiaphi moved through the camp, saying her goodbyes to each member of their party.

When she reached Lyric, the girl threw her arms around her. "Stay," Lyric whispered. "Please."

Neiaphi offered a sad smile and shook her head gently. "I can't."

She hesitated, then asked, "Have you decided? Will you go to Romota or Agartha?"

Lyric looked away, conflicted. "I don't know yet. I want to see Agartha before I make a decision. I just hope they'll allow me that chance."

A voice rang out from the top of the stairwell. "I can take you there first, if you wish."

Lyric spun around. Shalendra stood at the top, the wind catching the edges of her cloak. "We can go now?" Lyric asked.

"If it will help you decide," Shalendra replied with a nod.

"I think it will. If I see this land for myself, I can help others make their choice too." Neiaphi tilted her head. "But you've never seen Romota. How can you compare?" "Pelagios showed me images on his ship," Lyric said. "Romota is beautiful. I think many will be happy there. But some… some won't want to leave what they've always known. If I can describe both places—Romota and Agartha—maybe I can help them understand. Help them choose. That way, I'll feel like I've fulfilled my purpose. Even if it's not an easy decision for anyone."

Neiaphi stepped forward and embraced her again. "Wherever your path leads, I wish you the best. It's been an honor to know you."

"Give him a chance," Lyric whispered. "I can feel his attraction to me, but it isn't real. He loves you—I can see it. I'm just... an oddity. Something new. That kind of fascination fades. And when it does, the real heartbreak will begin."

Neiaphi turned away. She had nothing more to say. "Safe travels."

Lyric watched her go. "Safe travels, Neiaphi."

"How long will it take to reach Atlantis?" Neiaphi asked, as they rode away from the clearing where the communication machine had stood. Their horses moved at a brisk pace, the forest thinning behind them.

"You'll see," Asan replied, his tone teasingly cryptic.

Cypress trotted beside her, glancing back at the clearing, then up at her with a low whine. "It's just us now, boy. Come on," she said softly.

Beside her, Nexus shook her head, tugging against the reins. "Sorry, girl," Neiaphi murmured, loosening her grip.

"Fret not," Asan said, glancing sideways at her. "I have a feeling you'll see them again."

She gave a dry laugh. "How can you say that? It will take us moons to reach Atlantis on horseback. If I want to see them again before they leave in ten moons, I'd have to turn right around."

Asan simply smiled, not explaining. Neiaphi couldn't help glancing back one last time. At the edge of the clearing, Andonis stood alone, watching her go. He raised a hand in farewell.

She closed her eyes, turned forward again, and said nothing.

As they rode on, the silence stretched between them. Tears she'd fought to hold back slipped down her cheeks, unnoticed by the wind.

∞ 12 ∞
SEPARATED

"They're splitting up, sir. Which group do we follow?"

Rirmell cursed under his breath. "How many groups?"

The scout stepped closer. "Four in total. The woman and one of the new men left at midday—they're heading back the way they came. The rest divided into three groups: both men joined two centaurs and two newcomers; another centaur left with two more newcomers; and the last group—what's left of the centaurs and newcomers—departed together."

Rirmell narrowed his eyes, processing. "Send Zeus to Hades."

He paced in front of his scout, then glanced at the soldiers gathered in a loose circle, awaiting orders. His gaze landed on the two foreigners and the ragged group of centaurs.

"I don't care about the lone female or the centaurs breaking off. We follow the two men and their group. That pilot from Romota will be mine. And uncovering where this new leader hails from will do wonders for my career."

A society officer nodded toward the band of centaurs who had been traveling with them. "What about them?"

Rirmell waved dismissively. "Let them go where they will. Mount up."

Hepluosis bid the soldiers farewell as they moved out. Brutus approached him, asking. "Which path do you follow?"

Hepluosis paused before answering. "I'll follow Neiaphi. I don't know the men she traveled with. What about you?"

"I was sent after Cret," Brutus replied. "No interest in the others. We're going after the lone centaur—he's isolated, with only two humans. I want to find out what's going on."

Six shook his head. "Those others aren't human. They're too tall, and the way they move—it's like they float above the ground."

"Move out," Brutus commanded. "Safe travels, Hepluosis. And kill Cret if you see him again."

Hepluosis nodded. "You have my promise."

Captain Rirmell and his men moved swiftly back to the clearing where their prey had disappeared. He assigned two scouts to tail the pilot and mark their trail.

Before joining the pursuit, Rirmell wanted to investigate what had caught their attention in the clearing. But there was little to see—only a cold fire pit and a monolithic stone pillar standing alone.

He circled the pillar, stamping on the ground, then kicked at the stone. Somewhere nearby was a hidden entrance. He'd seen figures ascending what looked like stairs, but now no stairs were visible.

"Tassos, head back to the ship and bring two companies back to our last camp. When you return, keep watch over this clearing."

"Yes, sir!" Tassos snapped to attention and spurred his horse into a canter. Rirmell mounted his horse. "The rest of us will follow the pilot. Move out!"

Simandro moved briskly through the underbrush. Though they lacked mounts, the two Agarthans accompanying him kept pace without complaint. They had been traveling most of the day, yet neither had asked for a break.

As the sun dipped low, Simandro decided it was time

to rest.

They reached a small stream, bordered on one side by a dense bramble of berry bushes. "This looks like a good spot to stop for the night," he said, breaking the day's long silence.

"If you need rest, we can stop," one of the Agarthans replied quietly.

"I can keep going if you can, but I don't see the point. We've made good progress today.

Let's find something to eat and figure out where to go next." "If that is your wish," came the calm response.

They set out to gather firewood and berries. One of the Agarthans skillfully snared a couple of fish, then wrapped them in fresh grass collected from the stream.

As the fire crackled to life, the fish were placed on the hearthstones to cook, while the berries soaked in water nearby. Simandro settled down, easing the ache in his legs.

"I never caught your names before we left. I'm Simandro," he said.

The taller Agarthan—sandy brown hair and a pale, silvery-white complexion that seemed to glow faintly—answered, "I am Keryth, and this is Kolvar."

"If you have any questions as we travel, feel free to ask," Simandro offered.

"That won't be necessary. I've been to the surface many times," Kolvar said.

"Is it common for your people to venture into the sun?" Simandro asked.

"Not many come topside, but those who do visit regularly."

"So, what's it like down there? I imagine it must be pretty bright up here."

Keryth cocked his head and grinned. "We have a sun, but it's a little different."

Simandro's eyes widened. "There's a sun inside the planet?" he whispered in awe. "How so?" Simandro leaned in, curious.

"Our sun isn't as bright as this one when it pulses. It slowly brightens, then dims—just brighter than dusk here. No matter how often I experience your nights, I can't get used to them." Kolvar shivered slightly. "Some nights are so dark you can't see your hand in front of your face."   "Wow. That's a lot to take in."

Kolvar and Keryth exchanged a glance.

"If you decide to go to Agartha, we'd be happy to show you the best sights," Keryth offered.

"I haven't decided yet. It's not a choice to take lightly. As we travel, if you can tell me everything about Agartha, it might help. I saw pictures of Romota—it looks nice, but it's not home." He shook his head and ran his hands through his hair.

"Worry not, my friend. Your choice will become clear soon enough."

Talite peered through the darkness at Simandro's camp. Simandro and the two humans seemed relaxed, unaware they were being watched. The grey centaur melted back into the night to rejoin his companions.

"Did you learn anything?" Brutus asked.

"Yes, sir. The humans are telling him about their homeland—some place where the sun behaves strangely and the nights never fully darken."

"They must be from far to the north," Pena said thoughtfully. "I traveled north once in my youth, and during the warming moons, the sun never fully set."

Talite stared at Pena for a moment, mesmerized by how the firelight made her white haunches gleam against the coal-blackness of her hide. Shaking his head to clear his thoughts, he said, "They didn't say if this was only a warming moon phenomenon. But that's not important. The humans have offered him a choice—between their land and a place called Romota."

Brutus scowled, his jaw tightening.

Brackus stomped his hoof and huffed. "That's the planet Cret said they came from—the planet all centaurs came from as well."

"We'll keep following them and learn what we can," Brutus said grimly.

Neiaphi and Asan settled beside a small pond. The night sky was clear, the full moon casting a silver glow across the water. Somewhere in the distance, a lone wolf howled— sharp and haunting. Neiaphi jumped at the sound.

"Be calm," Asan said softly, stirring roots into the boiling water. "It's just a wolf. You're safe with me."

She shivered. "You haven't met the wolves I have."

They sat in silence for a moment before she asked, "Will we be walking the entire way?" Asan handed her a bowl, then settled on the other side of the fire and began eating.

Neiaphi watched him silently for a moment before clearing her throat. He looked up, smiled briefly, but said nothing.

Her gaze sharpened, and she nodded once. When he still didn't answer, she pressed again, "Are we walking the entire way?"

"You'll find out tomorrow," he replied, voice calm but unreadable.

She scowled. "Fine." Grabbing her bedroll, she curled up close to the fire, the silence between them thick with unspoken questions.

Hepluosis and Six sat shivering in the cold, their eyes fixed on Neiaphi's distant campfire flickering against the night. They kept their distance, wary of being spotted. Hepluosis prayed they wouldn't lose sight of her. Right now, she was his only link to finding Cret—or even glimpsing his parents again. The Pillars and Atlantis were mysteries he couldn't navigate alone.

Losing track of Cret had filled him with anger, but being this close to Neiaphi brought a flicker of hope. He vowed to make her pay for Cret's insolence—and to share in her suffering alongside Cret. The heartbreak that awaited before his end would be his sweetest revenge.

Andonis rode with his chin tucked to his chest, letting his horse choose its path as he drifted in thought.

"Heads up!" a voice shouted just before a branch whipped across Andonis's chest, nearly knocking him off and stealing the wind from his lungs.

He pulled his horse to a halt and leaned forward over its neck. "Are you all right?" Justic asked, trotting up.

Andonis nodded, sucking in ragged breaths. "I'll be okay in a moment."

"You need to watch where you're going," Justic laughed, giving him a friendly slap on the back.

Andonis grimaced and groaned. "You, my friend, are strong." He rolled his shoulder. "Play nice with us weak humans."

Justic laughed harder. "I'll keep that in mind. So, what's got you so distracted?" Andonis pursed his lips but said nothing.

"Oh, right—Neiaphi," Justic said knowingly. Andonis stared straight ahead, silent.

"Come on," Justic pressed. "You'll see her again. Give her some time to clear her head. She's headed to Atlantis. After we finish our mission, you can go there and win her back. She doesn't strike me as the type to choose a new love quickly."

Andonis sighed. "You're right about that. But there's already someone else in her thoughts. She thought he was lost when she said yes to me. We've recently found out he's alive—

maybe even already at Atlantis. If she reunites with him, I'll be nothing but an afterthought."

Justic glanced at him, a hint of sympathy in his eyes. "You sound pretty certain." Justic fell silent for a moment before continuing. "If her favor can be swayed so easily, then was it ever real to begin with?"

"I always knew her heart belonged to someone else," Andonis admitted, running his hands through his hair. "But I was certain she'd never see him again. Foolish of me, I suppose."

Justic nodded slowly. "The heart is a foolish thing. Even when it knows the truth, it still fights to hold on. You did everything anyone could've asked of you."

Andonis shook his head. "No, I could have done more." He hesitated, then added quietly, "Your sister... she's captivating. It could never be, I know that, but still—I let my thoughts and eyes wander." He hung his head in shame. "How could I have done that to her? I shamed her."

Justic shook his head gently. "Wandering eyes aren't something to be ashamed of."

Andonis's voice dropped. "When you're promised to someone, you should only have eyes for your betrothed. It's the first step in the commitment you're making. She had every right to leave me. I'm lost now. I can't go back to my family— I've disgraced them."

"Then stay with us," Justic said firmly. "You're not alone in this." Andonis reined in his horse and turned to face Justic. "Stay with you?"

"Yes. Help us gather as many centaurs as possible, then assist in settling them into their new homes."

"And where will you settle them? Have you decided?"

Justic shook his head. "Not yet. Lyric wants to see Agartha before making up her mind."

"That makes sense." Andonis nodded thoughtfully. "Well, for now, that's my plan too.

We'll see what the future holds."

Up ahead, the group slowed and began searching for a

campsite.

"Thought you might be hungry," Pelagios said, approaching with a sack of dried meat. "Thank you," Andonis said, taking a piece of jerky as he dismounted.

"Did Shalendra say how much farther?" Justic asked.

He shook his head. "No. Lyric keeps asking, but all she'll say is that we'll reach an access point soon."

"That'll have to do," Justic snorted.

"And what about you, Pelagios? Have you decided what you'll do when the transport ship arrives?" Andonis inquired.

"I'll be returning to Romota," Pelagios replied without hesitation. "You've thought this through."

Pelagios sighed. "No. Going home is my only option. I was supposed to do a slingshot trip and should've been back already. Everyone I left behind must be worried sick."

No one commented. They fell into a comfortable silence as they set up camp, the stars beginning to dance overhead.

The Society scout slid silently on his belly, retreating from the firelight. When he was far enough, he rose and sprinted back to Captain Rirmell to report the overheard chatter.

Rirmell would be pleased—they'd be traveling on foot for at least a couple of days, he thought.

Shaking off the thought, he pushed himself harder. He didn't want to be caught alone once darkness fully fell.

A wolf's howl shattered the eerie silence, startlingly close. A large shape flickered between the trees, matching his pace.

Shuddering, he faltered for a moment but forced his gaze back to the path ahead.

He took only ten more strides before sliding to a halt, falling hard on his behind. The largest wolf he'd ever seen stood snarling in the middle of the path, saliva dripping from its fangs and gleaming in the moonlight.

The scout scrambled to his feet, fumbling to unsheathe his bow. His fingers trembled as he struggled to notch an arrow.

"Be at ease, human, and you may live to see the sun," the wolf spoke.

The scout's mouth dropped open. "H… h… how, wh… wh… y… you…" He stammered.

From behind, Lars crept forward and struck him over the head with a heavy stick. The scout collapsed to the ground.

Staps growled, "You better not have killed him."

Lars knelt, checking. "He's still breathing."

"Grab him. We need to find cover before anyone comes looking," Staps said, disappearing into the shadows.

∞ 13 ∞
NEW WORLD

Nexus snorted softly, flicking her head up and down. Neiaphi reached out to scratch behind the horse's ear. "Easy, girl. Easy. We're almost there, I think." She glanced at the back of Asan's head as he rode ahead. They had been traveling since daybreak, the sun now dipping low in the western sky.

Asan reined his horse to a halt and dismounted. Neiaphi stayed mounted on Nexus, riding up beside him.

"Are we there? I don't see anything," she said, scanning the quiet landscape around them. "Come," he urged quietly.

She dismounted, following Asan along the narrow deer path, her horse Nexus moving steadily behind. Cypress darted in and out of the thick bushes, his tail wagging with youthful excitement.

The forest grew thicker, the underbrush choking the trail with fallen branches and tangled vines. Asan moved with surefooted ease, navigating around obstacles without hesitation, as if the path revealed itself only to him.

The sun dipped beneath the horizon, and dusk settled like a veil, shadows stretching long and dark. Visibility waned, making every step a careful one.

At last, they emerged into a quiet clearing. To one side, a small pond lay undisturbed—its surface smooth as glass, reflecting the soft shimmer of the rising moon like a delicate silver mirror.

The air felt still, charged with the promise of something new.

"What is this place?" she asked, eyes wide with wonder and a flicker of caution.

Asan remained silent as he led her to the far side of the pond. As they neared it, she saw a small structure take shape. It was a small stone hut with a wooden door and no windows. The roof was even made of large flat stones. It almost blended in with the landscape.

Asan approached the hut and moved a small bush to the right side of the door. Next to the door was a smooth black slate. He lightly touched it with the flat of his hand. The slate lit up. Neiaphi gasped, not expecting to see a mechanical screen in the middle of nowhere. Asan pressed a couple of symbols on the illuminated screen, and the door swung open—her breath caught as she stepped closer, the soft pink light spilling out like a gentle invitation. The hut, so unassuming from the outside, now felt alive with a quiet, mysterious energy.

Asan motioned for her to enter first, his eyes calm but unreadable. She hesitated for a moment, then pushed the door open wider, revealing a small interior bathed in the same warm glow.

Inside, the walls were lined with smooth stone, but interspersed were panels that pulsed faintly with light—like veins of energy running beneath the surface. A low hum filled the air, subtle but constant, as if the hut itself was breathing.

Neiaphi stepped inside, and Asan followed, the door sliding shut with a whisper, sealing them away from the dark woods outside.

Asan led his horse deeper into the confined space, but Neiaphi hesitated. Surprised, she saw that the floor instantly sloped down. Stones lined the inside of the small building, and all along the walls of the descending tunnel; the soft pink glow emitting from them. "Marvelous rocks, aren't they?" He asked without pausing, "Come, we'll be resting soon." He led them down the sloping tunnel deep underground.

Nexus nickered softly. Neiaphi placed a steadying hand on her neck, but they pressed deeper into the tunnel.

After what felt like an eternity, the path finally

leveled—yet they kept walking. Ahead, the tunnel ended abruptly, swallowed by complete darkness.

Asan halted at the edge of the void. He glanced back at Neiaphi, then muttered a few words in a strange, sing-song language. Suddenly, a blinding light erupted, flooding the cavern before them. Neiaphi shielded her eyes with both hands.

When her vision cleared, she took in the vastness of the cavern—so enormous that its far wall vanished into shadow. She searched for the source of the intense glow but found none visible.

In the center of the cavern rested a large metal ship, shaped like a long cylinder with one end tapered to a sharp point.

"What's that?" she asked.

Asan paused, then said, "That is our ride for the rest of the way. Come on." He gestured for her to follow.

In front of the ship stood a small obelisk. Asan pressed a few buttons, and a large door silently slid open on the craft's side. When it stopped, a ramp descended smoothly to the ground.

Without hesitation, Asan stepped onto the ramp the moment it touched down. Neiaphi approached more cautiously. Nexus stopped short, stretching her neck to sniff the ramp.

"It's okay, girl. Come on." Neiaphi coaxed gently. Nexus took a tentative step forward, then another.

"Good girl, that's it."

Nexus placed one hoof on the ramp, causing it to ring loudly. Startled, she snorted and tossed her head. Asan stood calmly at the top.

"Nexus, ta shaia, ta fauz. Ven hepd ta okava. Kip yevin czek," he said softly, his voice gentle and steady.

Nexus snorted again, shaking her head nervously. "Kip," Asan repeated, even more soothing this time.

Slowly, one careful step at a time, Nexus began to walk up the ramp.

Neiaphi stared at Asan, mouth agape. "What did you

say to her?" she finally managed. I told her to be calm, to be still. You'll be okay. Then I told her to come with me." "Amazing. Simply amazing. I doubt I'd get the same results with the same words."

Asan chuckled. "Most definitely not, miss. Please, have a seat while I secure the horses." "How long will this trip take?"

"Hardly any time at all."

Neiaphi glanced around. In the ship's center were a dozen chairs facing a long control panel with a large screen. Along the back and sides of the room, partitioned compartments lined the walls.

Asan led the horses into one of the rooms, then settled into the seat at the center of the control panel. He gestured for her to sit beside him.

Asan's fingers flew across the control panel, pressing symbols as they appeared and sliding over blinking lights. A low hum thrummed from somewhere deep within the vessel. Suddenly, a screen lit up on the wall before them, displaying the cave entrance.

Neiaphi watched as the gentle slope they had followed steadily rose until the exit disappeared from view.

"How are we getting out of the cavern?" she asked, eyes flicking to the panel. She tried to decipher the symbols, but the language was completely foreign.

"We're going down. Watch."

The humming grew louder, and a faint vibration hummed through the cabin.

Suddenly, Neiaphi's stomach lurched, as if it had flown into her throat. The screen went black.

"What's happening?" Panic threaded her voice as she tightened her hand on Cypress's neck.

"We're descending. Don't worry—this will only last a few moments. You'll feel a brief moment of weightlessness; that's normal. Please buckle the strap across your lap."

True to his word, a strange sensation made her feel like she was about to float away. The strap tightened just as her bottom lifted from the chair. But as quickly as it came, the feeling vanished, and the fall resumed.

Soon, the screen brightened again. Cypress whimpered softly but stayed close.

Neiaphi's mouth fell open. Before her stretched a world unlike anything she had ever seen. Their craft had broken through the Earth's crust into a vast underground ocean.

Fish swam past the vessel—some brightly colored, others bearing rows of sharp teeth jutting from their jaws. To their right, a coral reef burst with vibrant hues of blue, purple, orange, and red.

Tall strands of sea grass swayed gently between the coral, rocking with the passage of fish and the ocean's current.

Suddenly, a large head appeared before them. The serpent-like creature studied them with slow, blinking eyes before gliding away.

No, not a serpent, Neiaphi thought. The creature had a long neck, but its body and tail were equally long, ending in four strong legs with webbed feet.

As they emerged from the water, the sky came into view. "How do you have clouds?" she asked.

Asan chuckled but said nothing.

"Oh wow, look at the sun!" Neiaphi exclaimed. It was smaller than the sun she was used to, and dimmer as well. "Do you have a moon?"

"That's one thing we lack." "So, night doesn't exist?"

"Oh, we still have times when the sun dims, but it never gets fully dark—more like dusk on the surface."

Neiaphi pondered this. "I think I'd enjoy that. The dark can be frightening." Suddenly, she jumped up and rushed to the screen, placing both hands on it.

"Is that a Pegasus?" Neiaphi finally whispered, her throat tight with excitement, making it hard to speak.

Asan smiled. "Yes, that's a Pegasus. We have many creatures here that don't live on the surface. Some tried once, but it's more peaceful down here. Most find life easier in this realm. That's why we approached the centaurs. They'll flourish here."

They skimmed swiftly above the waves, moving at a speed Neiaphi couldn't begin to describe.

"How long will we be here? Will we see land?"

"We'll be heading back up soon," he said. "Sorry, no land visits this trip. Next time." "I can come back?" She tore her gaze from the screen to look at him.

Asan met her eyes. "Let's get you to Atlantis first. Then we'll talk more about that."

No sooner had he finished speaking than the craft plunged back beneath the waves, racing toward a dark hole in the rocky ocean floor.

∞ 14 ∞
THE KING

As the sun dipped below the distant western horizon, a city emerged from the fading light. Golden spires pierced the sky above towering outer walls. Waves crashed against the stone fortifications, sending plumes of spray high into the air. Large purple banners, edged in gold, flapped in the wind, partially obscuring the enormous mountain peak rising behind the city.

Alexa stood at the bow of the ship, eyes fixed on their destination. She had never seen a city so breathtaking. The walls shimmered in the sun's last light, as if inlaid with jewels.

The royal banners whipped in the wind—deep purple trimmed with gold. Though the seal was hidden from view, she already knew what it was: a silver griffin locked in battle with a golden pegasus.

Greish stepped up behind her and wrapped his arms around her waist. Without turning, Alexa smiled and leaned back into him, resting her hands on his.

When he bent down to kiss her neck, she giggled.

"You'd better make sure my betrothed doesn't catch us," she teased.

He laughed and spun her around. "And who else would be holding you like this?" he said, grinning as he tickled her sides.

She squealed and squirmed away, breathless with laughter. Holding her hands up in surrender, she grinned.

"You're the only one allowed to hold me like that."

"That's better," Greish said, pulling her into a fierce embrace and kissing her deeply. "Are you ready to see our new home?"

"I can't wait," Alexa replied, though her smile faded slightly. "But I can't help worrying about Neiaphi and Andonis. When do you think they'll arrive?"

Spinning her around again, he held her close as they both gazed toward the towering city walls.

"I'm not sure," he said. "I hope it's soon. We can't have a double wedding without them."

The ship veered toward a set of massive gates—crafted from interwoven iron and gold in intricate, gleaming patterns. The gates stood open, welcoming their approach without resistance.

The walls rose from a narrow strip of land, just wide enough for twenty soldiers to stand shoulder to shoulder. Beyond them, more water—about ten boat lengths across—stretched toward a dock directly ahead. Soldiers patrolled the pier, their armor catching the fading light.

Beyond the dock, the city unfolded in a dense cluster of single- and two-story buildings, packed tightly together. Colorful awnings stretched from windows and shop fronts, vibrant against the stone.

Grinning from ear to ear, Alexa could barely contain her excitement. She couldn't wait to explore the shops that awaited her.

Addident, Neiluios, Crelian, and a small guard detail disembarked and made their way onto the docks. They had been instructed to check in at the port entry office before continuing into the city.

The office sat conveniently at the end of the pier—a squat, weatherworn building with peeling paint and a single large window beside the door.

Behind the glass sat a portly man in a stained shirt, his

eyes cast downward. As they approached, he glanced up briefly, then looked away.

"Papers, please," he muttered, holding out a hand while tugging at the hem of his shirt with the other.

Addident handed him the papers that the inspectors gave them.

The port officer unfolded the paper with a snap, coughed loudly, and let out a sigh. His eyes skimmed the document—then froze.

For the first time, he looked up at the group before him, his expression shifting from boredom to disbelief. He glanced back at the paper, rereading it with widened eyes.

Clearing his throat with forced authority, he finally spoke.

"I'm afraid the hour is too late to send you directly to the palace." Addident's frown deepened.

"B-but," the officer stammered, clearly rattled, "if you remain aboard your vessels tonight, I'll arrange transport at first light, sir." His voice trembled, his fingers tightening slightly around the paper.

Addident and Neiluios exchanged a look.

"Be calm, my friend," Addident said gently. "I don't know what the letter says, but we are no threat."

The officer's hands trembled slightly as he held the document.

"Threat? This letter says you are to be taken to the King immediately upon arrival. Failure to do so would result in my dismissal." He swallowed hard. "But if I disturb the King at this hour... the consequences would be worse than death."

He paused, eyes flicking between them. "Unless... war is imminent. Is it?"

"Not that we're aware of," Addident replied calmly. Morning will be fine. How long is the walk to the palace?"

"Oh, no one walks to the palace," the officer said quickly, shaking his head. "I'll send a couple of carriages to take you to the central ferry."

He adjusted the paper in his hands. "How many will be

in your party?” “A dozen, I believe.”

“Good, good, sir. I’ll see to it at first light.”

“I wish I could come with you,” Alexa said softly, her lips trembling as she tried to hold back a pout.

Greish brushed a strand of hair from her face. “I’ll tell you everything when I return. Not everyone gets to visit the palace.” He kissed her cheek, lingering a moment before turning to join the others on the dock.

“Be safe. I love you,” she called after him, her voice catching.

He spun around mid-step and blew her a kiss, grinning, and for a moment, it was as if the rest of the world fell away.

Paragon, standing nearby with arms crossed, gave a half-smile. “Ah, to be young and in love,” he said, clapping Greish on the back as he passed.

Three carriages waited at the end of the dock, each drawn by a team of four matching horses. Purple blankets trimmed in gold lay under their harnesses, and tall plumes nodded on their heads with every movement. The horses snorted and stamped, eager to be on their way.

“This way, gentlemen,” the footman said with a crisp bow, holding open the nearest carriage door.

Each of the three carriages seated four passengers, with a driver and footman perched outside. With a flick of the reins, the horses trotted smartly into the awakening city.

Shadows stretched long across the cobbled streets. Shopkeepers began their morning rituals—throwing open shutters, sweeping stoops, and exchanging the first greetings of the day. As the carriages passed a bakery, the rich, comforting scent of warm bread and honeyed pastries drifted through the air.

Inside, Captain Hue, Undercaptain Seleo, and Lieutenant Greish scanned the streets from behind the windows, eyes sharp and hands on their belts where their swords normally rested.

Few people were out yet, but the city stirred with life—too slowly, perhaps, for their comfort.

The road curved gently to the left, hugging the circular edge of the island. Ahead, an elegant bridge arched across the water—a deep forest green veined with gold. As they approached, the intricate ironwork revealed itself: the golden veins were twisting ivy, with silver leaves woven between, catching the light. Tall flags fluttered from each of the ten posts, their colors rippling in the morning breeze.

Beneath the bridge, crystal-clear water rippled slowly, reflecting the soft morning light.

The horses stepped confidently across the span, hooves echoing softly on the stone.

On the far side lay another circular island, dotted with elegant two- and three-story buildings. Unlike the tidy simplicity of the first island, this neighborhood radiated wealth.

Gilded merchant signs hung from wrought iron brackets, their ornate lettering curling like delicate vines. Window displays dazzled with intricate carvings and shimmering jewels, each piece crafted to catch the eye—and the coin purse—of any passerby.

The street curved gently to the left, mirroring the path they'd followed on the first island. Soon, another bridge appeared ahead—its ironwork identical in design but painted a deep midnight blue, still adorned with twisting gold ivy and shimmering silver leaves.

Beyond the bridge lay a smaller island, bursting with lush gardens and heavy fruit trees. The sweet scent of honeysuckle reached them first, thick and intoxicating in the warm morning air.

At the island's heart stood a magnificent palace, its spires shimmering like molten gold, each crowned with the royal flag fluttering proudly. The palace rose from the center of a vast lake, reflecting the sun's rays in dazzling light.

The carriages came to a halt beside a modest dock,

where a sleek ferry awaited. Two dozen royal guards stood at attention, their armor glinting beneath the sun as they prepared to escort the party onward.

"Good day, sir. Papers, please," one of the guards said, stepping forward with a sharp nod.

Addident produced the same letter he'd shown the port officer, holding it out steadily. The guard scanned it, then gestured toward the ferry. "We'll take you across four at a time. This way, please."

The ferry was small but sturdy—capable of carrying them all at once, yet fewer passengers meant less risk.

"Atlantis takes their security seriously," Addident remarked, watching the guard closely. The guard gave a tight smile.

"Yes, sir. The King is a cautious man."

With a gentle hum from the ferry's engine, they glided smoothly across the lake. Before long, the opposite shore drew near, and all had safely crossed.

A slender man in a white robe trimmed with purple awaited them at the palace entrance.

His calm eyes surveyed the group as he stepped forward.

"Good morning, gentlemen. I am Fanis, one of King Thodoris's advisors. Please, follow me."

He led them up a grand stairway wide enough for twenty men to march side by side, its polished stone gleaming beneath their feet. The towering doors ahead stood as tall as five men stacked one atop another. Beyond them lay a cavernous hall, its walls soaring twice as high as the massive entrance. Rows of windows flanked either side, letting in shafts of pale light.

"All who enter these walls must be cleansed," Fanis said quietly, turning them down a long hallway to the right.

The hallway opened into a vast bathhouse, thick with warm steam that curled lazily from large bronze cylinders scattered throughout the room.

"You want us to bathe?" Addident asked, raising an

eyebrow.

Fanis bowed slightly. "If you wish to see the King."

Addident glanced around, then squared his shoulders. "We didn't come all this way to turn back now. Strip down, men."

Without hesitation, the group shed their outer garments, leaving only their underclothes—simple linen breeches. The heat from the pools enveloped them as they stepped into the steaming water, the warmth seeping into their bones.

A loud sigh escaped Greish as he sank into the warm water, the tension in his shoulders easing slightly.

"Now, this is refreshing," Paragon said with a chuckle, settling beside him.

Along one side of the bath, bars of soap and brightly colored sponges were neatly lined up. Two young housemaids slipped in quietly, unnoticed as they scrubbed away the dust and grime of the road. The housemaids gathered the discarded clothing and left behind fresh, clean garments.

Crelian was the first to climb out, a frown creasing his brow. "Looks like someone's taken our clothes."

Greish glanced down at his mostly bare frame and grunted, "Are we supposed to face the King like this?"

"No, they swapped our clothes for these," Crelian said, holding up a loose white robe. He slipped it on—its sleeves hung so long they nearly covered his hands. Nearby lay a pile of similar robes, each paired with a crimson sash.

After tying his sash, Crelian held out his hands and studied his reflection. "I look ridiculous."

"That's way too big for you. Are there any smaller ones?" Aner asked.

Crelian rummaged through the pile, holding each robe up against himself. "Nope. They all seem to be the same size."

Addident sighed and began donning his robe. "Well, then. I suppose everyone should get dressed."

Moments later, Fanis returned. "Excellent, gentlemen. Please follow me—the King awaits."

Fanis led them down the cool stone hallway into a vast courtyard garden, fragrant with the scent of ripe oranges and blooming jasmine. Every fruit tree imaginable—lemon, fig, pomegranate—and flowers in vivid shades of crimson, violet, and gold surrounded them.

At the garden's center stood a tall dais, crowned by an elaborate throne of gold and amethyst. Seated upon it was King Poseidon Thodoris, an older man whose piercing eyes surveyed them with quiet authority.

As they approached, Fanis dropped to his knees at the foot of the stairs, bowing his head until his forehead nearly touched the floor. The Loyals followed his example without hesitation. The Romotians, however, remained standing, the king's sharp gaze narrowing in displeasure.

Addident quickly scanned the group, then gestured for all to bow.

A faint smile curved the king's lips as he silently counted to fifty. Then, his voice rang out, clear and commanding:

"Rise, my children. Approach Fanis."

Fanis rose smoothly and ascended the stairs with measured steps. At the top, he bowed deeply, hands steepled before his chest in a gesture of respect.

"May I present the most wonderful and all-knowing King Poseidon Thodoris. My liege, may I present to you—Paragon, Aner, Mace, and Baccus from the Coastal Outer Realm; Simos and Tevin from the Northern Realm; High Officials Addident, Neiluios, and Crelian; Captain Hue, Undercaptain Seleo, and Lieutenant Greish from Romota," Fanis announced, his voice clear even as he remained bowed.

"Never in our lifetime have we witnessed such a gathering," the King said, speaking in the third person, his tone both proud and commanding. "All of you will confer with our map makers and update them as needed. It is costly to send out map makers—we shall make the most of your presence here."

All bowed in acceptance.

Paragon stepped forward and bowed again. The King waved a jeweled hand in acknowledgement. Fanis nodded and gestured respectfully. "You may speak."

"If it pleases Your Majesty," Paragon began, "we have an excellent map maker among us—Chartis from Romota. His skill is unmatched, and he has been charting our entire journey with some marvelous technology."

"Excellent. Bring him to us on the morrow," the King said, his voice steady but firm. "Now, to the problem before us: an invading army from Romota."

"Invading army? We are no such thing…" Addident began, but his words were cut short.

"SILENCE!" King Thodoris's roar echoed through the courtyard, his face flushed with anger. The gathered group froze, breaths held tight. "Do not speak to us without permission. Standing before us, we see several high-ranking representatives and esteemed Romotian guards. We have been told you travel with your families, yet the number of warrior-aged men is troubling. What are your intentions?"

Addident hesitated, the weight of the moment pressing down on him. After a long pause, Addident looked at Fanis and raised his eyebrows expectantly. Fanis's calm voice broke the silence. "You may speak."

"Thank you for your hospitality, Your Majesty. If I may, I will begin with our story." Addident paused respectfully before continuing. "King Titern of Romota received word from Atlantis requesting guards and officials. He chose those he wished to remove from competition—or those who had become a thorn in his side. Before our departure, a second message arrived, directing us to an alternate landing site due to a security concern. It was the Society that intercepted the original signal and altered our orders. Despite their efforts to eliminate us, with the help of these men"—he nodded toward his companions—"we have reached Atlantis, our true destination. We come not as invaders, but as allies, offering our assistance to maintain peace and support the advancement of Atlantis."

Addident bowed his head in respect as he finished.

King Thodoris remained silent, his gaze fixed on the floor as he weighed Addident's words. The garden fell into an awkward stillness. Finally, the King lifted his eyes, his voice low and sharp. "We sent no such message. You have been misled—again."

Simos stepped forward, bowing deeply. His tone was steady but respectful as he sought permission to speak.

"You may proceed," Fanis replied, his eyes flicking toward the King.

"We are certain the original message came from Atlantis, Sire," Simos said. "Our relay station monitors all communications as ordered by Royal decree. It originated here."

The King's scowl deepened. "We sent no such message," he repeated coldly. "You will be allowed to rest and resupply, but then you must leave—all of you. Enjoy the city's offerings, but be gone by the new moon."

With a dismissive flick of his jeweled wrist, the audience was ended.

Fanis hurried down the dais and swiftly led the group away from the lush garden. Instead of returning them to the front entry or the bathhouse, he steered them down a different hallway and into a vast dining hall. "Please wait here," he instructed briefly before disappearing toward the far side of the room.

"What's going on here?" Greish asked, his voice low but tense, eyes narrowing in suspicion.

"I don't know," Addident replied, determination tightening his jaw. "But I intend to find out." He strode toward the direction Fanis had disappeared.

At the far side of the hall, Fanis reappeared, urgency in his steps. "Please hurry, follow me." Without hesitation, he pressed aside a heavy tapestry, revealing a thick wooden door set into the wall. "Hold the tapestry for me," he said quickly to Addident as he produced a small key from his robes and unlocked the door.

"Keep to the right," Fanis instructed, "and go about fifty feet. Stop there. I'll light a torch."

Silent but obedient, they slipped into the passageway. The tapestry fell back into place, muffling the world behind them and plunging them into near darkness. The cold stone walls pressed close as Greish took the lead, moving cautiously until he halted at the designated spot.

Once everyone was gathered, Fanis stepped past them to the wall and struck a flint. A flickering torch burst into life, casting dancing shadows across their faces as he turned to face them.

"I'm truly sorry for the King's reaction," Fanis said quietly, his voice laced with genuine regret. "I had hoped the meeting would have gone differently."

"Where are you taking us?" Addident asked, his eyes sharp as he glanced down the shadowed corridor.

"To someone who can help," Fanis replied without hesitation. "Please, continue to follow me. We will be there soon."

"Are we in danger?" Greish's voice was low, edged with suspicion.

"This way, please," Fanis answered calmly but without offering reassurance.

They moved steadily through the dimly lit tunnel for nearly three hundred feet, passing several heavy doors and winding through a maze of turns. Finally, they halted before a large, unmarked door set deep into the stone wall.

Fanis cracked the door open just enough to slip his head inside, eyes scanning the room. "I am alone, Fanis. Please bring them in," a calm, clear voice replied.

He pushed the door fully open and motioned for the group to enter.

Inside stood an elegantly dressed woman beside a large

window that framed a sweeping garden below. Beyond it, the island's lone mountain rose majestically, perfectly centered in the glass.

She wore a floor-length purple gown trimmed with gold, her braided grey hair tossed gracefully over one shoulder. A warm smile curved her lips as she regarded the newcomers.

"I wish to apologize for my brother's manners," she said softly, her eyes shadowed with concern. "The King is unwell, and sadly, it shows in his demeanor. My name is Dyna, and on behalf of the people of Atlantis, I warmly welcome you to our city."

Addident stepped forward and bowed deeply.

"Please rise, Addident of Romota," she said with a gentle smile. "There is no need for such formalities between us. We are both royalty."

"You know who I am?" he asked, a note of surprise in his voice.

Dyna chuckled softly, her gaze steady. "I keep myself informed of all that transpires on Earth—and as much as possible on Romota. Please, have a seat. There is much to discuss, and little time to do it."

"Thank you for your hospitality, Lady Dyna," Neiluios said respectfully.

"It's my pleasure, Neiluios. Tell me—has Neiaphi made it to Atlantis yet?"

Neiluios blinked, caught off guard. "How do you know of my daughter?"

Dyna smiled knowingly and shrugged, motioning for him to answer her question.

"Not yet, ma'am. She's with the centaurs, helping alongside her betrothed."

"That's right. She should arrive in a few days," Dyna said softly. "Now, I know you all have many questions, but please allow me to speak without interruption. Fanis, would you bring the refreshments Lya left in my antechamber?"

She paused, her gaze steady. Addident opened his mouth to speak, but she held up a hand and continued, "Now, where to begin…"

"I am a descendant of Poseidie. My family has ruled Atlantis since he founded this city. We've seen our share of good and bad kings, but by my research, the last three—my brother, my father, and my grandfather—have been the worst." She paused, meeting their stunned expressions with sober eyes. "I know it's shocking to hear me speak so harshly of my family, but corruption and greed have taken root here, and it pains me deeply."

She shook her head slowly. "It was not always this way. My great-grandfather's sister—she would have been a kind, courageous queen. But alas, no woman has ever ruled Atlantis. That, I believe, has shaped much of our fate."

Dyna's gaze sharpened. "Now, Atlantis stands on the brink of war. Your arrival has only stirred the waters further."

She raised a hand just as Addident began to speak. At that moment, Fanis returned, carrying a tray of beverages, fruit pies, and their clothing.

"I am the one who requested your people. The original message—Addident, it was you I specifically asked for."

Her eyes locked on his, steady and unyielding. "I've been watching your career closely and I am very impressed. I know you stand in the line of succession to rule Romota, but I also know the current King well. You and I both understand you would never live to see the crown under his reign."

Dyna's voice softened but remained firm. "That's why I planned for you—along with loyal officials of the right bloodlines and a large contingent of honor guards—to come here to Earth. You were to land in the land of the Pyramids, where my contacts would prepare you to take the crown from my brother."

Her expression darkened. "When the Society intercepted that message, I feared the worst. My contacts in Romota panicked when they heard you'd gone missing. They threatened my life if I didn't find you. Some among your group carry ancient, long-lost royal bloodlines—if Romota discovered that, it would be catastrophic."

"We planned to train two usurpers: one for Romota, and one for Earth. When Pythia told me where you landed, I was beyond relieved."

She glanced at Fanis. "Pythia has been watching all of you for me. I instructed Fanis to bring you straight here, but my brother learned of your arrival first. My hands were tied. Now, you are in grave danger."

"Your brother gave us until the new moon to leave," Crelian said quietly.

Dyna's eyes darkened. "His word cannot be trusted. I fear you wouldn't have made it back to your people alive. We must get you all out of the city—tonight."

"Will our ships be allowed to leave?" Addident asked.

Dyna shook her head. "Not with your people aboard. You'll have to reach Mount Cleito first. I'll arrange transportation within the moon. It's my grandmother's former summer retreat—I haven't been there since I was a child. My brother won't connect the dots; the waters are heavily patrolled, but the island outside the city is overlooked."

She gave a grim smile. "I'll send your transports out of the city and have them destroyed.

My brother will believe you all perished."

"Fanis, please escort them back to their people quietly and without incident. I'll have additional men at the docks tonight to assist with your evacuation."

She sighed. "I'm sorry this isn't ideal. I'm truly sorry you're caught in this. My brother was once a good and caring king—when he first ascended."

Dyna shook her head, sadness shadowing her eyes. "But with the threat from the Lemurians, he's spiraling into despair and paranoia. Now go. I will visit you as soon as I can."

Fanis waved them toward the hidden tunnel and slipped away, disappearing from the castle. At the ferry, six men clad in the dark blue uniforms of the Atlantean Navy stood waiting. The sight of armed soldiers caused most to hesitate, but Fanis walked forward confidently.

"Greetings, Captain Iosif," Fanis said smoothly as he

approached the men. "Greetings, Council Fanis. Are these the ones Dyna spoke of?"

"Yes. Please get them back to their ships as quickly as possible. Commander Myron, summon Aggelos's and Kimon's platoons from the barracks. You're on watch at the docks tonight—a surprise rotation by order of the king."

Commander Myron snapped to attention. "As commanded by the king."

"Stay close to Iosif; he'll see you safely out of town. Be well, Addident. May the Gods grant us a reunion." Fanis bowed deeply, then vanished before anyone could respond.

Addident turned to Captain Iosif. "If you will lead us, we will be grateful for your help in getting us safely out by morning."

Iosif's gaze was sharp. "Don't thank me yet—you're still deep within the city." With a sharp turn, Captain Iosif led the group toward the waiting ferry.

∞ 15 ∞
ESCAPE

The dinner with King Luthais unfolded exactly as Cret had anticipated. The king remained silent, his gaze steady as his commanders filled the space with polite conversation. A harpist strummed softly in the background, weaving gentle melodies through the room. Three courses were served with quiet ceremony, culminating in a fiery wine paired with a sweet, delicate pastry that lingered on the tongue as the evening drew to a close.

After dinner, they were escorted back to the captain's quarters, where guards were posted firmly outside the door.

"What are we going to do?" Tivadarios asked, anxiety threading his voice. Cret ran a hand through his hair, frustration evident. "I don't know. Pavlina?"

She met his gaze steadily. "We're at Luthais' mercy for now. All we can do is wait and see. They'll notice we're gone eventually, but I don't know how soon. I wasn't even supposed to return to Atlantis until the next new moon."

"Can we do anything for Samira or her parents?" Tivadarios asked quietly.

Pavlina shrugged, her expression tight. "I doubt it. They're being held for crimes against the crown. I'm sure their security is tighter than ours. Do yourself a favor—forget about her. She's nothing but trouble."

"Trouble? What kind of trouble could she be in? She's only—what—fourteen?"

"I started my Naval training when I was twelve,"

Pavlina said, her voice low. "Few would suspect a young woman of being a saboteur. She's probably older than you think. And perfect, if you consider it: young, attractive, but not breathtaking—enough to distract, but not enough to be memorable." She shook her head. "No, she's perfect. I want to know her motive and who she's working with. I've never heard of any groups wanting to harm the Lemurians or Atlantis."

"Aten said he was trying to stop a war between you two," Tivadarios said.

"That war has been simmering for decades. I don't see how attacking both sides would stop it," Pavlina replied sharply.

Cret shook his head, muttering, mostly to himself, but loud enough for everyone to hear. "I think that's something we need to uncover. Pythia told me Atlantis needed me—and to find the Navy. I found them, and what I see is a three-way struggle. But somehow, I don't think helping Atlantis defeat the Lemurians and stopping this unknown group is the kind of help Atlantis needs."

"How do you know?" Bal-air asked, curiosity clear in his tone.

Cret looked up, surprised by the question. "Sorry, I didn't realize I said that out loud." He stroked his chin thoughtfully. "Honestly, I don't know how I know. It's just… a feeling. Like the first time I thought I saw a centaur—wasn't sure what I truly saw, but I followed anyway."

He glanced at Pavlina, who raised an eyebrow.

"Since landing on Earth, everything's felt like that. I pieced together what happened to the criminals Romota sent here, figured out what that processing plant was doing—" He trailed off, noticing Pavlina's expression. "Story for another time."

He smiled faintly. "But this feeling keeps coming back, like I'm following my destiny or something. Like I'm meant to do this, and there's no real choice."

"It's just what I'm supposed to do," Cret said quietly, "and somehow, I always seem to know where to go and what to do when I'm doing it. Sounds strange, I know. I can't explain it."

He sank heavily onto the edge of the captain's bed with a long, tired sigh. "I just wish we had more answers than questions."

The cabin settled into a comfortable silence, everyone doing their best to rest despite the weight of uncertainty.

Around midnight, Cret lay awake on the floor, staring out the single window at the full moon. His mind raced—what now? How to reach Atlantis? Should he even try? Where was Neiaphi? Was she safe? Were his parents and sister alright?

He closed his eyes and took a deep breath, trying to push the chaos away and drift off.

Then—a soft thud at the door made him snap his head toward it. The door creaked open just a crack, and a figure slipped inside, quiet as a shadow.

Cret stayed perfectly still, but his hand instinctively slid to the hilt of his sword at his side.

The unknown figure moved silently across the cabin, stopping just beside him. Cret held his breath, narrowing his eyes to peer into the shadowy outline.

"I know you're awake," the voice hissed, barely more than a whisper. "Do not make a sound."

Cret blinked, but still couldn't make out who stood there.

"Get up slowly. Wake Pavlina—quietly, but quickly. We don't have much time."

Cret nodded, heart pounding. Pavlina had the bed; he crept over, eyes scanning her form for any hidden weapons. Then, carefully, he placed his hand over her mouth.

Her eyes snapped open, wide, and wild, as she struggled to push his hand away. As recognition crossed her face, she relaxed and nodded.

Cret gestured behind him with a flick of his head.

Pavlina rose swiftly and approached the cloaked figure, while Cret lit a couple of candles from the single one that was left burning. The mystery person stepped into the light and pulled back her hood.

"Samira, what are you doing here? How did you get here?" Pavlina asked.

Samira's eyes flashed with urgency as she met their gazes. "There's no time to explain everything now, but if you want to live and keep fighting, you have to trust me."

Pavlina stepped forward, her expression hardening. "Why should we trust you? After all you've done?" She grabbed the other woman's wrist.

Samira's jaw clenched. "Because *I will not* kill you in the morning," she smirked trying to twist her wrist free from Pavlina's grip. "The choice is yours. I hope you make the right one.

Pavlina held Samira's arm firmly but not harshly.

Cret laid a hand on Pavlina's shoulder and squeezed. "We don't have much choice, do we? What's the plan?"

"What's all the noise?" Tivadarios grumbled sleepily. He rolled over with his hands over his head. Cret nudged him with his foot. "What are you doing?" He sat up, rubbing his eyes. "Samira? What are you doing here?" He jumped to his feet.

"I'm here to help you escape if you want to come," she replied, and then leaned in, voice low but steady. "To my ship. It'll be here before daybreak. Be ready to move." As silently as she had arrived, she departed.

Cret looked around the cabin; both centaurs were awake, but neither said anything.

"How did she escape?" Tivadarios asked, breaking the silence.

"I do not know and do not care at the moment. What will you do?" Pavlina inquired.

"Hmmm," Cret thought, "I don't trust the Lemurians. I don't necessarily trust Atlantis right now, either. I think we should go with her. Let's vote on it, though." He nodded to Tivadarios and the centaurs.

Tivadarios rubbed his chin, eyes narrowed in thought. "If Samira says she can get us out, that's something we can't ignore. But I want to be sure we're not walking into a trap."

Bal-air spoke up, voice calm but firm, "We came here seeking answers and safety. If Samira's ship is the only way out, then it's the path we must take. I vote to follow her."

Myreia nodded in agreement. "We must trust each other now more than ever."

Pavlina paced back and forth in the small cabin, her hands clasped behind her back, and her head bowed. On the third trip, she stopped and spun abruptly to face Cret. "I will join you. If I remain and all of you go, I will surely be executed."

"We could knock you over the head and tie you up to give the appearance you were not with us," Myreia offered.

A smile threatened to crack Pavlina's stony expression. "I appreciate the offer, but I think I'll just come with you and watch her closely."

Tivadarios shook off his sleep and rubbed his face. "Alright, I'm in. Let's get this done before anyone else wakes up."

Cret sighed and nodded. "It's decided. We prepare to leave before dawn."

The quiet cabin was filled with a new sense of urgency—tonight, they would make their escape. Time moved slowly, but sleep evaded them all.

It felt like an eternity later when the cabin door opened, and Samira stepped inside.

"Come, we have a short window in which to escape." She gestured for them to follow her.

"What about the guards?" Pavlina whispered.

"They have been dealt with, come. No more questions." They stepped onto the deck; the guards standing watch over them were slumped unconscious on either side of the door. Other lumps could be seen around the deck. Sailors and guards rendered unconscious littered the deck all around.

Cret's eyes widened at the scene. "How did you manage this?"

Samira's lips curled into a sly smile. "We don't have much time. Follow me."

Samira led them to the railing and pointed down. "We will lower the centaurs down first; the rest of you can climb the ladder. Once on board, we will push off. Our vessel is a short distance away. We'll be on board before daybreak. Come, we must hurry."

Four sailors approached and wrapped a harness around each centaur, preparing them to be hoisted overboard. Tivadarios touched Samira's arm. She looked at his hand, then up into his eyes.

His heart started to race, and he took a deep, shaky breath before asking her, "Did you get your parents out?"

She tilted her head to one side, "Yes, they are on our vessel. Thank you for asking." Leaving his hand where it was, she returned to the task at hand.

Myreia went down first, followed by Bal-air. Once he was halfway down the side of the boat, Cret, Tivadarios, and Pavlina started down the ladder.

"Let's move out, men, row like the kraken is almost upon us," Samira said sharply.

The little boat lurched away from the larger vessel when the four oarsmen used their oars to push them away, giving them clearance to start rowing.

"Welcome to my ship, *The Flying Scarab*," Samira said with a large smile. "She may not be much to look at, but no one can catch her. Please make yourselves comfortable. We'll make landfall at midday. Get some rest, you all look terrible." She tittered, turned, and left them to fend for themselves.

Cret gestured to the main mast with his head. Everyone nodded and walked the short distance to a group of large sacks and crates stacked near the mast. "This looks like a comfortable place to rest," Cret remarked.

Bal-air grunted agreement before laying down and leaning his torso against one of the sacks.

Tivadarios stretched out beside Bal-air, letting out a long sigh as he closed his eyes. Pavlina sat nearby, carefully pulling a small blanket from one of the crates and wrapping it around herself. The gentle sway of the ship and the distant calls of seabirds were strangely soothing after the chaos they'd just escaped.

Cret stayed upright for a moment longer, gazing out at the endless horizon. The rising sun painted streaks of gold and pink across the water, promising a new day—and with it, a new chance.

He finally settled down next to Pavlina, feeling the weight of the journey ahead but comforted by the company. "We're safe for now," he murmured. "Whatever lies ahead, we face it together. I don't know what awaits on that eastern shore, but I trust we'll find a way."

The ship creaked gently as it sliced through the waves. The morning light grew stronger, warming their tired bodies as the horizon beckoned with uncertain promise.

"So, where do you think they are taking us?" Tivadarios asked.

Pavlina shrugged. "Your guess is as good as mine." She shook her head and glared at him.

Tivadarios chuckled, "That's not true, I've never seen a map of where we are, so…" he held his hands out wide. "I have no idea where on the planet Earth we are."

Pavlina sighed, deepening the glare. A tense moment stretched between them before she broke out in a throaty laugh, "I'm sorry, you're right. That was a silly comment." She took a couple of deep breaths. "Oh my. I am tired. Sorry about that attitude; you didn't deserve it. I would venture to say we'll be making landfall on the continent east of Atlantis. I know of no settlements along that coast. We'll have to wait until we get there to see what's there."

"Wise words, two-leg," Bal-air grumbled before he drifted off to sleep.

∞ **16** ∞
STRANGER AMONGST

Hepluosis paced furiously around the hut's perimeter, his heavy boots leaving deep impressions in the muddy ground. His breath came in ragged bursts, the fury burning in his eyes like wildfire. He was fuming—swinging his sword left and right—slashing everything in the tiny hut where they lost Neiaphi. "She went in here. She couldn't have just disappeared. Yet she did," he growled.

Six waited outside the hut, letting his master take out his anger on the building instead of him.

Finally, Hepluosis fell silent. He burst out of the hut, ripping the door the remainder of the way off its hinges. Getting into the small building next to a pond in the first place had taken them nearly the entire day. Hepluosis was certain he would have found Neiaphi cowering in fear once he broke in. But the building was empty, with no windows and no back door.

He stomped away from the abandoned building and sat heavily beside the fire Six had prepared. "I don't understand where she went."

"Where do we go now, sir?" Six asked hesitantly.

"We'll backtrack and try to find the group with the two men."

"Then what, sir? Just follow them?"

Hepluosis thought for a moment before answering, "No, we'll approach them. The men don't know us." Hepluosis gave a grim nod, "It's a gamble, but it's better than wandering blindly."

Six adjusted the strap of his satchel and added, "We'll need new identities." "Why? They don't know us."

"What if Neiaphi told them about us, or mentioned our names?"

"Now, why would she have done that? I seriously doubt she spoke about us or even thought about us after we left for the processing plant. But… caution can't hurt." He paused for a moment. "We will change our identities. We'll say we are lost. We were with the processing plant group and got separated from the others. Furthermore, we approached their group because we hadn't seen centaurs on this planet and hoped they knew how to get to Atlantis. Hopefully, they will allow us to journey with them or at least point us in the right direction."

Six nodded; it sounded like a solid plan. "If anyone suspects us, it could end badly." Hepluosis agreed.

They settled near the dying embers of the fire, each lost in their thoughts.

They were able to make it back to the clearing before mid-morning the following day, and picking up the larger group's trail was easy to do. Not only that, but they did not suspect they were being followed. But followed they were by two different groups. Hepluosis and Six traveled at a quick trot for the remainder of the day and most of the next before they saw Rirmell's group ahead of them.

"At least their eyes are on what's in front of them and not what's coming up behind," Hepluosis remarked.

They veered off into the woods to circle the Society's men. They also wanted to make it appear they were traveling from the east to collaborate on their story.

Just before dusk, they spotted the strange group of centaurs and humans. They slowed their horses to a walk and cautiously approached the camp.

"Hello, the camp!" Hepluosis called out.

The two men from Neiaphi's group stood up, weapons in hand. "Hello, the travelers," one of them responded.

Hepluosis plastered a large grin on his face, holding his hands out before him, "I come in peace. We are lost. We're hoping you can help us."

"Dismount and come eat with us, strangers," the other man said.

The two strangely tall humans sitting close to the fire looked at them but made no moves to stop them.

Hepluosis and Six exchanged glances, then slowly dismounted. The campfire flickered, casting long shadows over the tall humans' features, which were oddly unfamiliar yet oddly serene.

As Hepluosis stepped forward, his smile never faltering, Six scanned the area, alert for any sign of danger. The air was thick with tension, but the invitation to eat suggested a temporary truce—or at least a chance to learn more.

Hepluosis nodded politely. "Thank you. We would appreciate your hospitality."

The group shifted slightly, and the humans and centaurs alike seemed to relax just a bit. It was clear this gathering was no ordinary band of travelers—something deeper and more complex was at play here.

The centaurs stood next to the four horses tied on a string line. Hepluosis handed his reins to Six and walked toward the fire.

"Thank you for the invite. We're starving. It's been days since our last meal," Hepluosis said, trying to sound desperate.

The two men shared a look. "Well, sit and warm yourselves, share your story for a meal," the taller man said. "My name is Andonis, this is Pelagios."

"It's a pleasure to meet you, my name is Heplin, and this is my friend Sexton."

"Where do you hail from?" Pelagios asked.

Hepluosis paused for dramatic effect, "I'm hesitant to

say. We're strangers in these parts and our story might be taken the wrong way. We only approached because we saw centaurs. We haven't seen or heard of centaurs in these parts," he said slowly with as much caution as he could put into his voice.

The two men glanced at the rest of their companions; the strange, tall humans said nothing, the women only nodded, and both centaurs shrugged their shoulders. "Do you know of Romota?" Pelagios asked quietly.

Hepluosis jumped up and quickly stole a glance at Six tying up their horses, "You've heard of Romota? I don't know you. Who are you?" He narrowed his eyes, trying to look suspicious.

Pelagios held his hands up, "Relax, friend. I'm from Romota. I work on a transport ship. I, uh, crash landed during a routine trip. We…" he gestured to his group, "will be going to Atlantis after we help the centaurs to meet up with some other new arrivals to this planet. I assume you were originally with them. How did you get separated?"

Hepluosis relaxed his shoulders. "My family was sent to the processing plant. We were rescued, but Sexton and I became separated from the others while hunting. I'm so glad I found you. May we travel with you?"

"I don't see any harm in that. This is Lyric, Justic, and our Agarthan friends. They are helping us get to Atlantis. They, uh, know a shortcut, but we have a small detour first."

"That's fine with me. I just want to get back to my family as quickly as possible." Hepluosis smiled, relief softening his features.

Andonis once again brought up the rear the next day, keeping a watchful eye on their new companions riding in the middle of the group. Heplin and Sexton had spoken little since their arrival. Andonis had pressed them with questions—simple things, really—like when they had last seen the other group from Romota, and whether they knew Chartis. Heplin always answered quickly and with confidence.

So far, his story held together. Yet Andonis still did not trust him. Something about Heplin felt off—too confident for someone who was supposedly lost on a strange world, searching for a city few even believed existed. Shalendra, however, showed no concern about Heplin and Sexton joining their journey to Agartha. Andonis could not shake his doubts.

After camp was set up for the evening, he sat beside Shalendra. "What's troubling you?" she asked.

"Are you sure no harm will come by showing us the path to Agartha?"

"Do you mean to harm my home?" she asked with a grin.

"Of course not, you know who I am speaking about."

"I know." Her smile grew, "Don't worry. The pathways to Agartha are well guarded. Only an Agarthan can access them. If they tried on their own at a later time, the access would be invisible to them. We have nothing to fear."

Andonis frowned, "If you say so. I still say we use caution around them." "Why do you distrust them so?"

"Neiaphi never mentioned them."

"I would venture to say she didn't mention most of them." Shalendra studied Andonis carefully. "We can't ignore our instincts, though."

Andonis nodded. "That's true. But she told me about all those close to her age. Heplin looks her age, and Sexton, not much older. I think she would have mentioned their names in passing, and if not her, then one of the others. From what I've learned, all the children taken to the processing plant were much younger. Only Cret and Hepluosis were close."

Shalendra thought briefly before speaking, "What about Sexton?"

"Hum, I don't know, he's quiet. Heplin called him his friend, but they don't act like friends, more like servant and master." Andonis's face lit up. "Hepluosis has a servant named Six. It must be them!"

"The names are similar," she agreed, "But even if it is

them, I still see no harm. All are welcome in Agartha."

I guess," he said absently.

Hepluosis was growing impatient after three days of riding with this strange, mixed company. Andonis distrusted both him and Six. Pelagios spoke with them the most, but his knowledge extended only to Romota; of Earth, he knew very little. The centaurs kept apart, while the women whom Hepluosis had begun calling the Tall Ones remained mostly among themselves.

At last, the Tall Ones halted and turned to face the others. Their hands were lightly clasped before them, small smiles playing on their lips.

"We're here," Arryn announced.

Hepluosis looked around where they stopped. They were in a small clearing with nothing visible except trees and rocks. "Where is here exactly?" he asked.

Arryn said nothing. She approached a large tree and placed her hand on a large, gnarled knot. The tree started to shimmer; the bark of the tree peeled away like it was nothing but a door. "This way, please."

The Agarthan stepped into the gaping hollow of the tree. As she crossed the threshold, light bloomed within the darkness, revealing a wide ramp spiraling downward. One by one, the others dismounted and led their horses inside. The soft glow along the ramp brightened as they descended, casting long, shifting shadows on the walls that seemed to pulse like living things. The horses shuffled uneasily, their hooves clicking against the stone.

Hepluosis motioned for Six to go ahead, leaving only Andonis behind him. When his turn came, he paused at the entrance and glanced back, meeting Andonis's sharp, unreadable gaze. The silence between them stretched, heavy with suspicion neither voiced. Hepluosis leaned out, peering toward the opposite side of the tree.

"Some illusion they have here, don't you think? He asked Andonis. Andonis gave no reply—just a curt jerk of his chin, urging him forward. Scowling, Hepluosis tugged his horse down the ramp.

Deeper and deeper they traveled, "Where are they leading us?" he asked Andonis. "Fine, you don't know either. Nothing to be ashamed of. How well do you trust those two?" Still no response.

Hepluosis sighed and shook his head. "Trust is a luxury we can't afford right now," he muttered under his breath.

Andonis finally spoke, voice low and cautious, "We watch each other. That's all the trust we need."

The ramp curved sharply ahead, opening into a vast cavern bathed in shimmering light. Stalactites hung from the ceiling like crystal chandeliers, their surfaces glittering in the glow. At the center of the chamber stood a massive cylindrical object of gleaming metal. Pelagios rushed forward, his hands trailing reverently across the smooth fuselage, his face alight with wonder. "How did you get this craft in here?"

"Craft? That's not a ship!" Hepluosis said.

"It most certainly is, young man," Arryn replied evenly. She pressed her palm against the surface, and a patch of metal lit up, revealing a keypad inscribed with strange symbols. Her fingers danced swiftly over it, and with a hiss, a door slid open on the vessel's side. A ramp extended smoothly to the cavern floor. "If you would be so kind," she said with a graceful sweep of her hand, "stow the horses in the rear, you'll find ample stalls prepared. Then, please, take your seats. I apologize in advance for the lack of appropriate accommodations for you." She inclined her head politely toward the centaurs.

Justic huffed, "That's fine, just treat us like horses."

Lyric punched him on the shoulder, "Ignore him. Any place is fine with us."

"I was only joking," Justic complained, rubbing his shoulder.

Hepluosis chuckled softly at their banter, though a knot of unease tightened in his stomach.

One by one, the horses were led up the ramp into the stalls at the rear. Their hooves rang against the metal flooring, the sound oddly out of place in the cavern. The centaurs inspected the cramped quarters with clear distaste, but kept their silence.

Andonis buckled his seatbelt after Pelagios showed him how. He studied the craft's interior—the walls, floor, and chairs were all a pristine, almost blinding white.

The low hum deepened into a steady vibration that seemed to pulse through every surface. Andonis's heartbeat quickened, matching the rhythm of the engines.

Shalendra took her place before a long counter, her fingers gliding across the illuminated surface as she adjusted the controls with practiced ease. Pelagios leaned forward, his eyes alight with both wonder and nervous energy. Then the wall before them flickered once and transformed into a view of the cavern outside.

"That's a screen. The ship is still sealed, and the screen allows us to see what is in front of us," Pelagios explained.

Andonis nodded, feigning understanding. Strange technology had crossed his path before, but this—this was by far the most unnerving.

The vibration grew stronger, sending a tremor through his seat. His knuckles whitened as he gripped the armrests. Swallowing hard, he braced himself against the unfamiliar sensation.

"The sensations you feel may seem strange at first," Arryn said calmly. "Just remain seated with your buckles fastened. We will be in Agartha soon."

"How are we going to fly there from inside this cave?" Pelagios asked.

"I never said we were going to fly there," Shalendra replied.

The screen went black, and the vibration increased. Suddenly, it felt like Andonis's stomach leaped into his throat with a plummeting sensation.

Lyric cried out at the sickening feeling.

"Hold on, you'll feel weightlessness next, and more diving. We are traveling extremely fast. We'll be in Agartha soon."

"Where in the world is Agartha?" Heplin called out, his voice quaking.

The feeling of weightlessness turned out to be somewhat pleasant compared to constant falling. Unfortunately, they continued to fall again far too soon.

Abruptly, the craft stopped vibrating and humming. A bell chimed, and then all was silent. Andonis opened his eyes, unsure of when he shut them, and looked around. The screen in front of them again showed him what was outside the ship.

It was a world unlike anything he had ever seen before. They appeared to be underwater. Brightly colored fish swam around their ship like it was nothing but another fish. Coral and seaweed littered the floor of the sea. With a great splash, their ship broke through the water's surface to reveal a sky, complete with clouds and a small sun. They rose higher into the air and then jetted forward with blinding speed.

The water blurred by them, and soon land could be seen. A city sprawled out in front of them. Tall, thin buildings were arranged in neat rows, and roads and paths ran between each building.

They approached a large meadow just on the city's outskirts, several ships just like theirs lined up along one side.

Shalendra guided her craft and set down next to one of the other ships.

"We have arrived. Welcome to Agartha. We can stay as long as you like," Shalendra said. "Come, let me show you around."

Everyone exited the subterranean ship, marveling at the bright, vivid colors. The grass was emerald green, and the leaves on the trees varied in shades of green and purple. The sky, although a very pale blue, seemed crisp and clear. Puffy white clouds hovered in the sky, unmoving. The warm sun bathed the land in a gentle light—bright and comforting, yet never harsh on the eyes. Birds of various kinds hopped across the mossy ground and flitted from branch to branch, their calls echoing softly.

The air was rich with the fragrance of blossoms,

mingled with the tang of the distant sea. One by one, they stepped out into Agartha, the ground beneath their feet a soft carpet of mossy green and silver that cushioned every step.

Andonis turned slowly, taking it all in. "It's like… Earth, but perfected."

Shalendra smiled. "Agartha is a harmony of science, nature, and spirit. This is what the world above could have been, had it chosen differently."

"Everything looks so peaceful," Lyric said quietly. "It is. We are quite proud of our civilization here."

"Don't you fear inviting others to live here?" Andonis asked.

Shalendra looked at him, puzzled, "Why would we? All are welcome here. We may live here and care for the land, but we do not own it. It is part of the Earth, just like any land on top."

Hepluosis shook his head, "One day, those who mean you harm will come here. You should be more selective."

Arryn waved her hand at them, "Nonsense. Come, there is much to see."

Shalendra led them toward the city gates, wide archways carved from ivory stone, guarded not by soldiers, but by serene figures in flowing robes. They bowed as the group passed, their expressions kind but unreadable.

Inside, the city buzzed with quiet activity. People of every shape, size, and color moved about with purpose, none rushing, none idle. Children laughed as they played in the numerous parks, while adults consulted glowing displays.

Arryn led them through a softly winding path lined with towering flowers that shimmered faintly in the breeze. The city of Agartha revealed itself slowly—not with towering walls or bustling chaos, but with quiet grace. Structures rose elegantly from the ground, shaped like petals, shells, or smooth stone, all seemingly grown rather than built.

As they walked, the sounds of a tranquil civilization wrapped around them—music without instruments, laughter without sharpness, language spoken in harmony with the wind.

"There is no currency here," Shalendra explained as they passed a market plaza where people traded goods with smiles and nods. "No titles, no politics, no ownership. We contribute what we can, and take only what we need."

Hepluosis scoffed softly, drawing a glance from Six. "Sounds like a dream. Dreams don't last."

"You are wrong," Arryn said gently. "If everyone has the same dream, the dream will go on forever."

∞ **17** ∞
ᘞILLA

As they broke free of the surf, a strange blend of relief and sorrow washed over Neiaphi. Overhead, the full moon hovered above the restless sea, casting silver light across the endless, heaving waves. The sky lay clear and vast, and on every side stretched nothing but open water.

"Where are we?" she asked Asan. "We're west of Atlantis."

"Shouldn't we fly higher? Won't someone see us?"

He shook his head. "No ships come this far. Only sea serpents and krakens roam these waters."

"How long until we reach Atlantis? Do you know if my family's made it yet?" Eager for a glimpse of land, Neiaphi scanned the horizon through the ship's screen. "I'll see if we've received any information," Asan replied.

"How?" she asked.

"We have eyes everywhere."

He placed his fingers on the panel before him, and a cluster of smaller screens flickered to life. One showed a harbor crowded with tall sailing vessels, their white sails billowing in the night wind. Another revealed a torch-lit palace rising against the darkness, its flames casting restless shadows across the stone.

"There!" Neiaphi pointed to the center screen. "Who are those people? Why are they moving through the forest at night?"

Asan tapped the image, enlarging it. A great column of

people and animals moved swiftly beneath the trees, their faces drawn tight with fear.

"There's my father, and Addident!" she exclaimed. "Where are they going?"

Summoning a map of Atlantis, Asan gestured to a coastal point on the far side of the island. "My guess is here. That structure may serve as a refuge. Look" he pointed to a glowing green dot creeping across the map, "that's your people."

"I'll take you there and stay with you until they arrive." "Thank you, Asan. I truly appreciate it."

"We've been walking for hours," Alexa said quietly.

Greish took her hand in his. "I'm sure we'll be there soon," he said, trying to reassure her. "I hope so," she whispered, her voice trembling with a sniffle.

"What's the matter?"

She shook her head, avoiding his eyes.

"Come on, you can tell me," he said gently, giving her hand a light squeeze. She looked up at him, unshed tears glistening in her eyes. "I'm worried." "About what?"

"Everything." She swept her hand through the air in front of her. "I've dreamed of seeing the great city my whole life, only to find it cruel and dangerous. Neiaphi is off, Gods know where, helping centaurs I never even knew existed. And now she's learned that Cret is still alive; he might even be on his way here.

"And poor Andonis… I've known him all my life. I don't want him to be hurt. But more than anything, I want my best friend to be happy. Now, we're trudging through a jungle in the middle of the night, heading to some royal hideaway— just to keep the King, my King, from killing us. I mean… what shouldn't I be worried about?" Her voice rose, tight with anger and panic.

Greish gently squeezed her hand and guided her off the path. Wrapping his arms around her waist, he held her close.

"I don't know what lies ahead, Alexa. But whatever comes, we'll face it together. I'll protect you with my dying breath."

"Let's hope it doesn't come to that," she muttered with a shaky huff.

He laughed softly, pulling her in tighter. "I love you. That's all that matters. Whether we end up in Atlantis or anywhere else… as long as we're together, I'm home."

"I love you too," she said, her voice cracking. "I just can't stop worrying." "I know. You care too much. It's one of the reasons I love you."

A fragile smile touched her lips, though tears still shimmered in her eyes.

He leaned down and kissed her—softly, slowly. Alexa melted into him, and for a fleeting moment, the fear disappeared.

"Better?" he whispered, breathless. She nodded, unable to speak.

"Good. Come on—we don't want to be left behind."

A grand villa loomed in the distance, perched on a steep cliff that overlooked the restless sea. Its many balconies jutted boldly over the roaring surf, as if defying the waves that crashed far below, sending spray into the night air. Torches ringed the villa and lined the winding path that climbed toward it.

Addident and Neiluios halted, their eyes fixed on the imposing edifice. "Is there a problem, sirs?" Captain Iosif inquired.

"Just wondering who might be expecting us," Addident replied.

Captain Iosif chuckled. "Fear not, Addident. You are in safe hands now. My Lady sent word ahead of your arrival."

In the villa's courtyard, a portly man with a broad, welcoming smile awaited them. "Welcome, Addident, welcome, Neiluios. I am Faidon. Please, lead your people around to the back. We can house many within, though not everyone will fit inside." He bowed deeply and motioned them toward a side entrance.

Beyond the archway, an ornate garden unfolded. Fountains leapt and shimmered among stretches of emerald grass, while flower beds, sculpted trees, and trimmed shrubs punctuated the landscape. The garden extended from the villa's stone steps to the cliff's edge, and off to one side stood another sizable building, set apart and safe from the precipice.

"Your animals can be stabled there," Faidon said, gesturing toward the second building. "And if you gentlemen will follow me, I'll show you the accommodations prepared for you."

"Greish, see to the animals," Addident ordered. "Undercaptain Seleo, keep everyone here for now. Captain Hue, you'll come with us."

The three men stepped away from the group and followed Faidon into the villa.

"I must admit," Faidon said as they entered the grand hallway, "I was quite surprised to learn we'd be receiving guests. It's been many years since any of true importance stayed here."

"No one comes here?" Neiluios asked, frowning. "Why keep the place staffed and maintained?"

"Oh, it's still used—just not by royalty," Faidon replied with a shrug. "Council members, the occasional general seeking peace… but no one of your rank has stayed here since Lady Dyna was a young girl."

He turned down a corridor and beckoned them onward. "Please—this way."

Faidon guided them through the entryway into the villa. The ground floor opened into three immense chambers: a sprawling kitchen with multiple hearths, a grand dining hall, and an opulent reception hall. The second floor contained a dozen stately rooms, while the third—equally vast—was reserved solely for royalty.

"Captain Hue," Addident commanded, his gaze sweeping the interior, "use the gardens and reception hall to establish quarters for your men. Neiluios, assign all mid- and low-ranking officials to the second floor. High-ranking officials will remain here."

Faidon hesitated, then bowed. "Forgive me, Aristos Addident, but these rooms have been reserved for your family. Only royalty may stay here."

"You were instructed to follow my orders, were you not?" Addident asked calmly. Faidon nodded slowly.

"Were you also told why I was brought here?"

Another nod. Slower this time. "You were summoned from our home world to usurp Lady Dyna's brother… and restore order to Atlantis."

"Good," Addident said, a faint smile touching his lips. "Then let me begin by abolishing the very idea of royalty. No more kings. No more monarchs."

Faidon blinked, clearly unsettled. "What should I call you, then, Aristos?"

"Addident is fine. But if you must use a title—let 'Aristos' be the highest." "Very well, Aristos Addident. I will see your orders carried out."

He bowed again, deeper this time, and left swiftly.

"Going to change the whole system?" Neiluios asked.

Addident nodded, pacing slowly across the richly furnished chamber. "It's long overdue. The systems that once governed Romota generations ago no longer function. I've had time to reflect on Lady Dyna's words as we walked here. Dynasties are steeped in corruption and deceit. The people deserve a voice in their own lives. Rules are necessary, yes— but they should be shaped by the community, not imposed from above."

Neiluios frowned. "The masses may embrace your vision, but those in power won't."

Addident's smile was grim. "Change is frightening, that much is true. It will not come overnight. Civilizations are not forged in a single day. But it must begin." He drew a slow breath, then turned toward the door. "Come—we all need rest. Our people are weary."

Asan landed the ship a short distance from the large villa.

"Why not land out front?" Neiaphi asked, glancing toward the building. "Surely people in Atlantis are familiar with technology by now."

"Asan shook his head. "Some are, some aren't. We have to err on the side of caution.

With tensions rising, we don't want to draw unnecessary attention—or create trouble."

"That makes sense," she replied, stepping down the ramp with Nexus following close behind. Cypress bounded ahead, alert and eager.

"I'll come with you," Asan said quietly. "There are many things I need to discuss with Addident."

"Halt! Who goes there?" a familiar voice called from near the villa.

Neiaphi threw back her cloak. "Neiaphi," she called out.

"Neiaphi? Impossible! Where did you come from? How did you get here?" Greish stepped closer to the torchlight, his face lighting up.

"It's so good to see you again, Greish. How's Alexa?"

"She'll be fine now that you're here. Where's Andonis?"

"He's fine. It's a long story."

"Well, come on—let's get you and your friend inside."

As Neiaphi entered the villa's garden, a sharp cry rang out. "Neiaphi!" Altesse sprinted toward her daughter, wrapping her in a tight embrace.

"I'm so glad to be back," Neiaphi whispered into her mother's hair. "Where's Andonis?" Altesse's eyes were filled with concern. "He's fine. Where's Father?"

"Inside, with Addident."

Neiaphi glanced toward the villa. "I have news. Mother,

this is Asan."

Asan bowed deeply. "Altesse, daughter of Tessa, it is an honor to meet you."

"How do you know me?" Altesse asked, her eyes narrowing slightly.

"Let's gather everyone first," Neiaphi replied, her tone calm but urgent.

"Did I hear someone say Neiaphi?" Neiluios called from the villa's entrance as he stepped outside. His eyes widened when he saw his wife and daughter approaching. A radiant smile broke across his face, and tears welled in his eyes as he rushed down the steps. He gathered Neiaphi into his arms, lifting her in a joyful embrace and spinning her around.

"I'm so glad to be home," she whispered.

"How did you get here?" he asked, concern mixing with joy.

"Father, this is Asan—from Agartha. He carries urgent news for you." Neiaphi cast a glance toward the villa. "Where's Addident? He must hear this as well."

"He's inside. Come on."

Once within the villa, Neiaphi made the introduction. "Addident, this is Asan of Agartha.

He brings us grave news."

Addident inclined his head. "Neiaphi, good to see you. Welcome, Asan. I wish I could offer you more hospitality, but we've just arrived ourselves."

Asan bowed deeply. "I require nothing. I am honored to be in your presence, Aristos Addident—third in line for Romotian throne and soon rightful leader of the Atlantean people."

Addident's eyes narrowed thoughtfully. "You possess vast knowledge. Please, let us sit and hear your tale."

"Asan bowed again. "It would be my honor. Please gather all your advisors and their families."

The reception hall seemed to grow smaller as more people pressed inside. High-ranking officials, with their wives and children above the age of twelve, claimed the seats nearest the roaring hearth. Overhead, candlelit chandeliers swayed gently, stirred by a faint breeze drifting in through the open windows that overlooked the garden. Mid- and lower-ranking officials crowded into the remaining space, their subdued murmurs filling the air.

"Asan," Addident whispered, nodding in encouragement.

Clearing his throat, Asan began. "Thank you all for gathering here. First, I would like to express my deepest sorrow and apologize for the hardships you have endured. Your journey has been long and arduous… and I fear it is not yet finished. My name is Asan. I am from Agartha. Before addressing the trials ahead, I would like to share a brief history, if you will allow me."

Addident's voice followed with steady conviction. "Please do. We have been deceived at every turn."

Asan nodded solemnly.

"Many generations ago, we Agarthans arrived on this world in search of a new home. We traveled far and wide, encountering primitive beings wherever we went. Unwilling to interfere with their young civilizations, we sought a place untouched by life on the surface. We found it beneath your feet.

"This planet—like many others—is hollow within, but far from lifeless. There, deep below, we made our home. And though we lived apart, we became guardians of this world, occasionally venturing to the surface when needed.

"On one such occasion, we discovered a new people had arrived—refugees from another star system—who chose to settle here. They called themselves the Lemurians. Peaceful and conscientious, they interfered little with the native species still in their infancy. Their presence was not considered a threat. But Agarthans live far longer than Lemurians, and in our time, many of their generations had already come and gone.

"A short time later—though only by Agarthan standards—another group arrived: the Atlanteans, led by Poseidie. Unlike the Lemurians or us, they were ambitious, aggressive, and driven by commerce. They built massive processing plants and began strip-mining the planet's surface, extracting and selling resources to other civilizations across the cosmos.

"Though these resources are, in theory, renewable, the rate at which the Atlanteans harvested them was not. The planet's balance began to falter. In time, the Lemurians reached a decision: they believed it was their duty to remove the Atlanteans from this world."

A sharp, collective gasp rippled through the room.

"Will the Agarthans stop them?" someone called out, voice cracking with urgency. Addident's frown deepened—he recognized Japster's voice among the crowd.

"We Agarthans are a peaceful people," Asan replied, his voice calm but firm. "We do not possess warfare technology, nor do we wish to. What we offer is not battle, but survival.

"We have opened our doors to all beings not native to this planet—centaurs, and others who were brought here from Romota. The Lemurian King, Luthais, has formally declared war on every creature of Romotian origin. However…" He paused, letting the silence stretch. "He has agreed to one condition: those who leave the surface and come below with us will be spared. No pursuit. No retribution. Safety."

He drew a breath before continuing.

"There is also a third faction—one that believes both Lemurians and Atlanteans will destroy this planet if left unchecked. They have worked tirelessly to prevent war… but their interference has only driven the conflict closer to the brink."

A murmur spread through the room.

"Who are they?" someone asked, leaning forward.

"They call themselves the Kemites," Asan answered. "They arrived around the same time as the Lemurians and have remained mostly in the shadows—until now."

"Are they not a threat?" someone asked warily.

"As of now, no," Asan replied. "They've remained isolated within the Kemi River Basin and have shown no signs of aggression."

"That gives us much to consider," Addident said, rising to his feet.

But Asan raised a hand, gently motioning for him to sit. "That was only the beginning. Please, there is more."

Addident hesitated, then slowly lowered himself back into his seat.

"Now, let us come to the present," Asan continued. "Lady Dyna—whom I believe you met briefly?" Addident nodded. "She has been working closely with the Kemites. It was she who sent a message to Romota, requesting your arrival."

A murmur passed through the room again.

"Romota," Asan began, his tone hardening, "is in turmoil—and not because of enemies beyond its borders. Its conflict is internal. The monarchy now teeters on the brink of collapse, not from rebellion, but because the rightful bloodline was displaced long ago.

"In time, that lineage dwindled until only a single child remained—a girl. To secure her survival, she was married into a powerful but ruthless family, one driven more by ambition than loyalty. She bore a son, but fearing for his life amid the treacherous court, she had him secretly switched at birth. Her fears proved justified: before his first year, the child thought to be hers was mysteriously killed. Whether it was truly her son who died has been lost to time.

"Her husband, consumed by greed and power, forced her to name one of his illegitimate sons as heir. From that moment, the throne of Romota has been ruled by descendants of a lie."

"What happened to the rightful heir?" someone yelled.

"He was raised in plain sight," Asan answered, "never knowing the truth of his birth. Only in recent years—through relentless study and advances in genetic tracing—has his identity been uncovered. Yet the bloodlines here are just as fragile as those on Romota. Addident, through your father's line, you are kin to King Titern—the very man who sent you here. But through your mother's blood, you descend from Poseidie.

"Over generations, those lines have been mingled with Earth-born humans. Though efforts were made to preserve them, purity was never absolute.

"The time has come for new leadership—leadership strong enough to restore peace. The Kemites have already reached out to King Luthais. They have made their terms plain: if King Thodoris is deposed and a worthy successor rises, they will end hostilities. That is where you come in, Aristos Addident."

At this, Phebis, Addident's wife, turned to him and gave a resolute nod. "He accepts," she declared.

Addident turned to her, his voice low with tension. "Phebis, shouldn't that be my decision?"

"No," she replied calmly, but with steel behind the word.

She rose, not just to her feet, but onto the chair itself, elevating her voice and her presence above the crowd.

"By a show of hands," she called out, "who among you believes Addident should take the mantle and lead us into a new way of life?"

There was a long pause. The room was thick with uncertainty. For most of them, their opinions had never been asked—let alone counted. But slowly, one hand rose. Then another. And another. Until the majority stood in silent agreement.

Phebis gave a curt nod. "Thank you. And to those who did not raise their hands—please, tell us why."

Japster pushed his way through the crowd, his voice cutting through the murmurs. "I don't think he's the right choice for the position."

Neiluios stepped forward, eyes fixed on him. "And why not?"

Japster shrugged, avoiding eye contact. "I'm not sure. I just... someone else would do better."

"Who?" Neiluios pressed.

Japster shrugged again, frustration flickering across his face. "I don't know."

"We've voted," Neiluios said firmly. "The majority has spoken. It's decided."

"That's not fair!" Japster snapped. "What if there's someone better out there?"

"Then bring them forward," Neiluios challenged. "We'll hold another vote."

Japster scowled but pushed his way back through the crowd, disappearing into the gardens.

Phebis turned to Addident, her voice steady and sure. "Then it is decided, my husband—you will lead us into a new era. An era where every voice counts."

Neiaphi spoke softly from nearby, her eyes thoughtful. "And what of the other royal line?"

Alexa, seated beside her, gave a slow nod.

"The Line will reveal itself when it's ready," Asan said calmly.

"Addident, Neiluios, may I speak with you and your families in private? A few trusted guards as well, if you don't mind."

"Of course," Addident replied and then turned to address the assembly.

"That will be all for now. We will hold further meetings in the days to come."

Addident led Asan and the others to the third-floor suites. Undercaptain Seleo and his son, Lieutenant Greish, stood guard outside, while Captain Hue joined them inside. Neiaphi pulled Alexa along, determined.

"I don't think Alexa should be here," Neiluios said quietly.

Neiaphi tightened her grip on Alexa's hand. "She's as much a sister to me as anyone. I want her here."

Asan cleared his throat, his voice cutting through the

tension. "The child may stay. All of you need to hear this." He let the silence stretch before continuing, his tone low and steady. "It's time you knew the truth about the missing royal line."

"But you said the heir would reveal themselves when the time was right," Alexa said, her voice tinged with uncertainty.

"That's true," Asan replied, "but the heir can't step forward if she doesn't even know who she is."

He turned toward Neiluios's family, his gaze unwavering. "Altesse, your mother carried the true royal bloodline—and through you, it passed to your four children: Neiaphi, Icarus, Annas, and Praxis."

Pausing, he locked eyes with Neiaphi. "Neiaphi, you are the rightful heir to the Romotian Throne."

Neiaphi's mouth fell open as shock rippled across her face. She glanced at her parents, their expressions mirroring her own disbelief.

"I don't want to rule," she said softly. "I want to stay here—on Earth."

Asan knelt before her, his voice gentle but firm. "No one is saying you must return. No one is forcing you to reveal yourself. If you choose, you can stay here and forget Romota entirely. But if you do, you must never share this knowledge with your children. They can never know—can never find out. As long as your line lives, Romota will keep searching."

Neiaphi swallowed hard and nodded. "That is what I will do."

"But what if they find out anyway?" Neiluios asked, his voice edged with concern.

"Then living among the Agarthans will be your safest refuge," Asan replied calmly.

Neiluios considered this for a moment. "Pythia, the Oracle, told me my sons would found a new civilization—a mighty one that would bring order and technology to the world."

Asan nodded slowly. "I've heard the prophecy. Only

time will tell whether it's a blessing or a curse. Stay here as long as you wish. We watch over you… well, on our time, at least."

Neiaphi tilted her head, curiosity breaking through the tension. "You said you live far longer than we do. How long, exactly?"

A faint smile crossed Asan's lips. "Almost a thousand years." "How is that possible?" Neiaphi asked, eyes wide with disbelief.

Asan spread his hands in a subtle gesture. "My race has its own ways."

Altesse stood and stepped closer, tilting her head up to meet his gaze. "Why did you mention Icarus?" she asked softly.

He gazed down at her, placing a gentle hand on her shoulder. "I'm sorry—I forgot you didn't know."

Slowly, he lowered himself to one knee, taking both her hands in his.

"Icarus is safe. The wolver sent to you before you left for Earth was meant to approach your entire family, to reveal who you truly are—and to help you all go into hiding on Romota."

He shook his head, sadness flickering in his eyes.

"But they chose someone young—valuing speed and stealth over experience and calm. She was startled when your husband came home. And when you screamed, her nerves broke, and she fled."

"So…" Altesse hesitated, her voice barely above a whisper. "What does that mean?"

"Icarus is alive—and still on Romota."

A sob broke free from Altesse. Neiaphi wrapped her arms tightly around her mother, and together they crumpled to the floor. Neiluios placed a comforting hand on Altesse's shoulder, squeezing gently.

"Will he be returned to us?" Neiluios asked, his voice thick with emotion.

"That has been debated," Asan said quietly. "But most

believe he should stay on Romota—to be prepared to take the throne…"

"But I thought you said I was the heir?" Neiaphi asked, looking up at Asan, tears of joy streaming down her cheeks.

He nodded solemnly.

"Yes, you are the rightful heir as the eldest. But no woman has ever held the throne.

Icarus would rule in your place until your eldest son comes of age." He paused, letting the weight of it settle.

"You would claim the throne on behalf of your family and appoint your eldest brother as King Regent—with you as Queen Heir. If you choose, you could rule alongside your brother."

Altesse looked up at Neiluios, a silent plea in her eyes. He gently patted her shoulder. "We want our son here beside us," Neiluios said firmly. "If what you say is true, it will be some time before he can claim the throne. Let him be with his family—and decide his own fate when he's ready."

Asan was silent for a moment, then nodded.

"I will arrange for the centaurs to bring him here in ten moons."

A sob broke free from Altesse as she trembled with joy. "My baby boy is coming home!"

Asan nodded again and rose.

"Now, I must depart. Shalendra will arrive soon with the centaurs. I wish you all the best of luck."

Asan stood and left before anyone could protest.

"What did he mean—arriving with the centaurs?" Addident asked, turning to Neiaphi.

"When I was with Lyric and Justic," Neiaphi began, "we traveled to the places where their mother was born—and where she fled, time and again. Enormous wolves attacked them, destroyed their communication machines, and slaughtered most of her people. We finally found a working communication device and made contact with Romota.

"They're sending a transport ship in ten moons—for anyone who wants to return with them," Neiaphi explained.

"That's when we met Asan and Shalendra. The centaurs—and us—seem to have three choices: stay on the planet's surface, return to Romota, or go underground with the Agarthans. From what little I saw, it's beautiful down there."

"You went down there?" Alexa asked, eyes wide with wonder. Neiaphi smiled faintly. "It was a shortcut, I suppose you could call it."

"What happened with Andonis?" Altesse asked gently, her voice filled with concern.

Before anyone could answer, Addident smiled and interrupted, "This is where I leave you. Have a good night. We'll talk more tomorrow."

With that, Addident, his family, and Captain Hue quietly exited the room.

Alexa sat beside Neiaphi, taking her hands in hers. Altesse gathered Annas from Net, while Cleop cradled Praxis.

Neiluios paced the floor. "Is he okay?"

"The last time I saw him, yes," Neiaphi replied. "It happened after we met the centaurs.

You've all seen Lyric? She's… a beautiful creature. Well…" Her voice faltered.

"He didn't," Alexa said sharply, her hands flying to her mouth.

Neiaphi held out her hands. "Only with his eyes. I can understand why he'd be fascinated—maybe even attracted—but I couldn't help feeling angry. And then to learn that Cret still lives and is on his way here… it was too much. I released him from our agreement."

Suddenly, the door slammed open, and Greish stormed in. "And he just let you end it?" he almost shouted.

"Greish, were you listening?" Alexa shot back, scowling.

"Hard not to," he snapped, gesturing angrily at the thin walls. "He just accepted you coming here without him—and letting him go?"

"I didn't give him a choice," Neiaphi admitted, "but no—he didn't want to be released. I told him I needed time to think. I'm so conflicted. How can I be in love with two men—and then get mad at him for letting his eyes wander?"

She hung her head, voice trembling. "I just have to see Cret again before I can decide."

"You're torturing yourself, child. Andonis is a good man," Net said softly.

"I know, Net. I do. But Cret and I… we have a connection I can't explain."

Cleop leaned forward, eyes curious. "What did The Oracle tell you?"

"She said my future isn't mine to choose—that others' paths will shape it," Neiaphi said quietly.

"That's not fair," Alexa said, frustration creeping into her voice.

"I agree," Neiaphi replied softly. "So far, Andonis has been the one deciding my path. All I can do now is wait and see what comes next."

∞ **18** ∞
𝒦EMITES

Cret woke with a start. Sailors rushed across the deck, their voices rising in a tangle of urgent shouts as the first mate snapped orders.

At the helm, Pavlina stood beside the captain, laughing as she clapped him firmly on the back. Nearby, Tivadarios remained curled into a tight ball, his rumbling snores oblivious to the chaos around him.

But it was the centaurs who seized Cret's attention. Their eyes were locked on the horizon, unblinking, as if they alone had seen what was coming.

"What's out there?" Cret asked as he stepped closer.

Bal-air pointed ahead. "Land."

Far on the horizon, a faint line marked the meeting of sky and sea.

"Are you sure that's land, and not just an optical illusion?" Cret asked.

Bal-air snapped, "I'm certain."

Myreia laughed and punched Bal-air lightly on the shoulder. "Forgive him. He hates the water. At this point, I think he can smell land even from this far away."

Bal-air scowled, rolling his shoulder. "I can not. But that is land." Myreia chuckled and shook her head.

Leaving the centaurs behind, Cret walked to the bow of the ship.

"Good morning," Pavlina greeted him warmly.

"Good morning. Is that land we see?" he asked,

pointing past the centaurs.

"Good eye," the captain said. "We're still a ways out—depends on the winds."

"Where are we headed?"

"You'll have to ask Samira." The captain glanced around the deck, then called out, "Hey!" to his first mate before striding over.

"So, what now?" he asked Pavlina.

She shrugged. "I guess we need to find Samira." Together, they set off to search the ship for their rescuer.

Deep in the ship's hold, they finally found Samira poring over maps in the mess hall.

"Where are you taking us?" Pavlina asked, skipping pleasantries.

"Good morning," Samira replied without looking up.

Pavlina crossed her arms, waiting. When Samira remained silent, her patience snapped.

With a swift motion, she drove her dagger into the table beside Samira's hand.

Samira didn't flinch. At last, she looked up. "We'll be making landfall here," she said, tapping a spot on the map.

Pavlina studied the map. "There's nothing there," she said flatly.

"You'll just have to wait and see," Samira replied, her tone guarded.

Cret frowned. "What's with all the secrets?"

Samira's eyes flicked toward him, narrowing. Her expression tightened with irritation before she exhaled sharply and sank into a chair.

"Fine. Sit."

"Cret, you and your people have endured much since arriving on this planet. I'm truly sorry for that—but the worst is yet to come. We stand on the brink of a war unlike anything this world has ever seen—one that will shake the very foundations of our civilizations.

"As you've no doubt noticed, most of this planet remains primitive—by Romotian standards, and by much of the universe's as well. My people want to keep it that way—at least for the next couple thousand years. Earthlings are still young, still finding their footing in the cosmos. They need to learn to stand and walk before they try sprinting up a mountain."

"You're not making any sense," Pavlina snapped.

"I am. Atlantis and Lemuria—they are doomed to destroy each other. Nothing anyone does can stop it. Believe me, we've tried. That's why we're changing course. Our mission now is to save as many lives as possible—and to help rebuild what remains once the war is over."

"Are Atlantis and Lemuria really that bad?"

Samira shook her head. "Not entirely. The Lemurians were once a peaceful people, helping many across this world. The Atlanteans, however, were selfish, taking whatever they wanted, whenever they pleased. If Lady Dyna ruled instead of her brother, I doubt we'd be facing this catastrophe. But that isn't the case. And that is why Addident was called here."

Cret's face lit up in surprise. "Whatever for?"

"To assume the crown and become King of Atlantis. He's related to Poseidie."

"Does he know this?"

"If they made it to Atlantis and spoke with Lady Dyna, then yes. But I don't know if they've arrived yet," Samira admitted, lowering her head. "I just hope your people are safe."

Cret swallowed hard, his thoughts racing to his parents, his sister, and Neiaphi's family.

Please be safe, he prayed silently.

"If you're not going to stop the war…"

"Unable to stop it," Samira interrupted firmly.

"Okay, if you can't stop it, what's the plan?" Cret asked.

"We're working with another group—peacekeepers called the Agarthans. Together, we're gathering good, decent people and moving them out of harm's way."

"Where to?" Pavlina pressed.

"Either somewhere safer on the surface... or underground, with them."

"Underground? They live in caves?" Cret's eyes widened in disbelief.

"Underground, yes. But caves? No. The center of this planet is hollow—and full of life."

"Impossible!" Pavlina exclaimed.

Cret shook his head. "No, it's possible. Are they helping both sides?"

Samira nodded. "Yes. There are good people on both sides who want a better life."

"How can I help?"

Samira studied him for a moment. "Why do you want to?"

"I spoke with Pythia. She told me I must go to Atlantis—that I'm needed there more than ever. This is my path. I need a ship, and I'll do whatever it takes to save as many as I can."

Samira smiled warmly. "I can help with that."

"If I'm never on a boat again, it'll be too soon," Bal-air grumbled, high-stepping through the surf.

Myreia trudged alongside him, water dripping from her.

Once her hooves touched solid ground, she threw her arms wide, spun in a circle, and laughed. "Nothing feels better than steady earth that doesn't move beneath your feet."

Bal-air smirked. "I always knew you hated the water more than I do."

"The difference is, I keep my thoughts in my head." She laughed, then bolted across the beach in a carefree sprint.

Cret smiled as he and Tivadarios hauled the rowboat onto the sand. "Looks like someone's glad to be back on land."

Bal-air grinned. "You have no idea." Then he was off,

chasing after Myreia.

"Centaurs," Tivadarios muttered, shaking his head.

"What now?" Cret asked Samira.

The boat scraped against the shore, and Samira leaped out with practiced ease. "This way." She led them inland.

The rocky shoreline soon gave way to sweeping grassland. Shielding his eyes from the bright sun, Cret scanned the horizon. "Are you sure this is the right place? I don't see anything." Samira only smiled, silent as she pressed forward.

The ground rose gently beneath their feet, the landscape shifting as the hours passed—sandy mounds dotted with low-growing trees appearing on the horizon. Still, she walked with unwavering purpose.

Finally, they reached a large rocky hill. Samira broke the quiet, "This way. We're almost there."

They climbed to the top and stopped beside a sturdy tree.

"Where to now?" Bal-air asked, scanning the area.

Samira glanced at Bal-air with a stoic expression, offering no reply. She knelt at the base of the tree and brushed aside leaves and debris until a lever came into view. Without a word, she pulled it.

A soft metallic click echoed from beneath their feet.

"Boys, if you could give me a hand," Samira said, gesturing toward the ground before the tree.

Cret crouched for a closer look and spotted two metal rings embedded in the earth. He shrugged, grasped one, and Tivadarios took the other. Together, they heaved upward, uncovering two heavy metal doors with a staircase descending into darkness.

Without hesitation, Samira stepped onto the stone stairs and disappeared below. "After you," Cret said, motioning for the centaurs to follow.

Bal-air narrowed his eyes, his face etched with suspicion. Cret sighed softly, shook his head, and began down the stairway. Tivadarios and Pavlina followed close behind, and after a hesitant pause, the centaurs reluctantly trailed after them.

The stairway lay cloaked in darkness, the only light spilling from behind as they descended. Samira led the way, her sandals scraping softly against the stone, the sound echoing through the tunnel. Gradually, a faint glow appeared ahead, accompanied by the gentle murmur of voices rising from below.

At last, the stairway opened into a vast chamber filled with people, some huddled around tables piled high with papers, others bent over consoles glowing with screens.

Samira's footsteps were quiet but purposeful as she crossed the room to a large table at the center. Twelve empty chairs circled it, but two men stood at its head, dressed in crisp uniforms. They moved small figurines across a detailed map, their faces set with concentration.

Cret, Tivadarios, and the centaurs hesitated at the foot of the stairs, exchanging uncertain glances. The low hum of voices and the shuffle of feet filled the air as they wondered where they were meant to go next.

After a pause, Samira looked up and gestured for them to approach, Pavlina already at her side.

Samira bowed her head to the two men. "This is Overseer Khati, commander of the ground forces who protect the lands near the Chief Sea and the Alta Ocean, and Admiral Asa, commander of the naval fleet." Both men inclined their heads.

"Asa has a vessel that can take you to Atlantis," she continued, "but the journey will be dangerous."

Overseer Khati's gaze was steady as he spoke.

"The seas around Atlantis are treacherous—not only because of natural hazards but also because of patrols and traps set by those loyal to the current regime."

Samira's eyes met Cret's with quiet determination.

"This is your chance. If you are willing to take the risk, we will help you reach it safely."

Cret swallowed hard, the weight of the mission settling

on him.

"I don't want to endanger anyone's life. But I feel I must reach Atlantis as soon as possible."

Admiral Asa nodded solemnly. His deep, commanding voice carried authority.

"Our vessel is fast and well-armed. My sailors are always ready for adventure—and I have long wanted an excuse to see the Great City. We will get you there."

"Thank you, sir. I wish there was some way I could repay you," Cret replied earnestly.

"The journey itself is payment enough. Rest up—we set sail in two days."

∞ 19 ∞
𝔄GARTHA

Lyric stood on the balcony, gazing over the broad pond that stretched before the house where she had spent the night. The air was warm and still, the pale, stationary sun was slowly brightening and casting its light across the landscape. She glowered; her eyes following the trees and bushes whose leaves glimmered in the glow—yet not a single breeze stirred them.

With a sigh, she rolled her shoulders and stretched her neck. Nights here felt strange—more like the faint glow of dusk than true darkness. She and the others barely slept. The Agarthans assured them they would adjust in time, but Lyric remained unconvinced. It wasn't only the brightness of night that unsettled her. There were no seasons here, no wind, no storms. Clouds gathered lazily during the brightest hours, and rain fell only every two or three days. Beyond that, the weather never changed.

It might have been a relief to live without harsh winters or scorching summers, but to Lyric it felt unnatural—wrong.

She shook her head, trying to clear her thoughts, yet still couldn't decide where they should settle—or what advice to give the others. Romota looked promising in the pictures she'd seen, but without visiting, she couldn't be sure.

"No closer to a decision, I see," Justic said, stepping quietly up behind her.

She shook her head again. "What are you thinking?" she asked.

He stopped beside her, folding his arms across his chest. "This place is nice, but I think Romota would be better for us."

She turned to face him, surprise flashing across her features. "Why do you say that?"

He shrugged, unease flickering in his eyes. "Everything here feels foreign—the weather, the light, even the creatures. I've never seen a pegasus before. I don't know what to make of it."

She hesitated. "This place is closer to home than Romota… at least in distance."

"That's the problem," he replied. "I can see most of us choosing to settle here, but the lure of the surface being so close might be too tempting."

Lyric nodded slowly, her decision finally forming. "Then I'll go to Romota, and urge the others to follow."

The next day, everyone was back onboard the Agarthan subterranean vessel.

Andonis and Pegalios had been unusually quiet since their arrival underground, and Lyric hadn't seen much of them during their short stay. Heplin and Sexton peppered the Agarthans with questions, and had Shalendra take them on a more private tour of the city.

"What do you think of this place?" Lyric asked the four two-legs.

Heplin and Sexton exchanged a glance, and Andonis shrugged. Pelagios, however, spoke up. "It's beautiful—and strange—down here. I'm glad I got to visit. I can't wait to tell my family about it. Have you decided where you want to settle yet?"

She nodded firmly. "Romota," she said confidently.

"Really? That's a surprise," Pelagios replied.

"Why's that?" Justic asked.

"I thought this place would appeal to you—closer to home and all," Pelagios said.

Lyric snorted. "That's the problem. It would be too tempting not to return to the surface."

"Just make a law banning return trips. The Agarthans would have to transport anyone who tried, and they'd simply refuse," Pegalios suggested.

"We wouldn't say no," Arryn said firmly, glancing back at them from the front of the ship.

"You wouldn't even if the centaurs passed a law forbidding return to the surface?" Pelagios pressed.

Arryn shook her head. "We don't keep anyone here against their will. If someone requests transportation back to the surface, we provide it gladly. To do otherwise wouldn't be moral. Agartha is not a prison. And though we built these vessels, they are available to everyone whenever they wish."

Pelagios sighed, shaking his head. "Well then, I suppose Romota it is. How many do you think will want to stay here?"

Lyric sighed. "I hope none," she said flatly. "What about you, Andonis?"

At the sound of his name, Andonis flinched. "Um, what did you say?"

"I asked—have you decided? Do you know where you'll go?"

"Atlantis," he replied, closing his eyes.

Lyric opened her mouth to press him further, but Justic's sharp look stopped her. She closed her mouth and nodded silently.

Shalendra stepped onto the ship as the centaurs excused themselves to prepare for the journey.

"Is everyone ready?" she asked, settling into her seat. "I didn't expect so many sad faces. Is everything all right?"

Silence hung in the air for a moment. Shalendra's gaze moved from one face to the next, her expression softening with concern.

At last, Lyric spoke. "We'll be fine. Just trying to take it all in—this place is… overwhelming. I'm ready to speak with the centaurs. Let's go."

Shalendra nodded and turned her attention to the console before her. Moments later, the ship gave a soft hum and lifted into motion, buzzing gently as it carried them swiftly through the underground sky, back toward the surface.

∞ 20 ∞
CENTAURS

The trip back to the surface was as strange as their descent. They were pressed into their chairs as the craft surged upward, then weightless for a few moments before being forced back again. To everyone's relief, they soon emerged in another cave—though none of them knew exactly where.

Shalendra and Arryn kept silent during the journey, refusing to reveal where they would surface. Shalendra led the way up the inclined ramp without a word. When they stepped out of the cave, everyone shielded their eyes against the blinding sun.

Lyric glanced around, Andonis standing beside her. "The sun looks strange now," she murmured. "We were gone barely more than a day, yet everything up here feels different— foreign, unwelcoming." She shook her head.

Andonis rested a hand on her shoulder. "It's because you've already chosen where to live. You've let go of this world, both on the surface and below. Your heart knows it, and now your eyes see it too."

"Thank you, Andonis." Lyric nodded, still staring at the glaring sun. Slowly, she lowered her gaze to meet his. "When will you leave for Atlantis?"

"As soon as I see you and the centaurs that will follow you off to Romota, I will head to Atlantis."

"Then what will you do?"

Andonis let out a heavy sigh, running a hand through his hair before shrugging. "I don't know yet. I need to see her one last time—to try and apologize again. After that, the choice will be hers."

Lyric nodded. "I have a proposal for you."

Andonis looked up at her, a look of hope in his eyes.

"If…" she paused, searching for the right words. "If you find yourself with nowhere to go, I invite you to come with us."

Andonis's eyes opened wide. "To Romota?" She nodded.

He hung his head and rubbed the back of his neck. A breeze stirred the canopy, rustling the leaves, and several small birds fluttered down to perch above them, chirping loudly.

"Thank you for the offer," he said, "but what would I do there? I doubt my skills would be of any use on Romota. To them, I'm nothing but a primitive."

"I'm not asking you to live among the other two-legs," Lyric replied. "I'm asking you to stay with us. We'll be strangers to everyone on that world. Even among other centaurs, we may seem backward. And before I met Cret, I had never even seen a two-leg. Having you with us would help.

"I've already asked Pelagios to help us settle in, but he may not have much time with his duties to the crown. Even so, you could act as our bridge—as our ambassador. You'll be a stranger, yes, but so will we. Don't decide now. Just keep the thought in your heart."

"Thank you, Lyric." Andonis closed his eyes and lifted his face to the sun, letting its warmth wash over him.

"It is time to continue," Shalendra announced, breaking the calm atmosphere.

"Do you know where we are?" Justic asked, walking beside Arryn.

"We will be at the location of your winter gathering very soon," Arryn said.

Lyric stopped short. "That far west?" she asked, frowning. "Only the Sage Clan will be there. Our own clan is the furthest east—we should really start there." Lyric remarked.

"Fear not. All those who gathered for the winter gathering are still there."

"Truly? Then why did we separate from the others and not travel together?" Justic asked.

"We didn't learn this until we returned to Agartha," Shalendra explained. "Otherwise, we would have journeyed with them. I'm sure they would have enjoyed seeing our realm."

"Why haven't they dispersed?" Pelagios asked. "I thought the gathering lasted only a few weeks."

"Usually it does," Shalendra said. "But this year the storms were harsher than usual, and wolver activity has grown. They've stayed together for safety."

"The Wers?" Lyric asked quietly.

"Yes. But don't worry. From what we have heard, no lives have been lost. The clans are protecting each other and holding off the threat. But it is only a matter of time before food becomes scarce, and they have to start expanding their reach to find resources. We must hurry."

"Then shouldn't we have arrived closer to them?" Lyric asked, her voice edging with panic.

Shalendra smiled at her moments before a voice called from the shadows.

"Halt! Who goes there?"

Shalendra stopped and raised her hands. "Friends, we come in peace and bring help for your current predicament."

"Come forward," the gruff voice said.

Lyric and Justic stepped in front of the two-legs. "Davic, is that you?" Justic asked.

"Justic? Lyric?" Davic emerged from the trees, eyes wide. "Where have you two been? Everyone has been searching for you—and for the others who left with you. The Sage Elder is still upset about it."

"It's a long story," Lyric said. "I'll explain everything soon. Can you take us to the Elders?"

"Why are you traveling with six two-legs?" he asked.

"Again, that is a long story and best told only once."

The Sage elder was in the main gathering area, waiting for them. Her white eyes stared straight ahead, and her face had a deep scowl.

"Why have you returned?" she asked as they approached.

Shalendra stepped forward and bowed at the waist. "Thank you for seeing us so quickly."

The Elder turned her sightless gaze on Lyric. "Why have you returned?" she asked again.

"I came to warn everyone here of a great danger that is fast approaching," Lyric said.

The Elder's expression hardened. "And what became of the two-legs you helped escape?" she asked, dismissing Lyric's warning.

"I helped him reach his destination."

"You defied me. You and all those who helped you? Where are the others?"

"Two have continued with the two-legs to assist them further. The others will be here shortly," Lyric said with her head held high. "Now, I must speak to all here. We are in grave danger. We have to flee. I will show you where…"

"ENOUGH!" The elder yelled. "Take them away. I will hear no more out of them."

"We will be heard," Justic stepped forward, unslinging his club from his back.

"Now you threaten me?" The elder's head snapped back.

"The only thing we are threatening is closed minds. We will be heard," Justic countered.

"You will not speak to me in such a manner. I may not be the elder of your clan, but you are within my territory, and that places you under my authority. No one will listen to your lies. You have allied yourselves with the two-legs." She sneered, gesturing toward Shalendra, Arryn, Pelagios, Heplin, Sexton, and Andonis. "From this moment, you are forbidden to speak to anyone. Your punishment will be carried out at sunrise."

"And what is this punishment?" Shalendra asked.

The elder's glare sharpened. "Lyric, Justic, and the others you claim will soon arrive shall be banished. As for you six—and any other two-leg brought here—you will be put to death."

Her words shattered the silence. The onlookers erupted in angry cries, voices rising in outrage. Lyric and Justic pushed forward, protesting the elder's decree.

"Silence!" the elder screeched. "I will have silence. Take them away! There will be no more talk of two-legs or of the dangers this child has imagined. The only danger we face is the Wers surrounding us…"

Her voice trailed off, fading into the uproar, as two male centaurs seized Lyric and her companions and led them from the gathering.

"Where are you taking us?" Justic demanded. His question was met with silence.

Lyric glanced around, frowning. They weren't being led toward the clearing where Cret and Tivadarios were housed. Instead, they were being taken deeper into the forest.

"Where are you taking us?" she demanded.

"Quiet," one of the escorts whispered.

Lyric and Justic shared a look and then nodded to their companions to continue following.

When they were finally deep enough that no voices from the gathering could be heard, the escorts stopped and turned to face them. The one who had spoken before folded his arms across his chest, while the other stepped forward and inclined his head.

"Forgive our silence," he said. "We had to get you away from the gathering as quickly as possible."

Lyric studied the two strangers in silence. One was taller than any centaur she had ever seen, his honey–chestnut coat gleaming beneath the light, flaxen hair falling in loose waves, and piercing blue eyes that seemed almost too vivid. The other bore such a striking resemblance to Justic that he could have been his twin.

"What's going on?" she asked.

"The Sage elder is not thinking clearly," the second centaur replied, his tone grim. "Ever since she laid eyes on your necklace, she has been obsessed with finding you—and the two two-legs you brought here. She refused to let the gathering conclude. Then the Wers arrived, forcing us to remain in this place." He shook his head in frustration.

The taller centaur scowled but answered. "From what we've learned from others of her clan, she harbors a deep hatred of your ancestor. Her brother was left heartbroken when she fled, and she has carried that bitterness ever since. I don't know exactly how she means to take that anger out on you—but whatever she's planning, most of us do not accept it. In truth, we had all hoped never to see you again."

Lyric snorted and shrugged her shoulders.

"Why have you returned? And with even more two-legs," the chestnut centaur said, his scowl deepening.

"I would prefer to tell as many as I can all at once, if possible."

The chestnut centaur nodded his head. "Go and discreetly gather the others. Meet in our usual place. My name is Eon. Come."

The night sky was pitch black, a heavy shroud of clouds smothering the moon and stars. The meeting place chosen by Eon lay far from the Sage Clan and the crowds still gathered for the Winter Gathering. Slowly, in pairs and trios, centaurs emerged from the darkness to join Eon, Lyric, Justic, and the six two-legs. Once all who were expected had arrived, a small fire was kindled beside a babbling brook, its voice drowned by the thunder of a nearby waterfall. The roar of the water carried far, masking footsteps and whispers alike.

Clusters formed around the fire, hushed voices weaving through the night as they waited for the meeting to begin.

"Thank you all for coming," Eon said finally.

"Why are we here, Eon?" demanded a black-coated centaur, stamping a hoof against the earth. "We risk discovery every time we gather like this."

"I know that better than anyone," Eon replied, his tone sharp. "But you all know why we're here. Lyric has returned. And you know what the Sage Elder intends for her—and for Justic." Every centaur nodded, and a few grunted in affirmation. "I, for one, wish to know why she has returned. Sage Elder will not listen because it matters not to her. I have assembled us to hear her words." He took a step back and gestured for Lyric to speak.

Lyric took a couple of steps closer to the fire and bowed her head for a moment to still her thundering heart.

"Thank you," she began, her voice low but firm. "I know what it costs you to be here. When I left the Winter Gathering and chose to help the two-legs I brought before the Elder, I didn't yet know why. Only that it mattered. Since then, I've learned what threatens us all—and I've found the solution."

Murmurs broke out and slowly grew into a quiet roar.

"Enough!" Eon said in little more than a whisper, but loud enough for all to fall silent once more.

"We have numerous threats, as do others on this planet. As some of you may know, we do not come from this planet. Those we left behind have been trying to reach us for some time and wish to see us return home."

"What about the threats?" An angry voice asked.

"We have two groups that wish to see our removal from the planet. The Wers…"

"That's nothing new. We've conflicted with them for generations," someone interrupted her.

"… and a group of two-legs known as The Society," she continued.

"All two-legs wish our destruction," a voice called out.

"Not all!" Lyric shot back, folding her arms across her chest. "A new group from our home planet has arrived. The two-legs—Cret and Tivadarios, the ones I aided—are part of that group. The Society seeks to drive them from this world, to erase them. The Society is trying to rid this planet of them. Pelagios…” she pointed to him, gesturing for him to step forward, “is also from our home planet. With their help, we have found missing technology that our kind had used to keep in contact with our King on Romota…”

“We have no King!” someone spat.

She inclined her head solemnly. “We do not have a king here because we already have a king on Romota. To crown another in this place would have been an insult to him. But that is not the point.” Her voice grew firmer. “The point is this: we stand at a crossroads. Three choices lie before us—but only one, in my heart, feels like the path to survival. Still, I will present them all, and each of you must decide for yourselves.”

A wave of murmurs rippled through the gathering, but Lyric raised her voice above them.

“Enough! Listen well. The first choice is to remain here, as we always have. But know this—the threats from the Wers and the Society will only grow stronger, and I fear that if we stay, our people may one day be wiped out entirely. The second choice is going to be difficult to understand.” She paused to compose her thoughts. “This world is hollow, its heart filled not with emptiness, but with life. The Agarthans— those who dwell below—have invited us to live among them. They brought us there,” she gestured toward Justic and the others, “and it is beautiful. Peaceful. A safe haven.”

She drew a deep breath before delivering the final choice. “The third is to return to our true home. A transport ship will come for us, to carry us back to Romota. This… is the path I believe we must take.”

Eon frowned, stepping forward. “Truly? I would have thought living with the Agarthans the wiser course.”

Lyric nodded. “I thought so as well, at first. And those who choose that path will be welcome. The Agarthans would never deny anyone the freedom to return to the surface. But up here, the danger grows too great for us to endure. Still, the choice is not mine to make—it belongs to each of you. Speak freely among yourselves and with the others at the gathering. At sunrise, I will depart. Those who wish to choose the second or third path must be ready then. If you choose to remain, I wish you luck and strength." She bowed her head and took a few steps back.

A large group was slowly gathering as the sun cast a rosy glow across the sky. Lyric counted heads as they mingled. There appeared to be members from each clan, as well as every member from a few of them. The most notable exception was from the Sage Clan – it didn't appear a single member was present.

Eon cleared his throat loudly, drawing all eyes to him. "Thank you all for assembling so quickly and being open-minded. You have all heard the story Lyric has shared with us. We leave at once and with haste."

Many heads nodded, and as one, everyone fell in behind Lyric and Shalendra, but they didn't get far.

"Traitors!" The Sage elder snarled.

Eon held up his hand to halt everyone. "Please step aside, esteemed elder," he said in a clear and unwavering voice.

"You are going nowhere," the elder spat. "Take them—bind their hands and legs. We will deal with their crimes one at a time." The elder ordered the four centaurs with her. Three held clubs in their hands, and one had a bow, but the arrow was not drawn. No one moved. "Don't just stand there!" She yelled. "I said, restrain them!"

A voice rose from among the crowd, firm and resolute. "We vastly outnumber you, Elder. We will not be stopped. We are leaving. It is what all centaurs should do."

"Leave? Where are you going?" she asked.

"Most of us will be returning to Romota," an older female centaur said, coming to stand beside Eon.

"You, child? You would abandon your own mother?"

The female bowed her head. "You have led us well, mother. But times have changed. We need to leave this planet, and now we have the means to do so. Come with us?"

"I will bow to no king," she replied with a scowl.

Eon shook his head. "Then stay and die at the hands of the Wers or the Society." He shouldered past the elder and her four guards. No one tried to stop them.

∞ 21 ∞
ATLANTIS

The small, sleek vessel sliced through the calm waters with unnatural speed. Cret and Tivadarios stood at the bow, watching a large mountain growing in the distance.

"That, my boys, is Mount Cleto," Admiral Asa said as he and Samira approached. "I haven't seen any Predators," Samira commented.

Asa gave a short nod. "We've been fortunate so far. But make no mistake—they are out there. Atlantis doesn't patrol this side of the island as tightly as the main entry."

"That doesn't sound smart," Tivadarios remarked.

"I agree with you." Asa nodded his head, clasping his hands behind his back. "Atlantis has gotten complacent during King Poseidon Thodoris's rule. His sister Dyna has been helping us and leaks information to us whenever she can," Asa said.

"Why is the king's sister helping you?" Cret asked.

"The royal line has been rotting under paranoia, leading to one poor decision after another," Asa replied evenly. "Dyna would make a wise ruler—fair, steady, strong—but Atlantis will never accept a queen. It was she who arranged for Addident and others to be sent here. You were all meant to land near the Kemite River. King Thodoris was to be removed, and Addident installed as the new king."

"King Addident?" Cret asked with his eyes wide. "That has a nice ring to it. But the Society intercepted the message, and here we are."

"Exactly," Samira agreed. "We'll take you to the Summer Villa and you'll wait there. Hopefully, the others from your group will make it there before long."

"Won't we be discovered at this Villa?" Bal-air asked from where he was lying. Asa shook his head. "No. It was Thodoris and Dyna's grandmothers' residence. Generals and visitors use it for recreation, but Dyna has reserved it for Addident's arrival currently."

"Predator off the port side!" The sailor in the crow's nest yelled, ringing a loud bell.

"Battle stations, men," Asa called out. "Engines at the max. We need to outrun them. Excuse me." He politely excused himself and headed to the helm.

Cret's gaze drifted to the mast rising above the waves in the distance. The larger ship sliced through the water with effortless speed, its bulk bearing down on them like a predator on the hunt. Movement near the top of its mainmast caught his eye. Sailors worked quickly, hauling down the purple-and-gold flag. At the base of the mast, more crew scrambled in a flurry of activity. Slowly, a new standard unfurled and climbed skyward—a black flag trimmed with purple fringe.

"They know who we are, men!" someone called out. "Get the scarab bolts ready, no holding back!"

Cret's pulse quickened. He glanced at Samira. Her knuckles whitened against the railing, her lips pressed into a thin line.

"They know who we are," she said.

"I heard that. What does that mean?"

"When Atlantis tangles with the Society, they use technology that is superior to the Society, but still not considered alien. However, when they face us or the Lemurians, they use technology very foreign to this planet."

"That seems strange to me. If they didn't hold back against the Society, they could eliminate the threat."

She shook her head. "They fear the Society capturing their tech. That would be disastrous for the planet."

Cret nodded, turning his eyes back to the much closer

Atlantean Warship.

"You and the others should get below deck. You'll just be in the way. If it comes to hand-to-hand, you'll know."

The first cannon shot thundered across the sea, erupting in a tall plume of water just off the starboard side. The four companions ducked below deck, the echoes still rumbling through the timbers. Tivadarios rushed to a porthole to peer out.

"I'm no expert on naval warfare," Bal-air drawled as he crossed to the opposite wall, joining Cret and Myreia, "but I'd wager that's the worst place you could stand right now."

"Didn't think about that," Tivadarios murmured.

Cret gave him a crooked smile and clapped him on the back. "I'm sure the Kemites have this under control."

"What if they don't?" he asked.

Cret glanced at the Centaurs. "You can both swim, right?"

Myreia nodded.

Bal-air growled. "I can if I have to," he said sharply.

"We might just have to," Cret replied grimly.

Cannon fire thundered across the waves, each blast followed by the explosive splash of water as projectiles crashed into the sea. For several long minutes, the two vessels exchanged fire without finding their mark. Then the first hits landed. The Kemite ship shuddered violently, timbers groaning under the strain.

Shouted orders rang out above deck, muffled by the thick oak boards overhead. A new sound joined the din—a deep rumble that made the floor tremble beneath their feet. The noise rose into a piercing whine, sharp enough to set their teeth on edge. Cret felt the hairs on his arms stand upright an instant before a blinding light flared through the portholes, followed by a thunderclap so powerful it rocked the ship from side to side

"That must be the scarab bolt they mentioned," Cret remarked.

"Electrical canon?" Tivadarios asked.

"That would be my guess."

Blast after blast was fired along with the more traditional catapult-style cannon projectiles. The Kemite vessel rocked, shook, and quaked with each impact. The four passengers below deck were unaware of the action and lost their footing due to the sudden motions. Bal-air growled in frustration and even screamed at no one in particular that he wanted off the blasted craft before he perished with it.

As the sun set, the battle persisted, neither side seemed to gain an edge over the other, until suddenly everything stopped. The ship swayed with the gentle motion of the wave swells, and now the only sound that could be heard was the water slapping against the hull, along with the creaking and moaning sounds of a seemingly deserted ship.

They shared a concerned look before nodding to one another and heading to the main deck.

The crew was still present, but no one was moving. They were frozen in place, their legs, arms, and facial expressions in unnatural poses for someone not moving. It was like the entire crew had been turned into statues.

"What's going on?" Bal-air asked.

Cret didn't reply as he jogged over to the Admiral. "Admiral Asa?" Cret asked, touching the man on the shoulder. He didn't move.

"Cret," Tivadarios said. He stepped in front of the Admiral and waved a hand in front of his face.

"I don't know," Cret answered the unasked question. "What manner of sorcery is this?" Myreia asked.

"Not sorcery, that I'm sure of. But I have never seen anything that can do this," Cret replied.

Bal-air stood at the railing, staring across at the Atlantean vessel, just a stone's throw off the port side. Both ships lay broadside to each other, yet no one moved—save for the four of them. Bal-air's eyes, however, were not on the human statues. His gaze was fixed on eight arcs of lightning, suspended in midair, frozen as they leapt between the two ships, each poised to strike its mark.

"How is this even possible?" he muttered.

A sudden gurgling sound rose from the water between the ships, startling them all. Cret's eyes widened as a small silver cylinder broke the surface, emerging from the surf. Its smooth hull glistened, catching the glow of the frozen lightning. None of them moved; every gaze was locked on the strange vessel.

"What is that?" Myreia asked quietly.

"I'm not sure," Tivadarios answered. "I hope it's friendly."

Bal-air snorted. "I doubt it."

Without a sound, a panel on the side of the vessel slid open, spilling a brilliant light across the four bewildered watchers. Instinctively, they raised their hands to shield their eyes.

Cret narrowed his gaze, straining to make out what lay beyond the glare. At last, a figure emerged—a person whose face remained hidden in shadow, framed by a halo of blinding light.

"Be at ease, friends," the woman said. "We are here to rescue you and take you to your families."

"You know who we are?" Cret asked.

"Yes, now please come with us if you wish to survive." She turned to reenter the vessel.

"Wait!" Tivadarios almost yelled. "We can't leave all these people here to die."

The woman turned to face them again, her features still masked. "There is nothing we can do for them. Fear not, however. I do not think these people will perish this day. Come now. Our device cannot keep them frozen for much longer. Please hurry." She gestured down to a ramp that had appeared at some point.

"Come on," Cret said. Bal-air and Myreia walked carefully across the ramp, almost eagerly at first. Cret was about to start across and then stopped. Tivadarios was walking away. "Darios, what are you doing? We need to leave."

"Not without Samira," he replied flatly. He marched up

to her and gingerly touched her shoulder. She didn't move. With a quick movement, he scooped her up in his arms and jogged back to Cret. "Now, I'm ready to leave."

Cret shook his head and gestured for him to cross the ramp before him. "I hope she doesn't kill you for this."

"That's a risk I am willing to take."

Cret could actually hear his scowl. As soon as Cret was aboard the cylinder craft, the panel behind him slid silently closed.

"Please take a seat. We will be on shore very soon. Centaurs, please follow me. We have more comfortable accommodations for you over here," the tall woman said. Cret looked at her closely. She was taller than him and slender, wearing a flowing white dress, and her platinum blonde hair almost seemed to shimmer.

Cret and Tivadarios made their way toward a cluster of seats, several already occupied. At the control panel sat another slender woman, dressed in a gown much like the first woman's. Directly behind her, two men were seated—one familiar, the other not. Farther back, in the last row, two more figures sat with their heads turned away.

The unfamiliar man in the first row rose and stepped forward. "Greetings. Welcome aboard," he said with a broad, toothy smile.

"Thank you. So, where did you all come from?" Cret asked, accepting his outstretched hand.

"Originally or just now?" the man asked.

"Pegalios, it's good to see you again," Tivadarios said. Slowly, he lowered Samira into one of the seats and buckled the belt around her.

"Likewise. I'd like to introduce you both to Andonis. Andonis, this is Tivadarios and Cret."

Andonis's back stiffened. "Nice to meet you both," he said through gritted teeth.

Cret nodded as they clasped wrists. Andonis squeezed Cret's wrist harder than necessary.

"I've heard a lot about you, Cret. Never thought I'd

meet you, though."

Cret squeezed Andonis's wrist in return. "I've heard a little about you, but if you're here, where's Neiaphi?" Concern laced his words.

"We parted ways a few weeks ago. She was taken directly here while I was assisting Lyric and Justic."

Cret glanced over to where the centaurs were taken. "Are they here?"

"No, they are waiting at the rendezvous location. We located the missing technology and contacted Romota. They are sending a transport. It will arrive in about nine moons," Andonis reported.

Cret nodded. "That's good news. Where were you two headed?"

"Atlantis—to join up with the others. Everyone who was not assigned along the way is waiting at some villa."

"We also found two more of your group that got lost along the way," Pegalios said.

"Oh, who?" Cret glanced over to the other two men. *Strange,* he thought, *they haven't greeted us.*

"Heplin and Sexton," Pegalios replied.

"Who?" Cret and Tivadarios asked at the same time. Both men in question looked up.

"Hepluosis? What are you doing here?" Cret asked, his eyes wide.

"Hello, Cret. Funny meeting you here," Hepluosis said sweetly. His smile was full of hatred and contempt.

"Hepluosis?" Andonis stood, whirling to face the two impostors. "I knew it!"

"Gentleman, please have a seat. You can speak more later," Shalendra said, taking her seat at the control panel. "We will be at the villa in just a few minutes."

"A few minutes?" Tivadarios asked. "How fast does this vessel go?"

Shalendra smiled but gave no answer. A soft chime echoed through the cabin, and a screen flickered to life above the control panel. Outside, the two warships suddenly roared back into motion. The eight lightning arcs, frozen only moments before, struck their intended targets with an ear-splitting crack and a blinding flash.

Just as quickly as it had appeared, the strange silver vessel slipped back beneath the waves. An eerie silence filled the cabin as they dove beneath the Kemites' ship and then shot forward, cutting through the water at staggering speed.

The quiet broke when Samira jolted awake with a startled cry. Tivadarios caught her by the shoulders, keeping her from leaping to her feet. He leaned close, whispering something softly. Her eyes widened, lips parting as if to speak, but no words came. Slowly, she gave a small nod, then glanced around. When her gaze met Cret's, he offered her a grin but said nothing. She nodded back faintly, though she didn't return his smile.

They reached the distant shore within only a few minutes, just like she said they would.

"Come along, gentlemen. We have much to discuss. Your families have been offered the chance to live with us, and I must learn how many are willing," Shalendra said.

The villa lay ahead of them, perched on top of a rocky cliff. Dozens of torches flickered, and numerous purple flags trimmed in gold fluttered in a gentle breeze that blew in from the ocean.

Cret peered into the darkness. Squinting his eyes, he was able to make out the forms of several guards walking the perimeter of the estate. A few of them held swords in their hands—the metal glinted in the torchlight.

"Are they expecting us?" Cret asked.

"No," Shalendra replied.

"Are we going to have issues?" Tivadarios asked.

"I don't believe so. When Asan brought Neiaphi here, he spoke with everyone," Shalendra told them. "While not expecting us, they will not be surprised by our appearance. You, Tivadarios, and the centaurs, on the other hand, will be a cause for celebration, I'm sure. Come, you have traveled a long way." Shalendra continued her measured pace up the path toward the illuminated villa.

The sentries noticed their approach, and soon, a sizable group was walking toward them. A large, imposing man took the lead, carrying a large sword.

"Captain Hue," Cret called, raising a hand. "It is I, Cret."

"Cret? How did you get here, and who are you with?" The captain asked.

"Long story. May we approach?"

"Of course. Come. Your parents are going to be relieved to see you."

"My parents? They're here?" Cret said, rushing up to the captain, closing the distance.

Captain Hue smiled broadly. "Yes, they joined with us before we left Krisa."

The rest of the new party approached. Captain Hue's face fell when he saw Andonis with them. "Welcome back, Andonis," the captain said.

Andonis nodded his head and then shook Greish's hand, leaning toward the young guard. Greish nodded, locking eyes with Cret.

"If you all will excuse me," Andonis said before sprinting toward the villa.

"Good to see you, Greish," Hepluosis said, grinning.

"I heard you had vanished one night. How did you meet up with this group?"

"Pure luck." He shrugged.

Cret looked between the two friends and then up to the fleeing form of Andonis. "What did he say to you?" Cret asked Greish. His tone had lost all warmth, his eyes narrowed with suspicion.

Greish sighed and shook his head. "I really don't want to get involved in this triangle."

"What are you talking about?" Hepluosis asked.

"Neiaphi and Andonis are promised," he said reluctantly.

Hepluosis bellowed out a loud laugh. "This is

wonderful news."

All eyes swiveled to stare at Hepluosis.

"What? Everyone knows I don't get along with either of them. I couldn't be happier. Come along, Six," he said and then strode away.

Greish shook his head. "I don't know why I was ever friends with him. We should get to the villa before he causes problems."

"What kind of problems?" Tivadarios asked.

"Andonis asked if Neiaphi's here. She arrived a few days ago. I'm sure that's where he's headed," Greish answered.

Cret hung back as the group started back up the hill. His heart was racing.

Should he go up there? Would she want to see him? What would he say to her?

Tivadarios looked back toward the sea and saw Cret standing there. "What's the matter?" he asked him.

"I'm not sure what to do," he said.

"Come on. It'll be fine, I'm sure."

Cret shook his head but followed him to the villa.

∞ 22 ∞
REUNION

Andonis sprinted up the hill, drawing the eyes of the sentry guards, though none moved to stop him. The villa sprawled across the hillside, its great estate glimmering in the torchlight. He paused only briefly, taking in the immaculately kept grounds stretching in all directions, before hurrying on. Unsure where to find Neiaphi, he followed the sound of voices toward the rear of the estate.

The path opened into a grand garden containing what appeared to be all his people and Neiaphi's.

"Andonis, is that you?" He heard his mother's voice.

He quickly zeroed in on her location and rushed over to her, embracing her in a quick hug.

"Have you seen her?" he asked.

"She's inside the villa. Third floor, I believe."

"I'll be back soon."

She patted him on the shoulder and nodded her head. "Go to her."

He nodded briskly and rushed toward an open door leading into the villa. His sandals slid across the polished marble floor, and he nearly fell—saved only by a firm grip on his shoulder and arm.

"Andonis, my friend. What's the rush?" Aristas asked.

"Thanks," Andonis muttered, steadying himself. He ignored the question, his eyes darting across the wide dining hall where clusters of people gathered in quiet conversation. "Where are the stairs?"

Aristas huffed and pointed to the far side of the room. "Do you need someone to hold your hand?" he asked with a smirk.

"Very funny," Andonis said, shaking his head in exasperation before striding toward the staircase.

He wove through the throng of people, muttering an apology when he brushed against a young woman carrying a sleeping baby.

The curved staircase was ornate—cream-and-black laced marble with a golden railing. He realized he stood in the villa's grand entry hall, the ceiling soaring more than three stories above. Placing one foot on the stair and a hand on the railing, he froze as vertigo swept over him. His heart pounded, and a sheen of sweat gathered on his forehead. What would he even say to her? Would she want to see him? Did he even want to hear what she had to say? Cret was just outside—should he tell her that, or remain silent? And if she discovered he had traveled with him but kept it hidden, would she hate him for it?

Too many questions rattled in his brain.

Drawing in a slow breath, he steadied himself and forced his legs to move, taking the stairs one at a time. A couple of people passed him on their way down, but thankfully, none stopped him. Whether it was courtesy or the intensity in his eyes, he didn't care.

Once on the third floor, he was unsure of where to go again. Which room was hers?

"Standing around waiting and wondering isn't going to get me anywhere," he muttered to himself. He went to the first door and knocked gently. He heard soft footfalls approaching, and then the door opened. It was Addident's eldest daughter, Nidora.

"Good evening, Nidora. Sorry to bother you, but do you know where I might find…"

"Two doors down," she interrupted before he could finish. "I don't know if she'll want to speak with you, but that's where she is. Good luck." Her lips curved into a shy smile.

He returned the smile with a grateful nod before

making his way down the carpeted hallway to the door she had indicated. Lifting his hand to knock, he froze once again, hesitation rooting him in place.

"Why is this so hard?" he asked himself softly. He glanced back down the hallway. Nidora was still watching him. When their eyes locked, her cheeks turned crimson as she ducked back inside her room. With a deep sigh, he rapped on the door gently.

Altesse answered the door. Shock flickered across her face, but she beckoned him inside without a word. Guiding him through their suite, she stopped at another room, knocked softly, and slipped her head inside. Though he couldn't make out her words, the door soon opened wider and she gestured for him to enter.

Neiaphi and Alexa sat together on a bench beneath a wide picture window. Both regarded him with cautious eyes. Alexa leaned close and whispered something to Neiaphi, who shook her head gently, offering her a reassuring smile before patting her hand. Rising, Alexa walked toward him. She paused, looking up with eyes that sparkled despite the sorrow etched across her expression.

"Be kind," she whispered, and then exited the room.

Neiaphi kept gazing out the window, fumbling with her skirt.

He stood there for a moment, taking in her beauty, trying to gauge her emotions. She sat with her back straight and hardly seemed to breathe. A breeze flittered in through the open window and tossed her hair.

He cleared his throat slightly, causing Neiaphi to visibly tense. "Can we talk?" He finally asked.

She nodded, still not looking at him.

Sighing, he crossed the room and lowered himself onto the opposite end of the bench. When she kept her eyes averted, he turned instead to the window. The vast garden stretched beneath them, where a dozen torches flickered in the gentle breeze drifting in from the ocean. The cool, salty air refreshed him. Closing his eyes, he drew in a deep breath. When he opened them again, Neiaphi was watching him.

"Did Lyric choose where to go?" she asked.

He nodded. "Romota."

She gave a small nod and returned her gaze to the garden.

"Agartha is beautiful. I… I wish you had been there with me," he said softly.

"I saw a little of it before coming here."

"We must have just missed you."

"I wasn't there long, and I never got close to the shore."

He hummed and nodded. "I'm so sorry, Neiaphi."

She looked at him with a serious expression. "For what?" she asked.

His mouth opened, but his reply died in his throat. After a few heartbeats, he found his voice. "For allowing my eyes to wander and hurting you."

"Your wandering eyes didn't hurt me. It is I who should apologize."

He slid a little closer to her and grabbed her hand tentatively. "You have nothing to apologize for…"

She raised her other hand, stopping him. "When I heard that Cret was alive and on his way here, my heart… it started to war with itself. I—" She hesitated, drawing in a shaky breath. "When I was with Cret before he went to the processing plant, I never would have said I loved him. Cared for him deeply, yes—maybe even more than a friend—but that relationship was never given the chance to grow. I know I love you…"

"But?" Andonis asked.

She looked at her hand clasped in his and then back out the window. "I have to see him again. I am older and have grown a lot in the past year, just like he has. I released you so you had time…" She trailed off and then stopped speaking, her breath coming in a sharp, almost panicked rhythm.

"Time for what?" He asked gently after her breathing returned to normal.

"Time to forget me and move on."

"Why would I do that? I love you."

She shook her head. "I'm not lovable. I'm too messed up in the head."

His laughter made her jump.

"Sorry," he said after a moment. "Comments like those are why I love you so much…" he paused, taking a deep, shuddering breath.

"But?" she asked, mimicking him.

The corner of his lips broke into a small smile, but it faltered quickly.

Neiaphi placed her other hand on top of his. He glanced down at their entwined hands and then squeezed his eyes shut. "My original offer still stands."

"I already rejected that offer," she said flatly.

"I know, but the time is upon us."

"What do you mean?" she asked, squeezing his hands slightly.

Without looking up at her, he answered, "I came here with Cret. We rescued him and Tivadarios out at sea. He's downstairs somewhere."

Neiaphi's breath hitched in her chest, and her hands went stiff. "Oh," she said quietly.

"I…I think you should go see him."

"I…" she began, but didn't know what to say.

"Do you want me to send him up here?" He offered.

For several heartbeats, she sat in silence, her breath shallow and uneven. A single tear slipped from her eye, clinging to her lashes before falling. When she closed her eyes, more tears streamed down her cheeks. Andonis resisted the urge to wipe them away. He stood and turned to leave. Neiaphi's hand on his arm stopped him.

"I…" she began, looking up at him with glistening eyes and tear-streaked cheeks.

"I'll send him up," Andonis finished for her.

She nodded; the movement was almost unperceivable.

Andonis walked down the carpeted hallway, staring at his feet, lost in thought. Did he do the right thing? "I should have just grabbed her and fled into the night," he whispered.

"Are you okay?" A voice broke into his thoughts, making him jump.

"Sorry, I didn't mean to startle you." It was Nidora. She was standing by a window near her room.

He stopped beside her and looked out the window, saying nothing. "Were you able to speak to her?"

He nodded.

"Since you're leaving, I assume it didn't go well," she remarked.

"Yes and no," he replied.

"Do you want to talk about it?" she asked softly.

Andonis raked his hands through his hair. "It's all my fault. I drove her away."

"I don't believe that," she replied.

He shook his head. "I let my eyes and mind wander and didn't consider her feelings."

Nidora placed a hand on his arm. He jumped slightly, looking down at her hand. "I don't think you ever truly had her," she said softly. "Neiaphi and I rarely spoke, but I saw the look in her eyes the day Cret rode away with his father. If she'd had a horse, I think she would have chased after him. She's been in love with him longer than she even realizes.

"You deserve someone who looks at you the same way. Someone who dreams about you."

"I used to think I had that person," he said sadly.

Nidora squeezed his arm and smiled sweetly up at him. "Where were you headed just now?"

"To bring Cret up here."

"Cret's here?" she asked with surprise.

Andonis released a shaky breath. "We arrived together. At first, I didn't know if I should tell her…But I figured the consequences of staying silent would be worse."

"I'll come with you."

"That's okay, you don't have to."

"I insist," she said brightly, looping her arm through his and guiding him to the staircase.

Arm in arm, they descended the stairs. A few people gave them puzzled looks, but no one spoke to them.

"Do you know where he is?" Nidora asked, looking around.

The low hum of quiet conversations drifted through the air as they stepped into the garden, where families and friends clustered around the glow of fire pits.

"I'm not sure," Andonis admitted. "As soon as we were spotted and welcomed, I rushed up here. He might be with his family."

"They're on the third floor too," Nidora said thoughtfully. Then her eyes lit up. "There's my father—he'll know." She raised her voice. "Father!"

"Good evening, Nidora. Welcome back, Andonis," Addident greeted them.

"Have you seen Cret?" she asked.

Addident turned his eyes to Andonis, who was staring at the ground. "I saw him walking the perimeter with his father." He nodded in the direction of the sea.

"Thank you, sir," Andonis said. "Thank you, Nidora. I can take it from here."

"Are you sure?" He nodded. "If you ever need to talk…" she trailed off.

Walking away, Addident glanced back, looking between the two, and shook his head.

Andonis nodded to Nidora, then walked briskly in the direction her father had indicated. Thankfully, he didn't have to go far before he spotted Cret and his father making their way back toward the villa.

"Cret," he called out, waving his hand.

Cret waved back, then murmured something to his father before breaking away and heading toward Andonis.

"Neiaphi wants to see you," Andonis said, his voice taut with restraint. "I told her I'd bring you to her."

Cret gave a dry chuckle. "Well, this is awkward. Are you certain?"

"No…" Andonis admitted, his jaw tightening. "But it's

what she wants.”

Cret nodded once. “All right. Lead the way.”

Andonis fell in next to Cret, and together, they returned to the villa.

Cret stood before the inner door in Neiaphi’s family’s room. The knotty pine door before him was painted a yellowish cream color, adorned with intricate gold and silver scrollwork. The golden hinges appeared freshly polished. He stood there for several moments, uncertainty gripping his heart and mind. He hadn’t seen her in so long. How much had she changed, if any? How much had he changed? Taking a deep breath, he rapped on the door with his knuckles.

“Come,” a soft voice said. His heart leaped at the sound of her voice. Slowly, he opened the door.

He pushed the door open slowly. The room was bathed in the warm glow of several oil lamps. Neiaphi sat before a wide picture window that framed the garden and ocean beyond. Her posture was straight, almost rigid, her back to him. She wore a gown of pale blue trimmed with gold, and her long brown hair fell loose except for a single braid at the center. A golden chain wound through the braid, dotted with tiny white flowers carefully spaced along its length.

A quick glance around told him they were alone. He moved slowly across the room, each step measured, his breath shallow and his palms damp with sweat.

“It’s good to see you again,” he said softly, his voice scarcely above a whisper. In the stillness of the room, anything louder would have felt like an intrusion. “I’m glad you made it this far…unharmed.”

“Yes, I made it this far.” She paused, her gaze fixed on the window rather than him. “Unharmed?” she echoed quietly. “I was so relieved to see your parents and sister again.”

“Me too… May I sit?”

She nodded her head and gestured to the bench where

she sat.

He moved to the bench in a quick, smooth motion. Her eyes were closed, so he let his gaze soak up the sight of her. Her face was the same. She was a little older, but she was still the Neiaphi he saw in his dreams. Her pale complexion and the slight rosy hue on her high cheekbones. She was just as slender as he remembered—everything was just as he remembered.

"I've missed you," she whispered. "Everyone told me to forget about you, to move on."

Tears slid down her cheeks.

"I was told the same thing, even after we escaped the processing plant," he said.

She dropped her chin to her chest and hugged herself. He saw her eyes open, and then she slowly lifted her gaze. Their eyes met—it was like being struck by lightning. His heart hammered in his chest; surely, she would have been able to hear it. Her deep blue eyes twinkled in the lamplight, glistening with tears.

They stared at each other, neither speaking, neither breaking eye contact.

Nothing needed to be said at this moment. Their eyes said everything.

After several precious moments, Cret slid across the bench to her and enveloped her in his arms. She crumbled into him, sobbing. Burying his head into her hair and holding her close, he felt a peace he didn't know existed.

∞ **23** ∞
ᴛHE ᴄHOICE

Neiluios watched Andonis and Cret ascend the stairs in uneasy, rigid steps. A deep sorrow slammed into him, a sorrow for whom he was unsure. He knew Neiaphi hadn't made her choice lightly, and now, having Cret back, he was uncertain what the outcome of the evening would be. Whatever she chose, he would support her, that he was certain of.

A few moments later, Andonis returned to the gathering hall. Neiluios watched him for a few moments and then approached.

"How are you doing, son?" he asked.

Andonis stiffened and then shrugged. "Not well, sir," he replied.

"You were able to see Neiaphi?" Neiluios pressed.

Andonis nodded. "I'm the one who told her Cret was here."

Neiluios was surprised at this revelation. He studied Andonis for a few heartbeats. Andonis was truly a decent man, and it was evident that he cared more for Neiaphi's feelings than his own. "You are truly selfless."

Andonis chuckled softly. "Thank you, sir. I just wish selflessness hurt less."

Neiluios clamped his hand on Andonis's shoulder. "Come, I think we both need a drink."

Neiluios led Andonis to a bar on the far end of the room. Andonis seemed to move only by his prodding. Going through the motions without thought. Out of the corner of his eye, Neiluios saw Nidora staring in their direction. When her eyes met his, she looked away, cheeks flaring bright red. *Interesting,* he thought. *I haven't seen her stare at anyone before. Maybe...* he let the thought drift off—a thought to ponder at a later time.

When he was certain Andonis was going to be okay—well, as okay as anyone could be in the same situation — Neiluios went to find Addident. He turned out easy to find, standing in the middle of the garden, speaking to two tall, slender women.

"Ah, Neiluios, just the man I needed to see," Addident said with an edge to his voice.

"Problem, sir?"

"Yes and No. Gather everyone for a meeting, please."

"Yes, sir."

Everyone assembled in the gathering hall. With so many in attendance, they were packed in tightly. Addident and the two women who arrived with Andonis, Cret, and the others stood in front, drawing all eyes to them.

The woman who appeared to be the leader took one step closer to the gathered crowd.

"Greetings, all. My name is Shalendra. You all met my associate Asan when Neiaphi returned to you. I am here to extend our invitation to join us in Agartha and also to inform you that the centaurs are sending a transport ship to return most of their kind to Romota. A great war is about to break out between Atlantis and the Lemurians, one that will be far more devastating than anything the Society has been trying to do. You have three choices, but only one is truly safe."

"And what choice is that?" someone called out.

"Japster," Neiluios muttered under his breath.

"Coming with us is the safest," she said flatly.

"To this unknown underground cavern!" Japster yelled.

Murmurs broke out amongst the gathered, the

volume growing until everyone was trying to speak over each other.

A sharp whistle grabbed everyone's attention, somehow slicing easily through the noise. All eyes went wide, heads swiveling to find the source.

Hepluosis strode forward with a smirk on his face. "Be at ease, my people," he spoke with confidence as he walked to the front of the room and stood next to Shalendra and Addident.

"I will handle this," Addident said.

Hepluosis grinned and shook his head. "Let me." Without waiting for permission to speak, he turned to the crowd and raised his hands. "I have been to Agartha, and Shalendra gave me a private tour of one of their cities. We will thrive there. While it looks different from what we are used to, it is where my family and I will be going."

"Son! I have not decided our future," Japster yelled from across the room. "Father, now is not the time."

"That's right. I am your father, and I set the rules for our family."

Neiluios looked at Japster; his face was red and contorted into a scowl.

"Times are changing, father," Hepluosis said with his chin in the air. His shoulders rounded backward, causing his chest to elevate. "All those who want to live in peace will be coming with me!" He declared loudly.

The room broke into a raucous of confusion and fear-fueled angry shouts.

"THAT'S ENOUGH!" Captain Hue bellowed. "Women and children are dismissed. All men will stay, and we will calmly discuss our options."

"That's not fair!" A woman shouted. "We have the right to voice our opinions."

Nodding heads and voices of agreement answered her.

Addident held up his hands. "I will have calm in this room!" His voice, while not loud, commanded attention, and a hush fell over the room. "All the men will discuss our options, and then we will return to our families. Each family will choose for themselves. We are charting a new way of life and a new way of decision-making. Everyone will have a say in the end. Dismissed!"

His words echoed throughout the hall. With barely a murmur, the crowd dispersed—all the women and children exited the room, while the men mingled quietly, slowly grouping themselves into their respective social classes unconsciously.

Addident and Neiluios stood in front of the room, with high- and mid-level officials closest to them, while low-level personnel and guards crowded in from behind.

Movement near the staircase drew Neiluios's eye as Cret descended alone. Wordlessly, he moved through the crowd to stand next to his father.

"I will open the floor to questions," Addident began.

With relative calm, questions were asked, and Shalendra, Andonis, and Hepluosis answered as best they could. After an hour of talks, the crowd of low-level, mid-level, and guards dispersed, everyone returning to their families.

Addident looked at those remaining and flicked his head to the stairs. The high-level officials remaining nodded in silent agreement. Some headed directly for the stairs, others grabbed another drink before joining them

Addident stood in the gathering room on the third floor, staring out a large door that led to an airy balcony. His back was straight, and his hands were clasped behind his back. His wife and two daughters sat on a sofa closest to him. The arrival of the high-level officials and their families caught his attention, as evidenced by a twitch in his jaw, but he still stared out the door.

After a few tense moments with no one speaking, he turned to face them.

"Our choices since coming here haven't been ours to

make until now…" he trailed off, looking each man in the eye. "Whatever you and your family choose will be yours and yours alone. What I do shall not influence your decision."

Nods and grunts of approval answered him.

"Neiluios, how do you suggest we announce our intentions?" Addident asked.

Neiluios sat still for a moment and then glanced over to his family. Neiaphi looked into his eyes and then nodded, as if reading his thoughts. "I say we place three pots in the gathering hall. One for each destination, and heads of households will place their names in the pot of their choice. We will announce who goes where tomorrow evening, and then we will make ready to leave."

"Agreed. Make it so," Addident said.

"Wait!" a high-level said quickly. "Shouldn't we tell each other? We need to make sure we have high-level officials going to each."

"Why?" Neiluios asked.

Kamkrates gave Neiluios a look of utter astonishment. "To maintain a sense of order, of course."

Neiluios and Addident shook their heads as one.

"We are a free people, and free people do as they wish. Whichever path is chosen, it will be up to them to mold into that society appropriately. They are grown men and women, and they have children. They have been through a lot to get to this point in time, and as such, they have earned the right to make their own decisions, right or wrong. Goodnight." He held out his hand to help his wife to her feet.

"Wait! We want to know what you chose, sir. I know my family will wish to stay with you," Amplios said.

Addident shook his head and led his family to their room.

"Neiluios?" Amplios asked.

"Everyone on this floor makes their own decision. Come," he gestured for Altesse and Neiaphi to join him.

Back in their room, Altesse rounded on Neiluios. "Where are we going?" she asked.

"You, our sons, and I will go to the centaur gathering to await our eldest son's arrival," Neiluios said with certainty, "and then we will go to the land Pythia showed me. Our sons will grow into great leaders and help build the most advanced society this planet has ever known—long after Atlantis has faded into myth and legend. As for our eldest, he will choose his own path when the time comes. I cannot say if he'll be able to return to Romota should he desire it, but I will help him however I can."

Neiaphi studied her father in silence, tension tightening her chest. Fear kept her lips sealed, yet the weight of her question pressed until she could no longer contain it. She lowered her eyes.

"What about me, Father?" she whispered

Cypress yipped, wagging his tail and then thrusting his nose under her hand. She smiled at him, scratching behind an ear.

"You met with Andonis and Cret," her mother stated flatly, no question asked. Neiaphi nodded.

"They both still desire you?" Neiluios asked. She nodded, returning her eyes to the floor.

"Who would make you happier?" Neiluios inquired, kneeling in front of her and grabbing her hands.

She raised her eyes and met his. "I don't know," she admitted.

Neiluios nodded, squeezing her hands gently. "We will be here a few more days, and then we will go to the centaur gathering. Take your time. If you haven't made a decision yet, you're welcome to stay with us until you're ready. The choice is yours. Your mother and I have done all we can to prepare you for adulthood. We are here for support, nothing more."

"Thank you," she whispered, her voice breaking as tears welled in her eyes. She leaned forward, wrapping her arms around her father while reaching to grasp her mother's hand.

"Would you like some company?" The voice caused Andonis to jump. He was still on the third floor gathering room, peering out the same door Addident had moments before.

"Sorry, I didn't mean to startle you," Nidora said.

He turned his head and gave her a tired smile. "That's okay. I was just lost in thought."

"Can I stay?" she asked.

He nodded and gestured to the sofa.

Once they were both seated, she cleared her throat. "Have you decided where to go?"

He shook his head. "Has your father decided?" he asked.

She nodded, "We are going to Agartha."

"Truly? That surprises me."

"Why?"

He was silent for a minute. "I just assumed he would stay 'top side' and lead those that stay here."

"Top side? That sounds funny." She giggled. "My father is in line for the throne back on Romota; he wants to be out of their grasp, and more so for my sister and me to be unreachable."

"That makes sense."

"I'm just sorry I wasted so much time."

"What do you mean?" he turned to face her fully.

"I've kept to myself, thinking everyone was in a station below me. I've been quite snobby, as my mother puts it. I wasted a lot of time I could have been getting to know others…" she trailed off, playing with the hem of her skirt.

He grinned slightly. "Who would you have liked to get to know?"

She sighed and then looked up. "You."

Andonis's eyes found Neiaphi's door. He stared at it for a moment and then slid his eyes back to Nidora. He had never really looked at her before. Neiaphi was tall for a woman, and Nidora was even taller—only a few inches shorter than him. Her platinum blonde hair cascaded over an icy blue eye. She was fetching. She looked up at him and batted her eyelashes. He smiled, causing her to blush and drop her eyes.

"I wouldn't mind getting to know you, but…"

"Her," Nidora huffed.

Andonis tentatively reached for her hand, and she didn't pull away, slowly lifting her gaze.

"It's complicated, and I'm not sure what's going to happen over the next couple of days."

"I understand completely. Take your time. If you want to talk, I'll be here for you."

"Thank you, Nidora."

She smiled again and then rose to her feet. "Good night, Andonis. I hope you sleep well."

He watched her walk away, her hips swaying slightly as she walked.

∞ **24** ∞
ᚦHE ᚲLIFF

Neiaphi wandered alone with only Cypress beside her. The sun was just cresting the eastern horizon. The manicured garden ended abruptly at the edge of a cliff that dropped quickly to the churning waters below. The white capped water sparkled in the early morning light.

Standing on the edge of the cliff, she looked down, and a wave of vertigo washed over her, causing her to take a few steps back. The cliff face reminded her of her first dream on the transport that bore her from Romota to this planet. She glanced around and, to her relief, she saw no paths leading down.

"Hello, little miss. Would you mind some company?"

She didn't have to look to know who came and stood next to her. "Thank you, Net," she whispered.

They stood in silence for a long while until Neiaphi shifted to stand a bit closer and placed her head on his arm. Slowly, he reached behind her and wrapped his arm across her shoulders.

"Why does everything have to be so hard?" she asked.

He shrugged. "The Gods have their reasons."

She looked up at him. "Do you truly still believe in the Gods?"

He shrugged again. "I think I have to. It's hard to explain, but knowing there is something bigger and better than me out there is comforting."

"I suppose…"

"Have you made your choice?" he asked after a few more minutes.

"No," she whined "Am I awful? I can't string them both along. I owe it to them. No… I owe it to Andonis. I need to pick him. It is the right thing to do. I already told him I would marry him. Cret and I were never anything more than friends."

"That's not true, maybe in the spoken world, but not in your heart." He turned to face her, placing his hands on her shoulders. "Do not worry about their feelings; they are both grown men, and they will survive. You need to pick the one your heart truly wants. Shut down your brain and listen to your heart. It doesn't reason, it doesn't worry, it doesn't think, it only feels. You can not live without your heart, so it is the thing that must make your decisions."

"That's silly, Net. You can't live without your brain either."

"Ah, not true." He waggled a finger at her. "I knew a man who had been struck in the head. He could breathe and walk, but that was about it. If his daughter hadn't told him when to eat and when to sleep, I don't think he would have done either. But a knife to the heart cannot be overcome."

She pondered his words staring at the ocean.

"Thank you, Net. I'll be back inside in a few minutes."

He nodded and left her standing on the edge of the cliff.

The wind increased, blowing briny sand into Neiaphi's face. She turned her head and lifted her arms to shield herself from the biting particles.

A noise from behind her caused her to turn. She saw Andonis speaking with Greish a little ways away. Greish's new dog was barking at something. She followed the dog's line of sight until she spotted Cret walking in her direction. Was she ready to speak to either of them? Sighing deeply, she returned her eyes to the ocean and then closed them tightly.

"Pythia?" she whispered. "Why don't I have any paths of my own?" she asked aloud.

"My dear child," a voice answered her.

Neiaphi's eyes snapped open, and she spun around

looking for the speaker. But she was still alone, though Cret was closer now.

Be calm, child. I am in your head, Pythia said.

"How is this possible?"

Ancient technology. Banned technology on Romota, I am told.

"Why did I not have a path of my own to choose?" Neiaphi asked again.

You have many paths.

"You told me that others would determine my path."

That was true back then. You had to reach this point without knowing how you would get here. You needed to learn about your ancestry in a more natural way. Everything you've been through has brought you to this moment. Now, you'll decide your future, and it will be yours alone.

Neiaphi smiled, and she started to laugh. Pythia's words rang true in her heart.

She knew what she wanted and who she wanted.

"That must be a joke I haven't heard before," a familiar voice said from behind her.

"Not a joke," she replied. "Just a realization." She turned to face Cret.

"And what is this realization?" he asked, walking up to her. He stopped in front of her, so close she could hear his breath. She tilted her head to look up at him. Over the past year, he had grown several inches. Even though she had seen him the night before, she had been sitting and hadn't really looked at him. His shoulders had broadened as had his cheeks and chin. He had an almost chiseled appearance now, still Cret but now so much more. A smile crossed her lips. He raised his eyebrows in question.

"That everything that has happened so far has been for a reason."

"What reason?" He chuckled softly.

"Everything that has happened, everything I have done and was done to me has helped turn me into the woman you see before you."

"I have to admit I do like what I'm seeing," he said quietly, his cheeks flushed slightly.

"And now I'm even more sure of my choice." Tentatively, she reached up and placed a hand on his chest. He reached up with both of his hands and clasped hers without breaking eye contact.

"Cret! We need to talk," a voice said.

Neiaphi looked first. Andonis was standing a short distance away with his sword drawn.

Cret looked over and nodded. "Stay here," he told Neiaphi.

"I will do no such thing."

"Please?"

The look in Cret's eyes made her heart jump. She had never seen such a mix of longing, fear, and sadness. "This will be handled between men."

Cret slowly started to walk toward Andonis. With a fluid and graceful motion, Cret drew his sword.

"NO!" Neiaphi shouted, running to place herself between them.

"Please, Neiaphi. Step aside," Andonis said.

"I will not allow this," she said, standing firm.

"This is between men. Don't worry about it," Andonis said, his voice icy.

"I will not allow you two to fight over me," she said.

"Trust me, Neiaphi, this is for the best. My path guides you, remember," Andonis said without taking his eyes off Cret.

"Not anymore. Pythia contacted me and revealed my true path. I am now forging my own. Please go back to the villa. I will speak to you in a little while. Please, Andonis."

He shook his head. "This has always been the path I was destined to take. There are two outcomes—one undesirable—but that's the risk I must accept. I need to see this through."

"If either of you truly cares for me, you will stop this madness." Neiaphi's face was red with frustration, her eyes wide with fear, and her heart was hammering so hard that it felt like a roaring river was racing through her ears.

Cret and Andonis took their eyes off each other, turning them to focus on her.

She nodded her head slightly. "Sheath your swords and let's talk like civilized people."

Cret nodded, lowering his sword but not sheathing it. Andonis shook his head and took a step closer to Cret.

Neiaphi held her ground and turned to face Andonis squarely. "Andonis," she said, her tone pleading. "Please, sheath your sword, let's go speak in private."

"I have to see this out. I can not rest until this path is nothing but a memory."

"To what end? Until either you or Cret is DEAD!" Her voice elevated, drawing the attention of others nearby.

Greish looked over and caught Neiaphi's eye. She flashed him the 'come' dog command. After she signed the command the third time, he realized she was communicating with him. Whistling for his dog to join him, he broke into a sprint.

"Neiaphi, I do not want to harm you. Please get out of the way," Andonis almost growled out.

"Neiaphi, please step aside." Cret's tone was soft with a hint of apology.

"I will do no such thing until each of you sheaths your swords and walks away. I will find you both later, and we will have civilized conversations." She stood firm, glaring at Andonis.

"Fine, stand there," Andonis said. He shifted his stance and, in a fast, fluid movement, he stepped past Neiaphi and advanced on Cret. Cret saw him coming and had his sword at the ready.

Neiaphi cried out, her voice breaking as she yelled at Andonis to stop. Neither man acknowledged her. Their swords were raised, each settling into a fighting stance, eyes locked in grim determination.

Panic surged through her. Greish was still too far away to intervene. Without a second thought, she lunged forward, desperate to force herself between them.

The clash of steel rang in her ears as their blades met for the first time. Sparks flew as Cret and Andonis moved in a deadly rhythm, trading blows with fierce precision. Step by step, their fight carried them closer to the edge of the cliff.

Cypress jumped to Andonis's side, hackles raised and teeth bared.

"Cypress! Leave!" Neiaphi commanded. Cypress looked at her and whined, but obeyed the command. Before she could second-guess her actions, she charged forward and jumped between them with outstretched arms. Cret saw her coming and immediately lowered his sword. Andonis, on the other hand, didn't see her. He sneered at Cret's appearance of weakness and raised his sword high, bringing it down in a sweeping motion, intent on cleaving Cret in two. As his sword lowered, he saw Neiaphi standing in front of Cret. A look of horror twisted her facial features, and a scream ripped from her throat. Cret reached out, grabbed Neiaphi's shoulder, and pushed her aside at the exact moment that he brought his sword up to block Andonis's slash.

Neiaphi stumbled with the force of the push and staggered a few steps. She stopped mere inches from the cliff's edge with her arms swinging wildly.

"Neiaphi!" Andonis cried out.

She glanced behind her to see both men rushing toward her, arms outstretched. "I'm okayyyy," she started to say as the ground beneath her gave way and she began sliding down the cliffside.

∞ **25** ∞
ᚻEALING

"What in the name of Hades were you two doing?" Greish yelled as he approached. With only a moment of hesitation, he slid down the cliffside on his backside.

"Look what you've done," Cret said.

"Me?" Andonis rounded on Cret. "You're the one who pushed her."

"If I hadn't, you would have killed her," Cret shouted, pushing Andonis back.

"ENOUGH!" Addident roared. "What is going on here?"

Andonis looked at his sword and then threw it on the ground, his face going as white as a sheet.

"I need a rope!" called Greish.

Addident rushed to the edge and looked down. "ROPE, we need a rope," he yelled.

Several guards ran over, one pulling a length of rope from his shoulder bag. Addident tied one end around his waist and threw the loose end over the edge. "You two in front of me, grab hold," Addident ordered. Cret and Andonis both moved toward him. "Not you two! You stay back; I'll have words with you both later."

"Okay, pull up slowly," Greish called up to them.

"Slow and even men," Addident ordered.

One step at a time, the three men slowly walked backward, pulling Neiaphi and Greish back to safety.

By the time Neiaphi was several feet from the edge, a

large crowd had gathered.

Altesse and Net rushed to her side.

"Careful, she hit her head pretty hard," Greish cautioned. "She might have a broken arm and leg, I can't tell."

Net nodded, then bent down and scooped up the unconscious Neiaphi.

Phebis, Addident's wife, started barking orders for boiling water, bandages, and ointments.

Altesse grabbed Neiaphi's hand as Net carried her back to the villa.

Outside her family's rooms, Cret paced restlessly, every step heavy with tension, while Andonis sat near the balcony in the adjoining gathering room. Each time their eyes met, Andonis dropped his gaze to his hands. Cret, however, only glared, fury simmering beneath the surface.

The nerve of him even being here. This is all his fault, Cret thought. He paused his steps and hung his head, shoulders slumping. *I could have stopped all this by walking away, as she had wanted me to. If she doesn't pull through, I will never forgive myself. I've fought so hard to get back to her. How could I let this happen?*

The door opened, and the family's female servant exited carrying a bundle of towels.

Cret rushed up to her, causing her to squeak in alarm. "How is she?" he asked.

Andonis stood and took a few steps closer, then stopped again.

The servant shook her head and tried to walk around him. "Cleop, please," Andonis said. "I…ah…we need to know."

"She's still unconscious. She's got a nasty lump on the head."

"And her arm? Her leg?" Cret asked.

"They don't appear to be broken, but we won't know

for sure until she wakes. Please, sirs, I must get clean towels." She curtsied and then hurried down the hallway.

Andonis and Cret both let out a loud sigh at the same time. Startling one another, they shared a look but quickly broke eye contact and resumed their worrying.

A stream of bright light cut through the haze and fog, painfully piercing. Neiaphi groaned, trying to open her eyes. Her head was pounding, and every joint and muscle ached. With each passing heartbeat, her anxiety grew. Why couldn't she open her eyes? Why did everything hurt so badly? She felt like she had wool in her ears. She heard sounds, but they were muffled and unclear.

She felt something cool and wet press against her forehead and cheeks, and then a trickle of water passed over her lips and slid down her parched throat. She groaned again, trying to open her eyes or sit up. Do anything other than just lie here.

A hand, at least she thought it was a hand, gently held her down, and then more muffled sounds. A voice finally broke through the cloud.

"Rest, you're safe. Sleep now," the voice said. Sleep pulled her back under.

The room was bathed in warm candlelight when Neiaphi was finally able to pry her eyes open. An almost unbearable pounding pulsed behind her eyes, and every limb felt heavy and stiff.

A moan escaped her when she tried to shift her weight.

"Let me help you." She heard her mother's voice. Altesse helped her into a sitting position, placing pillows behind her. "Are you thirsty?"

She tried to nod, but that only intensified the pain. A wince was all she managed. Her mother registered the intent and brought a mug up to her lips. A thick, warm liquid coated her mouth and slid down her throat. The honeyed tonic sent a wave of warmth through her body that seemed to settle into her fingertips and toes.

"Thank you," Neiaphi whispered. "What happened?"

"What do you remember?" Altesse asked.

"Andonis and Cret were fighting." Neiaphi's eyes widened, and she tried to sit up fully. "Are they both okay?" She managed after a groan.

Altesse placed her hand on her shoulder. "Both are fine. When you jumped in between them, Andonis didn't see you. Cret pushed you out of the way and barely managed to block Andonis's sword. You stopped at the edge of the cliff, and the ground gave way. Greish slid down and rescued you. You hit your head pretty hard."

"Oh." Was all she was able to say. She remembered jumping in between them, but everything else was a blur.

Slowly, Neiaphi glanced around the room. "How long ago?"

"Two days," Altesse replied.

"Two days? We were supposed to leave with Shalendra yesterday. Did everyone leave without us?"

Her mother shook her head. "No. Everyone agreed to wait until you were well enough." Neiaphi sighed and tried to move her legs.

"Where do you think you're going?" Altesse asked sharply.

"I have to get out of this bed. We need to leave, or we'll miss the centaurs."

"Don't worry. We still have time. Shalendra says we'll make it." Altesse placed her hand on Neiaphi's shoulder, pushing her back.

Neiaphi let herself sink back into the pillows. "All right. But why does everything hurt so much?" she whined.

Altesse chuckled softly. "You slid halfway down the cliff, remember? Wiggle your toes and move your hands for me."

Neiaphi obeyed, but winced at the effort.

"Do you think anything is broken?" Altesse asked.

She shook her head. "No, just stiff and sore—especially my left arm."

Her mother carefully lifted and moved the arm. Neiaphi cringed at the motion.

"Well, it's not broken, that's good. You were lucky."

"I don't feel lucky."

"Go back to sleep, I'll bring you something to eat in a little bit."

"Um, I…," she trailed off.

"What is it, dear?" Altesse asked.

"I need to speak to Andonis and Cret, but I don't know what to say now."

Altesse stood, keeping one hand on Neiaphi's arm. "Not now. I need you to concentrate on healing. There will be plenty of time to speak to them later while we travel."

"Are they…are they both going to the meeting place?"

Altesse nodded. "Yes, now sleep."

Neiaphi nodded and watched her mother exit the room. She closed her eyes and tried to relax. Unable to, she fidgeted in the bed, which only caused her pain. With a huff, she stilled and looked around the room. A few of the candles had burned down and snuffed out, leaving a single candle lit. The flickering light cast shadows throughout the room.

"Cypress?" she asked. Her voice was barely above a whisper. The air in the room felt heavy and oppressive—the dark room demanding quiet. A soft whine answered her, followed by the soft footfalls of her faithful dog. He approached the bed and placed his chin on it next to her hand. She smiled at him and then, with slow movements, reached over and scratched behind his ear. "I knew you'd be here." After a few moments, her eyelids became too heavy to keep open and she fell asleep.

∞ **26** ∞
𝔇ECISIONS

Crelian paced back and forth, shaking his head. "I don't like it," he said for the fourth time.

"It's what I have to do, Father," Cret repeated. I am an adult by Earth standards.

This is my life, and this is what I have to do."

Sephi placed a hand on Crelian's arm to stop him. "He has to forge his own path."

Crelian turned his eyes to his wife. "You're okay with this?" His voice elevated. She looked at Cret and then back at Crelian. "No, but I trust our son is doing what he thinks he has to."

"Pythia told me Atlantis needed me. She told me to find the Navy, but I wasn't meant to join them, like I thought. Atlantis doesn't need me…"

"But you just said…" Crelian cut him off, but Cret continued anyway.

"The Atlantean people need me. I have to figure out a way to get as many as possible off this island. The Lemurians will not be stopped."

"Have you told Neiaphi?" his mother asked.

He shook his head. "Altesse won't let anyone see her. I'll leave her a note."

Sephi shot to her feet. "No!" Her voice rang with such force that both Cret and Crelian flinched. "I will speak to Altesse. But you will *not* run off again, leaving only a note. You will look Neiaphi in the eye and tell her yourself."

"I think a note would be best," Crelian said softly. He opened his mouth to say more, but changed his mind when he saw the look on Sephi's face.

She nodded at his silence. "Good. I'll be back, and you'd better be here when I return." She pointed a finger at Cret and waggled it.

Cret held his hands out in surrender. "I'll be here." He promised.

Cret was once again facing the inner door of Neiaphi's family room. His mother, Altesse, and Alexa's mother were speaking in the gathering room not too far away.

He knocked on the door softly. Perhaps if Neiaphi were sleeping, he could avoid this confrontation.

"Come," a soft voice said.

Cret moaned and then opened the door. The scent of jasmine and rosemary assaulted his nose immediately. Neiaphi was sitting propped up in her bed. Alexa was sitting in a chair near the large window. She smiled at Cret and then stood.

"Please stay," Neiaphi said to her.

Alexa looked at Neiaphi. "Are you sure?"

Neiaphi nodded. "Hi, Cret. Please sit." She gestured to a chair next to the bed. Stiffly, he walked the short distance to the chair and sat.

"How are you feeling?" he asked.

"Sore." She winced as she tried to sit up a bit more. "Sorry, I haven't sent for you…"

"You have nothing to be sorry about." He glanced at Alexa, who was looking out the window, seemingly ignoring them.

"I do." She sighed and started to fidget with her sheets. "No, you don't. You did nothing wrong."

She chuckled dryly. "I have done plenty. But… thank you for saving me."

"Saved you and then almost killed you, you mean." His voice was full of regret.

She reached out and placed a hand on his arm. "You saved me. What happened next was a freak accident. Not your fault."

"I should have jumped down right after you." He hung his head.

"Greish was just faster."

"Speaking of Greish," he lowered his voice, stealing a glance at Alexa. "He's not the same man we knew back in Camp Roma."

"No, he's not. He's grown up a lot," she said with a smile. "He's become a wonderful friend."

Cret thought for a moment and then looked at Alexa again. Her back was tense, but her eyes were still outside. "I'm glad you were able to find so many close friends."

"I'm so happy you've returned," Neiaphi said, squeezing his arm.

Cret hung his head again.

"What's the matter?" she asked.

"I have to leave." Neiaphi sucked in a quick breath, so he continued quickly. "But I will return. Pythia told me Atlantis needed me, but it's not the island nor the government that needs me. I thought I was supposed to join the Navy and help them protect Atlantis. But I feel I have a higher calling."

"And what is that?"

"I must help the Atlantean people get off this island. The Lemurians are coming, and the innocent citizens here shouldn't pay for the King's failed diplomacy with their lives."

Neiaphi was silent for a moment, deep in thought. "I'm going with you," she said flatly.

Cret's eyes widened, and his mouth flopped open. "I don't..." Neiaphi shook her head. "I don't need your permission."

"But, surely your parents won't let you make this decision."

Neiaphi grabbed both of his hands and squeezed. "My life is for me to decide. No one can decide for me. I will be coming with you. I... I'm...." she hesitated.

"What?" He slid to the edge of the chair and brought her hands to his chest.

She closed her eyes. "I'm not supposed to tell anyone, but I can't have any secrets between us." When she opened them again, the worry etched into his face—and the shimmer in his eyes—softened her resolve. A faint smile touched her lips. Releasing one of his hands, she lifted her fingers to his cheek. "I'm sorry." A small chuckle escaped before her body clenched in pain, turning the laugh into a moan.

"Here, sit back. Relax," he said, pushing her back slightly. "What's so funny?"

"Nothing really. I just didn't mean to worry you so. My secret is nothing and everything."

Cret sat back down, shaking his head. "You are making no sense."

"I'm sorry. I'm still processing it all. Did you meet any of the Agarthans?"

He nodded.

"One of them, Asan—well, he told me… told my family and Addident's family that Addident is a descendant of Poseidon and was meant to come here to usurp the Atlantean throne."

"I heard about that," he interrupted.

"But what you didn't hear is that my family is actually the rightful heirs to Romota."

Cret leaned back. "Wow. Now that is news. If Neiluios is the rightful heir, then who sits on the throne now?"

She shook her head. "Not my father. The bloodline comes through my mother. One of her ancestors was switched at birth and hidden to protect the lineage. King Sil is not of the true royal line."

"So, what are your plans? Do you plan to return to Romota?"

"Oh, no! My place is here. I want to help our people here. My brother can decide to help Romota if he chooses."

"You mean brothers, Anis and Praxis," Cret replied. "I met them last night. Healthy boys." He nodded his head, shifting in his chair without letting Neiaphi's hand drop from his grip.

She squeezed his hand, pulling his gaze back to her. "You've missed so much." Her lips curved into a sweet smile. "Icarus lives—and he's coming here on the Centaurs' transport. He is the rightful heir to the Romotian throne. Anis and Praxis are destined to help build a new technological hub outside of Atlantis, sparking another era of growth for Earth. Until now, I wasn't sure where I belonged or what I was meant to do. But now…" her voice softened, "I see it all so clearly."

She fell silent, her eyes holding his. The seconds stretched, heavy with meaning, until an awkward stillness settled between them. Cret dropped his gaze to their entwined hands and cleared his throat.

"What have you decided?" he asked hesitantly.

Her smile deepened. "I'm surprised you need to ask. I already told you. I will go with you—to help our people. The people of Earth, yes, but especially those on Atlantis.

"They are my people. They are the ones I must serve. This is my path. And together, we will aid all who are willing to walk it. There are three roads before us, each with its own promise… and its own peril."

"You must have spent a great deal of time with Pythia," he said, lips pressing into a wry line.

Neiaphi laughed, the sound bright and genuine.

"Not in person, but I've had numerous conversations with her lately. Her technology is remarkable. I'll be ready to leave tomorrow. Go now and prepare for the journey. I must rest. Alexa, could you bring Greish and Andonis here?"

Cret's expression faltered at the mention of Andonis. Neiaphi gently patted his hand. "Do not fear. I choose you. You are the one I am destined to be with." Her radiant smile tugged the corners of his lips upward.

"I think he would disagree," he said.

Cret left Neiaphi's chamber, offering a polite nod to the three women still deep in conversation before descending the stairs. A soft sound of footsteps behind him drew his glance over his shoulder—Alexa was following a few steps behind.

He slowed until she reached him. "Will you and Greish

be joining us?" he asked her.

Without looking at him, she responded. "I'm not sure. If Neiaphi wishes it." She nodded.

"A lot of things are changing around here, it seems. What do you want?"

Alexa paused mid-step, turning her head to look at him. "Before meeting those from Romota, no one ever asked my opinion." She hesitated, then shook her head. "No, that's not entirely true. My father and the other men in our village listened to our concerns—but that was still different from being asked directly what we thought. I'm still getting used to having a voice. When Phebis asked everyone to vote on whether Addident should remain our leader, the women's hands were counted." She stopped, swallowing hard. Her eyes shimmered with emotion. "That had never happened before. Wherever Greish goes, I go. That is what I want."

Cret nodded and resumed walking down the steps, side by side with Alexa.

∞ 27 ∞
THE FOREST

The sky was dark, with only the faintest sliver of dawn beginning to brighten the eastern horizon. Thick clouds smothered the moonlight and hid the countless stars overhead. The Villa lay far behind them now, its dozens of torchlights long vanished into the night.

Neiaphi rode her sleek gray mare beside Cret at the front of their small party. Cret shifted restlessly in his saddle as the gelding beneath him plodded along the trail. Neiaphi had said the horse belonged to their servant, Net. The animal was tall and sturdy, but nothing compared to Rees. Cret had been forced to leave Rees behind on the Atlantean warship when the Lemurians took him and his companions. Rees drifted in and out of his thoughts—was he safe, and if so, where?

"Are you okay?" Neiaphi asked quietly.

He flinched at her voice, breaking his train of thought. "Yeah, I'm okay. I was thinking about Rees."

"Oh... that beautiful black stallion. Where is he?" she asked.

Sighing, he replied. "Not sure. He was on the warship when the Lemurians forced us to come with them."

Neiaphi gasped and then leaned close, placing a hand on his arm. "I'm so sorry."

Cret sighed and nodded. "Thanks."

An awkward silence stretched between them as they rode through the dark forest. Cret glanced around at the small group that was traveling with them. Andonis and Tivadarios were in the lead, with a loyal pair named Aristos and Bacceon just in front of them, with Greish and two additional guards in the rear.

"How long until we reach Atlantis?" he asked, his voice directed to no one in particular.

"I'm not sure," Aristos replied. "We traveled on foot, leading the horses."

"At this rate, we should reach the outskirts of the city before daybreak," Greish said, riding up next to them.

Cret nodded, a scowl creasing his forehead.

"I know we haven't had much time to get to know each other," Greish continued, "but I want you to know I'm nothing like Hepluosis. He was always…" He paused, searching for the right word. "Ambitious." He scratched his chin. "That's not quite it, but you understand. Since I've been away from him and spent time with these people…" He gestured to the group riding with them. "All his ideas and plans seem twisted. Truth be told, most of them never sat well with me anyway—but I always assumed it was just talk. After learning about the Society, I agree with Neiaphi—they'll use him however they can. I'm glad he was sent to the processing plant. Do you have any idea how he became separated from the others?"

Cret shrugged. "My father says he disappeared the same night Tivadarios and I left to help the centaurs. He was probably following us the whole time. After we joined up with Pelagios, he was left behind. Not sure how he ended up finding Andonis and the Agarthans…" he trailed off.

Silence stretched for several moments until finally they saw lights flickering in the distance. Greish and one of the guards spurred their horses forward, signaling for the others to hold back. A few minutes later, they returned and gathered everyone together.

"There are a few soldiers up ahead. I recognize a few of them," Greish told them. "I'm going to approach alone and see if we can get a meeting with Lady Dyna.

"If you think she can be trusted," Cret replied.

"She's the one who sent us out here. I think she's the

only one we can truly trust," Greish said with a short snort.

Cret narrowed his eyes. "Do you find this funny?"

Greish cleared his throat. "No, my apologies. For some reason, Hepluosis's face popped into my mind—utterly disgusted that I was speaking with you. The image struck me as funny. I'm sorry."

After a quick word with the two guards, Greish slipped into the darkness on foot.

The others stayed mounted, ready for a swift retreat if needed.

Neiaphi fidgeted in her saddle, glancing down at Cypress sitting calmly beside her. Sensing her eyes on him, he glanced up at her and whined softly. She smiled down at her loyal dog, repeating the hand command to stay and be silent. When Cret first met Cypress, she was amazed at how quickly the dog took to him; his intuition about a person's character marveled her.

She glanced around at their small band. Bacceon, Aristos, and Andonis huddled in low conversation, while Cret and Tivadarios spoke quietly a short distance away. The two guards Addident had assigned to accompany them scanned the dark forest, hands resting loosely on the hilts of their swords. Neiaphi shifted her bow, making sure it hung free of her cloak and could be drawn quickly if needed.

The longer they waited, the harder her heart pounded. Was Greish safe? Had he been captured? Were they about to be? How could they possibly convince an entire city to flee? Would the Atlanteans believe them—or laugh in their faces? Would she ever see Alexa, her parents, or her brother Icarus again? Or was she doomed to perish on this island, far from everyone she loved?

She squeezed her eyes shut and shook her head, trying to banish the storm of doubts. The waiting was unbearable.

When Greish finally returned—he was not alone. Eight soldiers, dressed in purple and gold uniforms, walked alongside him.

"Tie your horses up securely, and we might want to

leave Cypress here as well. We're going to have to walk from here," he told them.

They obeyed swiftly, tying off their mounts, and then fell into step behind him as the group began the trek toward the Great City.

They walked for what felt like an eternity. Neiaphi's breath was becoming labored, unaccustomed to walking for so long. Cret leaned over and whispered in her ear.

"Are you doing okay?" he asked.

She shook her head. "Too much time on horseback, not enough on my feet," she murmured. "But I'll manage." She forced a tight smile. Her toe caught on a root, and she stumbled forward with a startled cry she couldn't quite hold back. Cret's hand shot out, catching her and steadying her before she could fall.

"You okay?" he whispered.

The nearest soldier spun toward them, hissing a sharp warning for silence, his glare cutting through the dark. Neiaphi swallowed hard, nodded quickly, and fixed her gaze back on the ground ahead.

The soldiers led them into a small clearing on the edge of what appeared to be farmland. Andonis, Aristos, and Greish spoke in hushed tones, gesturing toward the fields. Cret approached, raising an eyebrow.

"We were just remarking," Greish explained, "we never noticed farmland behind the main city. The city captivated us. I don't know how much of it you'll get to see, but it truly is remarkable."

"So, do you know where they are taking us?" Cret asked.

All those from their small group gathered around to hear.

"They said there are two ways they can get us into the city. I chose to portray prisoners. This will allow us to walk through the barracks and into the dungeon."

Neiaphi's hands flew to her face in surprise. "And what was the other choice?" she asked.

"Sneaking in through the sewer," he said with a grimace.

"Well, my vote is the sewer," Neiaphi said, thrusting her nose in the air. "I will not be treated like a prisoner."

"I think you need to think about that a little bit harder," one of the guards said. "I don't think the sewer is going to be more pleasurable."

Neiaphi narrowed her eyes and then turned to face her friends. "Which way do you think we should go?" she asked them.

With one hand, Cret scrubbed his face, trying to think of how best to respond. "I think going through the prison will be less unpleasant."

"And what if this is a trap?" She leaned closer to him and whispered. "What if the king has found out about our whereabouts and he instructed these soldiers to capture us without drawing attention? This would be the perfect opportunity."

"Well, she does have a point," Greish chimed in.

Slowly, everyone nodded in agreement. Greish removed himself from their huddle and approached the commander.

The commander's eyes widened. "Are you certain about that?" Greish nodded. "All right, but don't say I didn't warn you. Change of plans, gentlemen. We're taking them through the sewer," he said to his soldiers. A few of the soldiers grimaced, and one openly groaned, causing his commander to glare at him. The soldier fidgeted and then snapped to attention. "That's better. Let's go," he ordered.

They turned away from the large building that they were heading toward and walked to the backside of what appeared to be the stable.

"These sewers were built when Poseidon first created the island. The palace and every residence in the city empty their waste into these underground tunnels. While they are regularly flushed and cleaned by prisoners, it is unlikely to be a pleasant sight. Are you sure you wish to proceed?"

He looked Neiaphi directly in the eye. She swallowed and tried to put on a serious expression, nodding her head. The commander glanced at Andonis, Greish, and Cret.

When they nodded, he shrugged and grabbed a torch. "Right this way." He opened a hatch on the ground and lowered his torch, allowing them to see a staircase spiraling down deep into the earth.

∞ **28** ∞
SEWER OR PRISON

The commander led the way down the staircase. Neiaphi hesitated for a moment before following Cret down.

The stairs were slick with condensation, and a slimy green mold lined the walls. As they descended, water dripped from the ceiling. Neiaphi cringed every time a droplet landed in her hair or touched her skin. *Maybe this was a mistake,* she thought, but kept her mouth shut.

The twisting staircase seemed endless, with no light other than the commander's torch in front of them and two more being carried by soldiers bringing up the rear. The soft clicking of the soldier's boots, scuffing from sandals, and shuddering breath from the drastic drop in temperature were the only sounds. Neiaphi tried to suppress a shiver that ran up her spine and crossed her arms over her chest, rubbing them vigorously.

The deeper they traveled, the staler and thicker the air became, and the smell worsened. Neiaphi gagged and was immensely happy that she hadn't eaten anything while they traveled.

A faint light glowed at the bottom of the staircase, but what awaited them was far from welcoming.

"I thought you said these tunnels were cleaned and flushed regularly," Greish muttered, his words muffled behind the hand clamped over his nose and mouth.

The commander's scowl spoke volumes. "They're supposed to be. I'll be checking the rotation logs when this is done. The way is long, but direct." He pointed down the tunnel to the right. "That path leads straight into the city proper."

"And what about that way?" Andonis asked, gesturing left.

"The barracks," the commander replied. "That's where the workers enter. About ten steps in, there's a ladder leading up to the cells. Only those convicted of minor offenses are sent here to labor—men the courts trust to work off their punishment in the filth."

Cret's group glanced around at the tunnel, marveling at the construction. The circular tunnel appeared to have been carved out of solid rock, but its walls were as smooth as glass, with no chisel or tool marks. There was a narrow ledge on either side of a channel full of brownish-green, slimy-looking water. The commander barked out orders to his soldiers and then gestured to Cret to enter the foul-smelling water. Cret looked over at Neiaphi and bowed, his hands flourishing.

"Ladies first," he said with a smirk.

Neiaphi peered down the tunnel and took a step toward the water. A thick, green film coated the top of the brown water, and a grayish foam clung to the edges, making the film resemble a foul-smelling island. "Coward," she muttered. The corner of Cret's lips curled into a grin.

"The sewer was your idea," he whispered.

She glared at Cret, then squared her shoulders. *I can do this… This was my choice,* she told herself, wrinkling her nose and forcing shallow breaths. She edged toward the narrow ledge, but before she could step onto it, the commander's voice cut in.

"I'm sorry, young lady. That won't do. Into the water. Walking along the edge will take far too long."

The look of horror on her face drew a few snorts from Greish and several soldiers.

Neiaphi glanced down again. Up close, the brown water was even more revolting. Excrement, food scraps, and a sodden clump of something that might once have been fluffy floated past in the sluggish current. She inched back toward the stairs, heart pounding.

"Please, miss. We need to be off," the commander urged impatiently.

Her stomach lurched. She stepped down one stair—then froze. Four rats, each nearly the size of a small cat, skittered along the far ledge. One stopped and stared straight at her. Its slick, beady eyes glistened in the torchlight, unblinking, almost daring her to enter its domain.

A shrill cry escaped her throat as she stumbled back, shaking her hands in frantic denial. "I can't. I… I can't go into that water. Shackle me, gag me, throw me over your shoulder like a sack of vegetables—anything but that!"

Her breath came in shallow gasps, chest tight, throat constricting as panic rose.

The commander's sternness softened. He placed a steadying hand on her shoulder. "Be at ease, miss. Right this way." He gestured toward the ladder that led up into the barracks.

Cret slipped an arm around her shoulders. For a moment, she leaned into him, grateful for the support—then she caught herself and straightened. A glance over her shoulder revealed Andonis watching her, his expression a mix of worry, hurt, and something she couldn't quite name.

"I'm all right now. Thank you, Cret." Her voice was steady, though her pulse was not.

Quickening her pace, she reached the ladder ahead of him. She thought she felt him stiffen as she pulled away, but she wasn't certain.

The short climb up the ladder brought them into a dim chamber lined with iron-barred cells along two walls. A few prisoners snored softly within, but no guards were in sight. Without pausing, the group slipped past and entered what appeared to be the main barracks.

The corridor sloped steadily upward, eerily quiet and empty. The air, though still stale, was a marked improvement from below. The reek of unwashed bodies, smoke from low-burning fires, and the acrid tang of torch oil clung thick on

Neiaphi's tongue like a bitter film. Yet she found herself grateful to breathe it—the irony was not lost on her.

The commander halted suddenly before a heavy oak door and motioned for them to hold out their wrists. One by one, he bound their hands with leather thongs. Another soldier moved down the line, draping each of them in filthy, foul-smelling cloaks and ordering them to pull the hoods low over their faces.

"Keep your heads down, gazing at your feet, and do not make a sound," he ordered them. "If we see anybody, I will deal with them. Now, we must hurry. Lady Dyna has been expecting you; we mustn't keep her waiting any longer."

They moved swiftly through the rest of the barracks, drawing little more than a passing glance from the few soldiers busy repairing gear and readying themselves for the next shift.

They exited the barracks into a small courtyard, where warm, humid air rushed over them. Neiaphi let out a long sigh, drawing in a lungful of freshness. But her relief lasted only moments. As they stepped into the prison proper, a wave of nausea hit her. The stench of sweat, excrement, and decay rolled over them, thick and oppressive.

The commander led the way through the entry checkpoint without a word. The guard on duty stiffened, snapping to attention with a salute as they passed. Inside, moans drifted from the cells lining either side of the dim corridor. Prisoners lifted hollow eyes to watch them but made no move toward the bars. Some shrank into the shadows, eager to disappear, while others stared with dull indifference. Neiaphi tried to glance around without drawing notice, her thoughts circling: *What had these men done to end up here?*

A sudden crash jerked her back to the present. Metal clanged against stone, followed by the shatter of ceramic. Up ahead, a man stood over a small child, shouting, his leg cocked back, ready to strike.

"Halt!" the commander yelled as they approached. The portly man with long, greasy blonde hair looked up at the voice. His eyes widened, and then he came to attention lazily.

The commander stopped a few feet away, glaring down at the child, who was picking up broken pottery and scraping some gray, pasty-looking food back into a bucket.

"What's going on here, Kostas?"

"Not that it's any of your business, Commander," the portly man started. "Just breaking in a new skully-boy, and this one appears to be a lost cause," he said, glaring down at the boy.

"A little honey attracts more bees than a pile of feces," the commander said sharply. The greasy jailer looked at the commander with confusion on his face.

"I don't get you, Sir," he finally replied.

"If you show the boy a little bit of kindness, he might learn faster," the commander barked out. "Now, throw away that mess and make a new batch of food for the prisoners."

The jailer choked out a laugh. "With all due respect, Sir. This lot will eat anything I give them. No sense wasting good food on the pigs."

"Who's in charge of the sewer cleaning rotation?" the commander asked to change the subject.

The jailer scratched his chin in thought. "It was Vlasis, but he died of consumption a few moons back. I don't know if he's been replaced."

"That would explain the conditions," the commander mumbled, mostly to himself.

"What was that, Sir?" the jailer asked.

"Get back to work," the commander growled. He pivoted on his heels and then paused. "Where's Captain Nikitas? I have some new prisoners for him."

"I believe he's taking his morning meal at Council Seraphim's residence. The councilor is off island right now," Kostas said with a wicked grin. The commander rose an eyebrow and then nodded briskly.

"Would you like me to go fetch him?"

"No… I will not meddle with that. I can take care of these prisoners."

They continued walking through the prison and started

to descend deeper underground. Cret slowed until he was side by side with Greish.

"Do you know where they're taking us?" he whispered.

"There's a passage that will lead us into a secret corridor in the palace."

Cret nodded. "I hope he's telling the truth, and Neiaphi's first instincts were not correct," Greish grunted in agreement.

"Stop here a moment," the commander said sharply when they reached a door at the end of a long, deserted corridor. He ducked inside the room and emerged a moment later. "Inside quickly."

Once they filed inside, he closed the door with a soft click.

"This way," he gestured to the rear of the large room.

Neiaphi's breath caught in her throat as she glanced around the room. There were several tables and chairs scattered about. Hanging torches were positioned over each, with a small table next to them, and a wide array of tools scattered on top. The tools looked rusty and dirty. Large dark stains were under each table and chair, but the thing that had caught Neiaphi's eye was that every single table and chair had straps attached to them.

"Commander… what is this room used for?" Neiaphi asked, her voice catching slightly.

The commander paused, letting his gaze sweep across the chamber before finally meeting her eyes.

"Interrogations, miss," he said with a calm and measured voice.

Neiaphi's eyes widened. "Torture?"

"Some might call it that. But times are tough, and we need answers that some are not willing to part with. Lady Dyna wishes to put an end to all of this. Please, we must keep moving, unless you wish to end up on one of those tables."

That threat was enough to get all their feet moving.

At the rear of the room, a tapestry portraying a cheerful family splashing in the surf was moved aside to reveal a door behind.

"Strange tapestry for a torture chamber," Neiaphi remarked.

"The king has a sick sense of humor. Come not far now."

He led them through a short, thankfully dark tunnel. The room they now found themselves in was small but well-lit and strangely comforting. Several large couches were arranged in a semicircle, with a large table situated in the center of the room.

"What is this place?" Andonis asked, spinning slowly as he gazed upward. A glass ceiling arched above them, its stained glass alive with constellations and planets painted across a deep purple and blue sky.

"I don't know its original purpose," the commander admitted, "but Lady Dyna uses it to ease the suffering of those her brother interrogates. She brings them here, gives them food and medical care. If they survive, she helps them escape. If not, she ensures their remains are returned to their families. This way, please.

He pressed his hand against a small panel on the wall. At his touch, it glowed, and a doorway slid open without a sound. Neiaphi, Cret, and the others from Romota smiled at the sight of technology they recognized, while Andonis's eyes widened in astonishment.

The commander gestured for them to shed their cloaks and had their bindings cut.

"Is this kind of technology common on Atlantis?" Andonis asked, rubbing his wrists as he walked through the door. Once the nine companions were inside a much smaller room with the Commander, the door closed behind them, leaving the rest of the soldiers behind.

"Yes. It is why we are very selective about who may come to Atlantis. The outer ring has the least amount, as that is usually the only place available to outsiders."

The Commander placed his hand on another panel, illuminating it. He entered a few numbers, and soon the lift began accelerating, carrying them upward. Andonis placed his hand on the wall to steady himself.

"Are you okay?" Greish asked.

"Yeah, that was just a strange sensation. How is this room moving?" Andonis looked around at the four walls and the low ceiling.

A chuckle escaped Greish. "This isn't the first tech you've seen." He slapped Andonis on the back of the shoulder, causing him to stumble forward a bit. Neiaphi glanced at them and couldn't help but giggle.

"True, true. But this is the first time I haven't been able to see or understand how it works. We're going up, right?"

"Yes, my friend. Don't worry. This is old technology, but it seems safe enough." Greish laughed heartily.

Andonis's eyes settled on Greish, and a moan escaped his lips. Neiaphi snickered again. Cret looked at her, then at Andonis and back again.

He found himself envying the friendship the three had built. The easy banter and good-humored teasing flowed naturally among them. He nodded to himself in reflection. He shared that kind of relationship with Tivadarios, but it was strange to see Greish this way. Back in Camp Roma, Greish had been... different, stern and serious at all times. But then, he had been in the earliest phases of his training, in an unfamiliar situation.

∞ 29 ∞
Lady Dyna

The lift came to a quick, shaky stop. A soft chime sounded as the door slid open silently. Warm yellow light revealed yet another small, empty room. Without a word, the commander stepped out and turned into a dark corridor to their left. His boots clicked against the marble floor, echoing through the narrow passage. The tunnel stretched on with many branches and turns. They passed countless doors without slowing.

At last, the commander stopped before a nondescript door and pulled out a key. A hush—and a sudden sense of awe—fell over the group as they entered a vast chamber. The opulence of the furniture and décor made it clear that this was a royal residence. Gold and jewels adorned every surface, making the room sparkle under the electric lighting.

A woman appearing to be in her late fifties sat near a large bay window. A breeze and scent of flowers drifted through the open window. The commander walked briskly toward her and snapped to attention, clicking his heels before she turned to look at him.

"My dear Tryfon. So good to see you again. Who have you brought to me?" She turned her gaze to the group of nine.

"Lady Dyna. May I introduce you to Neiaphi, daughter of Altesse and Neiluios."

Lady Dyna abruptly stood, approached Neiaphi, and then fell to her knees, pressing her forehead to the ground.

Neiaphi stared at the prostrated royal. "Please, don't do that." Neiaphi reached down and touched the woman's shoulder. "I am not accepting the throne. I'm just Neiaphi."

Andonis, Tivadarios, and the guards shared looks of confusion.

"Do you know what they're talking about?" Tivadarios whispered to Andonis, who shook his head in response.

Lady Dyna took Neiaphi's hand and stood. "Please introduce your entourage," she said.

Neiaphi looked at the men with her. She hadn't expected Lady Dyna's response when they met. She locked eyes with Andonis. She hadn't told him about her secret past. Asan had told her not to tell anyone. *I told Cret, though,* she thought. *He should have heard it from me. I'll have to speak to him when this is finished.*

"Lady Dyna, sister to King Poseidon Thodoris, the current King of Atlantis, I am pleased to introduce to you, my companions. Cret, Andonis, Lieutenant Greish, Tivadarios, Aristas, Bacceon, Alex, and Nik," Neiaphi told her.

"It is a pleasure to meet so many from Romota and our outlying settlements." Lady Dyna bowed her head.

"Lady Dyna, if I may," Cret said, stepping forward. "We have grave news and need your help."

She waved her hand with a smile. "Yes, yes, I know. The Lemurians are about to attack, and then my brother will launch a counterattack."

"You know?" Neiaphi asked.

She smiled warmly. "Pythia and I speak regularly. Nothing happens on this planet and even on Romota that I do not know about."

"What are you planning to do?" Andonis asked. "Me? Nothing," she replied.

"Nothing?" Aristas blurted out. "How can you say that you will do nothing?" Everyone nodded.

"I will not be doing nothing?"

"But you just said that," Andonis said.

She shook her head. "I said I was not planning to do

anything. That decision falls to another." She turned her eyes to Neiaphi.

"Me?" Neiaphi's hands flew to her chest.

"Yes, child. You may not wish to rule, but it is your destiny to save your people. Why are you here?"

"Cret found out about the Lemurians and felt he needed to save as many from Atlantis, and I'm here to help."

Lady Dyna chuckled. "While I'm sure that is correct, I also know that only you, Neiaphi, can convince the population to flee."

"Why would they listen to me?" Neiaphi asked. "Because of who you are, of course."

"But I do not want the throne. I don't want to rule. Asan told me to tell no one who I am if I didn't want that path. For my safety and that of my family, I must remain in hiding."

"Unfortunately, there is no other option. Once everyone knows who you are, they will follow you."

"I will convince them to leave with us," Cret stepped forward, stepping in front of Neiaphi. "That is why I was sent here. Pythia said Atlantis needed me. This is my path.

"Very noble of you, Cret." Dyna smiled sweetly. "But the people will not listen to you. Trust me—I know my people. Neiaphi, you must tell them who you are. I will help you. But you, and you alone, are the only one who can do this. Cret and Andonis may stand at your side, but it is you they will listen to."

Neiaphi glanced at Cret and then at Andonis. *Why did she mention both of them?*

"Okay, I will do what I must do," she said aloud.

"No," Cret said forcefully. "Asan told you to keep your identity secret for your safety." His eyes pleaded with her to reconsider.

She placed a hand on his arm. "I have to do this. These people must be saved. Our people must be saved."

They stared into each other's eyes for several heartbeats until Cret finally nodded.

"Wait a minute," Andonis said, closing the gap

between them. "How can you let her do this, Cret? I've only just learned about her identity and still have many questions. But this course seems risky and dangerous. If that Agarthan told us to keep it secret, I think we need to listen to him."

Neiaphi stepped forward until she stood directly before him. She lifted her chin to gaze up at him. He took her hands and pressed them to his chest. "I'm sorry I didn't tell you about the family secret we've just uncovered. My mother is from the royal line. An ancestor of hers was switched at birth and hidden from his father, the king of Romota, through marriage. That king's mistress bore him a son, whom he claimed as his rightful heir. That line became the current ruling family. I am the rightful queen-heir of Romota. My brother, Icarus, is the rightful king when he comes of age., until I bare a son."

Andonis shook his head. "No, Praxis is. The eldest of the twins." He looked at her with deep concern. "Icarus died on Romota, remember?"

"No. We've since learned he lives, and he's aboard the centaur transport on his way back to us. I will not be returning to Romota. My home is here, on Earth. And if, in order to save the people of Atlantis, I must reveal my identity—then that is what I must do." She released his hands and turned to Dyna.

"What do I need to do?"

"The first thing," Dyna said firmly, "is a bath and a new dress. Come, we have much work to do." She clapped her hands sharply, and the main door to her chamber swung open. Two guards and four chambermaids entered. "Take the men to my guest quarters—baths and new attire for all of them."

Both guards and two maids bowed in unison. The last two maids grabbed Neiaphi by the hands and led her through another door.

"I'll see everyone soon," Neiaphi called over her shoulder.

The sun was well above the horizon and already slipping into evening before Neiaphi found herself bathed, rested, fed, and dressed in a simple white gown. The soft cotton fabric felt cool against her freshly scrubbed skin.

She sat alone in Lady Dyna's antechamber, gazing through a wide bay window at an immaculately tended garden. Flowers of every color were arranged in careful patterns, while a cobblestone path wound gracefully among them. Benches and fountains dotted the landscape, adding to its serenity. Songbirds called from the trees, and squirrels and rabbits darted between shrubs and blossoms.

She could get used to a garden like that.

The door to Dyna's main room opened, pulling her attention away from the view. Lady Dyna entered, followed closely by the two chambermaids who had assisted Neiaphi earlier. "Are you ready?" Lady Dyna asked.

Neiaphi swallowed and then nodded. "I think so."

"Now, now. That is no way to think. A royal always knows what they are going to say, even if they don't. If you must pause to think, do so with a frown or a thoughtful look. The people will assume you are looking for the right words to convey your meaning. You must never let them know you don't know what to say."

"I'm not royalty."

"Maybe not in here." Lady Dyna tapped a finger on Neiaphi's forehead. "But in here you are." She jabbed her in the chest. "And that is all that matters. Now, let's go over what you are going to say again." Lady Dyna gestured to one of the couches and took a seat herself.

The chambermaids busied themselves laying out the gown Neiaphi would wear to the meeting. The newly altered gown and jewelry know awaiting her.

Neiaphi's heart pounded in her chest. The sun had set some time ago, and Lady Dyna had arranged a private meeting with the leaders and council members she trusted most.

They had journeyed into the city and now stood in a vast warehouse near Alta Bay. The air was thick with the mingled scents of sea salt and fish. Neiaphi glanced down at her gown for what felt like the hundredth time. The purple-and-gold fabric clung to her like a second skin beneath the voluminous cloak she wore. She had never dressed in anything so tight before, but Lady Dyna had insisted it was the height of Romotian fashion.

Neiaphi and her group waited in the shadows, allowing Lady Dyna to address the gathering first.

A man soon emerged before the assembly. He wore a simple tunic belted at the waist with a green sash. His black hair was slicked back, and his neatly trimmed beard tapered to a sharp point at his chin.

"Thank you for coming so quickly," he said in a rich bass voice.

"Why have you called us, Michalis?" someone asked from the crowd.

"Every time we assemble, we risk exposure," someone else called out.

Michalis raised his hands. "The time has come," he said simply.

"Time for what?"

Michalis looked at the man who spoke. "Don't act like you don't know what I refer to, Stelios. It is time to evacuate."

"Surely it can't be that bad?"

"Where would you have us go?"

"I can't abandon my business?"

"How will we leave? We have no ships."

These and many more questions rang out. Neiaphi covered her ears as the voices rose in anger, confusion, and fear.

Michalis waited patiently until the voices died down, having received no answers. "The Lemurians are going to attack soon. Some help for Romota has arrived. We are certain we can get everyone to safety." "But where will we go?"

Lady Dyna stepped from the shadows and approached. A hush fell over the crowd, followed by a growing murmur.

She smiled warmly, gazing at her subjects. "Thank you for risking so much by coming here tonight. As you all know,

I have devoted my life trying to undue the wrongs of my family." She hung her head for a moment and then looked back up. "Unfortunately, I have little to show for my efforts. I am happy to announce that I now have a plan that will work."

"You were supposed to remove the King," a quiet voice near the front of the room said.

"That was the plan, yes. But the Society foiled that. The descendant of our choosing has arrived and awaits us."

"Then who have you brought before us, if not him?"

"You have all learned our history—the history long hidden from most, both on Romota and on Earth," Lady Dyna declared. Her voice carried firmly through the warehouse. "Aristos Addident, also of Posidies' line, was brought here to usurp my brother. And you know that generations ago, the true heir to Romota was taken away and hidden. I am proud to say that we finally found that line. With the help of the Agarthans, the line knows their secret, and the eldest is here today." Lady Dyna turned to face the shadowed corner and held her hand out.

Cret and Andonis approached with Neiaphi following close behind, her cloak's hood hiding her face.

The assembly quieted.

"Before the heir reveals themselves. I would like to introduce a couple of their companions. Andonis, from the realm beyond the Chief Sea and Cret from Romota."

All eyes were glued onto Cret, and quiet whispers erupted. After the room quieted once more, Neiaphi stepped forward.

"We are beyond blessed to be in the presence of the rightful Queen Heir Neiaphi," Lady Dyna said, dropping into a deep curtsy.

Neiaphi lifted her hood and let it fall behind her.

"Why are you on Earth? You should be on Romota, assuming the crown," an angry voice called out.

"Where is your brother?"

"How old is he?"

"What's his name?"

A barrage of questions assaulted her, causing her cheeks to flare.

A loud, piercing whistle cut through the warehouse, echoing off the ceramic roof tiles.

"Let her speak and then ask your questions," Greish roared.

The warehouse fell into a tense quiet.

"Thank you, Lieutenant Greish," Neiaphi said and then took another step forward, squaring her shoulders. "My family and I did not learn about our heritage until only a few days ago. Back on Romota, my brother, Icarus, was approached by a loyalist wolver. She was young and timid and was chosen to contact my family because she was swift. She was spooked, and instead of speaking to us, she stole my brother. My parents thought he was killed."

A collective gasp rippled through the crowd. "But he lives, correct?"

Neiaphi smiled. "Yes, and he is on his way here as we speak. Please, allow me to continue," she said loudly when the room erupted again. "My brother will be allowed to choose his own future. At only four years old, he is too young to assume the crown, and I will not be returning to Romota."

"Then why are you here?"

"I am here to offer you a choice. The others who came from Romota with my family, and all those whose lineages trace back to Romota, have three options before them.

"The first choice will be to come with my family to the mainland—to the spot the Oracle Pythia has shown my father. My brothers, Praxis and Anais, are destined to build the greatest civilization known to Earth.

"The second choice will be to join the centaurs and return to Romota." Whispers surged again at the mention of the centaurs.

"The third choice is to go to Agartha with Addident and his family. For those who don't know, Agartha is located in the center of this planet." Neiaphi took a few steps back, standing between Cret and Andonis. Cret bumped her shoulder with his, smiling at her.

"Good job," Andonis told her.

"But how do we know the Lemurians are truly going to attack? There have been no sightings, no warnings," someone called out.

A chorus of agreement rang out.

"You will know it when you hear it from me," a woman said from the rear of the room.

All heads turned, and slowly the room parted. A woman, wearing a uniform, flanked by three uniformed men, strode forward. Cret walked forward and greeted her.

"Cret? By Zeus's favor, you're alive. Where did you and your companions go? One minute you were on the ship and the next you were gone," Pavlina said, accepting his greeting, grasping his wrist.

"The Agarthans froze time and escorted us here. How did you survive? I thought for sure both ships were about to be destroyed. Do you have my horse?" he asked in a rush.

"Barely, we survived only by the sheer will of the gods," Pavlina answered. "And yes, we have your horses. *The Gilded Pegasus* docked just last night."

Cret let out a relieved sigh.

"What about the Agarthans?" "

What about the Lemurians?"

The gathered grew angry once more.

"I have met with the Lemurian King. He will not back down. Even though Aristos Addident has arrived, King Luthais will not be swayed any longer. He will be attacking any day now."

"He told you that? How can you believe him?" Michalis asked.

"He knows I have no love for our king. My advice is to follow Neiaphi's suggestions and be on the move as soon as you can, no delays."

"To where? How do we get off the island?" Michalis asked.

Andonis took a step forward. "Venture to the other side of the island. There is a large villa. Our transportation will arrive in four days."

"What if we are detained?" someone shouted from the rear of the room.

"I'll be ensuring our defenses are occupied. No one will be looking at the populace, especially the king," Pavlina told them.

"Agreed," Lady Dyna said. "My brother will be in his bunker as soon as the fighting starts."

"Do you know when the Lemurians are going to attack?"

"No. But I know when they will launch their counterattack. We will be hitting them first—tonight. I know where their fleet is waiting. Make sure everyone you care about is out of the city. Atlantis will not survive the coming war."

"You sound so certain about that," a voice drifted to them.

"The Kemites have spies everywhere. The weapon they have will annihilate the island. Being behind Mount Cleto might save you."

"Might?" several people screamed at once.

"Don't be here to find out." Pavlina glared at everyone.

The group of men argued amongst themselves for several fingers of time, their voices rising and falling in heated bursts.

Cret, Greish, and Tivadarios stood apart, speaking quietly with Pavlina and Lady Dyna.

Neiaphi lingered off to the side, tugging at her gown and wishing it were not quite so tight.

"Would you like to sit?" Andonis asked as he stepped up beside her.

"I don't think this dress will allow me to," she admitted with a small wince.

He smiled faintly. "I hope you don't mind me saying—it suits you."

Her cheeks warmed, and she quickly dropped her eyes to the floor, shaking her head.

They stood together in silence, though Andonis's gaze never left her. At last, Neiaphi broke it. "I'm sorry."

He studied her a moment longer before speaking. "For what?"

"For wavering in my decision, and not being brave enough to voice my choice," she said barely over a whisper.

He shrugged. "I offered you this out and…" He paused. "I allowed my eyes to stray, shaming you."

She placed a hand on his arm. "You didn't shame me. I… I overreacted. Learning that Cret was so near, I…" She stopped talking, dropping her chin to her chest.

"What is it?" He pressed, taking one of her hands.

"I guess subconsciously, I was looking for an out without hurting either of us. I know now that was never possible. I… I hope we can be friends." She looked up at him, tears dancing in her eyes.

"I would like that, Neiaphi. Looking back, that's all I should have been to you—a close friend and nothing more."

He smiled down at her. A tear slipped from her eye, and before he could stop himself, he brushed it away, his hand cupping the side of her face. Her cheeks flushed once again, and he quickly let his hand fall back to his side.

Neiaphi excused herself, moving toward the rear of the room. "I need to be closer to the door… to the fresh air," she said softly.

When the debate finally ended and the decision for evacuation was made, Neiaphi and her companions followed Lady Dyna back to the palace.

They entered through a servant's entrance and were immediately stopped by the King's personal guard.

"Lady Dyna, the King has demanded your appearance," the captain barked, snapping to a quick salute.

"I will see him as soon as my guests are settled," she replied and started to walk past him.

The captain grabbed her arm, bringing her to a stop. She glared at the man's hand before looking up at him.

"Unhand me," she said with an air of command.

"I must insist that you and your friends come with me now."

She opened her mouth to protest, but closed it abruptly when two soldiers unsheathed their swords.

"Well then, Captain, why didn't you say it was so urgent?" Lady Dyna's tone shifted smoothly, though her eyes flicked toward Neiaphi's group with a silent warning. "My apologies, dear friends. It seems plans have changed. Let us see what my brother requires of us at this late hour."

The captain gave a curt gesture for her to move ahead, then fell into step behind her. The remaining soldiers closed ranks at the rear, blades glinting in the lamplight, their presence leaving no doubt that resistance was not an option.

"I'll think of something," Cret whispered to Neiaphi. Neiaphi nodded without speaking, not trusting her voice.

∞ 30 ∞
THRONE ROOM

They walked in silence through the palace corridors. Neiaphi's gaze swept over the marble and granite statues lining both sides of the vast hallway, each figure immortalized in a proud, eternal stance. To their right, tall arched windows, open to the night, let in warm air carrying the sweet fragrance of blooming flowers. Chandeliers hung at precise intervals overhead, their electric light dazzling against her eyes.

As they passed beneath one, she tilted her head back, marveling at its brilliance. How strange it felt—after a year of sunlight by day and fire by night—to stand beneath such artificial radiance.

The soldiers' boots clicking against the marble floor—the only sound.

Lady Dyna strode confidently ahead, shoulders squared and head high, her poise betraying no unease. Neiaphi forced herself to mirror that calm, though her heart pounded harder with each step.

At the corridor's end loomed two massive doors, their surfaces etched from base to peak with intricate designs traced in gold and silver. Four guards stood before them, armor gleaming beneath the chandeliers.

They clicked their heels together and crossed their spears, barring the entryway.

"Lady Dyna and guests to see the King at his demand," the Captain said.

As one, the guards nodded and moved aside. Two of

them grabbed gilded rope handles and pulled the doors open.

On well-oiled hinges, the doors opened wide. Lady Dyna walked through without prodding and marched up to the dais.

Inside, guards lined the throne room, standing rigid along a crimson carpet that stretched through the center. Between each soaring stained-glass window hung rich tapestries. Overhead, five chandeliers—three times larger than those in the hall—glittered two stories above. The white marble floor shone with blinding brilliance. At the far end, a dais rose ten feet high, crowned by a solitary golden throne. Upon it slumped the king, leaning heavily on one armrest. His broad frame filled the seat, purple robes rumpled from a restless night. A gaudy crown perched crookedly atop his head, completing his disheveled majesty.

"What took you so long?" The king barked.

The captain halted at the foot of the stairs leading to the dais and snapped a crisp salute before dropping to his knees and bowing.

"Lady Dyna was not in her quarters, sire."

"And where was she?" the king demanded.

Lady Dyna walked forward without speaking, stopping a length behind the captain before falling to her knees and pressing her head to the floor.

A quick glance at Andonis and Aristas confirmed that they should assume the same position.

"She was escorting guests to the guest quarters, Sire," the captain answered.

"What were you doing, sister?" The king asked, his voice dripping with venom.

"I was escorting guests," she answered without looking up.

"Rise," he said impatiently.

Neiaphi lifted her head and quickly lowered it when she saw only Lady Dyna rising.

"I was meeting with my spies, sire," she answered him.

"And what did your little birds tell you," he all but

growled.”

“War is coming…”

The king waved a hand at her. “We know about the coming war,” he said.

“But… have your spies told you that a fleet of Lemurian warships is less than a day away and coming in fast?” she asked calmly. Her voice was low, and her tone was like speaking to a child, not a king.

“RISE!” He yelled.

Every head shot up. The king's eyes were wide with fright.

“And you are just now telling us this.”

Lady Dyna held her hands out in a helpless manner. “I was not given the chance to come to you on my own accord. I was coming this way to warn you, sire. My utmost concern is for your well-being. Come, we must get you to the vault. You will be safe there, and your army and navy are more than capable of handling and thwarting this attack. The Lemurians have no idea who they are dealing with.”

A smile spread across the king’s face. “Flattery will get you nowhere, dear sister.”

She dropped into a deep curtsy. “I offer no flattery, only truth, my liege.”

The king studied her briefly before shifting his gaze to the group standing a few steps behind her.

“Explain,” he commanded, his voice sharp.

“We have two envoys that were onboard *The Gilded Pegasus* coming to see you with Royalty from the Centaur Nation…”

“Centaurs! Preposterous,” he spat. “Centaurs have long been extinct.”

“No, only in hiding, my liege.”

He made a rude noise with his mouth and then scrubbed his face. “If the envoys are here, where is the King?” His patience was waning.

Cret stepped forward and bowed at the waist, keeping his eyes on the ground.

"Speak," the king said.

"Thank you, King Poseidon Thodoris. My name is Cret. It is true that Tivadarios and I were traveling with the King and Queen of the Centaurs aboard *The Gilded Pegasus* when the Lemurians boarded and dragged us away. Though we managed to escape, the centaurs were taken captive. Fortunately, *The Gilded Pegasus*, sailing close behind, rescued us from the sea."

"Who are these others?"

"My invited guests from the outlying settlements," Lady Dyna replied.

"More of your spies?" He shook his head. "Meddling in affairs that are not your concern again?"

"The welfare of our people is my concern. However, your safety is my top priority right now. Please, brother—we must get you to safety."

The king's face reddened, and he squinted. "I will not cower in fear of the Lemurians. Atlantis is destined to rule this world, and soon the Lemurians will be nothing but a memory."

Lady Dyna gasped. "What have you done?"

"Soon… very soon, they will cease to exist. I have ensured it. Our ships approach even now, armed with my newest creation—Mazikos Thanatos. The explosion will dwarf anything the world has ever witnessed. We may even see the plume from here."

"How dare you?" Lady Dyna whispered.

"How dare I?" The king lurched to his feet, swaying before gripping the arm of his throne. His voice thundered. "How dare *they*! Poseidon claimed this planet for his descendants—for me. The Lemurians are pacifists. They are no match for us."

"Those pacifists will be attacking us in less than two days."

"Do not lecture me, woman!" he roared. "A worthless woman who refuses to marry, refuses to give me an heir, and meddles in affairs beyond her reach. Now, begone!"

"Just tell me you are going to the bunker," Lady Dyna

implored.

"We shall be going to my war chamber, not that it should be any of your concern.

Leave us!" His voice elevated.

Lady Dyna bowed and started to back away. Everyone mirrored her actions.

Once out of the throne room, Lady Dyna picked up the pace. "Come, we must get you out of the palace, quickly."

"What's the hurry?" Greish asked.

"My brother is extremely unstable in health, mind, and spirit."

"He appears weak," Aristas said, disgust lacing his words.

"He's been unsteady on his feet for moons now." She shook her head.

"Why hasn't he married?" Neiaphi asked, striding up next to Dyna.

"Oh, he has—three times. None bore him a male heir. The first two gave him daughters, and he banished both wives along with their children. The third failed to conceive, and her fate remains unknown. My spies have searched, but I fear the worst."

Soon, the palace came alive. Servants hurried from room to room, while soldiers raced through the corridors shouting orders. The Lemurians were attacking the harbor. Lady Dyna led them down a side hallway that opened into a circular chamber dominated by a massive golden statue of Poseidon in his chariot, drawn by four winged steeds. Broad arches framed a sweeping view of the city and harbor. The night sky blazed with cannon fire, burning buildings, and ships aflame.

Neiaphi's breath caught in her throat. Aside from the others standing with her, this was the very vision that had haunted her dreams.

"Atlantis is going to be destroyed. We have to get out of the city, now!"

Andonis rushed to her side. "Did you dream about this

day?" His eyes took in her frightened expression. He grabbed her hands—she was shaking.

She nodded her head and took a deep breath.

"It's a little different, but the burning city is the same. I know the way—come." Without waiting to see if anyone followed, she sprinted from Poseidon's tribute just as a blast shook the palace. She stopped before a tapestry of a former Atlantean king and pushed it aside, revealing a narrow doorway already standing open.

"Pythia has helped us this night," Lady Dyna said. "Quickly—go! Neiaphi knows the way. Stay safe. I pray I see you all again." She embraced Neiaphi and whispered in her ear. Neiaphi nodded, then stepped into the dark passage.

∞ **31** ∞
FLEEING

The tunnel led ever downward as it had in her dream. When they arrived at the staircase, she paused. Andonis shouldered his way to the front.

"What's the matter?" he whispered.

"In the dream, there were people down there waiting for me."

"Soldiers?" he asked, alarm causing his voice to crack.

"What's the matter?" Cret hissed.

"It's nothing," Neiaphi said. "There won't be anyone down there." "How can you be certain?" Andonis asked.

"Because none of you were with me in the dream. Come on." She gritted her teeth and started down the stairs, hoping she was right.

The staircase ended in a small room with dim lighting—just as she remembered—but it was empty.

"See? Now, come I feel the need to be far from this place."

Neiaphi headed to the left—a corridor cast in shadows greeted them.

To the right of the passage was an electric lantern swinging slightly. She grabbed the lantern and headed in.

Another blast hit the palace far above their heads. The tunnel groaned and vibrated, causing dust and debris to shower down on them.

"How long is this tunnel?" Tivadarios asked, his voice shaky.

"I don't know," Neiaphi answered.

"Didn't you dream about this tunnel?" Greish asked her.

"Well, no, not exactly."

"Wait, what?" Andonis asked.

"My dream ended back there." She gestured behind them.

"What?" several men asked at once.

"Quiet," Neiaphi hissed. " I see a light up ahead."

Cret slowly drew his sword, keeping the scrape of steel against leather to barely more than a whisper, and then shouldered past Neiaphi to take the lead.

Cret crept toward the light ahead of the others, halted at the intersection, and raised a hand to stop them. He peered around the corner, then gestured for everyone to follow.

No one needed Cret to explain where the tunnel was leading. The putrid stench of the sewer drifted over them. Bile rose in Neiaphi's throat, and a shiver of fear rippled down her spine.

The sickening odor grew stronger as they neared the intersection. Muffled retching echoed from the tunnel behind, making Neiaphi feel slightly better—at least she was managing to keep her stomach under control.

Dim yellow electric lights, set at intervals along the channel, made the greenish-brown water look even worse than it had under torchlight.

Neiaphi took the lead again, moving along the narrow ledge beside the murky channel. Her sandals slipped against the slick green mold, and her too-tight dress forced her strides short. On the opposite ledge, a cluster of rats mirrored her progress. Neiaphi's eyes flicked constantly between the rodents and the treacherous ground beneath her feet.

"You're doing well," Cret said quietly behind her. "Don't worry about the rats. They're more frightened of you than you are of them."

She chuckled dryly. "I seriously doubt that."

"Just keep walking, we'll be out of here soon."

Suddenly, there was a loud commotion from the rear of their procession. Several voices echoed together, making it impossible to understand, followed by splashes. The men from the rear of the group surged forward.

"RUN!!" They yelled.

Cret grabbed Neiaphi's shoulder, spinning her to face him.

"What—" She began to speak, but stopped when Cret seized the hem of her dress, ripping a slit up to her upper thigh before shoving her into the channel.

"Run." He jumped in behind her, grabbed her hand, and pulled her forward.

The waist-deep water wrapped around her like a slimy cloak. It felt like millions of fingers raking across her bare legs. Her sandals slipped and squelched in the muck—at least that's what she told herself she was running through. Fixing her gaze on the passage ahead, she surged forward, Cret tugging her slightly faster.

The sounds of their pursuers grew louder. Tears streamed down Neiaphi's cheeks, but she kept her eyes forward, forcing herself to ignore the filth she was slogging through.

The tunnel ahead brightened gradually with the flickering glow of torches. She gritted her teeth and pushed herself harder. Voices echoed ahead, but whatever was behind them sounded far worse.

The channel spilled into a broader passage, its water fouler still. Neiaphi's stomach gave way, and she emptied its meager contents into the reeking current.

"Halt! Who goes there?" A gruff voice asked. Neiaphi looked up, surprised to see two soldiers, a council member, and six prisoners.

The others closed in around her protectively.

"Lieutenant Greish, is that you?" The council member asked.

"Counsel Fanis? Interesting place to run into you," Greish said, sloshing ahead.

"Lady Dyna said I was needed down here. I assumed it was because of—well." He gestured at the condition of the sewer. "She is always so cryptic." He chuckled.

"We're being chased," Cret said, motioning for everyone to hurry.

"Come, come. I can help." Fanis rushed ahead of them and gestured for them to climb a ladder. He spoke quietly to his two soldiers. Both nodded and slapped their hands to their hearts, and then vaulted up the ladder without another word. After Neiaphi and her group reached the top of the sewer, they were ushered into a small cell off to the side. The second soldier had already gathered a few more men, and together they were descending back into the sewer.

"Come," Counsel Fanis said, approaching their open cell. "Let's get you back into the forest."

Neiaphi tried not to touch anything she didn't have to. Her hands were still coated in the slimy filth of the sewers. She gingerly held Nexus's reins and regretted sitting in the beautiful saddle her father had bought for her. For the hundredth time, she tugged at her dress, trying to stretch the fabric over her exposed leg. The garment had never been meant for riding, and if Cret hadn't torn the form-fitting skirt, she wouldn't have been able to mount at all. Glancing at the men around her, she chastised herself for such feminine worries.

They were all miserable, filthy, cold, and afraid. Yet Greish and his two fellow guards looked the least shaken. If she had to wager on their feelings, she would bet they were more angry than afraid.

Cypress whined up at her, and a smile cracked through her worried frown. "It's okay, boy. Everything's going to be fine. I hope."

The night sky behind them glowed with countless fires, while a cacophony of cannon blasts shattered the silence— mingling with the screams of horses and the distant drone of Atlantean voices raised in panic.

They rode at a measured pace, letting their horses

choose their own path through the dense underbrush. Nexus stumbled over an exposed root, snorted, and tossed her head.

Neiaphi patted her on the neck and glanced around. The thick canopy of trees blocked out the light and sounds from Atlantis.

Neiaphi jerked awake, startled to realize she had dozed off. A dim light shimmered ahead. Dozens of torches flickered in the ocean breeze, outlining the Villa's perimeter. She sighed deeply and hung her head. She was almost safe again.

Greish, Alex, and Nik led the horses toward the stables while the others made their way up the Villa's steps in silence.

"Would anyone like some tea?" Neiaphi asked. A few nodded.

"I need food," Tivadarios said.

"You always need food," Cret replied.

"What can I say? I'm a growing boy."

Neiaphi shook her head at the exchange. "I'll see if there's anything in the kitchen."

Soon, Neiaphi had mugs filled with lavender tea and a platter of sliced bread and cheese on a small table in the Villa's kitchen. She sat heavily on one of the chairs, trying to keep her eyes open while she waited for the others.

"You should head to bed," Andonis said, entering the kitchen.

"Soon."

"You couldn't find anything hot?" Tivadarios asked, walking in behind Andonis.

"Wow, really?" Cret chided.

"May the Gods strike you down for such an inconsiderate remark," Aristas retorted.

"I was only joking," Tivadarios whined. "Really, Neiaphi, really. I didn't mean it."

She waved her hand slowly. "Honestly, I'm too tired and dirty to care."

The room fell silent as everyone took a seat. With mouths full and a warm mug in their hands, the events of the night played out in their minds.

"We were lucky tonight," Greish said, breaking the silence.

"This planet is trying to kill us," Tivadarios remarked.

"The Gods are watching over us," Aristas said.

Greish snorted in agreement. "I pray we have such luck for the rest of our days."

"Darios? I haven't seen Samira around. Where did she go?" Neiaphi asked.

Tivadarios's face fell. "She went home. I tried to get her to stay, but she said she was needed. I thought about asking to go with her…" he trailed off.

"Did you tell her how much you liked her?" Neiaphi pressed.

He shrugged. "I didn't know how to bring it up. I don't think she felt the same way anyway. I'll be fine." He looked up and smiled weakly. "Really, I'll be fine." He patted her hand.

Neiaphi smiled and nodded. "Greish, do you know when we will depart?"

"I think the Agarthans are taking a group to Agartha in a few hours."

"Well then, I'd better get some rest. Thank you all for your help tonight." Neiaphi rose to her feet, prompting the men to stand with her. She waved her hands down with a smile. "No need to stand. I'll see you all soon."

"I'll walk with you," Cret said.

Neiaphi and Cret walked through the quiet gathering hall. "Let's head to the bathhouse first," Cret said.

"I just want my bed," Neiaphi said softly.

"You'll sleep better after your clean." He grabbed her elbow and led her past the staircase.

Her steps started to slow as weariness seeped into her

bones. Cret draped an arm around her shoulders to steady her.

The woman's bathroom was empty with the lateness of the hour.

"Can you manage on your own, or do you require assistance?" Cret asked.

Neiaphi looked up at him. He wore a playful smile. "I think I'll be able to manage just fine, good sir," she replied.

"I'm here if you need me," he teased.

She swatted his shoulder. "Be gone with you."

"Sir? Ma'am? Can I be of assistance?" A sleepy voice asked from the doorway. A young housemaid in her nightdress walked in, stifling a yawn.

"Sorry to have awoken you. I won't be here long," Neiaphi told her. Cret turned to leave.

"Wake me before everyone leaves," Neiaphi said.

Cret looked back at her. "You should sleep. Everyone will understand."

"No, I have to be there. I have to say goodbye. Please, Cret, promise me."

He walked back to her and grabbed her hands. "I promise I will wake you, and if you are too tired to wake, I'll drape you over my shoulder and carry you down the stairs."

She sighed, leaning forward until her forehead was on his chest. "I'll hold you to that."

Releasing her hands, he grabbed her shoulders and leaned her back. "Sleep well, I'll see you soon." He kissed her forehead and then left her with the attendant.

∞ **32** ∞
REFUGEES

The sun hung low in the eastern sky, casting a soft rose-gold hue across the puffy clouds. Everyone gathered on the beach, their mood somber as once again they said goodbye to friends. A gentle breeze ruffled the calm water, which lapped rhythmically against the white sand.

Four sleek silver cylinder-crafts awaited them, while numerous Agarthans stood along the shore, offering quiet welcomes and reassurances to those departing. When the last craft dipped below the current, several Loyalist women broke into a soft song. No one else joined the melody, but tears flowed freely from those left behind.

At midday, the first refugees from Atlantis began to arrive. Men and women—dirty and scared, with confused and terrified children—clinging to their parents.

Neiluios and Crelian took charge, showing the newcomers where their families could rest and escorting the men to the gathering hall.

Neiaphi, Alexa, and several other girls assisted their mothers in distributing food and drink, while Altesse and Phebis spoke quietly with a large group of women nearby.

As Neiaphi walked through the refugees, a quiet murmuring reached her ears. When she turned to hear better, she met large eyes and still lips. Neiaphi frowned and rolled her shoulders.

"Something wrong?" Nidora asked, walking up to Neiaphi.

Neiaphi startled, then shook her head. "Nothing, really. I'm just not used to this much attention. Yesterday, in Atlantis, they held a meeting…and I told them who I was."

Nidora raised an eyebrow. "Just who you are, or your link to the line?"

"My link. It appears the story of the line is well known here."

They continued weaving through the scared mass of people, handing out food and beverages.

"Have you decided what you will do? Where you will go?" Nidora asked. She handed a container of water and a loaf of bread to an elderly woman and then turned to face Neiaphi.

Neiaphi smiled and shook her head.

"What?" Nidora smiled.

"I think this is the longest conversation we've had…ever."

Nidora laughed. "I think you're right. I'm sorry. I've wasted a lot of time." She shook her head. "I think we could have been good friends."

Neiaphi nodded. "Are you going to Agartha with your parents?"

"I think so. Staying with my father until I'm promised is the smart thing to do. What about you? You have two vying for your affection. I've heard that Andonis is undecided where he will go. Has Cret made up his mind?"

"Not that I'm aware of. Helping Atlantis has been his driving force. We haven't spoken about what comes next."

"Have you decided who you want to be with?" Nidora dropped her eyes.

"I have."

"Oh really, who?"

"I haven't told them yet. I think I need to tell them first."

"When are you going to tell them?"

Neiaphi stopped walking and looked at her. "Why the interest?"

Nidora's cheeks flared. "I know someone interested in Andonis," she said quietly.

Neiaphi smiled and laid a hand on Nidora's arm. "He's a great catch. Has that person spoken to him much?"

"A little bit recently. I hope that's okay."

"Can we sit?" Neiaphi asked.

Nidora nodded and led the way to a quiet spot in the garden. They sat in silence for a few moments.

"I'll be telling Andonis that I have chosen Cret," Neiaphi said quietly.

Nidora looked at Neiaphi and tilted her head. "I knew you would."

"Really? How?"

"I knew it back in Camp Roma. You've always loved him."

"How did you know? I didn't."

Nidora laughed, throwing her head back. "Anyone who truly looked at you the day his father and he left for the processing plant could have seen it. Everyone was looking at the departed." She shrugged and dropped her eyes to her lap. "I…I feel horrible admitting this…"

"What is it?" Neiaphi asked, placing a hand on top of hers.

"I was jealous of your relationship with Cret. I…I didn't have anything like that. I felt everyone was beneath me."

"Oh, Nidora. I'm so sorry. I always thought that I should try to speak to you, considering we're only a few years apart in age. Closer than any of those younger than me."

Nidora sighed. "I know. I was foolish."

"Do you think Andonis likes you?" Neiaphi asked.

"I'm not sure. He knocked on my door when he first arrived, looking for you, and then I spoke with him after he saw you. I don't think he ever looked at me before."

They sat in silence, watching a small group of Laosian and Loyalist children dart among the refugees, trying in vain to draw others into their play. After several failed attempts, laughter finally broke out as a few willing children joined them.

A sharp bark drew their attention. Not far away, Greish

and Andonis sat with Cypress at their side. Neiaphi's gaze drifted across the Villa's grounds, seeing but not truly noticing—until movement caught her eye. Cret emerged from the stable, leading a coal-black horse.

Smiling, she stood. "I'll see you a little later," she said to Nidora.

"Bye," the other girl said, distracted. Neiaphi followed her line of sight—it led to Andonis.

"How about that ride?" Neiaphi asked, walking up the path.

Cret smiled. "Let's grab a saddle."

A few minutes later, Neiaphi was sitting astride Cret's horse, Rees. "He is a fine animal," she said.

Rees snorted and flipped his head. "Best I've seen," Cret replied. "Lieutenant Pavlina dropped him off this morning."

Neiaphi tapped her heels against Rees's sides, urging him into a trot. Rees responded immediately. She maneuvered in a figure-8 pattern and then asked him to canter. When she stopped in front of Cret, she was smiling from ear to ear.

"You can't have him," Cret said, returning her smile.

She laughed. "I would never give up my Nexus, but he is a fine mount." She dismounted and handed him the reins. "Better late than never."

A stable boy appeared and led Rees into the stable, leaving them alone. She glanced up and smiled.

"What?" he asked.

"You've grown so much. You've always been taller than me, but I never used to need to stand on my tiptoes to kiss you." Her cheeks flushed, and she quickly dropped her gaze as embarrassment washed over her. "Sorry… I shouldn't have said that."

Cret placed a finger under her chin and lifted her head to look at him. "I don't mind," he said softly.

"I…" She started, but Cret shook his head.

"Let me speak."

Neiaphi nodded, a shaky sigh escaping her lips.

Cret took her hand and walked to a bench in front of the stable.

"I want you to know that your happiness is all I've ever wanted," Cret began. "So, no matter what you choose, please choose with your heart…"

Neiaphi opened her mouth to speak. Cret placed a finger over her lips to stop her and shook his head.

"I don't want an answer today. We will all be traveling to the centaur rendezvous tomorrow evening. I haven't decided where I will go yet. You know that I would love to have you by my side, but don't make your decision yet. Think about it and tell me when we get there."

"I don't need to think about it. I know who I want and where I want to go. I've already told you."

"I know. But I need you to think about it some more."

She tilted her head. "Why?"

He sighed deeply. "Andonis needs the time to speak to you before you decide."

"I don't need to speak to either of you to know my heart, and I've already told him."

He grabbed her hands and brought them to his chest. "Speak to him first—as a favor to me."

"Why? You don't know him or owe him anything."

He looked into her eyes intently. "I was out of the picture—out of your life—when you met him. I've had time to consider his position, and if our roles were reversed, I would want, no, I would insist on the chance to stay with you. So, while we travel, please take the opportunity to talk to him, to spend time with him. He deserves that. I… I heard about Kayson." Cret dropped his gaze and squeezed her hands.

"Kayson has been dealt with," she said flatly.

"I heard a little about him and pressed Greish to tell me what happened. According to him, Andonis was singularly focused on your well-being, regardless of his safety. He truly loves you, and I—" He paused, eyes closing tightly. "If you make a hasty decision, I'll always wonder if it was truly what you wanted. I couldn't live with the thought that I broke you two apart. I need to know you're honest with yourself—that your choice is fully your own. Does that make sense?"

She thought for a moment before replying. "I see what you're saying. I will do as you request."

He squeezed her hands and sighed. "Thank you."

"Can you do one thing for me…to help me decide?"

"Yes, anything," he said.

"Kiss me."

Cret's eyes widened, and his cheeks flushed, but he nodded. Neiaphi looked up at him and closed her eyes. He studied her face for a moment before lowering his head and softly pressing his lips to hers.

A faint smile tugged at the corner of her mouth. Cret froze, uncertain, until she slipped her arms around his neck, drawing him closer. His hesitation broke; as he wrapped his arms around her, she parted her lips slightly, inviting him in.

∞ 33 ∞
Leaving

Two days later, Neiaphi wandered the Villa alone. A salty breeze drifted through the expansive estate, carrying silence in its wake. The Villa stood empty now; the last of her people had gathered in the gardens to await the Agarthans' return. She had chosen to linger, wanting to be the last one out. For at least a week, solitude would be impossible.

Her thoughts strayed to the path ahead. The quickest route was the shortcut she and Asan had once taken to reach the Villa—or something close to it. At least this time her people would glimpse Agartha before reaching the centaur rendezvous clearing. She hoped many would decide to stay there. Returning to Romota no longer seemed wise. The centaurs were fortunate; by leaving this planet, they would escape King Silsi and remain hidden from him. But her people—the Loyals and the Atlanteans—would not have such protection.

Exiting the Villa for the last time, she walked into the gardens. Alexa lifted her hand and gestured for her to hurry. Neiaphi smiled and joined her friend.

"There you are," Alexa said with a smile.

"Sorry. I wanted to walk through the Villa one last time. Are they here?"

"Greish just went to the beach to check, but they should be here shortly. I wanted to walk with you."

Neiaphi looped her arm through Alexa's, whistled for Cypress, and then started to walk to the beach.

Neiaphi and Alexa lifted their skirts and waded into the surf. The foaming, cool water swirled around their ankles as a gentle wave rolled in. A short distance out, a silver craft bubbled to the top of the water and then slid silently to the shore. A soft chime sounded a moment before the side of the fuselage disappeared, showing the inside of the vessel and the figure of a tall woman.

"Is this everyone?" Shalendra asked.

"Yes, ma'am," Alexa answered.

"Well, then. Let's get everyone aboard." Shalendra smiled broadly.

A ramp descended from the cylindrical vessel and rested lightly on the white sand. The late-afternoon sun bounced off the polished vessel, making it sparkle.

Neiaphi and Alexa were the first to step onto the ramp and take seats in the first row directly behind the pilot.

Soon, everyone was aboard.

"Welcome, everyone," Shalendra said, standing in front of the door. The opening vanished before their eyes, a smooth white wall replacing it. "You will be at your destination soon. Sit back and relax."

"Will we be taking the same route Asan took me?" Neiaphi asked.

"Yes," Shalendra replied. "Is that a problem?" She asked after she saw Neiaphi's face fall.

"Not really. This might be my last time visiting, and I was hoping to see more."

"Fear not. I have a feeling you will spend much of your life with us. But your time is not now."

Alexa leaned over. "What did she mean by that?"

Neiaphi shrugged. "You're going to love this part. It's going to feel strange, but the view is worth it." Her eyes swept across the passengers. Toward the back row, she spotted her parents seated with Cleop and Net. Andonis sat beside her father, flanked by his parents. Cret was farther forward with his own family, he smiled warmly at her which she immediately returned.

"Is this the same ship you were in?" Alexa asked.

"No. This one is much larger. Shalendra? Will this ship fit in the cavern?"

"Do not fret, child." Shalendra turned to address the travelers, her voice calm and measured. "When we enter the crust, you will feel a sensation of falling, followed by a breath of weightlessness, and then falling again. It is normal."

As soon as she stopped speaking, the display in front of the control panel winked to life. The Villa was in front of them, with the setting sun casting long shadows on the ground.

A red glow surrounded the mountain separating the Villa from Atlantis. "What is causing that light?" someone asked.

Shalendra swept her hand across the panel, and the image shifted. A gasp rippled through the cabin. Atlantis—or what remained of it—filled the screen. Every building was aflame. The docks had collapsed into blackened ruins. The palace, once gleaming and proud, lay in shattered heaps. Its towers toppled. The gardens, once lush and fragrant, burned like kindling. Thick columns of smoke strangled the sky.

Several women sobbed openly. Most of the Atlantean people had stayed behind.

Friends and some family members never to be seen again.

"The city can be rebuilt," a man called out.

"The Lemurians won't let that happen, I'm afraid," the Agarthan sitting next to Shalendra said.

Neiaphi felt the moment the ship plunged under the surf and cut through the current like a sharp blade.

A hush fell over the ship—breathing being the only sound.

Finally, someone spoke up, breaking the calm. "Why would the Lemurians keep us from rebuilding?"

Shalendra twisted in her seat to face them, her expression grave.

"We have recently learned the Lemurians developed a devastating device. Our scientists intercepted data from a small-scale test. If their full weapon is as large as we fear…the island itself will be erased."

"They can destroy an entire island?"

"King Thodoris claims to have a device he calls the Mazikos Thanatos," Greish said. He grabbed Alexa's hands and held them tightly.

Shalendra nodded. "We believe they each have the same device. It was purchased off-world."

"Can you show us Atlantis again?" a woman asked.

The monitor flickered. The smoking ruins vanished, replaced by a churning ocean storm.

There was no island. No city. No trace at all. "Where's the island?" someone yelled.

Shalendra pushed a few buttons on the console. The screen changed once more. Now they were looking at Atlantis.

"This was moments after we last saw it." Shalendra slid her hand across the panel, and the recording lurched forward. Bombs rained down on the city like an enraged hornet's nest had been struck. Then—a flash of light, and nothing. Shalendra pushed another button, and the image of the vacant ocean reappeared.

"What happened?"

Shalendra rewound the recording and then slowed the playback. A massive bomb the size of a carriage descended from the clouds. While still hundreds of feet above the crumbling palace. The bomb exploded, causing the screen to warble, and then a blinding light filled the screen. Shalendra pushed another button, and the image flickered for a moment.

What replaced the island was an enormous cloud that resembled a mushroom, extending high into the heavens.

When the cloud dispersed, the island was gone.

The Agarthan pilot gasped and flew her hands to her mouth, muttering something in their strange language.

"Is Lemuria still there?" Neiaphi asked in barely a whisper.

Wide-eyed Shalendra looked at her and then back at the console. Soon, another expanse of vacant ocean appeared on the screen.

No one needed the answer to Neiaphi's question.

∞ 34 ∞
RENDEZVOUS

The rest of the journey passed in silence. Each traveler wrestled with their own thoughts. When at last the vessel broke through into the underground world of Agartha, everyone's gaze was fixed on the screen. The few children traveling with them tried to stand on their seats to get a better view.

The ship sliced through the clear water, passing by colorful corals and strange-looking fish. When the ship shot up into the air, everyone gasped as one. The bright sky was clear with only a few puffy white clouds.

"Look at the sun, mommy," a little girl squealed.

"We have many wonders to see if you choose to live here," Shalendra said. "I'm sorry we won't be seeing more today."

The ship tilted once more, plunging back into the water and into the crust. That strange moment of weightlessness returned—groans of unease from the adults mingling with the bright giggles of children who embraced the sensation as if it were play.

One by one, they exited the cavern, where the hut once stood, into the small clearing Neiaphi and Asan had visited before. The hut had been almost entirely demolished. The door had been ripped from its hinges and sword slashes marred the inside walls. Outside the crescent moon was high overhead but barely visible behind the cloud cover. A makeshift camp had been set up for the night, but by the time the eastern horizon showed the faintest blush of rosy yellow, the group was on the move again.

Neiaphi and Alexa rode side by side, staying close to their parents. Up front, Cret rode near Shalendra, speaking softly to her. Neiaphi's eyes scanned the group, looking for Andonis. Although their group was small, the travelers kept close together, their horses moving in a tight cluster.

At last, she spotted him at the rear, riding alongside Greish. With a quick word of excuse, she guided Nexus toward the edge of the group and urged the horse back to him.

"Is there a problem?" Greish asked as he neared her.

She shook her head. "No, I just wanted to speak to Andonis. Can we talk?" she asked him.

He nodded, whispered something to Greish, and then fell in beside her. Greish reined up his horse to give them some privacy.

They rode in silence for a while, the only sound the steady rhythm of hooves on the trail. Neiaphi's thoughts churned as she tried to find the right words. Andonis kept his eyes fixed on her, his expression unreadable.

"I wanted to speak to you before I declare my decision," she said without looking at him.

"You've already made up your mind," he replied flatly. "You don't need to tell me. I know who you chose." He turned his head away, staring forward.

"I have been asked to speak to you before I'm allowed to declare my decision."

"Your father's or mother's idea?"

"Cret's."

His head whipped back to her. "Why would he do that?"

She sighed loudly and fidgeted in her saddle. "He wants to make sure I am true to my feelings. That I am making a decision that I can live with. I have to admit I feel I owe it to both of you—to pick you."

"To pick me?" His eyes went wide.

"In my heart, I have solid reasons to choose either of you. Cret professed his love for me after he left Camp Roma. I was told to forget about him…" she trailed off.

"I know. I've always known. I pressed you into deciding…into picking me…"

"No one forced me to pick you. I do love you, Andonis." She reined up Nexus, causing Andonis to stop his horse.

"But?" he asked.

"Numerous people have told me to listen to my heart, not my head. I've even heard of civilizations on Earth where a woman may have two husbands…" She paused, watching his reaction, then laughed at his bewildered expression. "I don't think I could handle that, and I doubt any man would tolerate it." She took a deep breath. "Have you decided where you will go?"

"I have. Have you?" he asked.

"I will go with the one I choose."

He chuckled. "You sound like Pythia, so cryptic."

"Where will you go?" she asked again, nudging Nexus with her heels to start moving again.

"Lyric asked me to go to Romota and be their ambassador."

"Really? You'll love it there…"

"I've decided to go to Agartha," he interrupted.

Neiaphi looked at him. "You spent a day down there, right?"

He nodded. "It's strange, but it's close to the surface. I could still visit. My parents want to try living there. If they don't like it, they said they'll find your father and settle with him."

"I'm glad you will remain with your family." She went silent for a moment. Uncertain how to broach the next subject she wanted to speak to him about without being blunt. Seeing no alternative she sighed and continued. "I heard you spoke with Nidora a while ago."

Andonis's back stiffened. He gripped the reins tightly, then dropped his chin to his chest. "Yes. Right after I saw you at the Villa for the first time. I… I should have told you. How did you find out?"

"Nidora told me. I haven't spoken to her much, but she seems nice, and she is tall and beautiful. If you like that type."

Andonis's cheeks flared, and he cleared his throat. "I never really looked at her before that night. But yes, I agree."

"Thank you for everything," Neiaphi said reaching over to him and touching his arm.

"No thanks are necessary."

"Yes, they are. You've done so much for me. Everything that happened with Kayson…"

"Don't even think about that monster," Andonis said. "I just want you to be happy. That's all I've wanted."

"That's what I want for you, too," Neiaphi said. Her eyes glistened in the early morning light with unshed tears.

"Hey now. No need to start crying. I'll be fine with whatever you choose." He leaned over and placed a hand on her arm. "I know you will make him happy, but will he make you happy?"

She stared at him for a moment and then nodded, not trusting her voice.

He gave a small nod in return. "Then I'm happy, as long as you are happy and safe. That's all anyone can ask for. Where will you two go?"

"I don't know yet. We never spoke about the after…only the present. Can you do me a favor?"

"Anything," he said. His voice sounded normal again.

"Spend time with Nidora, get to know her."

"I'll think about it."

"No, you said you would do me a favor…anything…remember?"

He smiled. "Okay, I'll get to know her for you."

"Don't do it for me. Don't do it for her. Open your heart and get to know her."

"I might not have much time, with her father staying topside and all."

"He's not staying topside. He wants his family in Agartha away from Romota spies."

"That's surprising, but I guess it makes sense. Thank you, Neiaphi." "For what?"

"For speaking to me. I knew who you would choose—I've always known, right here." He tapped his chest over his heart. "But speaking with you again… It has set my heart at ease. I'm sad I won't be the one beside you, but so grateful knowing you'll be okay."

By midday the following day, they reached the rendezvous point. Neiaphi hadn't seen Cret since the morning before. The men had remained deep within the forest, scouting the edges for any sign of danger.

When Lyric and the others first returned to the monolith, they reported signs of a battle—days-old—blood-soaked earth, discarded weapons, and the carcasses of a few horses. Strangely, there were no fallen men. The horses' throats looked as though they had been ripped out by wolves, and enormous tracks pressed deep into the ground confirmed it. The centaurs wasted no time establishing a perimeter and had kept a strict watch ever since. Members of the Wers Clan had been sighted from a distance, but so far there had been no clashes.

Now the communications clearing and its surrounding grounds were crowded with both people and centaurs. Neiaphi smiled to see the once-suspicious, solitary creatures mingling with the two-legs as if it were the most natural thing in the world.

The staircase was visible—two imposing centaurs standing sentinel on either side. Neiaphi handed Nexus's reins to Net and headed to the clearing.

"Halt. No one enters without permission," one of the centaurs said.

"She may approach," a voice said from the stairway.

"So good to see you again, Lyric," Neiaphi said.

"I'm happy to see you again as well. Where is

Andonis?" Lyric asked.

"Scouting. I'm sure he will find you when he returns."

Lyric tilted her head and smile forming.

"What?"

"You're different. You've picked your mate."

"I envy your acute senses."

"You picked Cret?"

Neiaphi nodded. "Although I haven't seen him since I made that decision official."

"Does Andonis know?"

Neiaphi nodded. "Cret made me speak to Andonis once more before making my decision."

"Then I must ask you a small favor before you tell Cret."

"What? Anything?"

"Let me see him again before you tell him."

"Sure, that's a simple request."

"Good. This is my fire." She pointed to their once-shared fire, which felt like an eternity ago, but in reality, was only a few moons passed.

Cret followed Neiaphi into a clearing with a simple stone obelisk at its center. Several centaurs were lying near it. Two he recognized.

"Greetings, Lyric. Hi, Justic," Cret said as they approached.

Justic nodded as Lyric stood.

"Welcome, my friend," Lyric said. "I would like to introduce you to my parents, Malix and Aleena."

"It's a pleasure to meet you both.

"Cret, walk with me?"

Cret glanced at Neiaphi. "Go, I'll be fine."

Lyric led Cret to the staircase leading underneath the obelisk. The staircase was well lit by torches and an ingenious channel that lined the passage.

At the bottom was a large room with nothing in it except a computer console. "Is this the communication machine?" he asked.

Lyric nodded, walking toward it.

On the screen, a countdown displayed the numbers 1-04.

"Is that when the transport will be here?"

She nodded. "When King Rees first sent word, he said they would arrive in eight Plexur moons. Pelagios translated that to ten Earth moons. But when we returned, there was a new message—two transports are being sent. The first will arrive in one moon and four suns. Neiaphi's brother and Prince Chi will be on it."

"Chi is coming here?"

"Do you know him?"

"Yes. He's my friend. Whenever I visited my grandparents, I spent most of my time with him. I never thought I'd see him again."

"I am looking forward to meeting this Prince Chi." Lyric nodded firmly and stamped a hoof.

Cret smiled, already imagining how easily they might get along. "My grandparents live close to the Centaur Nation. I'll give you a letter for them. They'll be glad to help you all settle in."

"That would be most helpful."

"Was there something else you wanted to speak about?"

"Have you decided where you will go?" she asked.

"To Rasenna. I want to help Neiluios and the twins build their new nation."

"What if Neiaphi wishes to go to Agartha?"

Cret raked his hands through his hair. "I don't know if she's chosen me yet."

A laugh echoed through the confined room. "That is the stupidest thing I've ever heard you say."

"Well, I don't."

"How much simpler your lives would be if you had the senses of a centaur. Yes, she loves Andonis, but her affection for you runs far deeper. Why did you send her to speak with him?"

"I want to make sure she's making a decision she can live with. That she's picking for herself, not for either of us."

"That makes sense, and she has."

Cret glanced at his friend and raised an eyebrow.

"You already know her choice."

A crushing weight seemed to settle on his shoulders. "Then I know what I must do," he stated flatly.

∞ 35 ∞
Duel

Neiaphi sat beside the crackling fire with Justic and his parents—her eyes fixed on the staircase.

When Cret appeared, her heart leapt at the sight of him, but something written on his face gave her pause. She resisted the urge to rise and go to him.

His gaze found hers. Stars seemed to dance in his eyes, yet his chin remained firm and set. Without a word, he strode to her and extended his hand.

She reached out without hesitation and was pulled to her feet.

He led her out of the clearing and back to their group's camp. His eyes scanned over the gathered, apparently looking for someone. He then led her to where her mother was sitting beside a large cooking fire.

"Please stay here," he said. The first words he'd uttered since meeting with Lyric.

He dropped her hand and left.

"Where's Cret going?" Altesse asked.

"I'm not sure. That was weird."

"Neiaphi, come walk with me," Neiluios said as he approached his family.

"Hello, father. Is something wrong?" she asked.

He motioned with his head and walked away from the fire.

"A young man has asked for you," he said after they were almost back to the clearing.

Her heart skipped a beat.

"So that's what he was doing."

"We have a bit of a situation on our hands."

"How so?"

"You are already promised, and breaking that is not something that is usually done."

She felt as if her stomach dropped to her knees. "So…what now?"

"Do you want this man?"

She opened her mouth and then closed it again just as quickly. He hadn't told her the man's name.

"I have thought hard about who I want, who I've always wanted. Cret and I are destined to be with each other."

Neiluios nodded.

"How are promises broken?" she asked quietly.

"Usually by a duel. With one man giving up, or in more cases than not—to the death."

"No!" Her hands flew to her mouth. "I've already spoken to Andonis. He knows my heart."

"Then he should yield without conflict. The duel will take place at sunrise. Please go to your mother to prepare."

"Prepare for what?"

He patted her shoulder. "Head back to the tent." He turned and walked away.

"What have I done?" she asked herself.

Neiaphi found herself sitting alone in her family's tent. Cleop and her mother attended the twins by the fire—Net and her father had been gone when she woke. The sun had yet to rise, but the camp was awake.

Her mother told her that she must stay in the tent and was not allowed to attend the duel. Her father and Net would be there to represent her. No matter how many times she asked, her mother wouldn't tell her what was going to happen. She supposed her mother didn't even really know.

While Romota established rituals and culture on Earth, significant changes occurred over the centuries.

The tent brightened as the sun crested the unseen

horizon, illuminating the sky above the still-dark forest. She heard the murmuring voices of men somewhere nearby, and then silence. Time dragged agonizingly slowly as she sat alone.

"Neiaphi!" Her father's voice drifted from outside the tent. "Exit my house and be presented to your husband-to-be."

A shiver ran up her spine at the coldness in her father's voice. *Is this how normal girls feel before meeting their betrothed?* Her heart and mind warred within her. Would Andonis have fought Cret for her hand, as he had started to back at the Villa? Or had he yielded willingly?

Her pulse quickened as she hurried to the tent flap. She paused, hand pressed against the coarse fabric, her breath hitching as panic and uncertainty settled over her like a wet wool blanket. Closing her eyes, she lifted the flap and stepped out. She smoothed her skirt and stood tall, her eyes opening.

Her father stood before her—blocking everything else from view. The stern look on his face made her wither inside. *Did something terrible happen, and was it all my fault?* She stood still and silent as her mother had instructed.

"Neiaphi, my daughter, I present to you your husband-to-be," her father said, his face stony, though she thought she glimpsed a twinkle in his eyes, as if he were suppressing a smile. He stepped aside. Cret was directly behind him, a large, goofy grin on his face.

"Cret, I present to you your bride-to-be. Let all gathered here know that two suitors dueled, and one prevailed. No other suitors may present themselves, following the Atlantean custom of the Chosen Promised. The wedding celebration begins now," Neiluios proclaimed.

Neiaphi's eyes widened at this declaration. Cret nodded to her, then bowed to Neiluios. "I accept and will bind our agreement." He spun on his heels and walked away.

Altesse approached, beaming. She took Neiaphi's hand and led her back into the tent.

"What was that?" Neiaphi asked when they were alone. "Your father was keeping to the Atlantean tradition."

"That's not how Alexa and Greish were promised.

What happened in the duel? I didn't see Andonis out there."

"I'm not sure. I wasn't allowed to watch. When Alexa and you were first promised, there weren't multiple suitors asking at the same time that your father approved of. I suppose this is the procedure when there is. Now, we have much to do."

"Wait! Alexa and I are supposed to wed on the same day."

Altesse smiled warmly. "Alexa is being prepared as well. Greish and Cret agreed to honor your wishes. Now, we need to get you bathed, and then I have a lot of cooking to do. The women's feast is tonight; tomorrow, we will feast with everyone."

That evening, all the women gathered at Neiaphi's family tent, gossiping and sharing stories of when the brides were little girls. Neiaphi and Alexa presented their childhood toys and threw them into the fire as an offering to Artemis.

Neiaphi watched with a frown as her terracotta doll's dress was engulfed in the flames.

"What's the matter?" Alexa asked. "This is a time of great happiness, not sadness."

"My father gave me that doll when we first arrived on this planet. I was far too old to play with such things, but the fact that he found the time to buy it meant so much to me. I had hoped to give it to my daughter someday."

Alexa looped an arm around Neiaphi's waist and hugged her. "I'm sorry." They stood in silence as their offerings were accepted by the goddess.

The feast continued well into twilight, reminding Neiaphi of the spring festival they had shared moons ago.

The following day began with another ritual bath, followed by a procession of gifts left in front of the girls' tents. Everyone contributed, even if it was only a pair of buttons. Neiaphi was overwhelmed, but Alexa accepted each gift with open and gracious acceptance.

The morning and early afternoon were spent cooking again.

Neiaphi muttered under her breath as she ground some

wheat to make bread.

"What did you say?" Cleop asked. Cleop was taking the freshly ground wheat and forming the dough.

"Oh, nothing. Just talking to myself."

Cleop smiled. "You are feeling bad about all the fuss?"

Neiaphi sighed. "Yes. We have limited resources; we shouldn't be wasting them on Alexa and me."

Cleop stopped and pointed a battered finger at Neiaphi.

"This feast is not just about you and your betrothed. It is a celebration for both families. Your family is losing a daughter, and his family is gaining one. This is a time of rebirth, a chance to start fresh. Since both of your marriages are rooted in love, it is a time to share that love with everyone. As you can imagine, marrying for love is rare—unless one is truly impoverished. Let us do this for you; let us share your happiness."

"Thank you, Cleop. I feel better now. What can I do to help now? The wheat is finished."

Cleop smiled. "That's more like it. Take these loaves to Sephi. Crelian made a rock oven."

∞ 36 ∞
THE WEDDING

As the sun set, Alexa and Neiaphi sat together before their friends, family, and fellow refugees—both two-legged and four.

The men ate first, while the women sat quietly at a separate table, permitted to eat only when the men were finished.

Cret and Greish were drawn into constant conversation and had not spoken a word to the girls all evening. Yet Neiaphi caught Cret's gaze lingering on her more than once, and the yearning in his eyes reflected her own. Still, she could not smile at him or return his look; her opaque veil concealed her face.

When she asked about it, Alexa simply explained that this was the way of things. Neiaphi marveled at the rituals and superstitions Earth's people clung to. Would they ever change? she wondered. Probably not.

Everyone she knew, and countless others she did not—approached her and Alexa, offering the Gods' Grace. Only Andonis was absent, which did not surprise her, though she could not deny the hurt.

As night fell and the feast came to an end, guests offered their farewells and slowly dispersed, until only family and close friends remained. The servants departed as well, leaving a torchlit path from the banquet grounds to two small tents.

"I know both of you wished for permanent houses

before the wedding, but tradition must be upheld," Alexa's father declared loudly from the head of the path. "Though a proper chariot could not be found in our present circumstances, we have secured carriages for you both."

He took Alexa's hand as Neiluios stepped forward and did the same for Neiaphi. Cret and Greish appeared, driving two carriages laden with their bridal gifts.

Altesse hugged Neiaphi tightly, tears streaming down her face. "Mother, I'm not leaving. Only sleeping in a different tent." Neiaphi's cheeks flared at her own words.

"My little girl is leaving forever. Tomorrow I will meet my grown daughter. You will be the same and different." Altesse smiled and patted her on the arm. "Cret is a fine young man. He was our first choice for you. I'm so thrilled he will be yours."

Tears welled in Neiaphi's eyes as she embraced her mother. She glanced over at Alexa, who was clinging just as tightly to her own.

Neiluios approached, took Neiaphi's hand, and led her to the carriage and Cret. "Neiaphi, I present to you your husband. The care you provide for him and his household is your sacred duty. Bear him many heirs. Cret, I entrust you with my only daughter. Guard her as your most precious treasure, honor her as you would your own mother, and give her both children and the means to nurture them." Neiluios placed her hand into Crets' and then kissed Neiaphi on her veiled cheek.

Cret, without a word, helped her into the carriage and then flicked the reins to get the carriage moving. Alexa's carriage followed closely behind. The torch-lined path branched into two, with Cret picking the left path and Greish following the right.

The small tent that awaited them stood apart from the main camp, with Crelian stationed outside and Cypress seated beside him. A warm glow spilled from within.

Cret leapt down, offering his hand to help Neiaphi descend. Still, he did not speak. She had been told that Sephi would greet her inside before leaving her alone with Cret, yet so much of the evening remained unexplained. The night felt more like a riddle than the wedding day she had imagined.

"Welcome, Neiaphi, daughter of Neiluios and Altesse. I am Crelian, your father-in-law. Welcome to your new home," Crelian said formally.

Neiaphi curtsied and then entered the tent. Sephi was standing next to the central fire pit.

"Be welcome, wife of my son," Sephi said warmly, embracing her before slipping away and leaving the two of them alone.

Neiaphi stood there, looking around her new home for the next few weeks. It was sparsely furnished, featuring a cooking fire, a rug, and a single bed.

Cret was standing behind her. He seemed equally as confused, or maybe waiting for her to do something. She saw a pot of near-boiling water next to the fire and two clay mugs beside it. *Well, I guess that's what I'm supposed to do.* She knelt beside the fire and fixed two mugs of tea. Cret came and silently sat beside her.

She sat quietly as she waited for the tea to steep. She wrung her hands in her lap. No one explained what happened next. Cret smiled and cleared his throat. She looked up and saw a playful smile on his lips. She returned the smile, but he couldn't see it; she was still veiled.

He reached over and took her hands in his. "Neiaphi, do you accept me?" he asked.

A laugh escaped her, which she quickly tried to stifle. "Sorry, I wasn't expecting that question. Of course, I accept you. What kind of question is that?"

"A question a man asks a woman when he loves her more than life itself."

"I accept you with my whole heart. I want you and no one else," she said.

Cret nodded and lifted her veil. Seeing his face again, free of the opaque fabric she had worn all day, felt almost like a reunion after their long separation. The firelight cast a reddish glow over his tanned skin, and his brown eyes shone warmly.

She handed him a mug, then took a cautious sip of hers. It was minty with a hint of chamomile and something else she couldn't identify.

"Thank you," Cret said before sipping from his mug. "Did you enjoy the celebration?"

"Um, yeah, it was nice," she said, keeping her eyes downcast.

Cret placed his mug down and lifted her chin with a finger. "That didn't sound right. What's the matter? You were going to choose me, right?"

She grabbed his hand and placed it on her cheek. "Of course, I picked you. It's just…it's just not how I pictured my wedding, that's all. Everything on Earth is the same yet different. Can we talk about the past couple of days?"

"Sure." He shifted his weight so he was facing her completely.

"I spoke with Andonis as you requested."

"I see it went well," he teased.

"Yes…Nidora likes him. I urged him to speak with her."

"Now, that makes sense."

"What does?"

"I saw them speaking together today. She wasn't hiding the fact that she likes him."

"I didn't see him at all today. I worried something might have happened to him during the duel. Can you tell me what happened after I brought you to Lyric? Until now, you've barely spoken ten words to me."

He squeezed her hands and pressed them to his lips. "Forgive me—that was never my intention. Lyric showed me the communications device, and she wanted to be certain I hadn't deceived you into choosing me. She's grown quite attached to Andonis."

"He is a likeable man."

Cret raised an eyebrow.

"What? Can't I say that—I've already wed you."

"The day before, while I was scouting with the others,

I was paired with Aristas and his twin, um, I can't place his name…"

"Bacceon," she offered.

"That's right. You came up in the conversation, and our… um… closeness at the stable. I learned that since you were already promised, even though you had released him from the obligation… what I did was unacceptable. Such things are simply not done here.

"Andonis never openly spoke of the breakup, so, my spending time with you—kissing you—was taken as a grave insult. They told me what I must do, and sadly, you had no say in it."

"No say? I hate this planet." She crossed her arms over her chest and huffed.

"After I spoke to Lyric, I went directly to your father to inform him of my intentions."

"You didn't even let me tell you I wanted you," she said softly.

"I'm sorry. I felt like I was walking on thin ice and didn't want to break any more rules. I told your father I was speaking for you—and I requested a duel."

"You requested it? After Andonis tried to fight you back at the Villa, and I almost died?"

He grabbed her hands again. "I was trusting his friend, Aristas. Aristas said he would back down graciously. He did, don't worry. We met at sunrise, and I declared my feelings for you. We drew our swords, and Andonis threw his at my feet and walked away."

"He didn't even say anything?"

"I guess it wasn't expected. I had no idea we would be married the very next day, though. That was news to me. Paragon told me that when there is a duel for a wife, the winner must be ready to marry immediately, or else the other suitor can request another duel. Waiting makes it look like the other man is stalling and is weak. My hands were tied," he said playfully.

"Oh, poor you," she teased, giving his shoulder a

playful smack. "And what about Alexa? Did she have any say in this rushed marriage? I hardly spoke to her with everything happening."

"Her father and Greish decided for her." He paused, noticing the grief that flickered across Neiaphi's face. "Don't worry. She wanted a double wedding with you. They both thought excluding her would provoke her wrath even more. She would understand why you were married off so quickly."

"That makes sense. I just wish I had had more time to prepare, that's all. So, what now? Are there more rituals for us to complete?"

"Only one, but we have the rest of our lives, so no rush." Her cheeks bloomed bright red at his implication.

"Like I said, no rush. Let's get some rest, and tomorrow we'll figure out the rest of our lives."

∞ **37** ∞
TRANSPORT

Neiaphi and Alexa entered the clearing side by side. Everyone they passed greeted them with warm waves and cheerful faces. Over the past few weeks, joy had become so constant it seemed almost infectious.

Lyric appeared, ascending the staircase. "The machine says today," she announced brightly.

"Already? That moon passed quickly," Alexa said.

"Are you leaving with the first ship?" Neiaphi asked.

Lyric shook her head. "No, I'll be the last to board a ship. I feel it's my duty to make sure everyone else has a place first."

"You have such a big heart," Neiaphi said.

"I haven't seen much of you two lately. Have you decided where you will go?" Lyric asked.

Both girls blushed. "We will be going with my father. I think we'll be leaving in a few days," Neiaphi said.

"So soon? I suppose that makes sense. Winter will be upon us before we know it. I will be sad to see you all go, but wish you much fortune and luck."

"Thank you, Lyric. We wish you much luck on Romota."

"How many more are going to Agartha?" Lyric asked.

"Not too many. Addident, his family and a few others. I think they will be leaving the same day as us," Alexa told her.

"And Andonis?"

"Agartha, I would imagine," Neiaphi answered. "He's

become quite friendly with Nidora. I think they'll be very happy together."

"I'm glad he found someone so quickly."

A sudden roar echoed above the treetops, startling everyone. A small transport ship descended and hovered over the clearing. With a hiss, the side door slid open, revealing a tall centaur with honey-blonde hair and a gleaming golden hide standing in the doorway.

A platform extended from the craft and slowly lowered to the ground with the centaur and four humans upon it.

"Welcome to Earth," Lyric greeted. "I am Lyric, and this is Neiaphi and Alexa."

"It is a pleasure to meet you, Lyric, and you as well, Queen heir Neiaphi." The centaur bowed low.

Neiaphi's cheeks burned. "Oh, please don't bow. I am not seeking the throne."

The centaur rose and nodded his head. "I meant no embarrassment. I am Chi of the Romotian Centaurs."

"Prince Chi?" Lyric immediately bowed.

"Rise, Lyric. Bowing is not done among our kind."

"Cret will be so pleased to see you again," Neiaphi said.

"Ah, Cret. It will be good to see my friend one last time. Have you discovered how many will be coming home?"

"Not fully yet. We have had a few more joining us over the past couple of moons, with reports that more are coming. How many can this ship accommodate?"

"Twenty comfortably."

"My parents and a few elders will be venturing home first." Lyric paused, her eyes glazing over. After an awkward moment, she shook her head. "I apologize. I said Romota was home—it struck me as odd."

Chi laughed, a rich, deep sound. "No worries. Let me put your mind at ease. Romota will become your home in every sense. I would be honored to meet your parents and the human leaders you serve under."

Chi's gaze lingered on Lyric—not casual, at least not to Neiaphi. It felt more like he was studying her, evaluating her. Lyric seemed to notice as well. Her tail flicked nervously, and she fidgeted with her fingers. Unless Neiaphi was mistaken, she was also blushing.

Neiaphi leaned over to Alexa and whispered in her ear. "I think Lyric has an admirer."

"Looks like it," Alexa agreed.

"Where are your parents?" Chi asked Neiaphi.

"I'm sure they'll be along shortly. Your ship will not have gone unnoticed."

The platform lowered from the ship again. Neiaphi looked at it suspiciously. When had it risen?

This time, two women stood upon it. The younger one bore a look of deep sorrow, her head bowed, her hands clasped tightly behind her back. Beside her stood a kind-faced elderly woman holding the hand of a small boy, no more than four years old.

As soon as the platform touched the ground, the young woman's form shimmered. Her clothes slipped to the earth as her body shifted into the shape of a great wolf. She lifted her eyes to the elder, gave a single nod, and then bounded into the forest.

Tears sprang to Neiaphi's eyes as she fell to her knees. "Icarus."

"Nephie?" the little boy asked.

Neiaphi nodded and held her hands out.

"Nephie!" Icarus shouted, wrestled his hand free from the woman, and ran to her.

"Icarus!" A woman shouted from the edge of the clearing. Neiaphi hugged her little brother tightly as her parents rushed to meet them.

A small group of humans and centaurs gathered in the communications room. Neiaphi and Alexa sat apart, near the fire by the obelisk. The night was calm, though the sharp chill of autumn was in the air. Thick clouds drifted overhead, blocking out the moonlight.

Engrossed in quiet conversation, they were surprised when Andonis sat next to them.

"Where did you come from?" Alexa squeaked with surprise.

"Sorry about that. May I join you?"

"Of course, my friend. Greish won't mind you speaking to his wife, not sure about Cret though," Alexa teased.

Andonis's eyes went wide as he glanced around, peering into the night.

"He's below with the others, be calm. He holds no grudge with you," Neiaphi said. "How have you been?"

"Good. Keeping busy helping Addident with preparations for their departure. A small group who went down on the first transport wants to come back up. They'll be here tomorrow, I believe."

"Any news?" Alexa asked, waggling her eyebrows.

Andonis rubbed the back of his neck with a sheepish grin, causing both women to break into a laugh.

"Nidora and I are getting along nicely, if that's what you're referring to."

"It is." Alexa smiled broadly. "I'm so happy for you."

"Me too, congratulations," Neiaphi chimed in. "Do you know who's coming back up?"

He shook his head. "I wanted to speak to you before we left and apologize. "He turned his gaze on Neiaphi.

"Apologize for what?" Neiaphi asked.

"For the duel."

"You don't have to apologize for that. Cret asked for it."

"Only because I didn't publicly announce our separation. If I had spoken to your father promptly, then the duel wouldn't have happened, and your rushed marriage wouldn't have been forced. For that, I must beg forgiveness from both of you. I know you both wanted permanent homes before wedding."

"While it was unexpected and at the time unwanted,

it's worked out," Neiaphi told him.

"Please be at ease, my friend. No hard feelings," Alexa chimed in.

Andonis nodded his head, and it appeared a great weight had been lifted from his shoulders. "Well, I'd better finish my rounds. Good night, Alexa. Good night, Neiaphi."

"Good night," they said together.

He melted into the shadows just as Cret appeared, coming up the stairs. "Who was just here?" he asked.

"Andonis. He stopped by while on rounds," Alexa told him.

"Did you know some of those who went to Agartha are coming back up?" Neiaphi asked.

"I heard something about that. Does he know who?" Both women shook their heads.

"Were you able to find anything about the young woman? The wolver?" Neiaphi asked Cret, her voice shaky.

"Chi says that she is the one who confronted your parents and took Icarus."

Shock swept over Neiaphi. "Why is she here?

"She volunteered. She was so ashamed of her actions with Icarus. She plans to appeal to your parents to let her stay and serve as his protector. If he chooses to return to Romota, she will help him reclaim the throne.

In the meantime, she will offer all the wolvers on Earth a chance to return home. They were never officially brought here. Long ago, they attempted to conceal their identities and lived quietly among the people of Romota. Generations ago, they chose to separate themselves, but they always maintained a close bond with the centaurs. The wolvers on Romota had no idea their kin were still here, living apart from humans just as they once did on Romota. Now, they want to reunite, if the others wish it."

"What's her name?" "Lycia."

"I hope for all of humanity's sake every single one of them chooses to travel back home."

Cret nodded in agreement.

∞ **38** ∞
ARRIVAL

Shalendra arrived early the next morning with a small group of people. The only one who surprised Cret was Hepluosis.

"Greetings, Shalendra," Cret said. "I didn't expect to see you again so soon."

"Greetings, Cret. I heard I missed the ceremony."

"What ceremony?" Hepluosis asked, walking over to them.

"Cret and Neiaphi were married," Shalendra answered.

"Ah, I'm sorry I missed that," Hepluosis said with a sneer.

"What brings you topside?" Cret asked, not bothering to mask the venom dripping from his words.

"Hepluosis has been a wonderful help with the resettlement of so many people. I asked for his assistance with this last trip. Some found Agartha too foreign," Shalendra said.

"So, where is the little wife? Have you finally adopted the culture up here and have her hidden from sight?"

"I would never treat her the way we were instructed. She is my partner in life, not my servant."

"Such a fool," Hepluosis muttered.

"Let's find Neiluios and get these people settled," Shalendra interrupted smoothly.

"The first transport to Romota leaves tonight, and everyone staying topside departs tomorrow morning," Cret said.

"Excellent. We can take any others who wish to venture

into Agartha with us tomorrow morning," Shalendra replied.

"Where's Addident?" Hepluosis asked.

"He's around. Why?" Cret countered.

"You mentioned finding Neiaphi's father and not him. I feared something had happened to him."

Cret barked a laugh. "Feared? More like hoped. Neiluios and most of the others are staying topside. Addident and a few will head to Agartha. If I were you, I'd tread carefully around him."

Hepluosis scoffed. "I am respected by the Agarthans and those who have already gone below. I have nothing to fear from his authority. Now, let's find Neiluios—I tire of your ramblings."

Cret gave a mocking bow and swept an arm forward. "By all means, lead the way." Hepluosis scowled but took the lead.

"Addident, I hear you will be coming with us in the morrow," Shalendra said in greeting.

Addident turned with a smile. "Welcome, Shalendra. I had hoped you would arrive before tomorrow. Yes—my family and a few others wish to depart from Romota's ever-watchful eyes."

"Agreed. I feel that is for the best. Cret, what about you and Neiaphi?" she asked.

Cret shook his head. "We'll be staying topside. If we change our minds, I'm sure we'll find a way to reach you."

"I will make sure we leave a communication system open."

"Thank you, Shalendra."

"There are a lot of centaurs here," Hepluosis remarked, looking around.

"More than anyone realized, it seems," Lyric said as she approached, a honey-blonde centaur walking at her side.

"Shalendra, may I introduce Prince Chi of Romota?"

Shalendra dropped into a deep curtsy. "Welcome to Earth."

"Rise, Shalendra. It is a pleasure to meet you."

Cret snickered and then clamped his lips tight.

"Something funny?" Chi turned to face Cret.

"I'm sorry, my friend. You have just changed since I last saw you."

"How so?" Chi looked at himself with his arms held out.

"You have just grown up, I suppose."

"It happens," Chi chuckled. "And look at you, married now, a sword at your hip, and able to wield it. I saw you sparring this morning."

Cret smiled. He'd missed his friend.

"Where did that other young man go?" Chi asked. Cret looked around—Hepluosis was gone.

Hepluosis wandered the camp. *She's around here somewhere, but where? There's a stream close, if I remember correctly.*

Making his way through the trees, he passed a few girls carrying baskets brimming with water. A few strides later, the sound of a stream reached his ears, mingled with the giggles of little girls. He slowed his pace and slipped behind a bush.

By the water's edge, several women and a dozen girls were busy—some filling baskets, others scrubbing clothes against the rocks.

He settled on his heels, watching and waiting.

To his delight, Neiaphi and another young woman were the only ones left at the stream as the sun began to sink in the western sky. He lingered in his hiding place for a few breaths longer before rising and striding confidently toward them.

The other woman saw him and nudged Neiaphi on the shoulder.

Neiaphi turned her head with a grin, but her smile faded

the instant her eyes fell on him. She whispered something to her friend.

"Hello, Neiaphi. I hear congratulations are in order," Hepluosis said, keeping his gait steady and one hand resting on the hilt of his sword. "I had hoped I'd get the chance to see you again."

"What're you doing topside?" Neiaphi asked, her voice shaking slightly.

"Where's your dog?" Hepluosis inquired, looking around. "I've heard he is quite protective of you."

"Cypress is close by," Alexa said loudly.

"Now, now. No need to yell. I'm no threat. Just an old friend come to say hello before I leave the top of this sorry planet forever."

Neiaphi stood abandoning her laundry and motioned for Alexa to do the same. "No sudden movements, you two. You wouldn't want me to get the wrong idea. Let's keep this civil."

"I have nothing to say to you. Leave us be," Neiaphi said. Her voice was slightly steadier, but fear was still laced in her words.

"But I have plenty to say to you. Cret, your beloved husband and I have unfinished business, and I realized long ago the easiest and best way to get to him is to get to you."

"Alexa, run!" Neiaphi hissed.

"Alexa, is it? Stay right where you are," Hepluosis drawled as he advanced. The women had chosen a dangerous place without realizing it. Slick boulders, glistening with spray from a small waterfall, cut off any hope of retreat. Their only options were to wade into the rushing stream or face him. He glanced at their heavy wool skirts and smirked. *They're not going anywhere.*

"Leave us alone." Neiaphi tried to sound brave and confident.

"Without your dog—or your husband…" he sneered the word, letting it hang in the air, "you're weak. You're mine."

Neiaphi took a few tentative steps out of the soft

sand. Hepluosis waggled a finger at her.

"Tsk, tsk, tsk. If you agree to stay and speak to me like a civilized woman, I will let your friend go."

"Do I have your word?" she asked.

Hepluosis smiled broadly. "Of course. I am a man of my word."

Neiaphi nodded to Alexa. The other girl waded onto the bank, leaned close, and whispered urgently, her hands gesturing wildly.

"Go!" Neiaphi ordered. *Find Cret.* She whispered the last words, but Hepluosis caught the movement of her lips.

Alexa hesitated, then edged past him. At the last second, Hepluosis lunged, seizing her arm and yanking her against him. Neiaphi's warning cry came too late.

"Now this…" Hepluosis grinned, tightening his grip on Alexa. "This is a beautiful woman."

"She's Greish's wife, Hepluosis." Neiaphi took a few steps closer.

"Is she now? I heard he caught himself a beauty, but I didn't believe the talk."

"You better let me go," Alexa tried to sound brave, but Hepluosis started to twist her arm, causing a whimper of pain.

"When we first came to this planet, he and I were the best of friends," he growled. "But this place has poisoned him. He isn't the man I knew. I owe him nothing." He wrenched her arm harder, drawing another cry.

"Stop this, Hep." "Or you'll do what?"

"I'll stay with you, we can talk."

"Nah, I'm done talking."

Hepluosis twisted Alexa's arm until a sickening snap rang out. Her scream split the air as she tried to wrench free, knocking him slightly off balance. With a furious growl, he flung her to the ground. Alexa fell with her arms outstretched. Falling on her broken arm—it buckled. She landed hard, and her head bounced on the rocky ground. Neiaphi cried out for her friend and started to rush toward her.

Hepluosis blocked her path. "Now it's just the two of

us. Let's have some fun while making Cret suffer." A cruel smile curled his lips. He drew a dagger from his belt and started walking toward her.

∞ **39** ∞
FIGHT

A woman's scream echoed through the forest—high, raw, filled with fear and pain. Men burst from their shelters, swords in hand, dogs racing ahead of them. Greish was the first to reach the stream, Ash and Cypress pulling him forward. The dogs suddenly veered, following the river upstream. Several men crashed through the trees behind him, sprinting to keep up.

They broke onto the bank where a figure lay sprawled on the ground. Ash and Cypress nudged the still form before throwing their heads back in a mournful howl. Greish's chest tightened—injured, but not dead. Relief washed over him as he recognized Alexa. She had said she'd be at the stream with Neiaphi. Where was Neiaphi?

Dropping to his knees, he slid to her side and grabbed her wrist, pressing for a pulse. Cret and Andonis reached him seconds later, both dropping beside him.

"Is she…?" Andonis started to ask, but couldn't finish the question. "She's alive," Greish answered. "Alexa? Alexa, can you hear me?"

"Greish?" she asked with a moan. "Where's Neiaphi?" Her eyes flew open, and she tried to sit up.

"Stay down, stay still," Greish said, pushing on her shoulder.

"What happened?"

"Where's Neiaphi? Hepluosis was…" Her eyes rolled backward, and she passed out.

"Hepluosis?" Greish, Cret, and Andonis said in unison.

Cret jumped up, looking around. Andonis crawled to the stream and cupped some water in his hands to drizzle over Alexa's forehead. Greish jumped up and started to look for tracks.

"Here!" he said, pointing to the soft sand in between the rocks. Neiaphi's small footprints led upstream. Hepluosis's tracks were not visible. He was most likely keeping his feet on the rocks.

"Ash! Cypress! Track," Greish said while giving the track command hand signal. Both dogs dropped their noses to the ground where Greish was standing and then took off upstream.

Hepluosis growled and shoved Neiaphi deeper into the trees. "Stop stalling. No one's going to find us—not until I'm ready for them," he snarled, pressing the dagger harder into her back.

Neiaphi glared at him. She resumed her measured pace—no slower, no faster. Hepluosis swore under his breath and then grabbed her wrist and spun her around.

"You think you'll be rescued? No chance of that. I'm counting on Cret finding us, but not yet." He tightened his grip and pulled her further into the trees.

The howling of dogs shattered the quiet. "They found Alexa. Cypress will find me," Neiaphi said through gritted teeth.

"I hope so. Cret can't truly suffer if he doesn't witness what is to come." Neiaphi moaned and tried to pull her hand free.

Hepluosis laughed and pulled her harder. " Come on."

Cypress and Ash darted through the dense underbrush,

with Cret, Greish, and Andonis only a few strides behind. Suddenly, the dogs veered back toward the stream, noses low to the ground as they stopped to sniff intently

"Did they lose the scent?" Cret asked.

Greish looked around. "They couldn't have just disappeared."

"Looking for something, boys?" A voice called from somewhere in the brush.

"Show yourself, coward," Greish yelled.

"This is between Cret and me. Greish, take Andonis and the dogs and leave us."

"I don't think so," Andonis said.

"If you want Neiaphi back in one piece, you'll do as I say."

Neiaphi let out a muffled cry. "Please do as he says," she squeaked.

Hepluosis stepped from behind a bush. Neiaphi clenched in front of him, his dagger at her throat.

"Back off, both of you. Hey, where's the other dog?"

"I'm not sure. Don't worry about it. Concentrate on the three of us," Greish said. "Let her go now, and I'll make sure we go easy on you."

Hepluosis laughed gruffly. "Sure, because the leadership so adores me. I think I'll take my chances here. One-on-one, I can take any of you. So, if the two of you won't back off and let Cret and me settle this, I'll have to resort to plan B." He twisted Neiaphi's arm a little. A moan slipped from her clenched teeth.

"Hepluosis, stop this madness," Cret said. "I have no wish to fight you. Just let Neiaphi go and be on your way. I won't say anything."

Greish glared at Cret. "Saying things like that is why I hate you so. You think you are so superior, so righteous." Hepluosis twisted his hand slightly, causing the tip of his dagger to nick Neiaphi's throat.

"I never thought that," Cret replied, holding his hands out and taking a step closer.

"Spoken like the righteous fool I've always known you to be. An arrogant dog. You pursued a woman who was already promised, then claimed and defiled by another. Yet you still married her. She is no better than a whore."

"Greish, Andonis, back off. This is between Hepluosis and me. Let Neiaphi go. Just you and me." Cret's anger was clear—his face flushed, his knuckles white around the hilt of his sword.

"No. They need to leave. Neiaphi will stay right here and watch." Hepluosis shoved her to the ground.

Cret's gaze locked on her. Her hands and ankles were bound, but she seemed unharmed aside from the thin trickle of blood running down her throat. He glanced at Greish and gave a single nod.

Greish and Andonis shared a look before they both sheathed their swords and started to back away.

"Don't forget the dogs."

Greish scowled, then whistled sharply.

"Now, it's just you and me, Cret. We will finally see who is the better man," Hepluosis sneered.

"I already know the answer to that question," Neiaphi said. "

Hold your tongue, woman." Hepluosis kicked at her legs.

Cret moved to his right and then dropped into a fighting stance. Hepluosis grinned as he advanced, his sword held high.

Their swords met with a reverberating clang of metal on metal. "I will cut you down to size," Hepluosis taunted.

Cret focused on his opponent's every move, waiting for the smallest opening.

They struck, parried, and blocked—each reading the other with precision.

Neiaphi watched as Cret defended her against Hepluosis. She hated this—hated the fight, hated this planet, hated Hepluosis most of all. He had been a plague and a bully for as long as she could remember.

Back on Romota, her father had been a low-level

official until just a moon before their departure for Earth—for the Krill Colony, as it was called then. With his promotion, she would have been moved to a higher class at school. But since everyone knew they were leaving soon, she was kept with the classmates she already knew.

If they had stayed, she would have been rid of Hepluosis, no longer forced to share a classroom with him. But it also would have meant losing Cret as a friend. At the time, she would have been sad, but it would have passed. Losing Cret now, though—that was unthinkable.

Hepluosis and Cret circled each other, trading blows. To Neiaphi's untrained eyes, their movements looked like a deadly dance. She knew little about swordplay, but to her, they seemed evenly matched.

Cret pressed the attack, driving Hepluosis backward. His opponent's boot caught on an exposed root, and he dropped to one knee. Cret hesitated, his sword raised but his strike slowed. Neiaphi's heart swelled—he was a good man, even in battle, honorable to a fault.

Hepluosis's lips curled into a sneer. He clawed up a fistful of dirt and hurled it into Cret's face.

"Weak," he spat.

Neiaphi cried out a warning, distracting Cret. Cret stumbled backward, momentarily blinded, rubbing at his eyes with his free hand while holding his sword before him. Hepluosis took advantage of the situation, jumping to his feet and running forward. Cret managed to side-step him, narrowly missing the arc of Hepluosis's sword. Cret slammed the butt of his pommel into Hepluosis's back as he stumbled past. Hepluosis grabbed hold of a tree to keep from falling to the ground. Cret rushed forward and kicked Hepluosis's sword out of his hand. Hepluosis spun, growling. He glanced around for his sword and then changed tactics. He lowered himself and ran for Cret, ramming his shoulder into Cret's middle, flinging them both to the ground.

Neiaphi covered her mouth to stifle a scream.

Swords now forgotten, the two men wrestled on the

ground, fighting to get the upper hand.

Hepluosis slammed Cret to the ground and pinned his arms. With no other option, he reared back and smashed his forehead into Cret's, stunning them both. Cret shook off the daze first, ignoring the hot stream of blood trickling down his face. Driving a leg between them, he twisted sharply, unseating Hepluosis and sending him sprawling to the side.

Still on the ground, both men groped for their weapons. Hepluosis found his sword first and lurched to his feet, towering over Cret with a sneer.

"Don't worry, Neiaphi—you won't see me kill your love," he said, lifting his gaze from Cret to her. "I'll only maim him, so he can watch you die first."

As Hepluosis focused on Neiaphi, Cret dragged himself backward across the ground, gasping for breath and struggling to stay conscious. Inch by inch, he reached out—until at last his fingers brushed the hilt of his sword.

When his focus returned to his target, Hepluosis growled and charged. Cret raised his sword just in time, steel clashing against steel.

"You will not ruin this for me!" Hepluosis roared.

A nearby howl tore his attention away for a split second—just long enough. Gritting his teeth, Cret forced himself onto his knees. Hepluosis lifted his sword high, but when he snapped his gaze back, it was too late—Cret drove the tip of his blade deep into Hepluosis's thigh.

Hepluosis roared in pain, dropping his sword and crumbling to the ground.

Cret stood with his sword leveled at Hepluosis, the tip steady before him. Sorrow weighed heavily on his chest. He held no love for the man before him, but killing him was something he could not bring himself to do.

"This…whatever this is between us ends now," Cret said, the point of his sword now at Hepluosis's neck. He said nothing to Cret, only glared. "This is OVER!" Cret yelled, repositioning his sword, resting the point on Hepluosis's chest. The man on the ground held his hands out. "I yield. This is over," Hepluosis agreed, closing his eyes.

Cret nodded and relaxed his arms. They stared at each other for a few moments before Cret fully relaxed and rushed to Neiaphi's side. He drew his dagger and cut her bindings.

A look of pure terror flashed across Neiaphi's face. Cret turned his head just in time to see Hepluosis lunging at him, dagger raised. Before Hepluosis could strike, a sword thrust through his chest from behind.

Hepluosis's face twisted in pain and shock. He staggered forward a few steps, gripping the sword protruding from him.

"That's for Alexa," Greish snarled from behind Hepluosis. Hepluosis crumbled to the ground…

∞ Epilogue ∞

Neiaphi stood on a balcony overlooking a lush garden below. Vineyards, farmland, and orchards stretched for as far as she could see.

The laughter of children reached her ears. She turned her head and peered down. A group of children ran through the garden under the watchful eye of Lycia, Cleop, and Altesse.

The eldest, now fourteen, was being tackled to the ground by twin ten-year-olds. "Annas and Praxis let Icarus get up," Cleop chided.

Neiaphi laughed at her brother's antics.

Three toddlers ran after the older boys, determined not to be left behind. Four-year-old Dimitris ran close behind with the slightly younger twins, Creluios and Andonis, on his heels.

Neiaphi sighed and placed a hand on her swollen belly. She lifted her gaze to the stars and prayed to any being that might be listening for her new baby to be a girl. Six young boys on one estate were getting out of control.

More voices caught her attention. Cret and Shalendra were coming up the steps to the house.

Ten years had passed since she last saw any of those who ventured into Agartha. Shalendra had arrived two days ago out of the blue with Addident and his family, wishing to revisit topside.

Andonis was with them as well. They learned that Nidora and he had taken their time getting to know each other and their new home, having wed five years prior and were expecting their second child about the same time as Cret and her were expecting their third.

Further from the villa, she saw Alexa and Greish near the stable, letting their second child, Alexis, see the puppies. Neiaphi could almost hear the squeals of delight coming from the fourteen-moon-old baby.

Since saying goodbye to the centaurs and those wishing to live in Agartha, life had calmed down considerably.

Neiluios and Paragon, Alexa's father, had led their group to a land shown to Neiluios by the Oracle Pythia. Rasenna, they called it. Over the years, more and more people began to settle in the area, eventually forming a city known as Etruria.

Pythia had originally told Neiluios that Annas and Praxis would build a great city on the seven hills of Rasenna. But, as with many of her foretelling's, the meaning was not as it seemed. Shalendra explained the night before that it would be a descendant of one of the boys, many generations later, who would fulfill that vision, many years to come.

Neiaphi, Cret, Alexa, Greish, and their children, along with their parents and servants, lived on a multi-villa estate north of the Seven Hills. The Etruscan people called this compound Rasenna—the home of their governor, Neiluios, and his extended family.

"Neiaphi!" Cret called from somewhere inside the Villa. "Out here," she called.

Cret walked onto the balcony, Cypress at his side.

She smiled at him, laying a hand on his cheek as he bent down to kiss her lightly on the cheek. Gray had begun to show at his temples, but the rest of his hair remained as dark as when he had returned to her all those years ago. Cypress padded over to her and rested his head in her lap.

"There's my good puppy," she cooed, scratching behind his very gray ear. His tongue lolled happily from his mouth.

"Are you ready?" Cret asked.

"I think so. How many will be in attendance tonight?"

"Most of the council and their families, I believe. Icarus is becoming a man. No one wants to miss his Liberalia."

Cret held out his hand and helped her to her feet, then led her out of the villa to the waiting carriages.

"Momma!" little Andonis shouted when he saw her coming. "Can I ride with Uncle Andonis?" he asked, bouncing up and down.

Neiaphi looked up at Andonis astride a pure white horse. "It's okay with me if it's okay with you."

Little Andonis scrambled into the saddle before she could even speak. She laughed, shaking her head, and climbed into her carriage. Nidora and Alexa were already inside, both holding their daughters.

She leaned out and looked up at Cret mounted on his current horse—a striking blood bay stallion—one of many they had bred from Rees. "Have I told you lately how lucky I am and how much I love you?"

"Only five times a day," Cret replied with a smile, leaning down to kiss her softly on the lips.

THE END...

Thank you for reading *The Chronicles of Atlantis!*
I hope you have enjoyed Neiaphi's and Cret's adventure.

Join my email list to be notified when future books are released.

Thanks again, and May the Gods Smile on You!

NeiaphisAtlantis@gmail.com

Sarah M Wasson

Within the shimmering embrace of Las Vegas, Nevada, I dwell with my beloved husband and son. My heart is imbued with the spirit of enterprise, juggling my pursuits as a pet groomer, amateur golfer, horse whisperer, falconer, and devotee of the fantastical realms of sci-fi.

Fantastical Realm Publishing
www.FantasticalRealm.com
FantasticalRealmPublishing@gmail.com